Welcome back to Memphis, where the sun goes down, shit starts popping off. The three major female gangs ruling the gritty Mid-South are the Queen Gs, who keep it hood for the Black Gangster Disciples; the Flowers, who rule with the Vice Lords; and the Cripettes, mistresses of the Crips.

The stakes are higher now, but the rules never change in a city where blood paints the concrete. Surviving is not guaranteed, even if you drop your head and mind your own business. Memphis's street divas are as hard and ruthless as the men they hold down. Their biggest mistakes happen when they fall in love.

Also by De'nesha Diamond

Hustlin' Divas

Heist (with Kiki Swinson)

Heartbreaker (with Erick S. Gray and Nichelle Walker)

Published by Kensington Publishing Corp.

Street Divas

DE'NESHA DIAMOND

Kensington Publishing Corp.
http://www.kensingtonbooks.com

This is dedicated to those surviving the Memphis struggle.

Acknowledgments

I really want to take this moment to thank the overwhelming support I've received for *Hustlin' Divas*. The evolution of this series has taken me by surprise, and I'm just so thankful of the many e-mails and Facebook and Twitter messages I've received. I apologize for the delay of the release; it has been an unbelievable year, and one can't plan for all of life's curveballs. Much love and thanks to the Creator. To Granny and my baby Alice, who continue to inspire me from Heaven above. My sisters Channon and Charla. My beautiful neice, Courtney—I love you. To Kathy and Charles Alba, absolutely the best. To Tu-Shonda Whitaker for keeping me sane, Evette Porter, Brenda Jackson, and Maureen Smith. Again to Selena James for still having the patience of Job.

And, of course, the Byrdwatcher family and The Diamond Girls Book Club—you lift me up. To anyone I forgot, it's the alcohol—really.

Best of love,

De'nesha

Cast of Characters

Detective Melanie Johnson is the daughter of the most decorated and crooked cop on the Memphis Police Department payroll. Unfortunately, the apple doesn't fall too far from the tree. She has her own skeletons in the closet, but none bigger than being the lover of both leaders of the dueling gangs, Python and Fat Ace.

Ta'Shara Murphy was once a straight-A student with dreams of getting the hell out of Memphis, but she took a detour on her dreams when she fell in love with Raymond "Profit" Lewis, the younger brother of Fat Ace. The war between the Vice Lords and her sister's set, The Gangster Disciples, puts her between a rock and a hard place. When she failed to take her sister's warning to heart, she was unprepared for the consequences.

LeShelle Murphy is Queen G for the Memphis Gangster Disciples. Not only does she love her man, Python, but she loves the power her position affords her and there is nothing that she won't do to ensure that she never loses any of it; that includes doing whatever it takes to keep her younger sister in line and handling the many chicken heads pecking at her heels.

Yolanda "Yo-Yo" Terry is an ex-drug mule turned stripper turned Python's latest baby momma. Convinced that she's the smartest chick on the block, her ambition has led her to cross paths with Python's real wifey, LeShelle. Her recklessness has already cost her her best friend Baby Thug, but this time, she stands to lose a whole lot more than she bargained for.

Willow "Lucifer" Washington is Fat Ace's right hand and as deadly as they come. A true ride-or-die chick to her core. The latest explosion between the sets will have her true feelings bubbling to the top, and when she's forced to step up to lead, she proves that you don't need a set of balls to wash the streets with blood.

Essence Blackwell, Ta'Sharra Murphy's best friend and once the lone voice of reason, now finds herself tripping over the same pitfalls that snared her friend. Of all things, she finds herself a pawn between the two biggest bitches in the game . . . with just a hope and a prayer of getting out alive.

Maybelline "Momma Peaches" Carver, Python's beloved aunt, believes and acts as if she's still wildin' out in her 20s. With an arrest record a mile long, Peaches is now confined to her shotgun home under house arrest. That doesn't mean that cards, fish fries, and blue light parties have ended. But when old family secrets start coming home to roost, her partying days may be well behind her.

Power

1

Melanie

I'm seriously fucked. That shit hits home the second I see Python, my baby's daddy and the leader of the Black Gangster Disciples, kick down my door to see his arch enemy, Fat Ace, head nigga of the Vice Lords, giving me a good dicking down.

I'm stunned and can't move.

"WHAT THE FUCK?" Fat Ace jerks out of my pussy and makes a dive toward the nightstand for his piece.

"YOU'RE A DEAD MUTHAFUCKA!" *POW!* Python's gun sounds like a cannon.

I blink out of my trance to dive in the opposite direction just as Fat Ace starts returning fire. Right now, I'm wishing that I didn't keep my own weapon locked in a safety box at the top of my bedroom closet. Judging by the look on Python's face, Fat Ace and I aren't walking out of this muthafucka alive.

POW! POW! POW!

Python ducks and twists away from the door before Fat Ace's bullets tear huge chunks out of the door frame. Unfortunately, that leaves me in Python's direct line of vision. Time crawls the second our gazes connect, while death skips down my spine and wraps itself around my heart.

"No, Python. Wait," I beg. I even foolishly lift my hands

like a stop sign as if that's really going to enforce a time-out. Python's black, empty, soulless eyes narrow. At this fucking moment, I'm no different from any other nigga on the street: disposable. I'm already dead to him, and my tears are nothing but water.

Fat Ace squeezes off another round.

POW! POW! POW!

Wood splinters from the door frame inches above Python's head, but that doesn't stop him from lifting his Glock and aiming that muthafucka straight at me. I'm a cop and I'm used to plunging headlong into danger, but I don't have a badge pinned to my titties right now, and my courage is pissing out in between my legs.

POW! POW!

Fat Ace misses again.

"Please. I'm carrying your baby." As a desperate act, I clutch the small mound below my belly, and I succeed in getting his eyes to drop.

To my left, Fat Ace's head whips in my direction. His voice booms like a clap of thunder.

"WHAT THE FUCK?"

I spin my head back toward Fat Ace. Why does it suddenly look like this muthafucka can pass for Python's twin? Anger rises off of him like steam. I open my mouth but my brain shuts down. It doesn't matter. There are no words that can save me.

"You fucking lying bitch!" Fat Ace's gun swings away from Python and toward me, while Python's gat turns toward Fat Ace. Both pull the trigger at the same time.

POW! POW!
POW! POW!

The bullets feel like two heat-seeking missiles slamming into me. I propel backward, and my head hits the wall first.

Across the room, Python's bullets slam into Fat Ace's right side, but the nigga remains on his feet and squeezes out a few more rounds.

Shocked, it takes a full second before the pain in my chest and left side has a chance to register. When it does, it's like nothing I've ever felt before. Blood gushes out of my body as I slowly slide down the wall and plop onto the floor.

POW! POW!

Python shoots the gun out of Fat Ace's hand.

POW! POW! POW!

"What, nigga? What?" Python roars.

Fat Ace clutches his bleeding hand but then charges toward Python real low and manages to tackle him to the ground before Python is able to squeeze off another shot. They hit the hardwood with a loud *thump,* and Python's gun is knocked out of his hand.

I need to get help. There's way too much blood pooling around me. *I'm dying. Me and my baby.*

"Is that all you got, nigga?" Fat Ace jams a fist into the center of Python's face. Blood bursts from Python's thick lips and big nose like a red geyser.

Tears rush down my face like a fucking waterfall. *I'm sorry, baby. I'm so sorry.* It's all I can tell my unborn child.

"Your ass gonna die tonight, you punk-ass bitch," Python growls, slamming his fist into Fat Ace's jaw.

Christopher!

My head snaps up. My son, Christopher, is in the other room. How can he sleep through all this noise? An image of Christopher, curled up in the bottom of his closet, trembling and crying, springs to my mind. *I have to get to my baby.*

I slump over from the wall but lack the strength to stop my upper body's falling momentum. My face crashes into the hard floor, and I can feel a tooth floating in blood in my mouth.

Covered in sweat and blood, Python and Fat Ace continue wrestling on the floor. Fat Ace, still naked, gets the upper hand for a second and sends a crushing blow across Python's jaw. A distinguishable *crack* reverberates in the room. To my ears, the muthafaucka should be broken, but Python ain't no ordinary nigga. And sure enough, in the next second, Python retaliates, landing one vicious blow after another. A tight swing lands below Fat Ace's rib cage. Its force not only causes another *crack,* but it also lifts Fat Ace up at least a half foot in the air and gives Python the edge in repositioning himself.

The punches flow harder and faster. The floor trembles as if we're in the middle of an earthquake. Python is shoved against the side of the bed, and the damn thing flies toward my head. Lacking the energy to get out of the way, all I can do is close my eyes and prepare for the impact. The bed's metal leg slams into the center of my forehead with a sickening *thud,* and a million stars explode behind my eyes.

The scuffling on the other side of the bed continues; more bone crushes bone. When I finally manage to open my eyes, Python is trying to stretch his hand far enough to reach for a gun, but it is a few inches too far. Fat Ace is doing all he can to make sure that shit doesn't happen.

Watching all this go down, I realize that I don't give a fuck if they kill each other. Why should I? I'm already sentenced to death. I can feel its cold fingers settling into my bones.

More tears flow as I have my last pity party. It's true what they say—your life does flash before your eyes. But it's not the good parts. It's all the fucked-up shit that you've done. Now that judgment is seconds away, I don't have a clue what I'm going to tell the man upstairs, that's a good sign that my ass is going straight to hell.

I have to say good-bye to Christopher.

Sucking in a breath, I dig deep for some reserved strength.

Determined, I drag my body across the floor, crawling with my forearms.

POW!

To my right, the bedroom window explodes, and shards of glass stab parts of my body.

Python and Fat Ace wrestle for control of the gun.

"Fuck you, muthafucka," one of them growls.

Still, I'm not concerned about their dumb asses. I need to see my baby one more time. However, I only get about half a foot before sweat breaks out across my brow and then rolls down the side of my face. How in the hell can I be cold and sweating at the same time?

POW! POW! POW!

More glass shatters. I turn my head in time to see Fat Ace's large, muscled ass dive out the window. Python runs up to the muthafucka and proceeds to empty his magazine out the broken window.

"CRABBY MUTHAFUCKA!" Python reaches into his back pocket and produces another clip. He peers out into the darkness for a minute. "I'ma get his punk ass," he says, and then turns and races out of the bedroom in hot pursuit, nearly kicking me in the head as he passes.

Relieved that he's gone, I drag myself another inch before my arms wobble and threaten to collapse. I need to catch my breath.

POW! POW! POW!

The shooting continues outside. In the distance, I hear police sirens. Then again, it could be wishful thinking. It's not like the department would respond this fuckin' fast.

Christopher. I gotta get to my baby.

Convinced that I've caught my second wind, I attempt to drag myself again. I try and try, but I can't move another inch. A sob lodges in my throat as I hear the sound of footsteps. *Christopher!* He must've gotten the courage to come see if I'm all right. "Baby, is that you?" Damn. That one question leaves me breathless. I'm panting so hard I sound like I just ran a marathon.

The slow, steady footsteps draw closer.

"Baby?" I stretch out a blood-covered hand. When I see it, I'm suddenly worried about what Christopher will think seeing me like this. Shakily, I look around. I'm practically swimming in my own piss and blood. It could scare the shit out of him, scar him for life.

He's almost at the door.

Tell him not to come in here!

"Baby, um—"

"Your fuckin' baby is gone."

Python's rumbling baritone fills my bedroom and freezes what blood I have left in my veins. My head creeps back around, and I'm stuck looking at the bottom of a pair of black jeans and shit kickers. More tears rush to my eyes. This nigga is probably going to stomp my ass into the hardwood floors.

"You're one slick, muthafuckin' bitch, you know that?"

"Python—"

"How long you been fuckin' that crab, huh?"

My brain scrambles, but I can't think of a goddamn thing to say.

"What? Cat got your tongue?" The more he talks, the deeper his voice gets. The sob that's been stuck in the middle of my throat now feels like a fucking boulder, blocking off my windpipe.

Python squats down. I avoid making eye contact because I'm more concerned about the Glock dangling in his hand. My heart should be hammering, but instead I don't think the muthafucka is working.

The gun moves toward me until the barrel is shoved underneath my chin, forcing my head up. Now it doesn't seem possible that I've spent so many years loving this nigga. How does a woman fall in love with death?

Python is not easy on the eyes, and his snake-forked tongue doesn't help. Big and bulky, his body is covered with tats of pythons, teardrops, names of fallen street soldiers, but more important is the big six-pointed star that represents the Black Gangster Disciples. He's not just a member. In this shitty town, he's the head nigga in charge—and my dumb ass crossed him.

"Look at me," he commands.

My gaze crashes into his inky black eyes, where I stare into a bottomless pit.

"You know you fucked up, right?"

I whimper and try to plea with my eyes. It's all I can do.

Muscles twitch along Python's jawline as he shakes his head. Then I see some shit that I ain't never seen before from this nigga: tears. They gloss his eyes, but they don't roll down his face. He ain't that kind of nigga.

"You fuckin' betrayed me. Out of all the niggas you could've fucked you pick that greasy muthafucka?"

"P-P-P—"

"Shut the fuck up! I don't wanna hear your ass beggin' for shit. Your life is a wrap. Believe that!" He stares into my eyes and shakes his head. "What? You thought your pussy was so damn good that I was going to let this shit slide? I got street-walkers who can pop pussy better than you. You ain't got a pot of gold buried up in that ass. I kept your triflin' ass around because I thought . . ." He shakes his head again and the tears dry up or had I imagined those muthafuckas?

Sirens. I'm sure this time. The police are coming.

He chuckles. "What? You think the brothahs and sistahs in blue are about to save your monkey ass? Sheeiiit. That ain't how this is going down."

So many tears are rolling out my eyes I can barely see him

now. I want to beg again, but I know it's useless. Time to buck up. Face this shit head-on.

"I can't believe that I *ever* thought you were my rib. You ain't good enough to wipe the shit out the crack of my ass," he sneers, releasing my chin and standing up.

The next thing I hear is the unzipping of his black jeans.

"You wanna live, bitch? Hmm?"

I nod but he still grabs a fistful of my hair and yanks me up. Next thing I know, his fat cock is slapping me in the face.

"Suck that shit. Show me how much you wanna fuckin' live, bitch. You fuck this shit up, and I'll blast your goddamn brains all over this fuckin' floor. You got that?"

I try to nod again, but the shit is impossible. Python's dick is so hard when he shoves that muthafucka into my mouth that he takes out another fuckin' tooth. I can't even say that I'm sucking his shit as much as I'm bleeding and choking on it.

"Ssssssss." He grinds his hips and then keeps hammering away. "C'mon, pig. Get this nut."

I don't know how in the hell I remain conscious, but I do, hoping this nigga will come sooner rather than later. But when Python's dick springs out of my mouth, I'm not blasted with a warm load of salty cum but with a hot stream of nasty-ass piss. I close my mouth and try to turn my head away, but this nigga holds me still and tries to drown my ass.

"Open up, bitch. OPEN THE FUCK UP!"

Crying, I open my mouth.

"Yeah. That's right. Drink this shit up. This is the kind of nut you deserve!"

By the time he lets my head go, I'm drenched from head to goddamn toe but still sobbing and trying to cling to life.

Python stuffs his still-rock-hard dick back into his pants and zips up. "Fuckin' pathetic. That had to be the worst head I ever had."

My eyes drop to the space in between his legs. There I see

my seven-year-old baby, Christopher. He stands in his pajamas, clutching his beloved teddy bear. "I'm so sorry," I whisper.

Christopher's eyes round with absolute horror.

He's going to watch me die.

"You're a fuckin' waste of space, bitch. Go suck the devil's dick," Python hisses, and then plants his gun at the back of my head and pulls the trigger.

2

Ta'Shara

"NOOOOOOOOOOOOOOOOOOOOOOO!"

Profit jumps and wiggles around as bullet after bullet slams into him. His face remains filled with rage as he glares at LeShelle. If he could reach her, he would tear her apart limb by limb with his bare hands. At long last, there's an audible *click*. This evil bitch has run out of bullets. However, to everyone's disbelief, Profit remains standing—but barely.

"What the fuck?" one nigga marvels.

The shit spooks the small crowd as they stare open-mouthed at Profit. A sliver of hope blossoms in my chest but then dies when Profit wobbles on his weakening legs and blood streams from both corners of his mouth.

"Profit." I take advantage of my shocked captors and scramble out of their grasp. But by that time, my man drops to his knees like a stone, and his eyes slowly roll toward mine. Our connection doesn't last longer than a second, but in that time I read so much in his eyes.

Regret.

Sorrow.

Love.

It's the love that I'm going to remember and cherish. At last he tilts over and collapses against the gravel and dirt.

"Whoa, ho, ho," Dreadlocks laughs. "Did y'all see that zombie shit? What the fuck?"

"Noooo," I moan, shaking my head as I crawl over glass, sharp rocks, and God knows whatever else. I have to reach him. "Profit . . . baby?"

"That nigga was a fuckin' soldier," another goon praises from behind me. "I ain't seen no shit like that in all my life."

My breath thins when I reach Profit. He looks like a broken mannequin, lying in a growing pool of blood. I try to take it all in, but I'm wondering how on earth to put him back together again. "Profit . . . baby?" My hands tremble as I reach out to touch his face.

"Fuck that nigga. He ain't no damn body," LeShelle snaps. "Grab Ta'Shara and let's get the fuck out of here."

I sit and carefully pull Profit's head into my lap. "I'm sooo sorry," I whisper as tears cascade over my lashes and fall onto his face. "This is all my fault. I knew better and . . . Please, I can't lose you like this. I love you. Oh, God, you don't know how much I love you." Lowering my head, I rain kisses across his still face. "Please, please forgive me." Once the sobbing starts, I can't stop. I no longer feel the pain in my jaw, my ass, or even in between my legs. The only pain that is threatening to kill me is the one that is in my heart.

"I SAID GRAB THE BITCH!" LeShelle yells. "What the fuck are y'all lollygagging for? We ain't chillin' out in Disneyland. We gotta get the fuck out of here."

"Profit, I'm so sorry," I repeat over and over again, rocking his head in my lap. "Please forgive me. Please." I'm vaguely aware of approaching feet. I lock my arms around Profit's shoulders. At this moment, I have one truth: I want to die here with him.

"You heard your sister. It's time to go!" An arm as hard as steel latches around my waist and jacks me up so fast that he also pulls Profit up as well. But I lose my grip, and Profit slams down onto the ground again.

"PROFIT, NOOOOOO!" I thrust out my hands, trying to reach him.

"Goddamn, this bitch got a fuckin' pair of lungs!"

"PROOOOOOFFIIIIIIIIT!"

"Get her in the damn limo! Shit," LeShelle barks.

Her girls scramble out of the way. The looks on their faces are ones of stunned disbelief.

"Damn, LeShelle," Kookie says, shaking her. "You're a cold-ass bitch."

"You didn't know? You should've asked somebody."

"No! No! No!"

The farther this nigga drags me away from Profit, the more I lose it. "Let me go!" I kick, punch, and try to claw my way out of his arms. It isn't until I get a couple of broken acrylic nails into his tough skin and slice that muthafucka open that he loosens his grip and drops me.

"GODDAMN IT! YOU FUCKIN' BITCH!"

I scramble back onto my feet and take off toward Profit again, but I don't get too far before one of the other rapists snatches me up.

"Now where the fuck do you think you're going?" he laughs.

"Let go of me! Profit!" Any minute, Profit is going to hear me and get up. He has to. I can't survive this night without him. I can't. "Please, let me go! Profit!"

LeShelle steps in front of me as her gangsta goon continues to lug me toward the limo. "Shut the fuck up! Goddamn!"

Angered by the very sight of her, I use this nigga's arm as an anchor and then hike up both legs and deliver a high-roll kick that snaps LeShelle's head back so fast that it looks like it's about to fly off her shoulders. "I fuckin' hate you! You're not my sister!" Hocking up a wad of spit, I launch that shit against the side of her face.

Her two homegirls and fellow Queen G's, Kookie and Pit Bull gasp and cover their mouths.

Ear Seeds

To stimulate the ear point, gently massage each Ear Seed for 10-30 seconds. You may do this periodically throughout the day.

When washing and showering, avoid vigorous scrubbing of areas where the Ear Seeds have been applied. If an Ear Seed becomes loose, do not try to reapply it.

Ear Seeds may be left on the ear for 3 - 4 days.

Remove Ear Seeds immediately if they cause you any discomfort.

Minor itching or irritation could indicate an allergy to the adhesive tape.

If any of these symptoms are present in the ear, remove and discontinue use, then make an appointment to see an acupuncturist at Stroger Hospital, Clinic B, for a follow up.

Semillas de Oreja

Para estimular el punto de la oreja, masaje suavemente cada semilla de oreja de 10 a 30 segundos. Usted puede hacer esto durante el día.

Al lavarse o ducharse, evite frotar vigorosamente las áreas donde se han aplicado las semillas para los oídos. Si una semilla de oído se suelta, no intente volver a aplicarla.

Las semillas para el oído se pueden dejar en la oreja durante 3 a 4 días.

Retire inmediatamente las semillas para los oídos si le causan molestias.

Una picazón o irritación menor podría indicar una alergia a la cinta adhesiva.

Si alguno de estos síntomas está presente en el oído, retírelo e interrumpa su uso, haga una cita con un acupunturista en el Hospital Stroger, Clínica B, para un seguimiento.

"You're dead to me, you hear me? DEAD!"

Slowly, LeShelle turns her head back around. Her dark eyes glitter with hatred as she calmly wipes the spit from her face and then touches the side of her bleeding lips. When she sees a dot of blood on her fingertips, she smiles. "Well, what do you know? Lil sister got some real balls." She steps closer. "But if you want to keep those muthafuckas, you better learn your fuckin' place 'cause it ain't shit for me to cut them off!"

I laugh. "Is that supposed to scare me now?" My laugh climbs another octave. "You think I give a fuck what you and your *weak* niggas do to me?" I hock up another loogie and spew it as hard as I can. The satisfaction of seeing it hit in between her eyes tickles the shit out of me. "Yeah. What the fuck are you going to do now, bitch?!"

LeShelle dives for me, but I rear back against her goon again and kick one leg straight up. My bare big toe cracks and bends painfully when it connects with her chin.

"Ahh. Shit!"

Mr. Dusty Afro releases me and then jumps back to watch Ta'Shara and I scrap. I rush over to her before she has a chance to blink the stars from around her head, and I send a punch across her nose. Her blood ejects across my face while I'm reeling back to throw another punch, but someone grabs the back of my hair and yanks so hard I'm probably bald-headed now.

"GET THE FUCK OFF OF HER!" Kookie yells. "Why y'all niggas ain't helping?"

Dreadlocks shrugs. " 'Cause my dick gets hard when I watch two bitches fighting."

The other dudes bob their heads.

I swipe at Kookie's legs and send her stumbling in the dirt, but when I turn, LeShelle jumps on me and starts pelting me with punches. Because of the beating I endured earlier, her assault renews and intensifies my pain.

"Goddamn it. I'm fuckin' tired of your ass!" LeShelle jumps up and then starts stomping me into the ground. "You're going to fuckin' learn, goddamn it, even if it takes all night. I'm in charge!"

Stomp!

"You're going to do what *I* say!"

Stomp!

"You hear me?"

Stomp!

"You're a Queen G for life, bitch!"

Stomp!

"And any goddamn time I feel like it, I'll take you out!"

Stomp!

I'm spitting and choking on blood while my head rolls to the right. Ten feet away from me is Profit's lifeless body while I take one stomp after another. *Soon. I'll be with him soon. Death is around the corner.*

LeShelle stops stomping me and kicks up a cloud of dirt in my face. "Now get this bitch in the goddamn limo before she *really* makes me mad."

3

Lucifer

The crowd at Da Club is jumping, which means the cash at the registers is flowing. That's usually all it takes for me to be in a good mood, but tonight I'm having trouble trying to fake the funk, since I know Mason, or Fat Ace as he's known in the streets, is rolling over at that pig's crib, getting his dick wet. And now that bitch is supposedly having his baby? I don't believe that shit. I know my nigga better be asking for a DNA test. I don't like *Officer* Melanie Johnson. I think she's as shady as her daddy. Everybody knows he's been sucking off the Vice Lord's teet for decades now. And Melanie used to date Python back in high school? C'mon, now. Is her pussy so damn good that niggas can't put two and two together?

Of course not. What the hell am I thinking? If Mason was so smart, then he'd know that my ass has been in love with him since Adam gave Eve his rib. But, no, I have a DO NOT TOUCH sign on my forehead as far as Mason is concerned. He and my brother Bishop have been best friends since grade school, which makes me like the sister he never had. It doesn't matter how hard I ride or how vicious I am in this street game. I am and always will be just his right-hand chick.

"Shit, Cutty. Give me a whiskey on the rocks," I say, pounding on the bar and then swiveling my head in a slow one-eighty to check out the dancing crowd. A few seconds later, I have my drink and start edging toward the back of the club. Damn. I should try to get fucked up or grab one of these punk-ass niggas to rub out some stress.

I find me a table in a dark corner at the back of the club and check out the scene. When my eyes land on one brother laughing with a group of niggas while quietly checking me out, I throw my head back to let him know that it's cool for him to approach me. He excuses himself, and I watch his confident pimp walk as he heads on back. Six foot two, chocolate, trim with a pencil goatee—I definitely see potential.

"Now, what's a fine woman like you doing hiding in the back of the club?" he asks.

So much for potential. "Never mind, I'm busy." I dismiss him and return to my drink.

"Whoa. Whoa." He holds up his hands. "I'm sorry if I didn't come correct, but a nigga gets nervous when he gets around a beautiful woman. Let me try again."

I glance up, annoyed that he's still standing there.

"My name is Justin, and you are . . . ?"

Holding his gaze, I reevaluate the situation. "Lucifer," I say. He doesn't laugh, which tells me he recognizes the name.

"How's your head game, Justin?"

Not sure he heard me right, he blinks and then glances around, as if there are going to be cameras jumping out or something. "Come again?"

"No. That's what I want you to help me with. How's your head game? Do you eat pussy?"

His smile returns. "I ain't had no complaints."

I lean back in my chair. "Then let me see what you're working with."

Justin's face twists in confusion as he checks around for those cameras again. "What? Here?"

"Why not?"

My cell phone starts ringing. It's Bishop. "Hold on a second," I tell Justin, and then answer the phone. "Whatever it is, I'm busy."

"They got Profit!"

"What?" The alcohol in my system disappears as I jet up out of my chair. "I thought he was at his prom tonight?"

"Hey!" Justin yells as I rush past him.

"He was. Those muthafuckas snatched him and his girl in front of witnesses on their way to the hotel! I'm trying to find Fat Ace, but he ain't answering his cell."

"Shit." I race through the crowd and then bolt out the front door. "Where you at?"

"We're out here looking for these niggas. We got a tip. . . . Hey, is that the building? Yo, I think we've found—there he go!"

I hop behind the wheel of my black Escalade. "Give me a fuckin' address, Bishop."

"Over off O'Donnell. Where the abandoned warehouse buildings are."

"I'm on it." I peel out of the parking lot while straining to hear every little thing over the line. "Talk to me, Bishop." When I hear nothing, I glance down at my cell to see I've lost the signal. I toss the muthafucka aside and slam down on the accelerator. Less than five minutes later, I make it over to O'Donnell and see Bishop and a string of brothers from the set.

"Tell me something," I shout, racing out of my SUV with my gat ready to blast. Niggas part like the Red Sea, and my gaze lands on the twisted, bloody body lying in the dirt. "Shit."

Brothers stand around and shake their heads. "Them grimy niggas gonna pay for this shit."

For the first time in a long while, I'm stunned. I liked Profit, even though I'd known him for only a little over a year. The lil nigga had heart. "We know who did this?"

"Who the fuck else? Those Gangster Disciples," Bishop shouts. "They want heat? We're about to bring it to them."

I kneel next to Profit's body and look down at his young face. *So much potential.* Leaning forward, I place a hand against the side of his neck, and my heart nearly stops.

"What?" Bishop asks.

I pick up Profit's wrist and then place my ear against his chest. "Oh my God. He's still alive."

4

LeShelle

"**Y**ou brought this shit on yourself." I cut a look over at my silent sister, who is slumped on the other side of the rented limousine. The foot soldiers I'd dragged in for tonight's job are all crammed in the front seat to give me some private one-on-one time with Ta'Shara so I can break down her new situation.

Ta'Shara, curled in a corner, stares at the dirt beneath her fingernails while a steady stream of tears rolls down her face. Now that she's finally in this bitch, she has stopped all that hollering. Her once-blue dress is now a nasty black and brown. Some of it is dirt, and the rest of it is drying blood. The pain in my chest grows while my own hellish memories try to resurface. Up until tonight, I had only one responsibility in life: protecting my sister. But in the last six months, Ta'Shara had made that shit impossible.

"I told you and I told you, but did you listen? No!" I grit my teeth and shake my head. "You just *had* to be hardheaded. The prom! You took that grimy Vice Lord to the muthafuckin' prom! What the fuck did you think was going to happen? Huh? You thought that I was going to let that shit slide?"

Silence.

I hammer my fist against my knee instead of swinging it at her head. I draw in a deep breath, but it doesn't do shit to calm my ass down. "Wait until this shit gets back to Python—just wait. He'll be looking at me sideways again. This kind of bull-shit is the main muthafuckin' reason he doesn't trust me. Me! After all these damn years of jumping when he says jump, fucking when he says fuck, and blasting when his ass says blast. Now here comes your tired and dumb ass fucking up every-thing."

Silence.

I draw in another deep breath. "Python is already out fuck-ing everything that's not nailed down. I got bitches and babies turning up like cockroaches." A lump clogs in my throat. Coughing, I strain to get the sucker back down while tears burn like acid at the backs of my eyes. I love my nigga. That's my first damn problem. In this crazy street game, love can only bring you disappointment and pain. I've played wifey to Python's ass for damn near four years. Still, my position as the leader of the Queen Gs feels just as slippery as the day my man moved my ass into his crib on Shotgun Row, the heart of the Black Gangster Disciples. I have some bitch cop on the scene and that retarded bitch Yo-Yo he got stashed somewhere in this shitty city, feeling herself and thinking that she's gonna replace me.

"I'm not going to let you fuck me," I hiss, making up my mind. "You got me twisted if you thought that shit. I've been through too much to lose it because you ain't got a lick of sense." My gaze slices back over to Ta'Shara. "I bet you'd like that shit, huh? Me back on the streets without a pot to piss in or a window to throw the shit out of." My glare hardens at the thought of the years Ta'Shara had been nestled up in her foster parents' nice little crib over in midtown while I was hustlin' on the streets like a gutter rat. We may be sisters, but our lives couldn't be more different.

We were brought up in foster care. Back in the old days, Ta'Shara and I were like two peas in a pod. There wasn't a damn thing that we wouldn't do for each other. Had to. No-body else gave a damn about us, especially not any of the sorry muthafuckas who took us in just for that little paycheck that came with us. The real nightmare began when I got tits and ass. Suddenly my foster daddies and play uncles wanted to play with my small nipples and hairless pussy.

Muthafuckas used to split my shit wide open on the regu-lar, leaving me crying and bleeding all over the place. Being two years older, I've always believed that it was my responsibil-ity to look after Ta'Shara—that is, until my baby sister flipped the script and started thinking that she was better than me, just because some Huxtable-wannabe couple was pumping her head with college bullshit. Since Ta'Shara's been living with them, they've been treating me like I'm something that is stuck to the bottom of their shoes. The sacrifices I've made over the years suddenly no longer matter, even the night I sliced one of our foster fathers up for eyeballing Ta'Shara's young titties. That shit landed me in a group home for two years.

At first I thought I fucked up. Getting separated from my sister meant that I could no longer look out for her. I had to toss that shit up to the man above and hope for the best. Meanwhile, I got educated into the street life quick, fast, and in a hurry. Ain't no sense in lying and saying that I didn't want this life. I did. After seeing all the power some of the girls had up in there. Those bitches said jump and everybody got their bounce on. What got me was how hard everybody was floss-ing. They were boosting shit and getting paid like a mutha-fucka. A bitch like me who ain't never had nothing was down with that shit.

The price? I got my ass beat and raped by a couple of car-pet munchers. Most of us did in that group home. The shit has been well worth it. I got cliqued up with a real family—a fam-ily that has my back and I definitely have theirs. We're together until the world blows up. That shit is a fact.

I hear a faint sniff, and my gaze cuts back over to my sister. My heart twists as if a knife has been plunged right into the center of it. *What have I done?*

Heat rushes up my neck. The time for babying her ass is over. "Stop playing the victim. *You* did this shit. Your boy's blood is on *your* muthafuckin' hands. You remember that shit!"

I watch as Ta'Shara's tears grow fatter and roll faster down her filthy face. I ain't doing nothing but spitting the truth. She refuses to look my way or say jack shit to me. That pisses me off more. "Put on your big-girl panties and own your shit. That nigga was neck-deep in the game. The *only* reason your ass ain't lying dead next to his ass is because we share the same blood. I did your ass a favor."

Silence.

Her blatant disrespect has my blood boiling. For the first time, I think I would've been better off if I'd capped her ass as well. After the thought crosses my mind, guilt attacks me. What the fuck is wrong with me?

"Shit." I drop my head and stare at the limo's floor. I don't like examining the shit I have to do out here in Murder City. A part of being a leader is about making some cold and bold moves and keeping your emotions out of it. But tonight . . . ordering Ta'Shara's rape . . .

It's a fucking new low.

I stare out the dark window. *I am my sister's keeper. I am my sister's keeper.* I feel the threat of hot tears burning the backs of my eyes, but once again, I fight those muthafuckas off. There's no point in crying about shit out here. You either get or get got. Plain and simple. I understand these rules and so did that pretty boy Profit. Only Ta'Shara has been acting like she doesn't know how shit works out here. Well, tonight she got a long overdue education.

Silence.

"That *little* shit that went down with you and my boys was a small price to pay for your life," I tell her. "Remember that shit. If you're thinking about opening your big mouth to the po-po, let's just say that I heavily advise against it. We got other muthafuckas we can touch." I scoot across the seat until I'm right up on her so I can whisper in her ear, "Like Tracee and Reggie."

Ta'Shara's head bounces up, and her large, brown eyes widen to the size of two silver dollars.

"Uh-huh. I thought that might catch your attention." My lips curl into a tight smile. "You know I'll do it, too, don't you? I'll be happy to take care of your precious foster parents. Then what will you do?" I ask, searching her eyes. "Mmm? Where do you think you'll end up? Out here on the street?" I laugh. "You think that you can handle that?"

Ta'Shara turns her head away, but I grab her swollen jaw and jerk it back toward me. "Look at me when I'm fucking talking to you!" I grind my teeth together while I try to get hold of my temper. "Real talk: you snitch and it's over for them. You got that?"

She tries to pull away, but I have her chin locked in a grip so tight it's a wonder that I don't break the muthafucka off.

"Got it?" I ask again.

At long last, Ta'Shara slowly nods her head.

I release her as the limousine rolls to a stop. A few seconds later, the door is snatched open and I jump out first.

"Is she cool?" Treasure asks, scratching his dry dreadlocks and peering down into the backseat of the limo.

"Yeah. She's cool. Back the fuck up, homey." I push him back and stare him down. "You done had all the pussy you're going to get tonight."

His black glare lands on mine. "C'mon, shit. What's another little taste going to hurt?" He smirks and grabs his dick. "I'll be quick. I promise."

"I *said,* back the fuck up." I shove him backward and pull my gat from the back waist of my jeans.

"Whoa. Whoa." Treasure's hands spring high into the air. "All that shit ain't necessary, baby girl."

"I ain't your fucking baby girl, nigga. Show the proper respect, muthafucka, and stay in your lane."

"A'ight. Chill." He tries to laugh the shit off, but I don't even crack a smile.

"Look. I don't want no misunderstandings," he says, trying again. I know his fake Rastafarian ass is more worried about Python than this Glock I have pointed at his skull.

"What you need to understand right now is that you need to hop your ass back in the front seat so you and Dog Pound can take this piece of shit limo somewhere and get rid of it."

"Cool. Cool." He steps back, crooked smile and all.

I shake my head and roll my eyes as I turn back toward the open door. "Get your ass on out here," I tell Ta'Shara. When she takes too long creeping out the vehicle, I reach down and jerk her out by her arm. "Shit. I ain't got all goddamn night." Beneath my firm grip, Ta'Shara is shaking like a leaf. I ignore this shit and drag her across a dark field behind a run-down, crack-infested apartment building toward my old but souped up burgundy Crown Victoria.

A couple of shots pop off in the night somewhere, but I don't pay it any mind. Shootings ain't nothing new out here.

"Where are we taking her?" Kookie asks, rushing behind us.

"Where else? My place," I say. Snatching the back door open, I yell at Ta'Shara, "Get in!"

Kookie don't look too comfortable with that decision. "Ain't they going to come looking for her there?"

I whip my head toward her. "No. Why should they?"

Face blank, Kookie bumps her gums while no words come out.

"Exactly." I return my attention to Ta'Shara, who is standing and quivering like an idiot. "What the fuck are you waiting for? I said get the fuck in there."

"LeShelle . . . please." Ta'Shara's cracked lips spew blood as she tries to talk. "Let me go. I p-promise I won't say anything."

"I know you're not going to say anything. If I thought that, I would've wasted your ass by now." I point my gun in her direction. "Now get your ass in the back of the car." She got moving then. After she was in, I slam the door and then turn to see Kookie looking at me and shaking her head. "What?"

"You're a cold bitch."

I laugh. "You said that already."

"It fuckin' deserves repeating."

Ten minutes later, we roll down Shotgun Row. Nobody creeps down this way unless they belong on this muthafucka. Even at this late hour, I spot the whites of niggas' eyes as they peep out my ride and then give me a casual head nod before going back to their business. Crackheads, college kids, and the occasional Caucasian persuasions are keeping the money flowing with the corner boys.

I pull the Crown Vic up against the curb in front of my and Python's crib and then kill the lights and cut the engine. However, instead of reaching for the door, I lean toward the glove compartment and pull out a Baggie of blueberry AK-47 and toss it over to Kookie in the passenger seat. "Roll that shit up."

"Aye, aye, bitch." She laughs, but it does nothing to break the tension layering in the car.

I glance up into the rearview mirror and stare at the top of my sister's head while her attention has returned to her dirty fingernails. I'm struck by how small she looks. I'm not completely emotionally detached, but I'm struggling to get there.

"Here you go," Kookie says, handing over a perfectly rolled

blunt and then whipping out her gold lighter. "Let's hit this shit. My nerves are fucking shot."

I take the blunt, plop it in between my lips, and then lean over while Kookie brings the small flame to the bottom of the blunt. The instant I draw in a deep toke, I feel my muscles relax, my heartbeat slow down, and my million fucked-up thoughts mellow the fuck out. I still keep my gaze focused on the backseat. "You want a hit?"

Silence.

"Cut the shit, Ta'Shara. I know that you hear me. You want to hit this shit or not?"

Silence.

I grind my teeth together and then hiss, "Fine. Fuck you, then."

Kookie shakes her head and reaches for the door. "I'm out. I said that I wasn't going to get involved in y'all family shit and look where the fuck I am."

"You ain't got to worry. I got this shit," I tell her.

"Yeah. We'll see. Catch you when the sun comes up, ho." Kookie jumps out of the car.

"I'm coming with you," Pit Bull says, and scrambles out of the car, too.

Ta'Shara and I are left sitting in a tomb of silence with the ghost of some dead nigga sitting between us. My mouth twitches for something to say, but this situation has gone beyond words. I jam the blunt back into my mouth and suck on the muthafucka until the front of the car is filled with smoke and I can fly instead of walk. "C'mon. Let's get the fuck up out of here." I toss the rest of the blunt into the ashtray and then climb out of the car.

Ta'Shara doesn't move and I have to jerk open the back door. "Don't make me go through this shit again. If I have to get you out of the car, you're not going to like it." Her ass moves even though it's slow as molasses. But when she pops up from my leather seats, I see a large smear of blood. I glance at the back of her light blue dress and see fresh blood soaking through and even trickling down her legs. Suddenly there's a large boulder in the center of my throat and my eyes burn as if they are marinating in acid.

Slamming the back door, I grab her left wrist and tug her toward the house. I fiddle with the lock and then rush her straight to the bathroom, despite the fact that she still makes a trail a blood through the house. I turn on the shower and force her to get underneath the spray of hot water. Even then she stands there as I rip off what's left of her dress. Her slim, curvy body is a tapestry of black and blue bruises, and the engraved initials on the side of her ass look nasty. It's probably going to get infected. I turn away from the shower and walk over to the vanity counter next to the sink and grab the alcohol. When I do, I catch my reflection in the mirror. I look like shit. Hair windblown and Profit's blood sprayed across my face and clothes. I press a hand against my cheek and smear some of that nigga's blood.

"Fuck!" I turn on the sink's faucet to wash this shit off when the front door slams and the whole house shakes. Python is home. "I'll be right back." I bolt out of the bathroom and up into the living room, but I stop dead in my tracks at the sight of Python's large, muscular body covered in blood.

I open my mouth to ask what the hell happened when he pushes a kid forward and tells him, "Go on into the back bedroom on the right and shut the door."

My gaze falls onto the kid's face, and I see Python's spitting image blinking up at me. "What the fuck?" I step back like they just one-two punched my ass. "Why in the hell you bring this lil nigga up here?"

"Watch your fucking mouth. That's my *son*." He shoves the boy again. "Go on and do what I told you."

"Oh, hell no." I stop the boy, turn him around by his

shoulders, and shove him right back toward his damn daddy. "He can't stay here. You need to take him back to the bitch you got him from."

"Don't start with me, LeShelle. I'm in some shit right now, and I ain't in the mood." He pulls up his wife beater and his complete left side looks like pulverized flesh.

"Shit. What the fuck?" I move toward him again.

"Chris, go on in the back. NOW!"

The kid jumps and then scrambles around me. I clamp my jaw shut. Clearly we're going to have to finish this another time. But one thing's for sure—that jizz baby ain't gonna be living up in here.

Python slumps his way over to the leather couch, and I rush to check out how bad the damage is. One plug above his hip.

"Who did this shit?"

"That ugly, punk muthafucka Fat Ace."

Thunderstruck, I bounce up. "What? When? Where?"

"Fuck, Shelle, squash the muthafuckin' questions and do something about this shit. My goddamn guts are bleeding out."

"A'ight. Calm the fuck down." I twist my face at his rude ass. "Did you at least earth that muthafucka?"

"Shit. I don't fucking know. Muthafucka flew out the damn window like he had on an invisible Superman cape." Python hisses and sucks in a deep breath as he presses a finger through the hole. "Are you going to get the molasses out your ass and take care of your man or what?"

"Hold up. Be back." I roll my eyes and storm back toward the bathroom. Removing bullets ain't nothing new to either one of us, but this shit couldn't have happened on a worse night. In the hallway, his seed is standing there crying and peeing on himself. "What the fuck?" I glance down at the piss on the floor. "Ain't your ass potty trained?"

"T-there's a snake in there," the kid whines.

"LeShelle, leave him alone and do what the fuck you're supposed to be doing! Goddamn!"

"Nasty ass." I roll my eyes and then push open the bathroom door and get another surprise. The shower is still going, with thick white clouds fogging up the place, but Ta'Shara is nowhere in sight.

"Ain't this a muthafuckin' bitch?"

5

Essence

Morris High School's prom is whack as hell. To get away from the lame bullshit that's happening on the crowded gym floor, I let Drey Faniel's fake balling ass talk me into sneaking up into the boys' locker room. I don't know why he couldn't come correct like the other niggas at the prom and spring for a muthafuckin' hotel room. Then again, it's probably because he spends all his corner money on sneakers. Sneakers. Not bling or a tricked-out ride, but fucking sneakers. He has so many of those muthafuckas I doubt that I've seen his ass in the same pair twice.

It's all right, I guess. Drey is all right. He ain't necessarily fine, but he ain't going to scare nothing out of the dark either. He got a nice, even caramel color and eyes the color of Milk Duds. Nothing special. Underneath his tuxedo, I know he got a few tats. Most he got after a couple stints in juvie—a couple of six-pointed stars and a few pitchforks repping the Black Gangster Disciples. At least I'm not in this piece with someone who's busted like my girl Hayley's man, Pookie. That brothah's complexion is the color of crude oil, and he has eyes and teeth the color of butter. Despite being ugly as sin, there are plenty of girls throwing panties his way because his hustle is tight and he loves raining money on bitches on the regular.

On the flip side, my girl Ta'Shara and Profit rocked the house. Hands down, they were the flyest couple up in here tonight. And the boldest. These weak niggas who rolled through were mad eyeballing the back of their heads. Vice Lords and Gangster Disciples don't fucking mix in this city. But I can't tell my girl nothing. Hell, *I* think Ta'Shara's ass is crazy, yet at the same time, I admire her, too. If you don't stand for something, then you'll fall for anything, right?

Shit. I can testify to that shit. That's why my ass has been in and out of juvie since I learned how to spell the muthafucka. It's not because I'm bad but because I'm a part of the Queen Gs' family, and you don't pay a membership fee to get in. You got to prove your ass is down for whatever, whenever. No questions asked. We're the Black Gangster Disciples' ride-or-die chicks. Period. In the course of keeping it real, I don't mind it so much. Family is important. My momma and daddy are both locked up, so me and my brothers and sisters are being raised by my grandma near Shotgun Row. We're all GD, and up until now, I've been proud of it.

The fact that Profit and his people are Vice Lords complicates the fact that Ta'Shara's sister is the head bitch in charge of the Queen Gs. Street politics clearly states that what's going on can't stand. I might not agree with my girl Ta'Shara dating a grimy Vice, but at least Profit's ass was willing to come out the pocket and get them a nice room at the Peabody. Instead, I'm with this broke muthafucka who got my ass up against this cold-ass locker with my red dress up around my waist and my panties jacked to the side.

"Hold up. Give me a sec." Drey pants as his softening dick slips and slides around my pussy. "Is this it?" he asks, jamming his dick against my clit.

"Nah, nigga." I pop him on the shoulder. We've been at this shit for twenty minutes. My shit is drying up. My buzz is halfway gone, and I'm starting to get the munchies. He's going to have to roll my ass through somebody's drive-through before he takes me home. "Ain't you done this shit before? Can't you tell that ain't a muthafuckin' hole?" I ask.

"Shit. Hold on." Drey fumbles around some more. "I'm going to get this shit. You know my ass is high as fuck—and it's dark in this muthafucka, too. Sheeiiit." He rams his shit forward, and a surge of pain has my ass jumping higher up on these hard-ass lockers.

"Oww." I slap him on the back of his head. "That's the wrong damn hole, you dumbass." Tired of the shit, I shove him away and pull my panties back in place. "Forget it. I'm out."

"*What?*"

Smoothing my dress back down, I march toward the door. To no surprise, Drey's desperate ass snatches me back by my hand and gets up in my face.

"Whoa. Slow down, baby. Where are you going?" His big lips stretch into a wide cheese-eating grin. "You promised me some pussy if I took you to this bullshit prom."

My face nearly twists off. "I ain't promised you no such damn thing. I just said I'd like to go. If you didn't want to take me, trust and believe that another nigga would have." He knows that I'm speaking the truth, too. I may be pocket size, but this year I got tits and ass with a tiny little waist. Whenever I walk by, more and more nigga's tongues be rolling out their damn heads. Sometimes even in front of their girlfriends. And what I do? Come here with this broke-ass nigga. "You see any other nigga up in here trying to get their fuck on in this stank-ass locker room?"

"Nah. That's why this shit is perfect. We got the whole place to ourselves, and we can still hear the music playing downstairs. And lookie over here." He releases me and runs over to one of the lockers.

I fold my arms as I watch him fiddle with the combination lock. After opening the muthafucka, he reaches inside and pulls out a bottle of MD 20/20 red grape. "You have got to be shitting me."

"What? This is the shit right here."

"That cheap bullshit? Negro, please. Nobody drinks that bullshit other than bums and winos."

"Don't trip. I got some Thunderbird, too." Drey reaches back into the locker and pulls out the other bottle. "Sheeiit. We're going to toss it up tonight."

"Drey, that shit ain't going to do nothing but tear up the lining in my stomach. Your ass couldn't even spring for no Grey Goose or Hpnotiq?"

"Tsk." Drey rolls his eyes as he crosses over to me. "C'mon now. Don't get all bougie on me. Trust and believe this shit is as good, and it's going to get the job done." He tucks both bottles under one arm and then makes a grab for one of my hands.

I pull my shit back and turn for the door. "Um. No. I'm out." Bolting out of the locker room, I try to wrap my brain around how fucked up this night is turning out while blocking out Drey storming up behind me.

"You're just going to roll out?"

"Later," I say, bolting back into the gym. Now I got to beg some muthafucka for a ride back to my grandma's crib. That shit is going to be hard since everyone is all grinding on each other as foreplay or getting ready to head out to the hotels to sweat out their girl's perms and weaves. Who in the hell is going to want a third wheel?

Drey keeps whining like a bitch behind me. "After all the money I spent on you tonight? This is how you act? Damn, girl. You're rude as hell."

"Whatever, broke muthafucka. You going to spend five dollars on some alcohol and call that money? You probably found that shit in between the cushions of your momma's damn couch." I thread through the crowd, trying to decide who I should hit up for a ride.

"Essence!"

"Get away from me with that bullshit." I stop in the middle of the floor and look around. There's got to be somebody up in this muthafucka who can help a sister out.

"Now what are you going to do? Your girl Ta'Shara has already left with that scabby crab Profit. How you getting home?" He reaches around me and slides a hand down to my crotch for a quick squeeze.

I spin around with fire boiling my blood. "Try that slick shit again and see if your ass don't be missing an arm next damn time."

"Spit that shit if you want. You ain't doing nothing but getting my dick hard."

"Now you just need to find a bitch who's willing to draw you a damn map so you can find a hole to stick it in. Me? I got better shit to do—like hook up with a nigga who knows what the fuck to do with pussy."

He snatches me by the arm. "Keep your fucking voice down." Drey looks around and catches a few eyeballs aimed our way. "WHAT THE FUCK ARE YOU LOOKING AT?"

Niggas laugh dead in his face. Shit. He ain't nobody major. Just a corner boy who can get you 10 percent off at Foot Locker.

Drey's grip tightens.

"Let go." I snatch my arm and glare up at his ass. I ain't scared. My being short is an advantage. I can tear up a nigga's kneecaps before he even knows what hit his ass.

"You know what? Fuck it. You do you."

"Believe that shit." I turn away, ready to storm out of this muthafucka. Shit. All I have to do is call up a cab and I'll be home to peep out *BET: Uncut* before midnight. Sad muthafuckin' way to spend a Saturday night. I reach for my purse that should be looped around my shoulder but grasp air. "Shit." Turning back around, I damn near crash into Drey's chest.

"What? Whatcha looking for?" he asks, and then holds up my purse. "You looking for this?"

"Boy, give me my shit back." I make a swipe for it, but

Drey pulls it up higher so that my five-foot-two frame can't reach it.

"Since I brought you, you might as well let me take you home."

"Ain't going to happen, broke ass."

"All right. Keep clowning and I'm going to stop being a gentleman."

"Nigga, who the fuck you think you're talking to?" I rake my eyes up and down his six-foot-three frame. "Newsflash, Einstein. A gentleman wouldn't have pulled that bullshit up in the boys' locker room with some fucking Mad Dog and Thunderbird whiskey. Shit, I think my great-great-great-grandfather used to drink that bullshit. I'm a fucking street diva, not some twenty-dollar trick, nigga. I deserve to be treated with some muthafuckin' respect."

"Stop breaking my balls and loosen the fuck up. Why the hell should I break off a chunk of my hard-earned shit for some pussy I'm only going to be up in for a couple of minutes?"

"Nigga, what?" Cobra-necking, I can't stop my eyes from rolling. "Sheeiit. If you're going to be nutting that damn fast, then you need to go ahead and step off the curb."

"Don't worry. I would've made sure that you came first." Drey flicked his tongue out, and the damn thing rolled out past his damn chin. My eyes perk up. Maybe this broke nigga actually has a hidden talent.

"All right. Fine." My eyes do another good roll. "Take me home. If you keep your mouth shut, I *might* let you get a taste. If it turns out that you know how to work that shit, I'll let you try to hit again."

Drey's eyes light up, his anger a distant memory. "For real?"

"For real. Now give me my purse and bring your ass on over here before I change my fuckin' mind." He hands me my shit, and I storm away, rolling my eyes. I'm going to let him eat my pussy, and I don't care if the muthafucka has me coming so hard I see Jesus—he ain't getting another chance to put that limp dick anywhere near my shit.

His smile spreads wider. "I thought that you might see things my way." He offers me his arm as if that's somehow going to make me forget that he tried to get me twisted off some fucking MD 20/20.

"C'mon before I change my fuckin' mind," I say, grabbing his hand and dragging him toward the exit. Out back, Khaled and his boys are tossing dice and smoking some serious shit that is forming muthafuckin' green clouds. "Goddamn," I saying, fanning that shit away from my face. No way anybody is going to convince me that shit ain't fucking up niggas' lungs. "What the fuck is that shit? Toxic waste?"

"Why?" Khaled barks, pulling his full frame up and twisting his face. "You plan on snitching, bitch?"

Quick as lightning, a pistol appears in Drey's hand and he's all up on Khaled like a soldier on the front line. "What you getting all swoll for, crab? My lady asked you a muthafuckin' question!"

Khaled laughs. "I ain't got to answer to your bitch!" He barely gets that last word out before Drey flips his gun and then swings that muthafucka across Khaled's jaw like a golf club. There's a loud *crack,* and Khaled hits the pavement like someone yelled, "Timber!"

The niggas Khaled was out here playing dice with jump up like a group of jack-in-the-boxes, but instead of coming to their homey's aid, they cover their mouths and crack the fuck up. Then one hollers to grab Khaled's shit and the muthafucka gets jacked while he's out cold.

Hell, I can't help but laugh my damn self.

Drey shakes his head and then wraps his arm around my waist. "C'mon. Muthafucka should be happy I didn't put a couple bullets through his head, talking to me out the side of his neck."

I slide into the passenger side of his rusted-out '72 Buick Electra. The car would be dope if Drey spread some cheese and got his shit hooked up. As it is, big gray clouds of smoke choke their way out of the tailpipe the minute the car turns over. There's also the stench of burning oil seeping through the vents. I ain't going to say shit. I want to get the fuck home as fast as I can.

Drey rolls his big-ass car through the school's parking lot, and when it comes time to make a right out onto the main street, he has to manually move the blinker lever up and down in order for his turn signal to work. It's all I can do to keep my eyes from rolling to the back of my head. I'm soooo over this shit.

He reaches over to the radio and blasts Lil Wayne's latest joint. But hell, even his speakers are all fucked up. Rattling and buzzing. Shit. What kind of nigga don't even keep his sound system on point?

"So where you want to serve up some of that good pussy at?"

"Take me home."

"What? You're going to let me sneak into your grand-momma's crib? Ain't you scared you're going to wake her up?"

"Nah, nigga. You can't come up in her spot. You can hit the lights in the driveway or some shit."

He cracks up. "Sho'nuff? You want me to eat you out in your grandmomma's driveway?"

"Not if you don't shut the fuck up and drive!"

"A'ight." He raises his hands off the steering wheel for a second, and the car starts to pull right. "I got to get the alignment fixed on Baby Girl," he says, reaching up and rubbing on the dashboard.

I swear to God this nigga could fuck up a wet dream. Now I ain't giving this nigga nothing. He can kiss my black ass and go find himself a chicken head. But hell. Even some cracked-out pussy is too good for his ass.

"What the hell is going on up here?" Drey asks, reaching over and mercifully turning down his fucked-up system.

A whole team of police cars with their blue strobes light up the whole damn street.

"Some nigga got capped," Drey says, rubbernecking.

"That shit ain't new," I say, bored. I hope this don't mean they're going to hold our asses up on this street all night. Just when I say that, I see two cops directing traffic to roll down alternate side streets. *Thank God.*

Drey eases off the brake while his tailpipe coughs up some more smoke. That shit is drifting toward the front of the car now, completing my humiliation as people twist their faces and look over at us. Drey is not embarrassed. He's still too busy trying to peek past the yellow crime scene tape to see if he can recognize the nigga being white-chalked.

"Is that nigga in a tux?"

That catches my attention. I pop up in my seat and try to get a good look myself. "I wonder who it is."

Bang. Bang.

Drey and I jump. A cop standing to the side of the car glares at Drey. "Keep this polluting piece of shit moving!"

"Damn, man. Careful before you fuck up my ride," Drey barks.

Both me and the cop give him an incredulous look. How can anybody fuck his shit up worse than it already is? This damn contraption looks and sounds like it has less than a mile before it just flat-out dies on our asses.

"I'm moving. I'm moving," Drey says when it looks like the cop is going to hit the car again. "These goddamn pigs. I swear I can't stand their asses," he complains, but finally heads off the main road.

I go back to ignoring his ass and wondering who's lying in the street. I don't know why, but Profit flashes in my head. Him and Ta'Shara took a big chance going to the prom together. It ain't like there were a whole lot of people happy to see them all hugged up tonight, and isn't this the route to the Peabody Hotel? There's a weird flutter in my gut. I grab my purse and dig out my cell phone.

"Who you calling?"

"None of your fucking business. Just drive."

"Damn, girl. Your mouth . . ." Drey shakes his head. "Rude as fuck."

"Whatever." I hit Ta'Shara's cell and it seems like the muthafucka rings forever before I'm transferred to her voice mail. "Uh, yeah. Shara, this is E. Look, um, I'm sure you and your boy are kicking it and everything, but I, um, I just wanted to make sure that you two made it to the hotel all right." I swivel around in my seat, trying to see past the yellow tape, but, the shit is now out of view. "I'm probably trippin', but, um, there is some shit going down not too far from your hotel, and I just wanted to check in." Now that I've put it out there, I kind of feel stupid. "Anyway, call me when you get this message."

After disconnecting the call, I hold the phone and wait for the knots in my stomach to unwind.

They don't.

I dial her number again. This time I start chewing my nails as I listen to the phone ring again. "C'mon, c'mon. Pick up."

Drey glances over at me. "What? You really think that shit back there has something to do with your girl?"

"God. I hope not."

Twenty minutes later, Drey squints and then leans over his steering wheel. "What the fuck is that?"

I hear the beep signaling me to leave a message on Ta'Shara's phone again as I glance up to see what has caught

Drey's attention. My mouth falls open, but I'm unable to speak as I see a slouched female, draped in a bloody robe, trembling and shaking as she half walks and half stumbles toward my house.

"Yo," Drey says, pointing. "Ain't that your girl, Ta'Shara, right there?"

6

Lucifer

I hate hospitals. I always have.

Besides being filled with a bunch of nosy muthafuckas who press you for the who, what, and why of shit, they're also greedy as fuck. All they want to know is how they gonna get paid. No money and they'll slap Band-Aids on your bullet holes and park your ass in the morgue when you finish bleeding out. I fail to see how their hustle is any different than the niggas out on the street.

Frankly, I would have liked nothing more than to take another trip out to Dr. Cleveland's private residence, but the amount of bullet holes Profit has is going to require a real operating table. Under normal circumstances, our asses would have done a drop-and-roll outside the emergency room to avoid playing twenty questions.

But Profit isn't a normal foot soldier. He's Mason's brother. His heart. There's nothing that he won't do for this lil nigga. With Profit being all fresh and new in the Vice Lord family, he hasn't been able to make a name for himself yet, but what most niggas do know about him is that he has fuckin' heart. The way he fought in his initiation fight is still being talked about among plenty of niggas up and down the ranks. No matter how hard Tombstone threw those punches, Profit refused to go down. And now he's looking like Swiss cheese and is still breathing? If he does survive this shit, he's going to have to change his street name from Profit to Jesus Christ because the brothah refuses to die.

The minute we pull up outside the emergency room, we shout that we need help. Two paramedics who are heading back toward a parked ambulance stop in their tracks while an old flashlight cop posted at the entrance glances over timidly. Not until we shove the hatch up and reveal Profit's bullet-riddled body do they all launch into action.

"What happened?" one of them asks.

"What does it look like?" I snap, and then glance to my side to see my brother giving me one of those looks that says *I told you so*. He was in favor of the drop-and-roll solution.

"Did you see what happened?" one of the paramedics presses as he helps transfer Profit onto a gurney.

"No."

"We have a pulse," the other paramedic announces.

My shoulders slump heavily. At least Profit didn't croak while he was under my care. We all take off into the hospital where an impressive number of people rush toward the gurney. IV bags, needles, nurses, and doctors pop up out of thin air. They all move in a weird, frenzied precision like they do on TV.

I stop jogging behind the gurney once they push through a double door, leading toward surgery. After that, I suck in a couple of deep breaths to calm my rattled nerves. This shit is in God's hands now. But as I stand, watching the swinging doors, a memory stirs. Just snatches at first. I was almost eight years old, standing in a hospital hallway just like this one while my mother wailed to Jesus not to let my father die on us. I knew that he was already gone. I had seen that light in his eyes vanish. Bishop cried, too, but not all hysterical like our Momma. His tears were silent as they rolled down his chubby face.

My eyes were as dry as a desert.

Maybe I was still in shock. My dad had been standing outside in our driveway, guzzling down his after-dinner beer and jaw-jacking with Cousin Skeet and Cousin Smokestack. They were brothers, but they weren't really our cousins; people just call each other that in our set. . . .

It was dark outside. The streetlight was already on, but I could hear deep baritones talking out in the driveway. I pushed open the screen and stepped out onto the porch. "Daddy?"

My dad turned toward the door while blowing out a long stream of smoke. Momma didn't like it when he puffed on those funny-smelling things that stunk up the whole house. "Yeah, what is it, Willow?"

I rushed down the stairs and then jogged over to hug his trim waist. That was my way of saying that I really didn't need anything, but I wanted to be around him.

"Well, aren't you a pretty young thing?" Cousin Smokestack said, glancing down at me. I was still dressed in my favorite yellow Sunday dress that I'd worn to evening service. I was supposed to have taken it off when we got back; Momma warned that she was going to beat me into the middle of next week if I got it dirty. But I wasn't worried about that, because I liked how the bottom flared out when I swung from side to side. Plus my father always said that I look like a yellow lily—his favorite spring flower. I suspected that he knew a lot about flowers, because my mom and grandmother spent hours in their gardens.

"What do you say, Willow?" my father asked.

He shook his leg to try and get me to answer, but my gaze dropped to my white leather shoes. I used to love how they clacked when I walked around. I'd pretend for hours that I could actually tap dance despite my brother complaining about all the racket I made.

"Willow," my dad pressed. "What do you say?"

"Thank you." I twirled my dress and hid my reddening face against my father's leg. I don't know why I was painfully shy when it came to compliments. I loved getting them, especially from Cousin Smokestack. He was nice-looking. I'd even heard my mom and Aunt Nicky say so in the kitchen one time. Hell, he knew he had it going on. He was real tall and had smooth honey-brown skin, big dimples on both sides of his face, and what most of us called "good hair."

Cousin Smokestack tossed me a wink. "You got yourself a heart-breaker right there."

"Sheeeiiit," my daddy swore. "These nappy-headed niggas better not come around here sniffing with their dicks out. I got something for they asses." He tapped at something on the other side of his hip that caused Smokestack's dimples to deepen when he laughed. I couldn't help but smile, too. He had that kind of effect on people.

Cousin Skeet nodded along, too. "I feel you. I wanted a boy my damn self."

I frowned up at him, but he tried to patch things over by smiling back. "No offense."

I rolled my eyes. Cousin Skeet wasn't one of my favorite people, though he seemed very popular. Maybe it was just me, but there was something about his eyes. They shifted a lot like he was always think-ing bad thoughts. He wasn't as tall as my daddy and Smokestack and didn't have as many muscles, but he still came across as a strong per-son. Someone not to fuck with, my daddy would say.

Dad was in a good mood, because he didn't order me to go back into the house so that grown men could discuss business. For the long-est time, I literally thought that my father made paper—like the kind we wrote on at school—because that was what he'd say all the time, but I finally caught on. "Yo, man. I'm about to go make this paper" or "I'm hustlin' for this paper."

This evening, I was trying to keep up with what they're talking about, but it was all gibberish to me—except when they started *cussing. Muthafucka this, grimy punk-bitch that. I thought that shit was funny and used it on my brother, Juvon, whenever he pissed me off, which was often.*

"So how things going with J.D.?" my father asked, pulling another drag on his funny-smelling cigarette.

"Humph!" Smokestack rolled his eyes before tilting back his forty. My dad laughed. "That good, huh?"

"Look, J.D. is J.D.: a fuckup of the highest order. But what can I do? He's blood, nahwhatImean?"

"I hear what you saying." Daddy shrugged. "Everybody has at least one fuckup in the family." He looked over at Cousin Skeet and cheesed.

"Ha-ha. You ain't funny, muthafucka." Skeet rolled his eyes.

"I call it like I see it," Dad said.

There was more laughter before my dad asked, "So he's still in rehab?"

Smokestack shook his head. "Nope. He got locked up over in Tupelo for knocking over a gas station out by the casinos. Dumb fuck got away but then remembered that he wanted to get some rolling paper and went back. Damn police was there taking the robbery report when he returned. Nigga behind the counter looked up, pointed, and said, 'Hey, there he go right there.' J.D. had the nerve to get mad and started screamin' that snitches get stitches."

Daddy and Cousin Skeet dropped and shook their heads. They did that a lot when they were talking about Smokestack's youngest brother. Of course, I've never met him. At least I don't remember ever meeting him. Momma said that he wasn't allowed to come around our house because he was too much trouble—or he was always in trouble. I couldn't remember which.

They continued talking about J.D. being a fuckup until Mom came to the front screen door. "Darcell, have you seen—Willow, child, get your butt in here and take off your good church dress." She opened the door and stared at me.

I hugged my dad tighter.

"Go on and do what your momma told you," my dad scolded, shaking his leg as a hint for me to let go.

I poked out my bottom lip and then hung my head lower.

"Evening, Lucille," Skeet called out to my momma.

She flashed him a small smile but then turned her attention back to me. "Giiiiirrrrl, if you don't get your narrow behind up in here, we're about to have a problem," Momma said, jabbing a hand onto her hip. "And pick up your lip before you trip over it."

Reluctantly, I released my father's leg but kept my head down and my bottom lip damn near on the ground. The men laughed as I dragged my feet toward the house. I made it halfway to the porch when the sound of screeching tires caught my ear.

"Who the fuck is these muthafuckas?" Smokestack asked.

Nosy, I turned around. A series of what sounded like firecrackers went off, and my dad fell to the ground while everyone else dove for cover.

Except for me.

I stood there in my favorite yellow dress, now sprayed with my father's blood, trying to process what had just happened and staring into my father's eyes and watching this strange light dim.

"SIX POPPIN', FIVE DROPPIN', NIGGAS," some boy shouted from the black car as it peeled down Ruby Cove.

Momma raced out of the house screaming, "DARCELL! OH, GOD, NO!"

From behind my father's bright red hoopty, Smokestack came up shooting at the fleeing car. "GRIMY, PUNK-ASS MUTHA-FUCKAS!"

POW! POW! POW!

"DARCELL," Momma wailed as she rolled my dad over.

Cousin Skeet dropped down next to Momma and tried to pull her into his embrace for comfort, but she didn't want anything to do with that and shoved him away from her.

I looked down at the ground and saw the odd angle at which my *father lay. It looked painful, and I couldn't figure out why he wouldn't try to get up.*

Smokestack kept shooting. POW! POW! POW!

It was useless. Those boys covered in blue were gone.

Time warped. I don't remember how long it took for my brother to race outside or who called the ambulance or even how we got to the hospital. I remembered standing in the hallway, watching the doctors and nurses rush my father through the hospital's double doors.

I turn away from the doors and the sad memories in time to see the flashlight cop mumbling and pointing two police officers in my direction. *Here we go.*

"Excuse me, miss. But were you the one who brought in the gunshot victim?"

He makes it sound like there was just one bullet. I want to go ahead and throw up the first brick wall, but their opening question isn't one I can just lie about. "Yeah," I say, folding my arms.

One cop, who looks like he's fresh off the boat from Africa, whips out his pen and notepad while the other one, a salt-and-pepper Italian, folds his arms and matches my stance. "You want to tell us what happened?"

"Don't know," I tell them. "I found him out on O'Donnell's and then brought him here."

"You *found* him?" Africa asks, lifting a brow.

"Yeah. He was crumpled up in front of an abandoned building. I stopped, realized that I knew him, and brought him here. I didn't see what happened."

The odd couple cut their eyes toward each other and share a look that clearly said, *Niggas.* Next, they fire one question after another, but I stick to my story, which happens to be the truth this time around.

When I get through wasting time with Dumb and Dumber,

I drift over to the waiting room with Bishop, Tombstone, Silk, and Gully.

"You think Lil Man is going to pull through?" Bishop asks, looking worried.

"Who knows?" I've never been one to give niggas false hope. "Did you call Fat Ace?"

Bishop shakes his head. "He's not answering his phone."

"Fuck." I dig my cell out of my pocket.

"Who are you calling?" Bishop asks.

"Who the fuck do you think?"

"But I told you—"

I signal for him to shut the fuck up when the call is transferred to voice mail. "Yo, man. Where the fuck you at? You need to get your dick out of that cop's pussy and head on over to the hospital," I blast into the phone. "Profit has been shot up pretty bad and . . . fuck, man, I don't know if he's going to make it. Hit me back on my cell when you get this message. I'm out." I disconnect the call and shove the phone into my pocket. "If he doesn't call me back in ten minutes, I'm riding out to that fake bitch's crib and snatching his ass out from between her legs my damn self."

The boys shake their heads.

"Jealousy don't look good on you," Bishop says.

"But you wear stupid well." I turn my back just as my cell phone starts ringing. Glancing down at the screen, I recognize Mason's home number. "It's about damn time. We've been blowing up your phone."

"Fuck! I don't have my phone. Shit." He groans. "I left it at that bitch's crib." He swears for a few more seconds. "You'd never fuckin' believe who that bitch has been smashing on the sidelines."

"Look. As much as I'd like to pretend that I'm interested in your bullshit relationships, I'd rather you hurry up and get your ass down to the Med. Profit has been shot."

"WHAT?" he thunders. "I thought he was going—"

"His limo got jacked. Bishop and his crew found him out off O'Donnell's." I lower my voice to inject sympathy. "It's bad, Mason. He's been pumped with a lot of muthafuckin' bullets."

There was a beat of silence. "Is he . . . ?"

"He was still alive when he got here. He's in surgery right now, but I ain't going to lie to you. It ain't looking too good."

"See you in a sec."

7

LeShelle

"FUCK! FUCK! FUCK!" I reach out and grab a curling iron from off the bathroom counter and hurl that muthafucka toward the vanity mirror. I don't even flinch when the bitch explodes into a million pieces. In the hallway, that pissy son of a bitch starts screaming and hollering, and it takes everything that's in me not to march back out there and give his ass something to really cry about.

"LeShelle, what the fuck is wrong with you?"

I ignore Python's ass as I stomp on broken glass in order to get over to the window. Sure enough, Ta'Shara's ass ain't nowhere in sight. *"Shit!"*

"LESHELLE!"

I turn around and storm out of the bathroom. The first muthafucka I see is that child hollering and snotting in the hallway. "Will you *please* shut the fuck up?"

"LESHELLE," Python thunders, limping into the hallway.

"What?" I shrug. "I fuckin' said *please*."

Python's eyes narrow as he grinds his teeth together.

I toss up my hands. "Fine. You deal with him. He's your kid. I have my own problems." Jerking away from his lil crybaby, I squeeze past Python to get out of the fuckin' hallway.

"And where the fuck do you think you're going?"

"I got some personal business I got to handle."

Python's face twists like I spat in his face. "Business? Bitch, what about me? I'm fuckin' bleeding all over the place."

"Then call your damn aunt Peaches over here to take care of it. I got shit to do, and that brat is really working the fuck out of my nerves right now." I try to snatch away my hand, but before I know it, Python's large hand locks around my throat and slams my head into the wall.

"Your mouth is out of fuckin' control!" His forked tongue slithers across his thick lips before he slams my ass again. "Do I look like some four-corner nigga who you can pop off to? Huh?"

Slam!

"I done capped one bitch tonight who thought she could play me stupid. You're welcome to join her ass in hell as far as I'm concerned. Now say something else slick."

Slam!

"Go ahead. I fuckin' dare you!"

Fuck. The way this nigga is squeezing my throat, I can't say shit. Plus, I think he has cracked the back of my head open. But if I'm not mistaken that loud-ass screaming has stopped. After the stars disappear before my eyes, I glare back into Python's black gaze, but I keep my muthafuckin' mouth shut. I'm not sure how long I'm pinned to the wall, but it feels like a long muthafuckin' time. While we're blowing invisible steam at each other, I realize that I do need to check myself. What's the point of making the moves I'm making just to lose Python to the next bitch he undoubtedly has on standby?

Python releases me and I slide down the wall and away from the big-ass dent my head made into the muthafucka. At my first gulp of oxygen, I start choking and hacking.

"Now fuckin' apologize," he barks.

"What?"

Python's open hand slams across my face, and I fleetingly think his ass gave me whiplash.

"I SAID FUCKIN' APOLOGIZE!"

Before his ass can hit me again, I throw up my hands as a sign of surrender. "I'm sorry," I manage to get out of a numb and bleeding tongue and aching windpipe. But when my gaze finds his again, I'm sure that he can still see anger in my eyes. His hand comes up again and I flinch.

"DON'T. TRY. ME."

Another standoff ensues, and luckily for my ass, his whiny whoreson starts sniffling. Python steps back but then starts ordering my ass around. "Take care of Lil Man. I'll take care of this plug my damn self." He turns and then storms into the bathroom. I hear him ask, "What the fuck happened in this muthafucka?" before he slams the door behind him.

I can't resist the urge of shooting my middle fingers at the closed door. I'm so sick of his ass always thinking that he's the only one with problems. I better find Ta'Shara and make sure she don't start blabbing to the po-po about her dead nigga. Then again, I know her ass ain't stupid enough to snitch. If she thinks my ass was ruthless earlier, she ain't seen nothing yet.

Sniff.

I jerk my head around, and once again, I'm staring at this ugly-ass kid. "C'mon here," I snap, turning toward one of the guest bedrooms. It's not really a guest bedroom since Python and I aren't exactly the type of people to be hosting niggas. The blue-painted room is more like a miscellaneous room, where Python stashes all his old workout equipment. There's an old treadmill with a mountain of clothes piled all over it. There's a stationary bike with the same problem and everything else that his aunt Peaches buys in the middle of the night from the Home Shopping Network and gives our asses. Basically, it's a room full of junk.

But there is an old bed in here as well—a twin bed that is as comfortable as sleeping on a pile of bricks, but that shit ain't my problem. "You can sleep in here," I tell him. "Just for the night—because I promise you that this shit ain't no permanent thing. I don't raise other bitches' bastards." I stare the kid down to make sure he gets my meaning, but then he blinks his big watery gaze up at me and I feel something tug in my chest. *Didn't some old bitch tell me and Ta'Shara that once when we moved in with them?*

An image of a woman with her nose in the air and a nasty, crooked-ass wig flashes in my memory. Yeah. It was the same bitch who fed us only one bowl of rice a day the entire three months we were there. It wasn't like we could steal shit either, because the evil woman kept food locked in a pantry and then kept the key tucked down in between her breasts. God, I hated that bitch.

I draw a deep breath and then shake off the memory. "Did you at least bring some clean clothes with you?" I ask, softening my voice.

He shakes his big, bowling ball–sized head while his bottom lip trembles.

"Fine." I huff out a long breath. "Take off your clothes and I'll go find something for you to wear." Now, just because I'm not snapping at his ass doesn't mean that I'm less annoyed. It's hard to get around feeling this goddamn disrespected.

I leave the kid alone and head to the master bedroom. Once there, I can't stop mumbling, "Fuck this bullshit" while I rummage around for something, anything, that would fit the child. Ten minutes later, I settle on one of Python's black T-shirts. Shit. At least the kid won't be naked. But when I walk back into the hall, I step in the kid's puddle of piss, and my blood pressure shoots right back up. I swear to God I don't see shit but red. "Guess I'm supposed to mop after this muthafucka, too," I snap at the closed door.

"Goddamn it, LeShelle. Shut the fuck up!" he shouts.

I roll my eyes. "Ain't this about a bitch?" I stomp into the blue room while still rolling my eyes.

"Put this shit on." I toss the shirt to the kid and then go back to the bathroom and knock.

Folding my arms, I shift my weight from side to side, waiting for Python to open the door.

"Yeah? What do you want?"

Are you fuckin' kidding me? "We need to talk."

There's a long pause and then, "C'mon in."

Still struggling to hold my temper in check, I reach for the knob and open the door.

Python is standing over the sink and picking at the hole at his side and bleeding freely all over the place. My concern for this nigga kicks in, and I toss all the other miscellaneous bullshit aside and move up next to him. "Stop. Let me take a look at it."

He glances down at me. "Oh. *Now* your ass is fucking concerned?"

"Shut up and move your hand." I lean in close and examine the wound. "The bullet is still in there."

"No shit."

I give him an irritated look. "You want me to help you or not?"

"Something tells me that you've been looking forward to paying me back for when I took the slug out of your arm a while back."

"They say karma is a bitch." I cheese up at him.

A smile hooks one side of his mouth. "A'ight. But make this shit quick because it's hurting like a son of a bitch."

"I can get it out, but because of the shape of this one, you might want to go with stitches instead of sealing it up with a hot knife."

"You know how to do that?"

"I can try—or we can probably wake up Momma Peaches to handle it."

"This time of night?"

"Please. You know her ass would do it for her favorite nephew." I wink at him, but his good humor has already faded from his face.

"Naw," he mumbles. "I don't need to bother her with this shit. Just do what you can."

I frown. Surely my smart-ass remark didn't have him thinking about his long-lost brother, Mason. The old-timers roaming around Shotgun Row told me plenty of times about how Python's cracked-out mother may have sold Python's baby brother for drugs. It's fucked up, but it's hardly a unique story around Memphis. This city is filled to the brim with a lot of trifling women who had no damn business spitting out babies—and I put my own momma in that same category. I've seen my fair share of bullshit around here with these strung-out bitches. If they don't toss it up themselves, they don't think twice about selling their kids wholesale. And trust and believe that you can't beat their asses sobbing and acting a fool in front of the news cameras when they report the children missing.

Getting that next hit is the only thing that matters to a crackhead. Only, let Momma Peaches tell it, the loss of his little brother really affected Python. To this day, he has never been able to forgive his mother.

Python resumes picking at the bleeding bullet hole.

I smack his hand away. "Stop it. You don't want to get an infection, do you?"

"Well, fuck. Get the molasses out your ass and handle this shit."

Ungrateful bastard. For the next thirty minutes, I concentrate on getting this bullet out of Python while waiting for him to tell me what happened. When I work the bullet out, we're both covered with blood.

"Let me see that son of a bitch," Python says.

I hand him the bloody bullet and then turn to get the alcohol and peroxide from beneath the bathroom counter.

"Soooo . . . do you wanna tell me what the fuck happened in here?" Python asks.

It's not like us to be tiptoeing around shit. I know that he's a real dog and that I'm the one kept on a short chain. But when niggas have a night like we clearly had, it's time to come correct.

"I did what you asked," I say flatly.

"Which is?"

I drench a hand towel with alcohol and start cleaning around his open wound. I know the shit has to sting, but Python doesn't flinch. It's small shit like this that gets my chest to swell with pride.

"Are you going to make me wait all night?"

"I took care of that situation between Ta'Shara and that Vice Lord muthafucka she was seeing."

His lips turn down as he rolls his eyes. "Yeah, right. Did she tell you that shit herself? You know bitches are some sneaky-ass muthafuckas. You need to bring her ass into the fold. Make her ass a Queen G."

"Done and done."

His black gaze finds mine again.

I smile. "I took a few niggas down by the school, and we jacked Ta'Shara and her nigga's shit after they left the prom."

"No shit?"

"No shit." I lean forward and plant a kiss on his thick lips. "I told you I'd handle it. Now it's done."

"Gangsta bitch." He slaps me on the ass.

"I did what needed to be done. Kind of like how you had to take care of your cousin Datwon."

Python cocked his large head. "What? You killed her?"

"Nah. I couldn't do that shit—but I earthed that grimy Vice Lord she'd been fuckin'." I cocked my hand like a pistol and placed the shit in the center of his chest. "Pow!"

Python's eyes lit up. "You're fuckin' shitting me. You capped Fat Ace's brother?"

"Fuck yeah. Dumped a full clip into that muthafucka! Lights out!" I laugh, remembering how good it felt to squeeze the trigger. My clit was thumping the whole time. Though it was eerie how that nigga remained on his feet like some black superhero. But his ass fell—and that's all that matters.

Python grabs hold of my face. "Goddamn. I fucking love your ass. You know that shit? You took that nigga's brother out! Fuck yeah!" He pulls me up against him and lays a kiss on me that steals my breath away. I melt against him and stretch my arms around his neck. Shit. Had I known I would've gotten this sort of reaction, I would have capped that young gun a long time ago.

"Oh." I push him back. "Your side. We need to get you stitched up. After that, we can finish this celebration in the bedroom."

Python flicks his forked tongue at me. "I wouldn't mind getting a little bit of that sweet ass, *Mrs. Carver.*"

My heart jumps. "What did you say?"

He reaches up and pinches me on my titties. "You heard me, Mrs. LeShelle Carver."

I scream and throw my arms around his neck.

"Ow. Fuck. Now that shit hurts."

"Oh, I'm sorry." I proceed to rain kisses all over his face. I can't believe it. I'm finally going to go from wifey to wife.

8

Ta'Shara

Profit is dead. Profit is dead.

I shove one foot in front of the other down a cracked and fucked-up sidewalk. Inside my head it's like there are two people—one who keeps replaying LeShelle firing bullets into Profit and another person vowing revenge.

Profit is dead. Profit is dead.

The only reason I know that I'm crying is because of my blurred vision. I make a lazy swipe at my face, and from the corner of my eyes, I catch two niggas hugging a street corner and pointing in my direction. My trembling, bloody hands clutch tighter the silk robe I stole out of LeShelle's bathroom while I inch toward the edge of the sidewalk. On this side of town, there's a good chance that these niggas are Gangster Disciples foot soldiers. If LeShelle discovers I'm gone, she's liable to put out a street APB and have my ass hauled back to Shotgun Row. Shit. She might even offer my captors another go at me as a reward.

Fear slithers down my spine while a sob lodges inside my throat and chokes the shit out of me.

Don't be stupid. LeShelle is your sister. She would never do something like that to you. She loves you.

In answer to that bullshit, the image of Profit's murder is replaced with the image of Dreadlocks pulling at my legs as if they were a wishbone and then pumping and grinding his stank-ass on top of me.

Your mind is playing tricks on you. That never happened. LeShelle would never allow something like to happen to you. She has always been your protector.

Then the image of Dreadlocks is replaced with Dusty Afro, and then another nigga and then another. Now my vision is completely fucked because tears are pouring down my face like a waterfall.

LeShelle wouldn't—

PROFIT IS DEAD, the other voice screamed.

I squeeze my eyes shut, trying to block out the voices in my head. I know what's happening. One part of my brain wants to submerge into denial while the other wants me to face reality. Right now, denial is so fuckin' attractive to me. Why wouldn't it be? Denial would mean that Profit is still alive, our limo was never jacked, and LeShelle . . .

I stop in the middle of the sidewalk and waver on my feet for a few seconds. *Profit is dead.* NO! *And it's all your fault.*

"T!"

My eyes pop open and my heart stops. *She found me!* Suddenly, I'm surrounded in a bright light and there's a loud *BANG!* I jump and take off running. I don't know where the energy comes from, but I'm eating up the ground in my bare feet.

Run! Run!

"T, wait up!" a voice yells out.

I hear the loud roar of an engine and then the stench of burning oil. I'm in full panic mode because I know what LeShelle and her rapist goons will do to me if they catch me. I release my hold on the robe so I can use my hands to swing and give myself more momentum. When I get a good stride, I clip something in the middle of the sidewalk, and the next thing I know I'm airborne. I don't have time to shift my hands forward to try and help break my fall, so I hit the concrete hard and slide for quite a ways. I'm aware of parts of my legs, arms, and even breasts scraping off, but I'm still physically numb and am able to jump back up and continue running.

"Goddamn it, Ta'Shara! It's me! Essence!"

It's a trick. Keep running! Hearing the car come up onto the sidewalk, I make a sharp right and hoof it toward a fenced backyard. It shouldn't be any problem jumping this mutha-fucka, but when I place my hand on the fence, this huge German Shepherd appears out of nowhere and jumps up.

"Ahhhhh!" I jump back in time to avoid the dog's vicious-looking teeth as they snap away at where my hands were.

Feet race up behind me.

"Ta'Shara!"

They are going to catch you! I take off toward the front of the house, with the dog running and barking from the other side of the fence.

"Drey, get her!"

No! No! No! An arm wraps around my waist and lifts me clear off the ground.

"Gotcha!"

Another scream rips from my throat as I twist around and rake my fingers down this nigga's mug shot.

"Aaaaaagh!"

His scream is like music to my ears as he drops me. However, my knees hit the backs of his legs, and we both tumble to the ground.

I land on something hard poking out of the ground, and the wind is knocked out of me. I can't even get my thoughts together.

"You crazy fucking bitch! What the hell is wrong with you?"

He grabs me by the shoulder, flips me over onto my back, and then pins my arms out like a crucifixion. The sight of another man straddling and pinning me down is all too much. I can't take it. I can't. Drawing a deep breath, I scream from my very soul while mentally curling into a fetal position and checking out of reality.

9

Essence

Ta'Shara's wild, gut-wrenching scream shocks the fuck out of me and causes each hair on my body to stand up. For a second, I back the hell up and look around to double-check that there ain't nobody thinking we're doing something to this girl. But as usual, the few dealers and crackheads who are hanging tough out here in the middle of the night are minding their business. They don't see shit, hear shit, and damn sure ain't about to call the po-po to come fuck up their cash flow.

"What the fuck is wrong with this bitch?" Drey shouts, still struggling to keep Ta'Shara pinned down.

I shake my head while my gaze falls back down to the ground to take in the whole scene. Despite it being dark as fuck, I am able to get a good look at T's bloody body and the dark, purpling bruises on her arms, chest, and face. Somebody worked her ass over real good. *What the fuck?*

Drey twists his head over his shoulder. "Essence! Are you going to help me with this bitch or not?"

Blinking and then mentally shaking myself out of shock, I rush over and drop down next to my girl. "T! Please calm down!" I try to still her thrashing head so that she can get a good look at my face. The shit ain't easy because she's strong as fuck and blasting my eardrums wide open.

"Let's let her crazy ass go," Drey shouts. "Clearly, she ain't right in the head."

"Have you lost your mind? Can't you see that something has happened to her?"

"Something happened to me, too! Look at my face!"

Crude, jagged, and bleeding scratches run down his face. "Shit. She did that?"

"Didn't you see her?" He pauses for a sec. "Wait. How bad does it look?"

I ain't about to tell him that Ta'Shara has fucked up his face. The vain nigga might retaliate or some dumb shit. "Let's get her to the hospital," I say, changing the subject. "T, look at me!" I lean down until we're nose to nose. "See, Ta'Shara, it's me."

"Hospital?" Drey echoes.

There isn't an ounce of recognition in Ta'Shara's eyes. Only fear.

Oh my God. Who did this to you?

"Look, Essence. I ain't taking this girl to no fuckin' hospital," Drey says. "Ain't no fuckin' way."

I whip my head around. "We *have* to take her to the hospital. Look at her!"

He's shaking his head the whole time while I'm talking. "Ain't going to happen. Those muthafuckas ask way too many questions, and I don't know shit. Don't wanna know shit and even if I did, I wouldn't tell them any goddamn way."

"But—"

"She's *your* girl. Not mine. I ain't getting involved in this bullshit. Look where the fuck we are. We're in GD territory—our shit. You think I'm going to help the po-po bring heat over here? Shit. You're out of your goddamn mind." He foolishly releases Ta'Shara's hands, and my girl comes up swinging, clocking both me and Drey on each side of our heads.

"Owwww!" The shit stuns the fuck out of me, and while I'm reeling to the side, I hear this loud *crack*!

"Goddamn it, bitch!"

While I'm blinking stars out from behind my eyes, I realize that Ta'Shara's screaming has stopped. I pick myself off the ground and look over to see Drey shaking his hand while T is knocked out cold beneath him.

"What the fuck did you do?" I check to see if my girl is okay.

"What the fuck does it look like? I shut her the fuck up!"

There's a pulse and she seems to be breathing evenly.

"You're welcome." Drey climbs off of her. "I'm getting the fuck out of here."

"Whoa, whoa. Wait!" I grab his wrist. "Where are you going?"

"Home. Fuck this shit." He tries to shake me loose. "This shit ain't my problem."

I tighten my grip. "You can't leave us here."

Drey laughs and snatches his hand free. "Watch me."

Jumping up, I chase after him. "Drey, please. You gotta help me!"

"I ain't gotta do shit." He strolls back toward his car.

"Goddamn it. *Please!* I swear, I'll do anything you ask. Just help me with my girl." That shit gets him to slow down. "Absolutely *anything* you want." I grab him by the shirt and pull him up against my body. "Anything *and* for however *long* you want it." I slide my hands down inside his pants and give his hairy nut sac a good squeeze. "Word is bond."

A small smile hooks the side of Drey's lips as he peeks down into my chocolate cleavage. "Any *freaky* shit I want?"

"Anything." I move my hand from his balls to grip his dick for a few strokes. Niggas around here don't do shit without getting something in return.

"A'ight, then." He nods before turning back around. "You better not renege on this shit neither."

My shoulders slump with relief as I follow him back. While she's still passed out, Drey has no problem scooping her up off the ground and carrying her to his rusted-out piece of shit, where he tosses my girl into the backseat like she's a rag doll.

"Goddamn it. Be careful," I bark, and then climb into the backseat, too.

Drey rolls his eyes. "Muthafuck that bitch," he mutters under his breath, and then slams our door. "Lucky my ass ain't dumping her ass into the trash."

Ignoring him, I turn my attention to Ta'Shara. I don't know whether I should wake her or let her sleep this shit off. *But what the hell happened to her? And where the fuck is Profit?* I close the robe she has on because her bruised chest and breasts are making my stomach churn and lurch.

Drey climbs behind the wheel and then shifts this death contraption into reverse, which of course causes his busted-ass tailpipe to complain with another loud-ass *BANG!* "Where to?"

"The Med. That's the closest, right?" I ask.

"Fine. But we're doing a drop-and-roll."

"But—"

"Save the bullshit. That's the deal or both y'all muthafuckas can get the fuck out of my ride right now."

"That's fucked up."

"Nah. Whoever done that shit to your girl is fucked up, but you need to stop and put two and two together before you start thinking about getting involved."

"What the fuck are you talking about?"

He rolls his eyes like I'm the stupidest muthafucka who has ever walked the earth. "The last time we saw your girl, she was rolling up out of the prom with that slob Profit. They were both cheesing and rubbing on each other like they didn't know they were violating a whole much of fuckin' rules. GD and Vice don't mix, you feel me?"

"Ta'Shara is not a Queen G."

"She is by blood. You know that shit. Don't play crazy."

I do know it, and I haven't wasted another moment's

breath trying to convince Ta'Shara of the dangers of her and Profit going public. Hell, even her sister had stepped to her and told her ass point-blank to end the shit. But my girl has been dick-crazy. The more you tell her not to do something, the more determined she is to stay with the muthafucka.

"That dead nigga we saw being chalked earlier," Drey continues. "Your girl's missing nigga and her ass looking like that tells me that some street politics has caught up with they asses and it was done by our people. Why else was she on this side of town? Huh?"

Everything this corner hustler is saying is making perfect sense.

"Check her ass."

"What?"

"You heard me. Check her ass and see if she's been branded." He hits a switch, and the interior light comes on.

I hesitate for a moment but then roll Ta'Shara over to confirm what we both already know. Sure enough, on her ass are the dirty, bleeding initials *GD*. My stomach stops churning and starts knotting at the sickening sight. Only one name floats to the top of my head. "LeShelle."

Drey nods. "Damn. Maybe you *are* a little smarter than you look."

"Shut the fuck up and drive," I snap, blinking back a few tears.

"Fuck. Don't get mad at me. I ain't had shit to do with this. But you think I'm going to be able to convince the po-po of that shit? They'll take one look at her ass and these tats on my neck and then haul my ass downtown. You, too, Lil Queen G. We'll either have to take the heat or snitch. How the fuck you think that's going to go down?"

Now I feel sick.

Drey shakes his head again. "We'll drop her ass outside the ER, and then we roll the fuck out. Cool?"

Torn, I glance down at Ta'Shara's face. T is my best friend.

I've had her back for a long time now, but . . . shit. This puts me in a bad situation—a life-or-death situation.

"MUTHAFUCK!" Drey leans forward to get a good look at his reflection in the rearview mirror. "Look at what that bitch did to my face!"

"Calm down!"

"Calm down? Fuck that. You need to clean that bitch's fingernails. Shit. I watch *CSI*. They can pull my DNA off some shit like that."

"What?"

"You heard me. Look around back there and find something to clean her nails. I ain't taking the rap for no goddamn body."

"Drey—"

"I FUCKIN' MEAN IT!" He jerks the steering wheel to pull over to the side of the road.

"All right. All right. I'll do it. Just fuckin' drive." I glance around the floor of the backseat and find a screwdriver. It's better than nothing. Satisfied, Drey continues driving while I try to dig the skin and blood from beneath Ta'Shara's fingernails. However, the act feels like a betrayal, and I feel a rush of tears threatening to flood my eyes. "Why didn't you fuckin' listen to me," I mumble low, shaking my head. I don't even want to think about what probably happened to Profit. No doubt the brothah is dead, but how he went out was probably brutal as hell.

Goddamn these fuckin' streets. I swipe my tears, but deep down I know that nothin' is ever going to change out here. If anything, it'll only get worse. Profit's death will only set off a vicious chain reaction. I hate to admit it, but Drey is right. The last thing we want is to be implicated directly in this shit. It would be like painting a target on the center of our foreheads for the Vice Lords.

"What the fuck is this shit?" Drey asks. He hits the dashboard, and the interior lights go out.

"What?" I glance up as he rolls into the hospital's parking lot.

"Those niggas right there . . . and over there . . . and there."

Sure enough, posted outside the emergency room are at least seven different groups of niggas, all flaggin' gold and black.

"It looks like a muthafuckin' Vice Lord convention out at this muthafucka." Drey huffs out a long breath. "SHIT! I knew my ass should have left you two bitches back there. I must have a neon sign over my head that says 'stupid muthafucka.' "

"Shut the fuck up!" I pop him on the back of the head while I peek out the situation. "Something has gone down."

"Duh! You fuckin' think?" This time he rolls his eyes so hard it's amazing the shit doesn't get stuck in the back of his head. "I'm getting the hell out of here."

"Wait! What—"

"We can't drop her off here. I'm willing to bet on my nanna's life that this shit here has a lot to do with your girl's missing man. All these muthafuckas gotta know that he took her ass to the prom. They catch us with her, they going to put two and two together and come up with six. Ya feel me?"

"Goddamn. This is some fucked-up shit." I'm starting to panic, too. The realness of this situation is hitting home like a muthafucka.

Beside me, Ta'Shara groans.

"Aw, fuck! If that bitch wakes up screaming, I'm personally going to put a bullet in her head."

I pop Drey again. "You ain't going to do shit."

"Fuck. I'll cap her ass before they cap me. Believe that shit."

"Whatever, nigga."

"Bet. You better makes sure her ass stays quiet back there."

Drey loops around, and his busted-ass shit catches a few niggas' attention.

My heart leaps into my throat. I have no idea what we'll do

if any of these muthafuckas decide to follow this smoking bucket of bolts. "Hurry," I urge, pushing his shoulder.

"I ain't going to speed through this muthafucka. They'll know that something is up."

A tall figure, dressed in all black but stacked with feminine curves, emerges from the emergency room and strolls across the parking lot toward a black SUV.

"Hey, I know that chick."

"Good for you," Drey mumbles.

I search my memory Rolodex, and it flies back to nine months ago, when Ta'Shara and I were down at this very hospital because Profit had gotten into some shoot-out with the police. When we went up to his room, that bitch there was standing outside his door along with a bunch of other Vice Lords like a string of personal bodyguards. Ta'Shara told me her name later on. *What is it?* "Lucifer," I whisper.

Drey's eyes bug. "Who? Her?"

I nod. "You know her?"

"Yeah. Fuck this shit." Drey slams his foot on the accelerator and peels out of the hospital like a bat out of hell.

"Hey!" I grip the backseat so that I don't fall back against my girl. "I thought you didn't want to draw attention?"

"I also don't wanna die tonight, so you need to shut the fuck up! You done got my ass into some bullshit. That's all I know. The sooner I get y'all out my damn car, the better."

"Well, then let's try another hospital."

"Fuck that! I ain't risking that shit no more."

"We had a deal!"

"And I drove y'all ass out here. It ain't my fault the place is crawling with cockroaches. Who to say they ain't got niggas at *all* the hospitals looking for that bitch?"

"Shit."

"Exactly. Shit." He shakes his head. "I say we just find some woods and dump her ass."

"Fuck naw. That shit ain't going to happen." And I mean that shit. I may be spooked, but I ain't going to punk my girl out like that. "We'll take her to her house."

"What? And tell her peoples what?"

I'm shaking my head and making shit up as I go along. "Nothing. We'll do a drop-and-roll there. Put her on the doorstep, ring the doorbell, and haul ass."

"What if we get caught? We'll be right back at square one."

"We *won't,*" I insist, but I don't have any fuckin' idea if that's true of not. All I know is that it's the best I can do for her right now. *Fuck.*

Fifteen minutes later, our asses roll into picturesque midtown. We loop around the Douglas' neighborhood a few times to make sure there aren't any roaming niggas hanging out to catch what the fuck we are about to do. In this blue-collar neighborhood, niggas are locked up and snug as a bug at this time of night. It's a mystery why Ta'Shara fucked with a nigga tied to the streets in the first place. The way I saw the shit, she was set. After growing up in foster care and being bounced around from one foster house to another, she'd landed a loving couple who was doing everything they could to steer her down the right path. A year ago, Ta'Shara was talking about college and getting the hell out of Memphis. *What a difference a man makes.*

"Is it this one?" Drey points to the two-level beige and gray stone craft bungalow.

"Yeah."

"Shit. It's nice out here," he comments, looking around.

"C'mon. Let's hurry up and do this." I tense up again. I can't believe that I'm about to do this shit.

Drey hops out of the car and opens the back door. When he pulls Ta'Shara out of the backseat, he almost bangs her head against the door frame.

"Hey, watch it," I snap, crawling out behind him.

"You stay in the car. The faster we do this shit the better."

I want to argue, but I know that he's right. "Make sure that you ring the door bell," I remind him.

Again, he rolls his eyes and then jogs up toward the door with Ta'Shara cradled in his arms.

I watch him like a hawk while he sets Ta'Shara down on the porch bench. He hesitates a moment but then rings the doorbell and takes off. He's halfway across the yard when the house lights click on.

"Hurry, hurry," I mumble under my breath. For a moment, I'm really fearful that he will be caught and ID'd for this shit.

But Drey is nimble as fuck as he jumps and slides across the hood of the car to get to the other side. "We're out of this bitch," he hisses, shifting the car into drive.

My eyes remain glued to the front door. When it opens, Drey jams his foot on the accelerator. Ta'Shara's foster mother, Tracee, opens the door and we're able to hear her scream, "REGGIE!" above the squeal of Drey's tires as we rocket into the night. I close my eyes against the gush of wind rushing through the open window, but it does nothing to brush away my shame. "I'm so sorry, Ta'Shara. I hope that you will forgive me."

10

Lucifer

Strolling across the dark hospital parking lot, I'm suddenly hit with the smell of burning oil. To my right, I catch sight of a rusted-out Buick Electra and twist my nose up in disgust. Some niggas really will ride around in any damn thing nowadays. Then something strange happens. A chick in the backseat points at me, and the driver's eyes get so fucking big that he looks like a goddamn cartoon. *Do I know these niggas?*

I stop at the curb and watch the car make an awkward U-turn. The hairs on the back of my neck stand up, and I cast a look at a couple of my flagged brothahs standing guard outside the ER, ready to shut down any potential drive-by bullshit like we had to deal with the last time.

"Yo! Go peep that shit out," I yell.

Like real soldiers, they take off to follow those shady-looking muthafuckas.

Satisfied, I resume my stroll toward Mason's SUV and hop into the passenger's side, but before I can launch my interrogation about where his ass has been for the past hour, I notice blood seeping through his white T-shirt. "What the fuck?!"

Mason groans as he tries to shift his massive frame around in his seat. "Don't worry about it. It's a scratch."

"A scratch?" I reach over the dashboard and turn on the interior light. I get in only one quick glance before Mason shuts it back off. "Damn. Chill out, Willow! I said it's just a fuckin' scratch. Tell me what's going on in there with my brother. Is he going to make it?"

For a few seconds I draw a damn blank, because I want to get to the bottom of what else went down tonight while I was getting my clit sucked at a goddamn club. At my hesitation, Mason's head jerks toward me.

"Is he . . . ?" His voice croaks.

"Nah." I snap out of it. "At least they haven't come out and told us one way or the other just yet. But . . ." I struggle on whether to reach for his hand. I'm not exactly known for my softer side. It's hard for me—has been for a long time. "Profit took a lot of bullets. Whoever did this shit tried to turn him into Swiss cheese. For real. But you have my word that we're going to find these muthafuckas and return the favor, and we're going to make sure that their asses ain't still breathing when we're through."

"What the fuck happened?" Mason growls. "Last I heard he was taking his lil girlfriend to the prom. Did a gang fight break out or some shit?"

"Not at the school, but a few of our young guns who go to Morris High filled me in on a few things I didn't know about. Not that it's my job to keep up with the drama that goes on in the high schools."

"What are you talking about?"

"Profit. Apparently, he and his girl, Ta'Shara, have been pissing a whole lot of people off—blatantly flaunting their relationship."

Mason's brows dip. "Okay. What's the big deal? They were all hugged at his initiation party, too."

"Profit has never talked to you about Ta'Shara's people?"

Mason pauses. "All I know is that he's crazy about the girl."

He thinks about it some more. "She's crazy about him, too. At least as far as I could tell."

I bob my head because that's the same impression I had, too.

"The last time we were up at this hospital," Mason continues, "Profit did get defensive when I tried to ask his girl a few questions. What the fuck were they hiding?"

"An awful lot," I tell him flatly.

"Are we going to sit here and play twenty questions while I bleed all over the place, or are you going to spit it out?" he snaps.

"I thought you said that it was a scratch? Let me see." I reach for the light again only to have Mason knock my hands away.

"Goddamn it, Willow! I'm not in the mood for this shit right now." He winces and grips the steering wheel. "I'm trying to handle one crisis at a goddamn time."

I watch uncomfortably while his arm muscles bulge to the point that I see veins popping out. Clearly he's in pain, but he's not going to admit it. Mason's pride is a monster. A minute later, whatever spasm that hit him subsides, but he's panting and sweating like he just finished running a marathon. *He needs a doctor.*

"The prom . . ." he reminds me, pulling out his flag from his back pocket and mopping his head with it. "Finish telling me what happened."

Sucking in a frustrated breath, I spill what I know. "Ta'Shara is a Queen G—by blood. Nobody knows if she's taken the oath personally but—"

"Who's her people? Anyone we know?"

"Oh, we know her all right. Ta'Shara's sister is Python's wifey, LeShelle. Head Queen G herself."

Mason snatches off his ever-present Louis Vuitton shades so

that his one brown eye and one milky eye can level on me and see if I'm serious. But I've always been a hard read. "Please tell me that you're fucking bullshitting me."

"I don't bullshit—you know that."

"That mutha—" Mason bites down on his bottom lip and shakes his head. "Why the hell would Profit keep something like that from me?"

"You really have to ask? What would you have done had you known?"

"Tell him to dump the bitch!"

"Exactly—but since when do you Lewis men listen to reason when it comes to pussy?"

"Fuck!" Mason rolls eyes. "He invited that bitch out to my crib. For all we know, her ass was sent there to spy on our asses. You know how hot the streets have been this past year. Those pussy muthafuckas have been dropping our people like flies." He pauses for a moment. "Come to think of it, her ass showed here that night just before the Gangster Disciples came blasting up the damn hospital. Remember that? She crept in and surprise, surprise, guess who was waiting for our asses downstairs ready to light our asses up?"

I nod, but then toss out, "Or . . . Profit and Ta'Shara really do like each other and didn't want people telling them who they can and can't be with."

Mason cocks his head at me. "What? You're a muthafuckin' romantic now? You going to try and tell me that you grew a heart when I wasn't fucking lookin'?"

That jab hurt.

"In case you forgot," Mason sneers, "Romeo and Juliet died at the end of that fucked-up story."

"Doesn't change the fact that they still loved each other."

Mason rolls his eyes as he turns his head away. "Love . . . it's all bullshit. Trust me. I got a fucking reminder of that shit tonight."

"What are you talking about?"

"Just don't talk to me about that love bullshit. One bitch is as good as the next. Smiling bitches lie to your face and then creep around and be squashing your enemy behind your back. FUCK!" He punches the steering wheel and the horn blares, breaking the night's silence.

"Where's the bitch?" Mason asks.

I frown, confused as to which bitch we're talking about.

Mason's large head rolls toward me again, and I swear to God I can see anger simmering off his body in waves. "The girl," he spits. "Where the fuck is the girl?"

Blinking, I'm surprised that the obvious question hasn't even crossed my mind. I've been so focused on Profit and Mason that . . . "I don't know."

"You don't know?" he repeats, nodding his head for a few beats. "You don't *fuckin'* know?" he explodes, and then unleashes a fierce torrent of punches against the steering wheel. "Aaaarrrrgggh!"

Stunned, I lean back and watch while each solid punch causes the horn to blare in protest. I understand his frustrations, my own emotions are all over the place. But after a full minute, I worry. "Mason, please. Calm down." Awkwardly, I reach out and place my hand against his shoulder. "We're going to handle this shit. Trust me. Those fake gangstas are going to pay for this shit. You got my word on that!"

Mason throws his hands up and shrugs off my touch. "I want *every one* of those muthafuckas dead. You hear me? Every. One." He's panting so hard he looks like he's getting ready to pass out.

I bob my head, but we still have one more thing left to discuss. The big black elephant in the SUV. But Mason can be stubborn, and he damn sure doesn't like asking for or accepting help. "You need to see a doctor," I toss out. "You look like shit."

"What doesn't kill me makes me stronger." He sucks in a deep breath.

"But a hard head makes a soft ass," I remind him.

"It's gonna take a whole lot more than this shit to take me out."

"Let me see what type of damage we're dealing with."

"Willow—"

"And you got one more fuckin' time to call me by that damn name and then we are going to have a fuckin' problem."

Our eyes lock and I know him well enough to recognize pain.

"You still think that you can beat my ass, don't you?" he asks.

"Don't front. You know I can take you down anytime, any-place," I tell him.

He laughs, but the shit sounds painful. After a minute, his laughter dies out and he sits there thinking for a long while. "I fucked up," he says. "I really fucked up tonight."

Whatever the hell he's talking about, I know this shit ain't easy for him to admit. "Is that right?"

Another long silence and then, "Yeah."

I don't like the way his breathing sounds. It's too choppy, and sweat is still pouring down his face. What had he said earlier? Bitch has been fucking someone on the sidelines? Was he talking about his precious Officer Melanie Johnson?

"So who was the other dude?"

A muscle twitches along his temple. "That reptile wannabe muthafucka."

"Why am I not surprised?"

"You knew that shit?"

"They dated back in high school, Mason. She confirmed that shit to you not too long ago. She said it was over—you chose to believe that bullshit. I didn't."

"You never really liked that bitch, did you?"

That was an understatement. "Like father, like daughter," I tell him.

Mason rolls his eyes.

"I know that . . . but—"

"Like I said, when it comes to pussy—"

"You made your point," he growls, looking like he's on the brink of another spasm. "Squash it."

Of course I don't. "Was Python there when you went over there?" I press.

"He busted in on us." Mason coughs. "Nigga started blasting while my dick was still swinging in the muthafuckin' air." He coughs again and then chugs in a deep breath. "Bitch started begging for her life and admitted that the baby she's carrying is his."

"Muthafuck! What kind of soap-opera bullshit are you involved in?"

"None. I blew a hole in that ass."

I blink. "You killed her?"

"Don't know. Her ass was still breathing when I jumped out the window in my fuckin' birthday suit." Mason's cough sounds like he's trying to hack up a lung. When he stops, blood trickles from the corner of his mouth.

I panic. "That's it!" I pop open my door and hop out of the car. "Yo!" I holler to the guys posted outside the ER. "Y'all niggas come over here and help me."

"Willow—"

"Time-out with that 'Willow' shit. You need to see a doctor."

Mason shakes his head and tries to talk again, but I take full control of the situation. I rush around the vehicle, and when I open Mason's door, he spills out.

I barely catch him before he hits the concrete.

It takes six niggas to help get him back into the SUV, and by that time Mason's entire T-shirt is soaked through with blood. I can't take him into this hospital. Not if he possibly killed a cop tonight. There's only one place I can take him.

"Don't you fuckin' die on me," I say, struggling to get the upper half of his body back into the car while tears burn the backs of my eyes. "Don't you fuckin' dare."

Shelter

11

Momma Peaches

It's official. My ass is no damn good. But to tell the truth, after six decades of being on God's green earth, I'm okay with that. I am what I am, and if people don't like that shit, they can lick the crack of my ass. That's right. Not all of us senior citizens try to act like we're angels, crying and hollering in somebody's church five times a week and hoping that's enough to get God to forget about all the hell we done raised back in the day. Nah. I don't believe in faking the funk like that. I've done my dirt and haven't tried to wash it off. I've also made some mistakes, terrible mistakes, but the way I see shit, that's the only way you're gonna learn.

I've also been hardheaded about a lot shit, too. And that usually revolved around men. I've had them all—young, middle-aged, or old—because I've kept my body tight and right. And that's all most niggas want—that and a hot plate every now and again.

I suck in a deep breath and then try to decide whether I want to satisfy my craving for a plate of flapjacks or stay right where I am. After all, the mattress is comfortable, the sheets are soft, and Cedric's thick-ass dick is hard as a brick and nestled nicely in my pussy.

Okay, maybe I shouldn't have fucked my parole officer, but

everybody must play the fool sometimes. Yeah, maybe I've played it more times than most, but last night I couldn't help myself. Once I made the connection that Cedric is the son of my first love, Manny, I had to have him. Shit. Looking into the face of Manny's mini-me while I was nuttin' up was fuckin' sweeter than anything I could've ever imagined. It was almost like I was sixteen again.

Cedric doesn't eat pussy like his daddy, but he sure as hell can fuck like him. Who would've guessed that knowing how to sling dick could be in someone's DNA? I chuckle at my scientific discovery, but when I hear my stomach rumble, I know that it's time to un-ass the bed. However, the moment I peel back the top sheet, Cedric stirs.

"Where you going?"

Fuck. I get a little wetter hearing his deep bass up against my ear. "To the kitchen."

He chuckles. "Pancakes?"

"We call them flapjacks around here. What? You don't want any?"

"Now, what man have you ever known to turn down a hot plate first thing in the morning?"

Cedric pulls me back by the shoulder so that I'm lying flat against the bed. He stays lying on his side but props his head up on his folded arm. "But I thought that we should talk first."

I roll my eyes and pray that I don't have another one of those sensitive niggas who always wants to talk about feelings and what every fuck means in our relationship. Shit. I just went through that bullshit with my last lover, Arzell. He got hot because he wanted to marry me when everybody and they momma knows that my ass is already married. Yeah, my nigga, Isaac, might be behind bars, but fuck, whose man isn't nowadays?

"What do you want to talk about?" I ask flatly, and hope he picks up on my little attitude and drops the subject.

Cedric frowns. "What the hell do you think I want to talk about?"

This time I'm more dramatic when I huff out a long, frustrated breath.

"Oh. Damn. It's like that, huh?" He shakes his head and then rolls out of bed. "Forget it. A brothah can take a hint."

Shit. This is the type of shit I want to avoid. "Wait." I grab him by the wrist and pull back. "I didn't mean it like that," I lie. "I'm just a grouch before breakfast."

His sexy green eyes narrow and then scan my ass like a human lie detector. "Yeah. Whatever." He jerks his wrist back. "Squash it. I'll put in for you to be transferred to another PO first thing Monday morning."

Alarmed, I sit straight up. "Why?"

Cedric laughs as he climbs out of bed. "Oh, *now* you want to talk?"

I steal a second so that my gaze can rape his fine, red-bone ass. Mmm-mmm. Just like his daddy. "C'mon now. I didn't think that you were going to say no ridiculous shit like you didn't want to be my parole officer no more."

He snatches his clothes off the floor. "Under the circumstances—"

"Oh God, don't tell me that you're one of those brothahs who does everything by the book."

He chuckles. "All right. I won't tell you."

"Well, don't that beat all? The last Boy Scout." I reach over to the nightstand and pull open the top drawer. A few seconds later, I'm lighting my morning joint.

Cedric shakes his head. "You're just going to smoke that shit right in front of me?"

I smile and shrug. "It's your fault. I always smoke when I get some good dick."

His smile stretches wider. "I could have you arrested."

Holding the blunt in the corner of my lips, I press my

wrists together and then offer them up to him. "You can slap those Coco Chanels on me any time you feel ready, Daddy."

I love the way the light catches his eyes while we flirt. "Oh? Is that right?" He pulls out a pair of handcuffs from the back of his rumpled jeans pocket and then walks over to me. Did I write a check that my ass can't cash? We're still smiling at each other when he snaps each silver bracelet closed around my wrist.

"They're kind of tight."

"They're supposed to be." He removes the blunt from my mouth and then casually plops it between his own lips for a long toke, but then he snatches it out and starts choking. "Holy shit. What the fuck is in this?"

Tossing my head back, I can't help but laugh. "That's some bad shit," I brag. "Special blend from one of the girls who used to hang around here. I had her hook me up with a whole box full not too long before she passed."

"This shit didn't kill her, did it?"

I laugh. "Nah. It had something more to do with someone emptying a whole clip of bullets into her pussy."

"Fuck," he says. "Are you for real?"

I shrug, letting him know that it is what it is. "You live by the streets, you die by the streets . . ."

"Is that what you do?" he asks, cocking up a brow.

I only give him half a smile this time. "I'm different."

Disappointed, Cedric shakes his head. "Everyone out here thinks that they're different. They hustle and gangbang, thinking that they'll be able to jump out of the movie just before the part where Tony Montana is pumped full of holes."

"True." I bob my head. "But look who you're talking to, baby. I look damn good, but I ain't exactly a kitten. I'm an old alley cat, and I learned a long time ago that these streets don't love me. I'm a survivor, through and through."

"Is that right?" Cedric takes another long toke. His eyes are already starting to look glassy.

"You might want to take it easy on that, Boy Scout. It has a way of knocking you on your ass."

"All this shit is doing is getting my dick harder." Smiling, he places it back into my mouth so I can take another hit.

"Well in that case"—I blow a stream of smoke straight into his face—"let's get you as hard as possible."

Cedric snubs out the blunt, grabs my bound wrists, and jams them high over my head until I'm pressed into the mattress. With him hovering above me, I can testify that he is indeed as hard as steel. When he slides that fat cock into my wet pussy again, I swear to God my mind goes straight to the moon. It doesn't make no sense for no dick to be this goddamn good.

"Awww, shit," Cedric pants, rotating his hips and hitting my G-spot. "You got some good-ass pussy."

The sweet, heady funk that our two bodies generate is as intoxicating as the blunt we just smoked. I don't even fucking mind that this young brothah is banging my head against the headboard. All that matters is this nut I feel forming in the very tips of my toes and rolling up my good leg. It never matters to these niggas that I lost half of my left leg years ago. Though I have had some niggas say that it helps them get easier access to this pussy I'm dishing out to a few chosen ones.

"OH GOD!" My nut courses up my thighs and gains momentum as it heads toward my clit. I lock up my pussy muscles, and Cedric's mouth drops into a perfect circle.

"Yeah. That's it, baby. Yo shit it so fuckin' tight."

Damn right it is. I stay up on my muthafuckin' Kegels. A nigga can forgive a lot of things, but never a funky or busted-out pussy.

Cedric hunches his back and keeps churning this sticky honey like his life depends on my ass coming. Somewhere along the way, I sink my nails into his big, smooth back and rake them all the way up to his fuckin' shoulders.

"Awwww shhhhhhheit," he hisses, but his wonderful hips don't stop.

At long last that nut reaches the tip of my clit and explodes like a nuclear bomb over Afghanistan. I don't mean to scream and shout, but I do both of those muthafuckas at the same damn time. "Aww, shit, you muthafucka."

Cedric isn't far behind my ass, especially when I pluck my nails out of his shoulders and then start caressing his muscled ass cheeks. When I think he's ready, I slip my finger straight into that tight ass. Instantly, he roars and pops his dick out of my drenched pussy and shoots his hot, gooey white bullets across my flat stomach like an AK-47.

To show how much I appreciate our morning workout, I reach down and slide my fingers across the pretty mess he's made, and then bring them up to my mouth so that I can have a taste. "Mmmmm."

Cedric laughs. "You're a nasty freak."

"Are you bragging or complaining?"

"Since I'm the one fuckin' you, I'm most definitely bragging."

We lie in bed for about another hour. I even get another go at his mad head game and practically drown his ass in pussy juice before we actually take off the handcuffs and climb out of bed. I hit the shower first and then head toward the kitchen, stopping briefly in the living room to turn on the television. A few minutes later, I hear someone sneaking up behind me.

"Go on and sit down, baby," I say. "Momma Peaches is going to fix you up some of her famous flapjacks."

"Flapjacks?" Arzell thunders. "What, you got another nigga up in here?"

I jump and turn around so fast that it's a wonder my prosthetic leg don't fuckin' pop off. Sure enough, there's Arzell's tall ass glaring at me like I owe his ass money. This is exactly what I get for fuckin' around with my best friend's twenty-three-year-old grandbaby. Once you pussy-whip them, they become emotional hotheads.

"Arzell, what the fuck *you* doing in here?" I bark.

"Nah, bitch. The question is what the fuck are *you* doing in here?" Arzell looks straight crazy, like he ain't shaved or washed since he rolled up out of this muthafucka with his ass up on his shoulders.

"First of all, I ain't no nigga's bitch. And second of all, I suggest you get that bass outcha voice when you're talking to me."

"I'll fuckin' settle this shit." He jerks away from the kitchen door and snatches out his signature .50-caliber magnum from his sagging jeans and starts toward the bedroom.

"Arzell, no!" I rush after him, but this young nigga's long legs have him halfway down the hall before I can even catch up with him. "Stop, boy! Stop!" I grab him by the arm and start bopping him on the back of the head. "Take that foolishness up out of here."

"FUCK, NIGGA, WHERE YOU AT?" Arzell shouts, shrugging off my flailing arms like he's fending off flies. Why the fuck I didn't grab my muthafuckin' skillet, I don't know. Niggas listen when cast iron whacks they heads.

"Move, Peaches!" Arzell barks, knocking me into a wall and kicking open my bedroom door.

I stumble and fall just as my door bangs opens so hard that the top hinge breaks off.

"Muthafucka!" Arzell shouts, pointing that long-ass barrel straight at a wide-eyed Cedric who has one foot in and one foot out of his blue jeans.

Arzell fires.

"Shit." Cedric ducks and then charges forward like a fucking linebacker. His shoulder rams into Arzell's chest, propelling his ass backward. When he hits the same wall I'm lying down against, I swear I hear a couple of ribs snap in his chest.

I scramble away as Cedric slams a fist across Arzell's glass jaw. He drops the gun and it knocks me in the head. "Y'all, niggas need to stop playing."

Cedric, clearly pissed off for having my young buck shooting at him, sends another punch dead in Arzell's mouth. Blood splatters everywhere—on me, on the walls, and on Cedric's ramming fist.

"All right, enough!" I pull at Cedric. "Leave the boy alone. He's had enough!" I tug on one of Cedric's meaty arms, and I think he's starting to ease up a bit when from the corner of my eye I see Arzell's right hand retrieve the magnum.

"ARZELL, NO!"

This muthafucka starts shooting. I ain't quite sure what the fuck happened. I must've blacked out because the next thing I know, I'm pulling my face off the floor and Cedric is stomping the shit out of Arzell.

"YOU FUCKIN' TRYNA KILL ME, LIL PUNK?"

Kick!

Kick!

Stomp!

Stomp!

Arzell curls into a fetal position and takes his much-deserved ass-kicking like a child.

I try to move but can't. I look down and I see my prosthetic leg splintered to hell and back. "MUTHAFUCKA!" I pick up my shit, stare at it, and then start whupping up Arzell's head with it myself. "Nigga, you done fuck up my damn leg. You know how much one of these damn things cost?"

I hear my front door burst open, and my house fills up with Gangster Disciples and Queen Gs ready to start blasting.

"Momma Peaches, you all right?" McGriff shouts. "What's going on up in here?"

Cedric's hands fly up into the air in surrender at the sight of my nephew, Python's right-hand man, storming in with his gun cocked and swinging between Arzell and Cedric.

"Y'ALL NIGGAS CHILL!" I shout before they start blasting.

"Shoot this nigga!" Arzell shouts, uncurling and making another dive for his gun.

An army of guns go up.

"NO!" I wave my arms and manage to stop everyone's fire as well as kick out my good leg and send Arzell's gun sliding away from him.

"Momma Peaches, what the hell is going on?" McGriff asks, his black gaze darting back and forth.

"Just some dumb shit," I hiss, and then smack Arzell over the head again. "See, I need to stop fuckin' with you young muthafuckas. Y'all always wanna solve shit with a gun." I whack him one more time. "We cool—just get this nigga out of here."

The guns go down and niggas start snickering. But McGriff reaches down and grabs Arzell by the collar of his T-shirt. "C'mon, Romeo. You heard Momma Peaches. Kick rocks."

"But . . . but—"

McGriff jams his gun under Arzell's chin. "Nigga, does it look like I'm fuckin' asking yo ass?"

Arzell holds up his hands to signal his surrender. He may be mad, but he's not stupid enough to buck up against McGriff and think his ass is gonna be able to walk out of this muthafucka alive.

Cedric bends over and chugs in deep breaths. He's eyeballing Arzell so hard I know that he wants another go at him or at the very least to haul his ass down to jail. But our little rendezvous is a bit problematic and in all likelihood could cost him his job. He's sweating like a muthafucka, too. While Cedric struggles to calm down and catch his breath, a few of the Queen Gs help pull me up off the floor.

"You all right, Momma P?" Kookie asks.

"Yeah. Just help me over here to this chair." When Kookie and her friend Pit Bull help me on over, one of the other girls hands me my busted prosthetic. I can't help but be a little embarrassed.

"Now is everything cool here?" McGriff asks, swinging his gaze over to Cedric. On Shotgun Row, niggas are suspicious of every new face.

"Yeah. We cool," is all I say. It ain't nobody's business who the fuck I allow in my house. "Now y'all muthafuckas go. Shit. This ain't no damn family reunion." I wave them toward the door while twisting my head with a whole lot of attitude. That's when I catch sight of that punk-ass bitch who locked my husband up on the television screen. *Is his ass crying?*

"Yo, Kookie. Turn that up!"

This slow bitch Kookie looks around like she doesn't know what I'm talking about.

"The television. Damn. Hurry up!" I'm going to miss what the reporter's saying.

"Captain Johnson," a reporter shouts. "Does the department have any leads in your daughter's murder?"

Despite being in a sharp, highly decorated police captain uniform, Captain Melvin Johnson looks like a train wreck. There're bags under his eyes, his bottom lip is trembling and he's having a hard time spitting out whatever it is he's trying to say.

"At the moment, the department is carefully combing through the crime scene. Given the violence of . . . of my daughter's heinous murder . . . the amount of blood, bullets . . . the total destruction that happened there last night . . . I am . . . we are confident that we will be able to secure an arrest soon."

"What the fuck?" I can't believe what I'm hearing.

"Captain Johnson," another reporter calls out while a series of flashes flickers across the screen. "Do you know anyone who would want to kill your daughter? Did she have any enemies?"

A tear skips down the captain's face as he shakes his head. "Being a police officer herself, I can't say definitively that Melanie . . . Officer Melanie Johnson . . . didn't have any enemies, but I can't imagine it. And I can't imagine who would want to kidnap"—his lips quiver—"my grandson." He presses his lips together and then proceeds to break down.

"Kidnapped?" My mind zooms to Python. *He wouldn't.* But the way my stomach starts twisting, I know that I'm trying to lie to myself. "Holy shit! Somebody get my other prosthetic leg out of my closet. Hurry!"

12

LeShelle

"Sssssssssss."

Heaven is the feel of Python's thick, forked tongue sliding in between my ass cheeks while his hand pumps steadily in and out of my pussy. This shit is so good that I'm willing to forgive this nigga of all past transgressions—and, Lord, there have been plenty. I have long had the respect of being his number-one wifey, Queen G, his ride-or-die bitch, but soon I'll have the papers and his last name. It'll make it official that I belong someplace—belong to someone. Truth be told, that's all I've ever fuckin' wanted.

With Jacki-O's fierce lyrics playing from the Bose on the nightstand and my nigga dicking me down, I feel like the queen of the universe. My legs are trembling while warm honey slowly drips from my pussy and coats Python's big-ass hand. We've been at this shit off and on for hours. Neither one of us is afraid to put in work when it comes to funkin' up these sheets. When my body is convulsing and exploding, I ain't thinking about shit other than what I got going on right here in this bed. Now, if we didn't have to get out of this muthafucka, everything would be all good. I grew up feeling like someone's unwanted trash, tossed into the foster care system and forced to fend for myself . . . and my sister. But fuck that bitch. Looking out for her ass has done nothing but cause me a lot of heartache and misery. From this day on, I'm looking out for number one, and I'll mow down any bitch who gets in my way.

Pretty soon, all Python's jump-offs are going to know what time it is, and they're going to get back or get smacked down.

"Sssssssssss."

My eyes flutter open as Apollo, Python's six-foot red-tail boa constrictor, slithers by my head. Usually it's just us and two small ball pythons, Beauty and Beast, in the bed. They're harmless, but Apollo creeps me out. Seeing his ugly ass ruins this orgasmic high. I scoot back when I notice his ass coiling like he's getting ready to attack.

"Ba-by, does he have to be in the bed?"

Python's warm tongue slowly pulls out, but instead of answering me, he slaps my ass so hard, the *whap* reverberates throughout the room.

"Ow!" I jump up as Apollo strikes. Bastard barely misses sinking those ugly fangs into my titties.

"Python!"

He laughs and smacks my ass again. "What the fuck? Your ass scared, Ma? Get your ass down!" He pushes my head back onto the mattress and then peels my ass cheeks open. "I'm gonna get me some of this good shit you got."

I don't know where Apollo has slithered off to, but best believe I'm keeping an eye out for that muthafucka. In no time at all, I feel the head of Python's big cock squeeze into my back door, and I suck in a deep breath. I ain't gonna lie—this shit is painful, and it reminds me of all those pedophile muthafuckas who used to creep into my bed late at night and then leave me crying and bleeding. But those memories don't last but for a second, because the next thing I know, I'm embracing the pain. It's the only thing that's real and consistent in this life. If a bitch don't learn that shit, she will forever be played out.

"Sssssssss." Python sinks all his shit in with one long-ass stroke.

With his balls resting on the back of my ass, I hear him taking in air with small sips. I take it as a cue to squeeze my ass muscles like I'm about to snap his shit off.

"Ssssss. Goddamn, baby. Goddamn." His hand locks tight on my waist. "Do that shit, baby. Do that shit."

Whap! Whap! Now both of my ass cheeks are on fire.

"Lock that shit up, baby!" he pants.

My nigga is a true-blue ass freak, and I know how to give him exactly what he wants. While his mind is spinning, I start rocking and throwing everything I got onto this fat dick. "That's right, baby. Fuck me. Show me how much you love this shit."

He ain't said nothing but a thing. I arch my back, bite my bottom lip, and pound his shit. I steal a glance at his fuck face, and that shit is so twisted I know his ass is completely sprung. "You like that, Daddy?"

"Sssssssss." His hands slide up from my waist and stretch all the way up to close around my neck. I lift my head because I know what's coming, and he doesn't disappoint. He starts squeezing gently at first, but it don't take no time before his grip starts tightening. Before I know it, my head feels like it's twice its normal size, and I can literally hear my heartbeat racing inside my head.

"YEAH! YEAH! YEAH!" Python roars.

I'm numb and tingling everywhere. Then suddenly a blinding pain pierces my upper inner right thigh, but I can't scream out and Python seems content to try and turn my asshole into a murder scene. Yet, the pain isn't going away. If anything, the shit seems to be spreading down my leg.

Hold on. Hold on. He's going to blast his shit off in a few seconds.

Just hang on. But damn, each second feels like a goddamn life-time. Then Python hits the right corner at the right time and I come so hard it feels like I'm pissing on myself. A second later, Python pulls out and hoses down my ass as if the shit is on fire. At last, he releases my neck and I collapse while sucking in so much oxygen I choke on the shit.

The pain in my thigh is unrelenting. I turn and look down. At the sight of Apollo, dangling with his fangs still locked onto my thighs, I freak the fuck out.

"Goddamn it, Python! Get this muthafucka!"

"What?" He turns to see what the hell is going on.

He's too fuckin' slow. Swinging my hand out to the night-stand and knocking shit over, including the Bose, I grab Python's gat and then come back around, blasting.

POW! POW! POW!

I'm trying to hit this muthafuckin' snake but not really thinking this shit through.

"WHAT THE FUCK?" Python scrambles out of bed.

POW! POW! POW!

Once he collects his thoughts, he knocks the gun out of my hand. It hits the wall with another loud discharge. "What the fuck is wrong with your stupid ass?"

"GET HIM OFF!"

He chuckles and then sits down on the edge of the bed. "Calm down and hold still."

I can't. I'm kicking and trying to knock the muthafucka off.

"CALM DOWN!" He grabs both my legs, but I'm still squirming and bucking from the waist up.

"PYTHON!"

"All right. All right." Still laughing, he reaches for the snake's head and then squeezes the sides of his mouth together before slowly pulling him up until his two thin fangs slide out of my thigh. "There we go," Python coos to Apollo. "Did Momma scare you?"

I shiver and then squirm away. "Get that muthafucka out of here. His ass can't come back up in this bitch!"

Python cocks his head at me and pushes out his bottom lip. "What happened to my fearless Queen G?"

"Fuck you, asshole. I mean what I said. That muthafucka stays out!" I examine my thigh and the two crimson puncture marks.

"Chill out. He ain't poisonous."

I glare at him. "The shit still hurts."

"Put some alcohol on it and you'll be good to go." He lowers Apollo onto the floor and then allows him to slither away.

I chug in several deep breaths and then feel stupid for freaking out. Four years I haven't blinked an eye about all these pet snakes. I've taken bullets and murked bitches and niggas like my ass gets a W-2 for the shit. Now I get one bite and I start screaming and hollering like a bitch.

Python leans over and cheeses in my face. "You finished pouting now?"

"Fuck you."

"Again?" He grabs his meat and starts stroking himself. "I might have another round left in me."

BANG! BANG! BANG!

"Who in the fuck?" Python pops up off the bed and walks over to the window with his dick swinging.

I roll over to my side of the bed and then reach down on the floor for my robe. When I snatch it up, I jump at seeing Apollo's coiled ass and I'm tempted to get that gun again.

BANG! BANG! BANG!

"Who is it?" I ask Python, since he's looking out of the blinds.

He frowns and turns toward the dresser. "Momma Peaches."

"Shit. Why is she banging like the fuckin' police?" I huff. "I'll go see what she wants," I say, sliding on my robe. Before hopping out of the bed, I glance around the floor to make sure that Apollo's sneaky ass ain't nowhere around. Sure enough, he's slithered off somewhere. After that, I dart out of the bedroom and race toward the door.

"Morning, Momma—"

"Where he at?" she asks, shoving the door out of my hand and storming into the house like a tornado.

"Please, come in," I say sarcastically, and then slam the door behind her.

"Save the attitude, honey. I ain't got time for no bullshit. Where's Python?"

Python strolls into the living room, clutching his wounded side. "Hey, what's up?"

"What's up?" Momma Peaches rolls. "What's up?!" She swings her hand so fast I don't really see it. I hear the *SLAP* when it connects to Python's face.

I jump and then shut the front door.

"Nigga, have you lost your fuckin' mind?" Momma Peaches roars. "You killed a cop? And not any fuckin' cop, but the captain of police's daughter? You really think that your ass is going to get away with that shit?"

Python holds up his hand and steps back in case her ass gets to swinging again. "Whoa. Chill out for a second."

Fast as lightning, Momma Peaches closes the small space and swings again.

SLAP!

"Don't fuckin' tell me to chill out! I'll stand here and knock sense into you all goddamn day if I feel like it. And you know what? You're gonna stand your ass right there and take the shit. You got that?"

Python clenches his jaw.

SLAP!

"Boy, I asked yo ass a question!"

He shoots a look at me, and I drop my head like I ain't seen shit.

When Momma Peaches's hand rises back up, Python jumps back and again starts talking. "I got it. I got it. Damn!"

SLAP!

"Don't be fuckin' cursin' at me, boy! Now where the hell is my grandbaby?"

Python looks to me again, and then Momma Peaches swings her attention to me as well.

"He's in the blue guest room," I confess before she knocks my ass into the middle of next week—and I don't doubt that her ass would do it either.

"Were *you* in on this?" Momma Peaches digs a fist into her right hip.

"N-no." My eyes bulge wider.

Momma Peaches cocks her head.

"I swear."

"Uh-huh."

Her gaze rakes over me, and I'm not too sure her ass believes me.

Momma Peaches turns back toward Python. "So what happened?"

Python draws a deep breath. "With all due respect, Momma P. I don't think—"

"Nigga, if you were thinking, you wouldn't have done no stupid shit like kill a cop and kidnap her kid."

"He's *my* kid, too."

"Great, he and all his other brothers and sisters can visit yo ass at the federal pen—that is, until they stick a needle in your damn arm. A cop? The captain of police's daughter?" Her hands come up.

"Fuck," Python explodes, jumping back before Momma Peaches starts swinging. "It ain't like I planned that shit," he thunders. "I went over to that muthafucka to find out if she was carrying my seed."

"You *were* still fucking her? I can't believe this shit," I grumble.

Python glares. "Squash it!"

I clench my teeth together and simmer.

Momma Peaches looks sick. "She was pregnant, too? What, she said it wasn't your baby so you shot her?"

"I didn't get a chance to ask her—she was too busy riding Fat Ace's dick."

The laugh is out of my mouth before I have a chance to stop it. Once that shit gets started, I can't stop. I know the gun battle happened, but I didn't put two and two together that it went down like this.

"What the fuck is your evil ass laughing at?" Python barks.

"Why the fuck do you think? You're always roaming from bitch to bitch and never appreciating what the hell yo ass got at home. Then when you see all these hoes for the triflin' bitches they are, you slither your ass into my bed like everything is everything."

"Yeah. Whatever." He waves me off and twists his face like I didn't spit the truth at his ass. "I don't remember hearing no complaints last night—or ten minutes ago."

"Just like a nigga to think that his *dick* is gonna solve all his problems," I snap back.

"Chill with that shit. I wasn't the only one capping niggas last night."

"Nigga—"

"Will y'all two stupid muthafuckas shut the hell up?" Momma Peaches yells. "Let me go see this baby. He's probably scared out of his mind, and I don't fucking blame him. If I had y'all silly asses looking after me, I don't know what I'd do."

We watch her storm off and then give each other a final glare before marching behind her. When we reach the guest bedroom, I'm surprised and taken aback to see the lil boy trembling like a leaf and huddled in a corner behind boxes and piles of clothes.

"Hey, you can come out," Momma Peaches coaches softly. "Nobody is going to hurt you."

The kid doesn't move. I pull in a deep breath and then roll my eyes. This bastard is making us look bad.

Momma Peaches turns toward Python. "What's his name?"

Python clears his throat. "Christopher."

"Christopher," Momma Peaches calls softly. "Do you know who I am?"

The boy's large eyes lock onto the older woman.

"Hmmm? Do you know?"

Still a little wary, the kid slowly shakes his head.

"I'm your *great*-auntie. I'm your grandmother's sister."

Christopher twists up his face with disbelief while fat tears skip down his face. "I want my momma," he whines.

I ain't gonna lie—something in my chest starts hurting and I look away.

BANG! BANG! BANG!

"Who in the fuck is that now?" Python hisses.

"I don't know." I storm back toward the front door. "Who is it?!"

"MEMPHIS POLICE!"

13

Essence

Curled into a ball at the foot of the bed and still dressed in my prom dress, I feel like a zombie. I didn't sleep a wink last night. It ain't every fucking day that someone finds their best friend after they'd been brutally raped and beaten and trying to hoof it home in a bloody silk robe and barefooted. Shit. I still can't believe last night happened, just like I can't believe that Drey and I didn't get Ta'Shara to a hospital. Instead, we dropped her off on her doorstep like an unwanted baby.

How could I fucking do that to my own best friend?

What makes it worse is that I know Ta'Shara would have never done no fucked-up shit like that to me. But no matter how many times I review the shit in my mind, I can't see what I could've done differently. If those fucking Vice Lords were mobbin' that goddamn deep outside an emergency room, I got to believe that it was because one of their own was up in there, and in my and Drey's paranoid minds, we concluded that someone had to be Profit.

If not, then where in the fuck is he? He has to be dead. I can't believe for a second that he would've allowed his girl to be raped and beaten the way she was when he still drew breath. He loves her too much for that shit to go down like that. Profit is cool, even if he is a grimy Vice Lord.

"GD and VL don't mix," I moan, burying my head into my hands. But how many times had I told Ta'Shara that shit? Too damn many to count, if I want to be real with it. So why is this shit hitting *me* like it's such a fucking surprise?

I rest my head on my knees and start rocking back and forth. *What am I supposed to do now?* Should I call or should I drive over to the Douglas's?

Maybe I should do nothing, mind my own business. It ain't like niggas don't die every day, sticking their noses in shit where it don't belong. I agree with myself to stay out of it, but two seconds later, I'm dying to pick up the phone. But if I call, it might raise suspicions. What if I drive over and pretend that I was dropping by to talk about the prom last night?

That might work.

Then again, I don't know if I'm a good enough actress to pretend that I don't know what happened to Ta'Shara last night. Fuck. What if I start crying before I even ask to see if she's home?

"Goddamn it, T. Why didn't you stay away from him?" My throat squeezes tight and I nearly choke on a sob.

My door explodes open, and my older sister, Cleo, in all her ghetto glory charges into the room and dives into the lower bunk bed that we've been sharing for far too damn long. Her boyfriend must've just dropped her off because she's wearing the same clothes that she left out of here in last night.

I sniff and wipe away the last of my tears.

Cleo pops her head above her pillow. "What the hell is the matter with you?"

"Nothing," I lie, and struggle to pull myself out of bed. Maybe I can hide in the shower before—

"Essence! Essence." My five-year-old lil brother, Jamie, runs into the room. "Nana said for you to fix us some breakfast!"

Behind him comes my six-year-old cousin, Kay, who has

one half of her hair braided while the other half is sticking up all over her head. "I want some waffles!"

Jamie turns around and pushes her. "No! I want pancakes!"

Goddamn it. I don't feel like dealing with this shit. "Cleo?"

"Don't look at me." She plops over and then buries her head underneath the pillow.

"Thanks a fucking lot." Cursing and rolling my eyes, I climb out of bed and stomp my way up to the kitchen so I can feed these brats like they are my kids. When I pass the living room and see two of my brothers and their girlfriends lying around, I get even more heated. All these niggas around and none of them can feed these kids? But sure enough, when I start cooking, here they come.

"What are you cooking?" Kobe asks, reaching over and pinching off a piece of bacon.

I slap his hand away and bark, "None of your business. Now go on."

He laughs and steals an even bigger piece. "What? You must be mad because that nigga Drey didn't spring for no hotel room last night. I told you his ass was cheap. Muthafucka be bitching and complaining about the prices on the ninety-nine-cent menu at McDonald's."

Any other time, that shit would have cracked me up, but right now I just want his ass to leave me alone.

"Damn, E. Don't pout. I'm sure there's other niggas out here in the jungle. You'll get laid one of these days."

"Ha-ha." I flip his Katt Williams wannabe ass the bird.

"I know your girl got plenty of dick last night."

I stop cold. "What the fuck are you talkin' about?"

"Ta'Shara. That's your girl's name, right?"

He steals another strip of bacon, but this time I snatch it out of his hand. "Yeah. And?"

Kobe shrugs. "*And* I heard she got busted into the set last night. Her sister sanctioned the shit—even took those big niggas, Treasure and Mario, to do the honors."

"What?" I feel sick.

"Some other niggas got the honors, too. I wish that bitch would've called me. Your girl got a thick ass. Fo real." He chuckles as he chews on his bacon.

I pop him dead in the mouth.

"What the fuck?!"

"You sick muthafucka!" I wail on him, landing punches on his head, mouth, and even his right eye. "That's my fuckin' friend, you stupid fuck!"

Kobe throws up his hands and tries to cover his face while backing out of the kitchen. "Chill, E! Damn!"

Nobody comes to his defense. Those lazy niggas on the couch do what they always do first thing in the morning. Light up, blaze, and watch the action. When I'm tired of beating his stupid ass, I run to the bathroom and just barely make it in time to dry-heave over the toilet.

Treasure and Mario? I know those nasty niggas *very* well. They're enforcers. When Python or McGriff say do, they do without question. Most of the time they like to get their hands wet when they do their blood work. I have no trouble picturing them making those brutal bruises all over Ta'Shara's body and that crude GD carved into her ass. How the fuck could LeShelle do something like that to her own sister? Does blood mean nothing to that bitch? The Gangster Disciples and Queen Gs are my fam, too, but my blood, trifling and nerve-riding they may be, still trumps all this street shit.

My stomach clenches again and I shove my head closer to the toilet water, but again nothing comes out.

"Is your ass drunk or some shit?" Cleo barks, appearing in the doorway. "You left bacon burning in the kitchen. What if the muthafuckin' house caught on fire?"

I pull my head back up and crawl over to the door and slam it in her face.

"Well, fuck you, then." Pause. "Are you coming to feed these kids or not?"

I roll my eyes. Let her ass figure it out. I'm tired of these muthafuckas acting like they can't do shit. I peel out of my clothes, shower, and then rush to put on something clean. Hell, the ends of my hair are still wet when I race toward the front door, and niggas are still bitching and lying around in the room.

"Where the fuck are you going?" Kobe shouts.

I slam the door so hard that I'm surprised the muthafucka doesn't break in half. Once I hop into my old, hand-me-down '89 Ford Escort, I pray real hard that the muthafucka starts up.

It doesn't.

"C'mon. C'mon. Don't do this to me," I beg. "I swear, I'll take you in for a tune-up, wash you—anything you want, just please, please start." I turn the ignition; it hesitates but finally starts up. "Thank you, baby. Thank you." I peel away from the curb with a small white cloud puffing out of my tailpipe. During the ride to the Douglas's, I practice what I'm going to say and how I'm going to say it, but when I pull into the driveway, I can't remember a single sentence.

There's a car there, but not one that I recognize.

Climbing out from behind the wheel, I suck in a nervous breath. However, it isn't enough to stop the hot tears burning the backs of my eyes. *Ring the doorbell or knock?* That one question trips me up for another full minute, so I decide to do both.

The ten-second wait feels more like an hour, and when the door cracks open, it's this older, silver-haired woman. It isn't until my eyes meet hers that I see a little of Tracee Douglas in her sad, kind eyes.

"Can I help you, young lady?"

My mouth goes dry and my tongue feels like it's ten inches thick. "Um, yes. Is Ta-Ta'Shara here?"

Instantly, the older woman's eyes tear up. "I'm sorry. Not at the moment. Are you a friend of hers?"

I nod as my throat locks and my vision blurs.

The woman opens the door farther and then steps up to the threshold and touches my arm. "Do you know anything about what happened last night?"

I try to jerk my gaze away, but her large brown eyes are like a supermagnet and I just can't. "N-no. I . . . heard some rumors," I lie, and then hope that she isn't able to read me like I think she can.

"Yes. Well . . . I'm sorry . . . um . . . Ta'Shara and her parents are still down at the hospital right now."

"Which one?"

"I don't know if it's a good idea that you go down there."

The knots in my stomach tighten, and I fear that she's about to turn me away. "Please. I need to see her." Against my will, a tear skips down my face and I see that it's enough to soften her resolve.

"The Med," she confesses while her hand moves from my arm to grip my hand. "If you go, you should know that Ta'Shara may be . . . different."

I know. "Okay . . . thank you." I pull my hand away and then rush back to my car. This time it spares me the stress of pretending like it's not going to turn over. Once again, I'm racing back over to the hospital. It's frustrating because my ass catches every red light and manages to pull up behind every senior citizen putt-putting along.

I remain a bundle of nerves the entire time I park and get Ta'Shara's room number. The first thing I hear when I approach the room is a woman crying and then a man trying to calm her down.

"It's going to be all right, Tracee," a broken male voice comforts.

"How is it going to be all right? Did you see what those monsters did to her?" she cries. "How can anything *ever* be all right again? She's dead."

My heart drops as I stop outside the door. *Dead?*

"She's dead inside," Tracee moans. "You can just look into her eyes and see that there's nobody in there."

"Shhhh. It's going to be okay."

Slowly my heart starts pounding again. *She's not dead. She's not dead.*

I'm so entangled with my own thoughts that I don't hear the footsteps coming up from behind me, but suddenly, a hand locks around my arm and starts dragging me away from the door. I turn around to bark, "Hey!"

But my protests shut down.

"We need to fuckin' talk," Lucifer announces, and drags my ass to God knows where.

14

Lucifer

"Where in the hell are you taking me?" this little girl squeaks while I drag her down another hospital hallway.

When I ignore her, her body starts trembling like she's suffering from some epileptic seizure. I ignore that, too. Mainly because muthafuckas tend to start shutting down when they think or realize that death is around the corner.

I hit an exit door that leads us outside and then shove her through it. Once I ram her tiny ass up against the back of the building, I unsheathe my Browning hunting knife and plant it against her throat.

Her eyes bug, but she don't say shit as my sharp blade bites into her skin.

"I got your attention?"

"Y-yes."

"Good." I fake a smile. "Now, I'm going to ask you a few fuckin' questions, and I'd appreciate if you just answer them and not waste my time by spitting out lies or testing my patience—mainly because I don't have any. Understand?"

She swallows, and as a result, her soft skin presses against my knife and a thin drop of blood rolls over the jagged blade and then drips to the concrete like a single, red pearl drop.

"Good." I cock my head. "How was the prom last night . . . Essence, isn't it?"

She whimpers.

"That good, huh? Get laid?"

More whimpering.

"Probably weren't in the mood after all that . . . shooting and raping and shit . . . right?"

"Oh God," Essence whines.

"No. Lucifer, honey." I press the knife a little harder and watch a few more blood pearls drip to the concrete.

"No—What? Shit. You got it all wrong."

"I do?" I cock my head to the side and watch the fear expand in her eyes. "What part did I get wrong? The shooting or the raping?"

"I didn't have shit to do with any of that."

"So it wasn't you and your boy *Drey* who dropped Ta'Shara off all beaten and battered at her parents' crib last night?"

"Fuck. H-how—"

I press my knife deeper and watch the pearls turn into a rivulet. "No patience, remember?"

"Drey and I didn't have anything to do with the shooting. We found my girl walking in my neighborhood with hardly any clothes on and acting crazy and shit," she confesses. "Drey had to knock her out just to get her into the car so we could take her to the hospital—but when we saw you and some other Vice Lords, we got spooked and decided to take her to her parents' place. I swear. T is my best friend and shit. I wouldn't do anything to hurt her. You gotta believe me."

Fat tears roll down homegirl's face at a fucking serious clip. Since I have a good bullshit detector, I have no problem believing this bitch. I ease my blade back an inch. The girl's shoulders droop in relief, but our eyes remain locked.

"Where you stay at?" When she hesitates, I return the pressure on the knife.

"On Woodfield."

"Near Shotgun Row?"

She bobs her head.

"You a Queen G?"

She sucks in a breath and then bravely nods again.

My lips twitch. "Is your girl Ta'Shara a Queen G? Did she set Profit up?"

"Not by choice," she whispers faintly. "She got branded last night."

"Who sanctioned that shit last night?" I press.

Essence shakes her head. "I don't know."

"You don't know?" I repeat, smirking.

The lil girl shakes her head.

I close my eyes and tell myself to count to ten, but I only make it to two. "That better be the one and only lie you tell me." I open my eyes and our gazes lock again. "Who?"

The girl goes back to trembling so bad that the knife is easily slicing her soft neck. "I ain't no snitch."

"Do I look like the muthafuckin' po-po to you?" I tilt my head to the other side while she takes a moment to reassess her situation. "Look around."

The girl's doe eyes dart all around the back of the building.

"Either you start talking or this here is going to be your fuckin' resting place until someone starts complaining about the stench back here being so bad they have to come out and investigate. I'd imagine by then a few rats would've done a good number on those big damn eyes you got staring at me. Your skin will be a kind of bluish green color. Your internal gases will bloat your face up, and your bowels will probably empty out of you in one long shit stream. Not a good look." I have to admit, fucking with this young girl's head is like torturing the neighborhood stray cat. It's kind of fun. "So who was it?" I press.

Tears leap over the girl's lashes while I watch her digest how fucked up her situation really is. If she is hoping for sympathy, she's staring at the wrong bitch. And frankly I ain't going to stand my ass out here too much longer before I slice her shit and go about finding this information out through other means and channels. In these fuckin' streets, a snitch ain't that hard to find.

Then ever so slowly, this tiny bitch starts tilting her chin up. A small vein pulses against her jawline as she grinds her back teeth together. She's trying to prepare herself to meet death with whatever courage she has left.

Before I know it, a smile hooks one side of my mouth while I cock my head. "You got heart. Is that what you're trying to show me?"

She doesn't say anything, but she's still trembling like a muthafuckin' leaf.

"Yeah." I bob my head and ease the pressure off the knife a little bit. "You got heart. I can dig that shit."

The girl's shoulders relax again.

"Doesn't mean that I'm going to let you walk your small monkey ass up out of this back alley, but I can give you kudos for it. I'm used to bitches snitching when they get scared, especially Queen Gs and their fake-gangsta asses. The only damn thing they ride hard is those kiddie dicks those grimy GD muthafuckas think they got sagging."

Essence's jaw twitches again.

"What? You got something to say?" I challenge.

She swallows and damn near starts choking on that little bit of courage she's trying to gather up.

Yeah. It's too damn easy fuckin' with this bitch. "Check it. Your heart is misplaced in this scenario." I come at her from a different angle. "You claim that girl in there is your best friend, but you'd rather taste steel than get her some street justice? You'd rather let the niggas who dug her out get away with giving her a few broken ribs, a collapsed lung, a broken jaw, and whatever petri dishes of diseases they probably had? Let's not even talk about how fucked up her mind is right now. You'd be lucky if she even knows who the fuck you are if she pulls through this shit."

More tears race down the girl's face.

I go in for more. "But I guess that's okay with you, because that's the kind of *friend* you are. You let shit slide."

Essence shakes her head.

"If I had a friend like you, I'd slice my own damn throat."

"It could've been anybody," the girl says. "The whole damn school didn't like them flaunting their shit in front of them like they did at the prom. GD and Vice don't mix. I *told* Ta'Shara to leave Profit's ass alone. A lot of people told both of them. Now I gotta put my neck on the line and become a snitch? How the fuck is that fair?"

My jaw twitches. "Bitch, my name ain't Oprah. I don't want to hear your silly-ass problems."

Essence whimpers.

"Now, this is the last time I'm going to tell you: give me a fuckin' name."

15

LeShelle

Shit. It's the police!

I whip my head around to see if Python heard this shit as well. Sure enough, his ass is already reaching for one of his spare gats stashed in one of the end tables by the sofa.

Momma Peaches jumps into the action and smacks his hand away from the drawer. "What the fuck? You think you're going to blast your way up out of here?"

Me and Python give her a Hell-the-fuck-yeah look.

"Just play the shit cool," she snaps. "Y'all don't even know what the fuck they want yet. If it was what you two think it is, they would've came at the door with a battering ram. See what the fuck they want first." She nods her head toward me. "Open the damn door."

This bossy old bitch is getting on my nerves. I shift my gaze to Python, and he gives me the okay nod. Frankly, I'm still with the notion of shooting first and asking questions later, but my ass is outnumbered, so I turn back toward the door. Ain't no use in praying because God has long stopped answering my calls. I open the door.

On the other side, two police officers in crisp blue uniforms stand erect with blank faces.

"LeShelle Murphy?"

I swallow and stiffen my spine. "Why you want to know?"

The short white one pokes out his thick barrel chest. "Answer the damn question. Are you LeShelle Murphy?"

Folding my arms, I thrust out my left hip. "Yeah. Now what you want?"

Officer Asshole looks over his shoulder at his partner before turning back toward me with a serious attitude. "We're here to talk to you about an incident involving your younger sister, Ta'Shara."

That fuckin' snitch! "What about her?"

"Ma'am, do you mind if we come in?"

"As a matter of fact, I do," I say boldly. "Me and my nigga were in the middle of fucking, so we ain't exactly decent."

The cops exchange looks again.

"Now what is this shit about my sister?" I ask, hoping by shocking the shit out of them that I can throw them off my nervousness. From the looks on their faces, it works.

"There was an incident—"

"Yeah. You said that part already."

White Cop reaches for a small pad and pen from his chest pocket. "Your sister Ta'Shara and her boyfriend Raymond Lewis were carjacked leaving their high school prom last night. The driver of their limousine was killed at the scene."

They stare at me, and I try to show the required concern. "Well . . . is she okay?"

"No," the older black cop says. His penetrating black gaze sweeps my face. "I'm sorry to inform you that your sister was brutally beaten and raped."

I gasp and cover my mouth with my hands. *Too much?*

The black cop nods. "She's alive," he assures me, and then pauses. "Her foster parents have taken her to the hospital. Things are a little shakier for the young gentleman who took her to the prom, though. He took seventeen bullets."

"Shakier?" My brows dip. "So . . . he's alive?"

They both nod.

Fuck! Fuck! Fuck!

My hands ball at my sides while I damn near grind my back teeth down to powder. I think about the number of bullets I pumped into that nigga, and I can't figure how in the hell that muthafucka is still breathing. My world just got considerably more fucked up. Ta'Shara I'm sure I can handle, but if that grimy Vice Lord starts talking, my ass is a dead bitch. Period.

"I'm sorry," the black cop says. "I know that all of this may be coming as a shock to you."

"You have no fucking idea." I exhale a shaky breath while my brain scrambles for a new plan.

White Cop continues. "Your sister is currently unresponsive. We haven't been able to get her side of what happened last night."

At least there's some good news.

"We're not even sure if she's aware of her surroundings."

"Well . . . I appreciate you coming by to tell me." I nod, anxious to get these pigs the hell off my porch. Yet, when I try to close the door, Officer Whitey shoves his foot inside and blocks it. I glance down at his foot and then arch a single brow up at him. "Is there something else?"

"Your sister sustained some interesting markings on her body. In particular are the initials 'GD' carved into her butt cheek." His blue eyes level on me. "Those mean anything to you?"

I stare at him like his ass is stupid. "Should it?"

Only one side of his lips hook into a smile. "We have strong reason to believe that those initials stand for 'Gangster Disciples.' "

Silence.

"This area here is a stronghold of the Gangster Disciples, isn't it?"

I keep my expression blank. "You tell me. You're the one with all the information this morning."

Their expressions return to being blank canvases.

"Any reason why Tracee Douglas believes that *you* may have something to do with what happened to your younger sister last night?"

"Is she the one that sent you over here?"

"She gave us your name and we looked you up in the system."

I laugh in his face. "Let me get this right. That silly bitch told you that I actually had something to do with having my flesh and blood beaten and raped?"

Silence.

"Uh-huh. Well, did she also tell you that she's had a grudge against me ever since she caught her man coming on to me when I lived with them? And instead of getting rid of his pedophile ass, she kicked me out on the streets?" It was a huge lie, but fuck it.

The cops look at each other.

"No. I didn't think so. Maybe you should be looking at *his* sick ass. Where was he last night?" I give them a nasty sneer. "Look. Me and my sister might have our differences, but I *love* her. We might not live together, but our bond is deep. I'm sure when she snaps out of whatever daze she's in that she'll tell you the same thing." I got these cops so fucking twisted it's clear that they don't know what the fuck to think.

The black cop breaks their silence first. "Ma'am, we came over here to talk to you. We're not making any accusations."

"Really? That's not the way it sounded to me. I know the game. You came over here to accuse me of some bullshit. Well, you can carry your ass back on over to Ms. Tracee's Fantasyland and tell her to stop spitting my name out her neck. I'll roll my ass over to the hospital later and see what time it is for myself. Now, if you don't mind, I'm about to close this door and go back to fucking my man. Either one of you got a problem with that?"

These muthafuckas blink like a couple of deer caught in headlights.

"Good. Now move your foot," I tell Whitey.

Slowly, he drags his shit back. I can tell by the look in his eyes that he wishes he can haul my ass in on something—anything. I smile and then slam the fucking door in his face. I wait and listen to them walk off the porch. When I turn, Python looks impressed while Momma Peaches is shaking her head.

"Lawd. Lawd." She tosses up her hand. "I don't even want to fuckin' know what the hell that shit is about."

Good. Because I ain't about to tell you shit nohow.

Momma Peaches faces Python again. "Take care of that damn baby before the next time those pigs roll over here looking for him." She continues shaking her head as she moves past him and heads toward me and the front door. "I gotta get the fuck up out of here before the po-po slaps the handcuffs on me for being caught up in y'all bullshit." She snatches open the door and cuts another look over at me.

I'm not blind or stupid. I recognize the look of disgust when I see it. As Momma Peaches marches out the door, I swear I hear her mumble, "Your own fuckin' sister."

Once the door slams shut behind her, my head whips in Python's direction. "What the hell is her problem?"

"You didn't make sure that he was dead?" he asks, ignoring my question.

"I dumped an entire clip into his ass."

He shakes his head. "Pack your shit. We're rolling up out of here."

16

Yolanda

Somehow I got to get my shit together. At least that's what I've been telling myself since Baby Thug's funeral. There hasn't been a day that I haven't heard her voice inside my head, telling me about how much I'm fucking up by hanging all my hopes and dreams on Python's ass. But for as long as I can remember, I've wanted to lock down one of the big players in my set. A governor, a lieutenant, an enforcer—some goddamn body. Maybe then bitches will start looking at me with respect and not like I'm some slow retarded bitch who used to suck boys' dicks for Lemonheads back in junior high.

Growing up, I never really had any friends. It could've been because I was a Ritalin-popping, short-yellow-bus-riding, desperate bitch with a crazy-ass momma. I didn't blink twice about sexing my way into the Black Gangster Disciple set and then hoing my pussy out to mule drugs into the prison system. The only niggas I pulled were four-corner street soldiers who had their hands in my pockets more than I had mine in theirs. Weak niggas who only lived for the next fly-ass sneaks to hit the shelves while dabbling in their own product to get high. Fucking niggas like those just kept me looking like a joke to the other Queen Gs.

Keeping it real. I know my ass ain't smart, but I'm fine as

fuck and I can handle any dick tossed my way. Surely that's the foundation of a boss bitch. Shit, that's all Python's wifey, LeShelle, is working with. Hell. Without him, she ain't nobody, and she certainly ain't better than me. If she was, then her nigga wouldn't have plucked me out of the Pink Monkey, set me up nicely in my own place, and dropped out his next seed in my belly. Fuck, she's been with his ass for damn near four years, and she ain't spit out nothing but piss and blood clots. She ain't no real woman, and she's kidding herself if she thinks she can ever keep her nigga out of my bed.

Don't get me wrong. She spooked my ass pretty good at Baby's funeral with all that *ticktock* bullshit. But she's going to have to come harder than that if she's hoping to get rid of me. Now, did she have something to do with the police finding Baby's pussy pumped full of bullets? Maybe. But Baby was a part of the streets. She could've run up on any kind of trouble. Most likely she got caught fucking some other nigga's girl. Not everybody gets off on the idea of two carpet munchers together.

I ain't worried about LeShelle. I got her man, and I don't have to live off shitty Shotgun Row in order to keep him. As long as I keep serving up this good pussy and ass and then turn around and fix him a hot plate, it's all good. Every time he leaves my place, there's a fat-ass knot of cash on the nightstand. So far, I got three Gucci shoe boxes filled to the brim with loot. That's gotta be more than enough for me to try and get my kids back from the Department of Children's Services.

At least that's why my ass is up here at the booty crack of dawn, trying to see this social worker. I told Baby that I would stack this paper and get my kids, and that's what the fuck I'm going to do. If she is looking down from heaven, this shit is gonna make her proud. But these muthafuckas need to hurry the fuck on. It's already ten past nine and there's gotta be like twenty other bitches waiting in line for them to unlock the doors.

We know their asses ain't doing shit, because we can see them walking around laughing and bumping their gums through the glass doors. This type of shit is so typical. They let everybody know that we're on their muthafuckin' time.

Ten more minutes pass and another twenty people line up. Everyone is grumbling and asking what time they open. I'm tempted to take my ass home and try this shit tomorrow because my feet is starting to hurt in these five-hundred-dollar designer shoes.

At exactly 9:32, this wide-hipped heifer unlocks the doors and we all rush inside like a herd of buffalo. After signing in, I plop into a chair and wait another hour and a half before that same heifer calls my name. When I follow her double-wide hips back to her cubicle, I have a serious attitude.

"Yolanda Turner," she says, flipping open a fat manila folder that's falling apart at the seams. "Long time no see."

"Yeah, I know. It's been a while." I plop down into the chair next to her desk and try my best to force on a smile. These bitches start tripping the moment they sense you coming at them sideways.

"It's been more than a while." She flips through a few more papers and then reaches for the pair of black-rimmed reading glasses on her desk. "Ten months." Pause. She riffles some more papers. At long last, she turns toward the computer.

I don't know what to do while she's doing all of that, so I start nervously crossing and uncrossing my legs. Five minutes later, when her gaze slides over to me, she simply asks, "So where have you been?"

"Oh . . . well . . . around." I should've had a better answer than that. I mean, fuck, how long have I been waiting?

"Around?" she echoes, staring over the top of her glasses.

I swallow hard like a dummy and nod.

"I see." She tugs in a deep breath and then closes the folder. "So what can I do for you, Ms. Turner, while you're just . . . hanging around?"

My hand starts itching because I'd like nothing better than to slap the holy shit out of her. "I came to see about getting my kids back."

Silence.

I clear my throat. "I mean . . . I'm doing better now. I can take care of them."

Slowly, this bitch pulls off her glasses and then leans back in her chair to study me.

"I have money," I blurt out, and then grab my purse. Before I can pull out a knot of cash, she reaches over and places her hand over mine.

"Don't." She shakes her head at me.

"What? I was about to show that I can afford to take care of them now."

She leans back again. "So . . . what? You're going to toss me a wad of money like this is where you come to buy kids off the rack?"

What the fuck is she talking about? "They're my kids," I remind her.

"Technically, yes."

"Technically?" I glance around to see who the fuck she's talking to. It sure in the hell can't be me. "Look. No disrespect, but, duh, I was the only bitch on that hospital table shitting and pushing those babies out. They're mine—and I want them back."

"Then maybe you should've brought your butt back up in here before they were eligible for adoption."

"Wait. What?" I know damn well I didn't hear this bitch correctly. "Who's up for adoption? Y'all can't give my babies away!" I jump up and start looking around. "Who the fuck is your supervisor? You done lost your damn mind."

This bitch pops up, too, and I reflexively yank my earrings out of my ears. Pregnant or not, I know I can take this heifer out.

"Oh. What are you going to do? Fight me?" She laughs. "Clearly you *don't* want to see your kids again."

"I'm trying to, but you're telling me you're giving them away."

"Clean out your ears. I said that they are eligible for adoption. And you don't have anybody to blame but yourself. We've been calling you for *months*. You're never home and you never return our calls."

"Ain't nobody called me."

She glances down at the folder again. "Are you still living at 1315 Utah Avenue with your mother, Betty?"

My eyes roll to the back of my head. "No. And of course my momma didn't tell me y'all called. She's probably pissed that I'm not there no more for her to leach off of."

"I see." Her eyes rake over me. "You want to take a seat, or are you getting ready to leave?"

I chug in an impatient breath and then sit my ass back down and wait for more bullshit to be shoveled my way.

"Ms. Turner, I'm sorry that you haven't received our numerous calls; however, it is your responsibility to make sure that we have an updated contact number. What if something had happened to one of the children? There would've been no way for us to contact you."

I shift in my chair but promise myself that I'd get ghost if I have to sit here while she lectures me about how bad of a mother I am. "Tell me what I have to do to get my kids back. Ain't nobody adopting them nowhere." I blink back tears.

Her eyes fall back to that damn folder. "It says here that the last time you were in, that you were told to enroll into parenting classes. Have you completed that?"

"Classes." I roll my eyes.

"Yes. Classes," the woman instructs. "You want your kids, you're going to have to prove to us that you can take care of them."

I reach for my purse again. "What? I said that I have money. That means I can cook and buy them new clothes now." The thought of having to sit up in some damn class touches off some old childhood memories. I ain't good with all that school crap. Reading and writing—that shit gives me a headache.

"Look, Ms. Turner. If you're serious about getting your kids back, then you'll take your butt to parenting classes. No one here is going to beg you to do the right thing. You need classes. You need counseling. We need to see how you're going to provide for them, and we need to inspect your home to make sure that the children will be living in a safe environment."

The more she talks, the more my face twists. "Damn. You want some blood, too?"

"As a matter of fact, you will have to pass a drug test."

"Are you for real? I'm fuckin' pregnant. I ain't on no drugs."

"Ha!" She rolls her eyes. "Like that makes a difference. If you saw *half* of what I see roll up in here, you wouldn't have even said nothing like that to me."

I suck in a deep breath. This shit is already giving me a headache.

"How far along are you?" she asks, picking up a pen.

I place a hand over my belly. "What? You eyeballin' this one, too?"

She lifts her brows as a silent answer.

"I don't believe this shit. Humph. I'm startin' to think that I shouldn't have bothered to come up in here."

She shakes her head and lowers her pen. "Nobody has a gun to your head. You're more than welcome to leave. And when you do, I will type in the system for this case to proceed with your children being eligible for adoption."

I feel trapped.

"But if you're serious . . . I'm willing to work with you. I can file an extension and we can set up a goal for reunification." She tosses up her hands. "It's up to you."

Fuck! I blink back a few more burning tears and sit there like a dummy.

"What do you want to do?" she presses.

"Fine. I'll take the damn classes."

She nods and gives me a weak-ass smile. "Good. Now let me get some updated information on you."

For the next hour, I sit there while the woman gets all up in my business. Of course she looks at me cross-eyed when I tell her I don't exactly have a job no more, and she doesn't want to hear about how much money I have. If I want my kids back, then I have to get a J-O-B. Preferably, one that hands out W-2s. By the time she stops handing me pamphlets and listing all this shit that I have to do, I really do have a massive headache.

Outside, I hop into my new silver Terrain and suck in a deep breath. When that feels good, I do a few more. *Can I really do all this shit?* I don't have an answer. At long last, I start the car and pull out of the parking lot. Not until then do I reach underneath my seat and pull out a much-needed blunt. It's not until I get that first good toke that I even begin to relax.

17

Lucifer

I stroll into the Pink Monkey, unrecognizable in a leather skirt so short that both my ass cheeks are poking out the bottom of the muthafucka. My long legs are greased with the right amount of baby oil and cocoa butter while I glide on a pair of six-inch heels like I was born with the damn things on my feet. Every nigga up in this grimy-ass hole-in-the-wall damn near twists their heads off tryna get a good look at my brick-house curves. No. I don't like dressing like this, but it's not like I don't know I'm blessed with a banging body. I do—and for tonight's mission, it's going to come in handy.

"Goddamn!" One nigga approaches, having a hard time tryna decide whether to focus on my perky 34C-cup titties or my hypnotizing onion booty. "Please, please, please tell me I ain't dreamin'."

"Depends," I tell him with a fake smile. "Is your name Treasure?"

"My name is any damn thing you want it to be." His gaze rapes my frame while his face twists like he's about to bust a nut at any second.

"Then why don't I call you *Get Ghost*?" I step past him.

"Aw, shawty. You ain't got to be like that." He places his hand on my shoulder, and before his ass can even blink, I have that muthafucka on his knees with his arm twisted behind his back.

"Did I give you permission to touch me, muthafucka?"

"Ow. Ow. Shit. Damn, shawty. I'm sorry."

"Keep your muthafuckin' hands to yourself." I twist his shit harder.

"Owwww. Shit. All right!"

I reel in my urge to break his shit but give in to the impulse to plant my heeled foot in the center of his back and kick his ass to the floor. Niggas at the bar hoot and holler at the extra entertainment. A few of them even wave dollar bills in front of my face. I just roll my eyes and work my way over to the bar.

"Buy me a drink," I tell this big Mufasa-looking muthafucka with dreads.

He turns his huge, dusty head toward me, and though his eyes are hidden behind a pair of black sunglasses, I know his ass is checking out the goods. "A'ight, Ma. I'd say a peek at those sweet titties is worth seven-fiddy." He signals the bartender. "What will it be, Ma?"

"Martini—apple."

"You heard the lady."

Not only is this muthafucka allergic to soap and water, but also apparently he has never met a toothbrush or mouthwash his ass liked. Somehow I manage to smile and not throw up.

"So where you from, baby? You work here?"

"Not yet. I'm hoping to get something, but I ain't been able to catch up with the owner yet," I lie.

"Humph. You might be waiting a while," he laughs.

"Why you say that?"

"Shit. Where you been at—under a rock? There's a fuckin' war going on, Ma. Those fake paper gangsters are gunning for our man. The streets are hot. That nigga gonna be ghost until we got this shit handled with those grimy Vice Lords."

"We? You GD, too?"

He tosses back his head and laughs. "Fuck. You better act like you know. I stack that long green all day and pop caps in those VL pussies like it's a part-time hobby. You feel me?"

My eye twitches. "Is that right?"

"You know it, baby. Treasure goes for his shit."

My brows cork up. "Treasure, huh?"

"Mmm-hmm." He turns toward me. "As in, you show me your private treasure and I'll show you mine."

That fuckin' line actually works on silly bitches? "Tempting," I lie with a straight face. "Especially if your treasure is as big as I think it is."

"Fuuuuck." He grabs his dick in his baggy clothes and flashes me two perfect rolls of yellow teeth. "You can give it a test feel now, baby girl. I ain't shy."

Without missing a beat, I reach over and grab his shit. To my surprise, the muthafucka is walking around with an anaconda in his pants.

"Think that you can handle that shit, Ma?"

I wiggle in my seat. "The real question is whether you can handle me, Daddy."

"Fuuuuuuck." Then he hits the guys on the arm sitting next to him. "Yo, Mario! I'm going to have to catch up with you later."

Mario? "Why don't you invite your friend?"

Mario jumps up so fast that his stool falls out from underneath him. "Fo real?"

Treasure's cocky smile dips.

"Why not? I'm always down for a double stuffing." I wink and give his cock another good squeeze.

"Well, all right now. This must be our lucky night." He stands, giving his boy a quick fist bump.

"I know that shit's right. Where in the fuck have you been all my life?"

"All that matters is that I'm here now. So, are we going to do this?"

"Fuuuuuck yeah," they chorus like a ghetto version of Dumb and Dumber.

"Then let's go." I turn from the bar and take my time strolling and working my hips toward the exit. The moment we make it outside, Treasure's hand is underneath my skirt and his middle finger is injected into my dry pussy.

"Damn, baby. We're going to have to get you ready for Big Papa or this shit is gonna to hurt."

I grind my teeth together. "You want to do this in the back?"

"Here?" He looks around. "You don't want to go to a hotel or nothing?"

"Maybe I like doing it outside. You complainin'?"

"Fuuuuuuck no!" He wiggles his finger around. "I'll watch you slob on my nigga while I get up in this fine ass. My shit is already fuckin' hard as a brick."

"I had my mouth watering for you first, baby."

His lips hitch up higher. "A'ight. Shit. Whatever." He removes his hand, and I make a mental note to douche as soon as I get my ass home.

Once we reach the back, Treasure looks around, laughing. "All right. Let's get this shit started." He unzips his pants and pulls out this long, black and brown cock and gives it a couple of strokes. "Let's see what you're working with, Ma."

"Absolutely, baby." I spread my legs and proceed to bend down while twerking my ass up in the air.

As Mario moves behind me to pull out his shit, my hand slides beneath my right hip and withdraws my Browning hunting knife. I take Treasure's erect cock and pull it to my lips. "You ready, baby?"

"You know it." He thrusts his hips upward, greedy and anxious to get this show on the road.

Smiling, I pull his cock with my left hand and slice upward with my right.

Treasure's eyes bug out of his skull at the same time I hear

Mario gagging and choking on his own blood. I don't have to look back to know that Bishop is in the middle of removing Mario's neck from his shoulders.

"What the fuuuuuuuck?"

"How about you suck this yourself, muthafucka?" I take his detached cock and shove it hard into his mouth. "By the way, Profit and Ta'Shara send their love, nigga." With one quick slice, I split Treasure's throat open. He gags, his eyes wide as fuck as he hits the concrete like a falling tree. Now that he's down, I straddle his body and squat down so I can carve an upside-down pitchfork into the center of his head. I completely miss watching the light go out of his eyes, but the vision of him with his own cock in his mouth is priceless.

When I'm done, I cock my head and try to admire my work. "Do you think that's crooked?"

"Uh, we ain't got all fuckin' night, Willow," Bishop barks.

I jerk my head back at him. "What's with this Willow shit again?"

He shrugs and twists up his face. "You're the one who's dressing up like a girl all of a sudden. What did you expect?"

I stand back up, sheath my bloody knife, and tug my skirt down so that it covers my ass. "Fuck you."

Bishop laughs.

18

Momma Peaches

"**P**eaches. Peaches! PEACHES!" Josephine screams, and pounds on my front door.

I hear her, but I ain't paying her ass any mind since Cedric is back to trying to pound the lining out of my pussy. But when I'm like three strokes from busting my latest and greatest nut, Cedric's hips stop their jackhammering. "Who the fuck is that now?"

"Who gives a fuck?" I throw my ass back on the dick and get two good strokes in before Josie straight up sounds like she's the muthafuckin' police.

"PEACHES, I KNOW YOUR ASS HEARS ME. GET THAT DICK OUTCHA ASS AND COME AND AN-SWER THIS DAMN DOOR!"

"Oh no, this bitch didn't!" Pissed, I slide my wet pussy off this fat chocolate log, grab my prosthetic leg and robe, and march my ass to the door. This fuckin' lack of privacy is seri-ously getting out of control. "If it ain't one thing, it's another," I mumble under my breath as I stomp my way to the door.

BANG! BANG! BANG!

"PEACHES! GET YOUR ASS OUT HERE!"

I snatch open the door and don't wait two seconds before I bust Josie in the mouth. Her head reels back and shifts her wig off center. Unlike me, Josie's fine brick-house curves have long morphed into a big-ass brick wall. She has more fat rolls around her neck, waist, and ankles than she knows what to do with.

"What the fuck is wrong with your ignorant ass?!" I glance up and down Shotgun Row and see bitches creeping out onto the porch, and that causes my blood pressure to jump a few more notches. *Lawd, this bitch is gonna cause my ass to catch another case out here.*

Josie pulls out a small travel-size pack of Kleenex and tries to catch the rest of the blood that's squirting all over my front porch. "What the fuck? Are you crazy?"

"You hammering on my door like the po-po and you got the nerve to fix your face to ask me if *I'm* crazy? Bitch, you must've lost your mind out here." I start looking around. "Where it at? Huh? Where it at?"

To double down on this foolishness, Josie charges back at me. I guess to try and run me over because that's really all that a Mack truck can do at the end of the day, but my next punch nails the center of this bitch's throat, and it shuts her ass down. I don't know why from time to time niggas forget who the fuck I am and try to test me.

"Slow your roll, baby girl." I step out onto the porch while Josie struggles to wheeze in some air. "Now, I'm gonna assume that your big ass is over here because you're upset about that little piece of drama that went down over here with your grandbaby."

Wheeze. Wheeze.

"And you know what? I'm gonna let you have that because I can respect it. I'm having a little bit of trouble with my own blood right now. You want to protect him. I get it. But what I can't and won't abide by is you rolling over here and disturbing my peace—putting my business all out on Front Street." I bend over and make sure that we make eye contact. "You feel me? I don't pop up at your prayer meetings, Bible studies, or whatever else you're doing to try to convince God to let you into the pearly gates after all the hell you done raised and all the fucked-up shit that you did to try to break up my marriage. So I'm not gonna have it. You hear me? If I feel like fucking your children, grandchildren, or even dig up your dead husband for a damn dick ride, that's just what the fuck I'm gonna do. Is we clear?"

Wheeze. Wheeze.

I reach over to lift her head back up and temporarily forget that she's wearing a wig and snatch the muthafucka off. "Shit!" I blink at that head of wiry silver curls smashed down by a sheer nylon wig cap. The shit makes her look closer to ancient. "Now that's a damn shame. Girl, where's your pride? Get your shit fixed." I toss her two-dollar wig back at her, but before I can go back into the house to get tangled back into my bed-room sheets, police sirens fill the air—and not just one or two but the whole damn squad blazes down Shotgun Row, look-ing like a blue army.

"What in the world?" Josie pants, pulling herself up and struggling to shove her synthetic wig back onto her head.

Niggas jump out of the street and then scurry about like cockroaches tryna get out of the way. They don't go too far be-cause let's face it, we're some nosy muthafuckas on this street. But I know what's up.

"Oh, fuck," Josie says, forgetting all about her busted lip. "Is that who I think it is?"

Captain Melvin Johnson. His ass springs out of the first pa-trol car, looking like a black hurricane as he bears down on Python and LeShelle's place.

Fuck. Fuck. Fuck. Fuck.

Now let's get it straight. Python getting arrested is nothing new. Shit. I have a hidden safe in my closet specifically set up to bail his ass or any other family member out of jail. But this shit—getting caught with a missing child, who happens to be the grandson of Memphis's supercop—has the potential of putting my favorite nephew on death row.

A fresh wave of guilt attacks my conscience. Wasn't my raising Terrell supposed to save him—give him a fighting chance to survive in a world that didn't have any love for the black man? Or is this another one of my fuckups in a long line of fuckups?

I move to stand next to Josie and watch with bated breath as the police rush the door with a battering ram. Two seconds later, they bust it down. Knowing Python and LeShelle's Bonnie and Clyde's tendencies, I'm not surprised that in the next second gunshots rings out.

RAT-A-TAT-TAT-TAT! RAT-A-TAT-TAT-TAT!
RAT-A-TAT-TAT-TAT! RAT-A-TAT-TAT-TAT!

Niggas duck.

It sounds like a fucking firing range out here.

But as fast as those muthafuckas ran into Python's place, those pig bastards come running right back out.

"Fuck! Shit! Shut the fuckin' door," Melvin yells. "Someone get Animal Control down here. This house is crawling with snakes!"

A smile hooks the side of my lips, and I'm able to breathe a sigh of relief. Now all I have to hope for is that Python comes to his senses and drops Christopher off at a hospital or fire department. If not, Captain Melvin Johnson is gonna stay on his ass like white on rice. Just as that thought drifts across my mind, Captain Johnson's gaze cuts in my direction.

"Aw, shit." I roll my eyes. The last muthafuckin' place I want to be is on this nigga's radar. The next thing I know, his ass is on the move toward me. "This day keeps getting better and better," I grumble.

"Look, girl. I'm gonna catch you later," Josie says, wiping her mouth and damn near tripping over her feet to get off my porch.

I don't respond because it ain't like I issued her ass an invitation over here in the first place. The only thing I have time to do is tighten the belt on my robe before Captain Johnson is in my face.

"Peaches."

"Melvin." He eyeballs me like my ass calling him by his first name is just cause to haul my ass downtown.

"Where is he?" he barks.

"Who?"

"You know damn well who. Your gangbangin' nephew Terrell. Tell me now and I might go easy on him."

"First of all, Terrell is a businessman. What he does around here is handle his *business*. And do you mean by *going easy* that you won't beat him down and plant shit on him before you arrest him?"

Melvin takes another step and is standing so close I think he's about to French kiss my ass. "It's more like I *might* not put a bullet in the center of his forehead before I slap the cuffs on him." For emphasis, he plants his fingers in the center of *my* head and pushes me backward. "Especially since locking you Carvers up is a complete waste of time and taxpayers' money."

My eyes narrow, but I hold my tongue.

"Of course, your *husband* would probably like a little company in the big house. Who knows, maybe if they were both there, you'd find the time to stop in for a visit every now and then, and Isaac wouldn't have to resort to cracking niggas' asses open to get that nut you used to give him?"

"Get off my porch," I hiss.

Melvin's face inches down toward mine till our noses touch. "Or what? You know I can haul you in on general principle. I'm sure if I get you in the interrogation room for about five minutes, I can get Terrell's whereabouts out of you or you can at least slob on my dick like you and your sister used to. You remember those days, don't you? Pussy in exchange for bail money. Thanks to you, I've grown quite fond of one-legged bitches."

My hands ball at my sides.

"If you're out breathing fresh air, that can only mean that you're on parole. Play ball and maybe I won't have to call your parole officer."

Behind me a throat clears.

Melvin lifts his head and shifts his attention to the front door where Cedric stands with his arms crossed. "Now who do we have here?"

"Cedric Robinson," he answers for himself. "Maybelline Carver's parole officer."

Melvin's gaze shifts down to Cedric's bare chest and open jeans and then back to me before an evil smile curves his lips. "Guess it's true what they say: you can't teach an old *bitch* new tricks."

It takes everything I have not to punch this nigga in *his* throat.

Melvin places his captain's hat back onto his head. "I'm sure I'll be seeing you around." He takes one step off the porch but then stops and turns back. "Make sure you tell Python that there's not a rock in Memphis his ass can slither under that I can't find."

"Seeing how that's where you live, I don't doubt it," I shoot back.

A thin smile cracks his lips before he struts his ass off my property.

"Bastard."

19

Yolanda

I know that my ass is taking a chance rolling over to Shotgun Row. It ain't too far-fetched to believe that LeShelle's most faithful Queen Gs won't jump my ass the minute I step out of my SUV. And it's not like Baby Thug is around to act like my personal bodyguard anymore. If shit pops off, I'm on my own. But for now I'm relying on the fact that I have Python's baby baking in my oven to shield me. Still, that doesn't stop my heart from jumping into the center of my throat the minute I turn onto Shotgun Row. First off, there's an awful lot of niggas roaming around—more than normal for a Monday afternoon. Then I see why. The po-po got the whole damn street lit up with blue lights.

"What the fuck?" I roll to a stop outside my momma's crib. When I hop out of my vehicle, my eyes zoom in on Captain Melvin Johnson leaning all up in Momma Peaches's face. He's so close I can't tell whether he's about to kiss her or spit on her.

My momma is on the porch with a smile as big as the whole state of Tennessee.

"What's going on?" I ask, creeping up the stairs while trying to make sure that I don't miss shit.

"Who gives a fuck—as long as they lock that old bitch's ass up, I'll be happy."

I cut my eyes over at her and shake my head. The beef between these two goes way back to the time when Momma Peaches lopped off an ear on one of my momma's ex-boyfriends. Since she had done it to protect me, it made the old lady gangsta a hero in my eyes, but I'm not so dumb not to know that she has plenty of enemies and that going back to jail ain't nothing but a thang. Hell, she done floated in and out of that muthafucka so many times, I wouldn't be surprised if there is already a cell block named after her.

When Captain Johnson turns and marches back down the porch steps, my momma emits a disappointed moan before heading back into the house. The front door slams behind her with a loud *bam!*

I don't budge. I watch Memphis's much-bragged-about supercop with my own disgust curdling in my blood. Every soldier around here who has ever had handcuffs on their asses knows that Melvin Johnson is not the nigga to fuck with. The muthafucka is as dirty as they come.

Trust and believe that back when I was trafficking, I had to slob on that old man's dick more than my fair share or cut his ass in on the action to get a few charges dropped. The only difference between him and the other hustlers out here is that he carries a badge. I have to hand it to him—the couple of times I've seen his ass on the news, the old man was slicker than a can of fucking oil. With all that cheesing and grinning, the only thing that was missing was a pair of tap shoes. But his little show must work 'cause he got white folks believing they got the right nigga in charge for the job.

Judging by his and Momma Peaches's faces, there is still no love lost between them two. Even I've been around long enough to remember how hard the relentless cop came down on Momma Peaches's man, Isaac. Hell, he made most of his high-profile busts off the backs of the Gangster Disciples, which in turn gave that crooked nigga most of his stripes. You'd think he'd at least send us a Christmas card every now and then.

But something else is going on. I can tell by the way the lines in his face are deepening. Before I can think too hard about it, a white truck turns down onto Shotgun Row, and I'm barely able to make out the words ANIMAL CONTROL on its side before it screeches to a stop in front of Python and LeShelle's crib.

That catches my attention as I realize that the other police cars aren't around Momma Peaches's place but around my man's crib. "What the fuck?"

All thoughts of cussing my momma out for not relaying the messages from Children's Services fly out of my head. My nosy ass drifts toward the action like the rest of these muthafuckas out here. Shit. My whole upgrade situation is totally dependent on Python's ass being able to draw breath. Until this moment, I really haven't given much thought to anything actually happening to that nigga. The muthafucka is a legend in these streets. Superman with two Glocks in his hands. Ain't nobody been able to take his ass out, and many have tried.

But what if he gets locked up?

Fuck. Niggas get locked up every day all day. What will happen to my ass then?

No man.

No money.

No apartment.

No job.

Fuck. That taste of money I got saved up ain't gonna last that fuckin' long. My mind zooms so fast, I have a migraine in two seconds flat and my stomach starts to churn violently. I try to hold it together, but then I see these Animal Control muthafuckas scrambling around with long poles and rounding up snakes. Niggas are pointing and laughing until a few of

Python's babies get loose and start slithering out into the yard and into the streets. Suddenly niggas scream and run in every direction.

I lose it and slap a hand over my mouth. There's not enough time for me to turn around and race to my momma's place to throw up, so I drift off the cracked sidewalk and hurl onto Momma Peaches's front lawn.

"What in the hell?" Momma Peaches's sharp voice cracks like a whip from her front porch. "Child, are you all right?"

Before I can even attempt to answer, I'm hit with another wave of nausea and I lose the last bit of that bean burrito I had on the way over here. Before long, my stomach muscles lock up and I clutch my big belly like I'm about to go into premature labor.

"Lawd. Lawd." Momma Peaches shuffles off her porch. "If it ain't one damn thing, it's another."

In the next second, she's there brushing my blond braids back from my face and rubbing my lower back.

"Now don't you get yourself all upset," she consoles. "Everything is going to be all right." She turns and hollers up at her porch. "Cedric, help me get this child into the house."

I pull in several deep breaths, but when I manage to push myself upright, I lock gazes with Kookie and Pit Bull across the street. These bitches are staring at me so damn hard that I'm surprised my ass hasn't just dropped dead on the spot. When Kookie lifts a phone to her ear, there's no doubt in my mind that the snitching bitch is on the phone with LeShelle.

"You look pale," Momma Peaches says, checking me over. "C'mon into the house and let me get some food and fluids in you."

This tall dude comes up behind me and asks in this sexy-as-hell voice, "Can you walk, or do you need me to carry you?"

Fuck. Where in the hell did Momma Peaches find this fine nigga at? "I . . . I can walk."

"Lean on my arm, sweetheart."

Hell. I'll lean on whatever this muthafucka wants. He may be old but . . . fuck! "Thanks," I say, and then allow him to direct me toward the house. On the way, I flash Kookie and Pit Bull the bird and then smack my fat ass. Let them run and tell that shit.

Once we're up the porch stairs, Mr. Fine tells Momma Peaches, "We need to talk."

"Later," she says dismissively. "I gotta help settle this child's stomach. She's carrying my nephew's seed."

Judging by the look on his face, her answer annoys him, but it sure as hell shuts down any conversation he thought he was about to have. Now that's the kind of power I wish I had over niggas. Momma Peaches knows how to work her gangsta shit. Absently, I wonder what the hell happened with Arzell, but I know better than to ask Momma Peaches about her personal business. I certainly don't want her cussing and checking my ass in front of everybody.

"It's been a minute since you've been around here," Momma Peaches says when we enter the kitchen. "I was beginning to think that Python stashed you in another country."

I frown, disappointed that Python hasn't kept her up to date about what's been going on with me and the baby. My thoughts must be written on my face because Momma Peaches adds, "Of course, I don't ask Python too many questions about his personal business. The less I know the better—especially nowadays."

I nod and try to see what's going on outside the kitchen window. "Is Python around?"

"You want some flapjacks? I'm in the mood for some flapjacks," she says, ignoring my question. Still it puts a smile on my face because everyone knows the 411 on Momma Peaches and her flapjacks. My eyes dart to her new man, and I can't help but wonder why she ain't in bed and riding this muthafucka until she got saddle sores. I know I would. He's fine. "Nah. I'm cool, but if you got a Sprite and some crackers, that would be great."

She smiles and winks. "Coming right up."

I laugh and inwardly reaffirm how much I love this old woman. Growing up, I lost count how many times I wished that she was my real momma instead of the one I got. Peaches is tough and she always stands up for her own, which gets me thinking about Captain Johnson again. "I saw Supercop leaving. Now, that's someone who really hasn't been around for a minute."

"Humph!" Momma Peaches plops down a sleeve of crackers and a canned Sprite in front of me. It's no surprise she doesn't cough up information. She doesn't roll like that. If I want to know something, I need to come direct.

"What's going on down at Python's? I mean . . . is it something I should be concerned about?"

Momma Peaches shrugs as she lowers herself into the chair across from me. "That shit ain't for me to say. If you need to know something, you're going to have to ask him yourself."

I discreetly settle a hand on my belly as a sly way of playing the pregnant card, but Momma Peaches shakes her head. "Please, child. Don't embarrass yourself. Dick Cheney couldn't waterboard information out my ass if he tried, so you giving me those big puppy-dog eyes ain't doing shit. Believe that."

"Can't blame a bitch for trying," I say, smiling and scooping my cell phone out. I hit Python up on my speed dial. No surprise, my ass goes straight to his voice mail. "Hey, Python, baby. It's me, Yo-Yo," I say. "I'm checking in. I haven't heard from you, and I'm down here on Shotgun Row and, like, the whole damn Memphis Police Department is down here, breaking your shit in. So, um, give me a call and let me know what's going on or if you need me for anything. All right. Bye." I disconnect the call and smile at Momma Peaches.

"See. That wasn't so hard, was it?"

"No. I guess not." I pull a cracker out of the sleeve and pop the top on my soda.

Two seconds later, Ms. Josie busts through the door. "Maybelline," she yells, racing into the kitchen all wide-eyed with a busted lip and bruised neck.

"Damn, bitch." Momma Peaches jumps out of her chair. "What the fuck I gotta do to stop your ass from rolling up in here like you paying the muthafuckin' bills around here?"

"You don't think Python had anything to do with Captain Johnson's daughter's murder, do you?" Ms. Josie asks, ignoring Momma Peaches's question.

I spew out my drink.

Momma Peaches jumps back and nearly topples over the chair behind her. "Goddamn, girl." Irritated, she turns around and grabs a roll of paper towels.

"Sorry," I say, but then turn toward Ms. Josie and her crooked wig. *Damn. Has someone been beating her ass?* "Captain Johnson's daughter has been murked?"

Josie is eager to keep bumping her gums. "It's been all over the news for the last couple of days. They found that girl in her bedroom shot the hell up. Blood everywhere. And there's a city-wide hunt for her missing son."

Momma Peaches jabs her fists onto her hips. "Anything else you feel like broadcasting, Ms. Reporter?"

Josie blinked. "What? The shit is all over the television. What did I do?"

I hop up and race into the living room to turn on Momma Peaches's TV. Sure enough, Officer Melanie Johnson's picture is the first thing I see on Channel 5. It's a face I remember very well, mainly because she'd walked in on Python busting a nut all over my ass in his office at the Pink Monkey sometime back.

As I stare at her picture on the news, the tiny hairs on the back of my neck start standing up. *She's dead?*

LeShelle's last words to me at Baby Thug's funeral echo in my head. *You ain't me. You ain't never gonna be me. And you're not always gonna be pregnant. Ticktock.*

I feel sick again. Turning, I race away from the television to find the small bathroom down the hallway. I barely make it in time to throw up that one cracker, and then I dry-heave until I get another stomach cramp.

"Damn, child. What's wrong with you?"

By the time I lift my head, I'm trembling like a leaf.

"Child, do you need me to take you to a doctor or something?" Momma Peaches asks, handing me a cool towel to press against my forehead.

I shake my head, though I ain't too sure that I don't need a doctor. *Or a mortician once LeShelle gets finished with me.* "I better get home," I mutter under my breath.

"You're more than welcome to lie down here," Momma Peaches says. "I'm worried about your color."

Struggling to get off the floor, I shake my head and use the towel to wipe the drool from my mouth. "I'm all right," I lie. "It's just one of those days."

"Well, at least stay over at your crazy momma's house until your nerves settle," she insists. "I'm sure she'll let you do that much."

The way her dark brown eyes roam over me, I can tell that she really cares and is concerned. That kind of shit makes me smile. Momma Peaches is tough on the outside but soft where it counts. "I'm fine. Really." I flash a smile and ease past her to exit the bathroom.

As I shuffle back through the living room, the news still has Officer Johnson's picture up as they go on about the horrific, bloody crime scene. How can I not think about Baby Thug's murder scene? She had been discovered in a bloody bedroom as well. The only difference I can tell is that this cop was allowed to meet her maker with her pussy bullet-free.

Tears blur my vision, but when I rush outside, the late

spring air does wonders against my clammy skin. That relief is short-lived because the heavy weight of Kookie's and Pit Bull's gazes lands back on me. This time, when our eyes connect, fear skips down my spine. Suddenly, I don't feel Python's blanket of protection at all. In fact, I feel like a crumbled up Flower who has wandered over onto the wrong side of town. Baby Thug's voice fills my head. *You're in over your head, and you don't even know it.*

As I rush down Momma Peaches's porch steps and then hightail it back toward my SUV, police cars start rolling out. Shit. I want to be right behind them so they don't have to come right back and white-chalk my ass.

Tap. Tap.

I whip my head back around to my rolled-up window, and these two ugly, jacked-up bitches are sneering at me through the glass.

"TICKTOCK, TRICK," Pit Bull shouts.

My hand trembles as I turn over the car. Still I got a little bit of pride left and I can't let them know that I'm seconds away from crapping in my panties. I flip them a bird and yell, "Sit and rotate, bitches!" I shift the car into drive and whip away from the curb.

Behind me, those evil hoes shout, "TICKTOCK!"

20

LeShelle

"That bitch is over there right now?" I ask, and then curse under my breath. What I wouldn't give for five minutes alone with that retarded muthafucka who thinks she's going to take my spot. My taste for blood these last couple of days has only gotten stronger, and I know that Yo-Yo is just the bitch I can feast on to give me the little satisfaction I need.

"She's walking into Momma Peaches's place right now," Kookie tattles.

My eyes cut over toward the bedroom door. Python is busy talking to McGriff in the living room. Hell, my ass is even doing a mental calculation on the odds of being able to sneak out of this West Memphis crib, float out to Shotgun Row, murk that pregnant monkey, and make it back here before Python suspects a muthafuckin' thing.

"Fuck. Watch her ass and let me know what happens."

"Cool, girl. You know we got your back."

I roll my eyes at that shit. Anybody who boasts that kind of shit usually is looking for a soft spot to plant a knife. "Don't talk about it—be about it" is my motto. "A'ight. Get back at me." I disconnect the call when Kookie shouts. "What now?" I ask, irritated. I want to get in Python's face about all these loose jump-offs he still got floating around here. This foul shit has got to stop.

"Giiirrrl, I hope y'all plan to stay away from down here for a while because Supercop got the whole damn police force down here. They done busted down y'all's door and everything."

My survival instincts kick in, and I sneak another look toward the door. "Who are they looking for—me or Python?"

"Python—from what I hear."

I exhale a quick breath but know all that shit can change if Ta'Shara and her Vice Lord lover start snitching. I need to find out what the hell is going on with that situation, but no doubt if I pop up, Tracee and Reggie will be in my face bumping their gums and riding my nerves. "Yo, Kookie. See if you can find Ta'Shara's friend for me."

"Who dat?"

"Um, Essence, I think it is. She stays around the block." At Kookie's silence, I add, "Cleo's little sister."

"Oh. A'ight."

"Tell her I need her to peep that situation with Ta'Shara and her man, and then I need for her to get back at me."

"You think she'll do that? I mean, if they friends and all."

"Persuade her ass," I snap. "If she has a problem fulfilling her obligation to the Queen G family, then put your foot in her ass."

Christopher suddenly appears at the door, looking like an ashy and nappy-headed mess. "I'm hungry," the bastard whines. Why didn't Python grab this nigga some clothes while he was kidnapping muthafuckas?

I cut my eyes over at this annoying lil fuck. I can literally feel my blood pressure jump. "Hold on, Kookie." I drop my cell phone from my ear and yell, "Tell your damn daddy that you're hungry. I ain't y'all's damn cook and maid up in this bitch!"

He drops his head lower, and that shit gets me rolling my eyes harder. "I don't believe this shit." I put the phone back up to my ear. "Kookie, girl, let me call you back. I gotta feed Python's whiny-ass son. Looks like the only name change I'm gonna get is *Mammie* around here."

Kookie laughs. "A'ight, girl. You hang in there. That nigga is gonna do the right thing."

"Humph. It better be soon. That's all I know. Handle that situation for me and call me back." I disconnect the call and drag in a deep breath. "Seven-years-old and don't know how to feed himself," I huff under my breath. "This is bullshit."

Stomping across the large bedroom in a pair of booty shorts and a tight tee, it takes everything I have not to shove the boy out of my way. When I storm into the huge open space that's currently serving as our living room, Python is running on a treadmill, with his top lieutenants, overseers, and enforcers huddled around talking business as well as strategy.

At the sight of Python's chiseled hard-body covered with tats and sweat, my clit starts jumping. Sure he looks like a massive pit bull running on that muthafucka, but he has my ass trained well to respond when he's pumping that much testosterone around. If none of these niggas was up in here, I'd be trying to relieve some of my own stress.

"C'mon in here," I tell Christopher, and lead him into the kitchen. But when I open the fridge and then the cabinets, there ain't shit up in this muthafucka. "Ain't this about a bitch?!"

Storming back out of the kitchen, I make a beeline straight toward Python, who's stepping off the treadmill and toweling the sweat from around his neck. "That nigga is some fuckin' where," he growls. "Big muthafucka like that ain't just disappeared into thin air."

"Yo. We're trying. We got a couple of plants at the hospital, but there's as many Vice Lords crawling around that mutha-fucka as police officers. This shit ain't easy. Not by a long shot. Unless we're rolling up in there like we did last time, we're going to have to be patient with this one," McGriff says.

Python's face damn near twists off. "Fuck that. We're in a him-or-me situation now. I can't rest until I know that nigga is six feet under. This ain't about money, drugs, territory, or even bitches right now. You feel me?" he barks at McGriff. "As many plugs as I put in that muthafucka, he should be down. But I'm starting to think he and his brother eat bullets like mutha-fuckin' vitamins."

McGriff nods. "I feel you. That young nigga took a whole damn clip. Them niggas must've made a deal with the devil or something."

Python flings his towel, and the shit snaps against the right side of McGriff's face. The nigga jumps, his eyes bug in shock.

"You finished admiring those niggas?" Python barks, thrusting out his chest and looking like he's two seconds from jumping his own right-hand man. The whole room goes quiet. If a fly floated between these two niggas right now, bul-lets or fists would start flying.

McGriff swallows and finds his voice. "Nah, man. It ain't nothing like that. I'm thinking we need to come at them with something harder, is all. I got no love for none of those hooks. You know that."

Python remains in a fighting stance. It's clear in his face that he'd rather fight this shit instead of hug it out.

"C'mon, Python," McGriff says, flashing a nervous smile. "You know how I feel about those fuckin' slobs."

Python grunts and then turns his back on his nigga. De-spite his two-hour workout, we can all still see the tension coiled in every inch of his body. "I want that muthafucka found—*today*."

Normally, I would try to stay away from him when he's in a black mood, but not today. I'm pissed at his ass. Folding my arms, I huff an impatient breath to get his attention.

Python glances over and gives me the shut-the-fuck-up look and then turns back toward his nigga.

McGriff clears his throat. "We also need to see about bringing Momma Peaches out here. It ain't safe with her alone on Shotgun Row right now. I'm concerned about a blackout being ordered."

"Blackout on me?" Python's chest swells up while outrage twists his face. "Those muthafuckas want to murk my whole family? Fuck that. We're going at this nigga hard. I want that nigga's family tree wiped clean. Feel me? I want the streets red with blood."

McGriff tosses up his hands. "We've tried that shit before, remember? Ain't a whole lot known about that nigga. Hell, we were all surprised to learn that the muthafucka even had a brother last year."

"Well the bastard didn't crawl out from up under a rock."

"Maybe, maybe not. Those fuckin' hooks did a good-ass job hiding his peoples. Our best bet is to go at his soldiers hard, take out as many of those muthafuckas as we can. We do that, we're liable to smoke that big nigga out."

I can tell by reading my nigga's face that shit ain't good enough. He wants to go medieval—put that nigga's head on a pike and roll through every hood in the city to let those niggas know that the nasty fuck was murked and who the hell did the shit.

"If you want to get a king's attention, you don't go after pawns," I tell McGriff. "You go after the nigga's queen."

Python smirked. "I already did that, remember?"

Melanie wasn't his queen. She was yours. "Shit. That crooked pig could've just been his jump-off . . . or a way to keep tabs on you."

Python's jaw tightened. I struck a nerve.

"What about that other bitch I've heard so much about? That right-hand evil bitch they call Lucifer. Maybe she's really his queen." I fold my arms. "Most ride-or-die chicks are." My gaze raked Python up and down. "Even when the man they're banging for don't realize it."

All the niggas start exchanging looks, like this shit never occurred to them.

For the first time in days, Python smiles. "Beauty and brains." He glanced over to his boys. "McGriff—"

"I'm on it," he says, hopping up from the edge of the sofa.

"And about Momma Peaches," Python barks. "Beef up security. The only way she leaving Shotgun Row is by body bag—she already told me that much."

McGriff sucks in a deep breath and shakes his head like his boss. "Done. But I gotta tell you that between them hooks and the po-po rolling through, they're gonna take a serious hunk out of our cheese. Niggas are gonna gripe about tryna eat."

Python looks unmoved as he sits down on a weight bench and starts on his arm curls. "Tell them niggas to squash that bullshit. We are at war. We lose and ain't nobody gonna eat." He does a few more curls and shakes his head. "What's with these young, pussy-fucks? Niggas need to man up, show that they're down with the cause. This shit is not a drill. The first soldier who steps up with that bullshit you put your foot in that ass. I mean that shit. Get them niggas to fall in line."

"Done," McGriff says, looking eager to leave.

Python's gaze cuts back over to me and what I got on. "Speaking of which, what up, Shelle?" He slaps me on the ass and then watches it jiggle. "What have I told you about parading around in shit like this when my niggas are over here?"

Nigga, is you for real? "Your *son* is hungry," I say, clucking my tongue.

Python's face twists up. "And?"

I roll my neck. "*And* what do you think?"

"Ain't this about a bitch?" he swears under his breath, and then looks at McGriff. "Niggas ain't shit. Bitches ain't shit."

"Excuuuuse me?"

A vein twitches along his jaw as his black gaze returns to mine.

"Who the fuck you callin' a bitch? That bastard is yours not mine. Dig his damn momma back up and tell her ass to breastfeed him."

Python drops his barbell and comes up swinging. I hear the *slap* probably a good three seconds before I feel the pain explode on the left side of my face. By that time, I'm on the floor and blinking stars from my eyes.

Quick as a black panther, Python's massive frame crouches over me. "Look around down there and see if you can find your damn mind, bitch. Who the fuck are you talking to?"

I touch my bottom lip and see that it's bleeding. "Fuck you!"

Chairs screech all around us, and suddenly niggas start making excuses to leave.

"Yo. We catch up with you later, man," McGriff says, holding his fist up for a quick bump before rushing toward the door.

"Ayo, G." Python calls McGriff back while I pull myself off the floor.

"Whassup?"

"Take Lil Man with you. Get him a Happy Meal or something while Shelle and I discuss a few things for a minute."

"A'ight, cool." McGriff turns toward Christopher. "C'mon, Chris. You heard your old man."

Christopher hesitates, but when he sees Python reach for his weight-lifting belt, a fire lights under his ass and he scrambles out the door with the other GD niggas.

I have an idea of what Python thinks he's about to get started, and I turn back toward the bedroom.

"Now where in the fuck do you think you're going?"

"Fuck you, Python. I ain't in the mood for your bullshit."

WHAP!

I jump at the feel of the silver spikes on his leather belt biting into my skin. "OW! Stop it, Python! I don't feel like fuckin' with you right now!"

His other hand whips across my right side, and another explosion of stars flashes behind my eyes, but this time I come back around with my claws out. My clit starts thumping the moment my nails sink into his lower left cheek and then rake upward.

"FUCK!" he roars.

The sight of blood pouring from the four large jagged lines before my claws are extracted from his face gives me this crazy-ass high that has me laughing like a maniac. In the next second, Python backhands me so hard that it actually lifts me off the floor and sends me crashing into the glass coffee table. Glasses, dishes, and even a toolbox and some other shit crash down around my head, but I still can't stop laughing.

"Oh. You like that shit, do you?" He touches his face and sees the blood, but then a sinister smile carves its way onto his ugly face. "You want to play rough, baby? I got something for your ass. I'm tired of you always talking shit." He lunges with his fist soaring toward my face like a locomotive.

A rush of adrenaline surges through me, and I shift my head out of the way and hear Python's fist hit the hard floor littered with glass. His painful roar has me convinced that there's nothing but concrete beneath this thin, cheap-ass carpet. If he hadn't just been trying to knock my ass out, I might feel sorry for him. As it is, I push him over to the side while he tries to shake the pain out of his bruised hand.

"Serves your ass right," I tell him, getting up.

He rolls over onto his back—now half laughing and moaning.

I want to stay mad a little longer, but a smile tugs at my lips and I end up climbing on top of him and straddling him. "Aww. Did you hurt your hand?"

Python's black gaze shifts over to me. At the same time, I can feel his fat dick inching up against the back of my ass. "Let me see it." With a pout, I reach for his hand. When I see his bleeding knuckles, I moan in sympathy. "Aww. Poor baby." I bring it up to my mouth and then mop up the tangy blood with my tongue. "Mmmm."

Python hikes up a brow, but then another smile tugs at his lips. "Your ass is fuckin' out of control."

"Don't act like you don't like it." I take his hand and then plant it underneath my shirt. Like a good boy, he squeezes my shit and gives me that little taste of pain that I've been dying for. Reaching behind me, I slide my hand beneath the elastic waist of his black sweatpants, and I grab that fat cock and start beating that shit to get him ready.

"Ah. That's why you've been mouthing off. Your ass wanna get fucked."

"You know it, nigga." I tighten my hold on his shit. "Why the fuck I always gotta beg for what supposed to belong to me?" Fast as a whip, I grab a pair of pliers from the floor and lock that shit on his fat meat before he has a chance to process it.

Python jerks up with a loud hiss. "Ow! What the fuck?"

"Oooh. Looks like I finally have your attention."

"Fuck! Ease up!"

"Nah. Fuck that shit," I yell, and give his shit a good yank. "I'm tired of this fuckin' bullshit. You're still messin' with that retarded yellow bitch?"

"W-what?" He tries to grab my hand, but my next yank has this muthafucka seeing stars.

"Stop playing me stupid, Python. You know I'm talking about your girl Lemonhead. Why is this bitch still in the picture? Ain't you learned your lesson about fucking with these fake-ass bitches?" I yank on his shit some more. "Every time I turn around, these bitches are crawling out of the woodwork like roaches. You like roaches, muthafucka? Is that it?"

"Shelle, baby, please."

"Aww. I'm your baby now? What happened to all those bitches you were calling me a little while ago?"

"I-I'm sorry."

"You sorry?" I cock my head. "Damn right you're sorry."

He yelps and bangs his head back on the floor. As long as I got his ass like this, I'm definitely running shit. When I let go, I know we gonna go at it. That shit is okay. As long as I make my muthafuckin' point, it's all good. "You're in the trouble you are in now because you can't stop digging in these other bitches' asses. That cop told you she was carrying your baby and now this ho. What makes you think that bastard is yours?" While he writhes beneath me, I yank again. "Because she told you so? Didn't McGriff and Tyga stretch her shit out at the Pink Monkey, too? What makes you think that baby ain't their seed—or any other nigga who'll toss her ass fifty cents?"

Through his pain, our eyes connect again.

"Uh-huh. You didn't think I knew about that shit, did you? I ain't forgot how shit works down at the Pink Monkey. I used to toss your salad in the VIP, remember?" I take a chance and release his dick and then mush him in the head. "Get your head off her fat ass and start thinking for once."

"Chronic," Python's ringtone, starts blaring, and I look around until I see his phone vibrating in a pool of broken glass that used to be the coffee table. I reach for it and sure enough, *Lemonhead* is stretched across the screen. My eyes narrow as I toss the phone over and let it hit him in the center of his chest. "Handle that bitch . . . or I will. That's a muthafuckin' promise."

21

Essence

Niggas are talking.

In fact, for the last two days there's been more bullshit shoveled around than anyone knows what to do with. Topics jump around the Python and Fat Ace showdown, the captain of police's dead daughter and his missing grandson, the botched hit on Fat Ace's lil brother, and the fact that LeShelle sanctioned her own sister's rape into the Queen Gs, which landed the girl in a mental hospital. It all sounds like a soap opera on crack. The tension on the streets has never been thicker. Muthafuckas keep reminding each other to constantly watch they back. Retaliation is coming; we all know that much—it's the when and how that has us all staring at our own shadows sideways.

Even in FabDivas Hair Salon, bitches have their faces all twisted while they toss in their two cents.

"Shit. I think the fat bastard is dead," my sister Cleo says as she lowers her head back over the sink.

Ms. Anna, the shop's owner, starts attacking her scalp like there's three years' worth of dirt caked on her head.

"Shit. That would be a blessing *and* a curse," Pit Bull says, shaking her head. She is finally getting that tacky-ass silky-straight weave out of her head. "A blessing because the ruthless bastard has been put down and a curse because those Vice Lords will be coming at us with everything they got, especially that evil bitch Lucifer. Word on the street is she's worse than that one-eyed monster in charge now."

"Shit. She can't be any worse than LeShelle's medieval ass." Kookie laughs. "Hell, if y'all knew half the shit this bitch has sanctioned, y'all be running up in somebody's church tryna get saved."

Ms. Anna surprises everyone and pipes in, "Both those bitches have bigger balls than most niggas I know."

Pit Bull grabs her crotch. "Speak for yourself. My shit sags real low."

Everyone chuckles uncomfortably because it's been rumored that the butch bitch is either a transvestite or one of those weird muthafuckas who have both man and woman private parts. But who the hell knows. As much as she talks about her balls, she flips the script and talks about her pussy just as much. I don't know what the hell she got going on down there, and I sure as fuck don't give a damn.

"Somebody gotta know something," Kookie says.

I flip through the pages of one of these old-ass magazines, but then I get this weird sense that everyone is looking at me. I freeze and wait, but the hairs on my arms and on the back of my neck start rising, and I decide to sneak a quick peek over the magazine. Sure enough, Kookie and Pit Bull are looking dead in my face.

Oh, shit. They know. A lump suddenly materializes in my throat, and all the swallowing in the world isn't getting that muthafucka to budge.

"Well?" Kookie asks.

"Well what?" My gaze shifts around.

Slowly, everyone else picks up on the growing tension.

"Surely you heard something. Isn't Ta'Shara like your main girl?"

I frown. "Whoa. We don't get down like that."

"Ain't nobody saying that y'all bump uglies or nothing—just that you two hang and shit," Pit Bull says.

The music is turned down, and heads start coming out from under the dryers. Ms. Anna needs to change the name of this salon to Nosy R Us.

I keep trying to swallow this huge lump, but I think this muthafucka is getting bigger not smaller. Same goes for my eyes.

"Damn, small fry. Whatchu looking all scared for? We asked your ass a simple question. Are you friends with LeShelle's sister or not?"

"Y-yeah." I shrug. "We're cool."

Kookie and Pit Bull share a look.

"Just cool?" Kookie asks. "You ain't been down to the hospital to check up on her or nothing? Her or that lil Vice nigga she was fucking around with? I mean, let all the lil Queen Gs tell it, you two are thick as thieves."

"Yeah. That means that you knew those two were gettin' it in waaay before anyone else did. Right?"

I force myself to be calm—well, to *look* calm anyway. "Nah. I was surprised like everybody else."

They call me a liar, though their lips don't move. It's all in their eyes and in the swivel of their necks. Instead of engaging in a staring contest that I know I'll lose, I lower my head and pretend that this is the most fascinating shit I've ever read, but these bitches' gazes remain locked on me. When I hear them get up from their chairs and walk over to me, I damn near have a heart attack.

Aw. Fuck. Am I about to get my ass beat?

Pit Bull sits to my right, while Kookie plops down on my left.

I look up and catch Cleo's worried gaze, and for a brief moment I wonder if she even has my back. The way other muthafuckas' families have been acting, I think I have good reason to be concerned.

"Whatchu reading?" Pit Bull asks, snatching the magazine out of my hands. She doesn't even bother to take a look at it before tossing it over her shoulder.

"What do you want?" I ask with attitude, which could get my head knocked off my shoulders.

"Why don't you come outside with us and let us holler at you for a minute?" Kookie says.

"For what?"

Her face twists. "I guess you'll find out once we get outside, won't you?" She stands.

Pit Bull stands up, too.

I look up at them, torn between telling them to kiss my ass and bawling like a fucking baby. *I knew this shit was going to fall back on me.*

Cleo climbs out of her chair, her hair wet and dripping down her back as she walks over to where I'm sitting. "Is there a problem?"

"Nah. There ain't no problem. We just want to holler at Essence outside for a minute."

Cleo plants her feet and folds her arms across her chest. "For what?"

The two Queen Gs flanking my sides turn their hard gazes toward her, but to Cleo's credit, she doesn't flinch and she doesn't budge.

"It's a personal matter," Pit Bull says, rocking her head.

"You ain't got personal business with my lil sister. Anything that you want to talk to her about, you can say in front of me," she tells them.

"No offense, Cleo. I respect what you're doing and all, but this shit doesn't have anything to do with you."

Cleo's face gets harder by the second. It's her angry face, a look I know well since she'd been known to go off on me more than a fair amount of time growing up. "Like I said, anything you have to say to my baby sister, you can say in front of me. We're all Queen Gs. Family is family, but blood is blood. You feel me?"

I don't think I've ever been more proud to have Cleo as my sister than I am right now. This is how family is supposed to act. At least I know now that if there is some shit about to pop off, she'll most definitely have my back.

"Fine," Kookie spits. "Let's take this shit outside."

"A'ight," Cleo agrees, and then shifts her hard stare at me. "C'mon, let's go, E."

I climb up onto my wobbly legs, and these muthafuckas feel like they're filled with Jell-O as we walk across the shop toward the front door, with every eye following us. One person who looks relieved is Ms. Anna. I know she's tired of bitches fighting up in her shop.

Cleo and I follow Kookie and Pit Bull to the side of the building. When we stop, I make sure that I'm standing close to my sister, with my hand stretched into my jacket and locked around my gat. After my run-in with Lucifer, I vowed that it was going to be the last time a bitch caught me slipping.

Pit Bull snickers like she knows what's going on in my pocket. "Slow your roll, lil momma. Ain't no reason for bullets to start flying . . . yet."

Cleo glances over at me. If she's surprised that my ass is strapped, it doesn't show on her face.

"Like I said, we just came out here to talk," Kookie says.

"About what?" Cleo asks, folding her arms again.

"About Ta'Shara and Profit," Kookie tells her. "LeShelle wants to know if your lil sister has any new information. That's all. She's concerned."

"Humph!" I roll my eyes.

"What?" Pit Bull says, shrugging. "Ain't she got a right to be concerned about her own blood?"

Not if she's the one who landed her in the hospital in the first place. Everyone's eyes land on me again. "I ain't got nothing to tell you."

"You haven't been to see her or nothing?" Kookie presses.

I shake my head but then wonder if I'm about to walk into a trap. *What if someone had seen me there—seen me talking to Lucifer?* My stomach twists into knots. If that shit got out, would Cleo switch sides then? "I didn't talk to her," I hedge, trying to buy time.

"But you *can* go see her, right?" Pit Bull says. "Her foster parents will let you talk to her, right?"

Kookie adds, "Yeah . . . and maybe you can get in to see what's going on with her boyfriend. Find out if that nigga gonna pull through. Is he gonna wake up, or is he gonna be a vegetable or some shit."

"Wait," Cleo jumps in. "That place gotta be crawling with Vice."

LeShelle's girls bounce their shoulders. "So? Her rolling up to the hospital is legit. She can see Ta'Shara—maybe she can tell what's going on. If not, she can always claim that she's friends with that nigga as well. It's worth a shot."

"So you want her to play snitch?" Cleo says, trying to make sure she understands what they're saying.

I'm already a snitch. My gaze drops for a second, but I pick it back up in case they read guilt on my face.

"So? She ain't snitching to no cop or nothing. She's tryna get some information for LeShelle—our *queen.* Damn. Muthafuckas do covert operational shit all the time in the GD family. Why are you sweating this lil bullshit?" Pit Bull barks.

"She a kid," Cleo says. "And you're talking about sending her ass into the lion's den with those Vice niggas. With all that's gone down these past few days, these niggas gotta be jumpy as fuck. They'll probably shoot first and ask questions later."

"Bitch, please. We got niggas much younger than her neck-deep in dirt and wallowing in that muthafucka without complaint. Fam is fam. We're all sisters in these streets. If the head queen asks for a favor, what's with all this negotiating shit?"

Cleo rolls her eyes. "Please. This ain't street shit. This is family shit. Ain't nothing more dangerous than niggas getting in the middle of family shit. Ask Tyga. He tried to help Datwon and Python bridge some family bullshit, and the muthafucka took a bullet to the skull while Datwon got fed to Python's pet snake Damien. If LeShelle wants to see about her sister, why can't she roll over there and see her for herself?"

Kookie and Pit Bull look at each other while amused grins stretch across their faces.

"Uh-huh." Cleo bobs her head. "So it's true, then. She's the damn reason her sister's up in that bitch in the first place, ain't she?"

Kookie shakes her head, but her grin refuses to falter. "Look, Cleo, we ain't out here to discuss all that. We're asking nicely for Essence to go in and try to get the four-one-one. Surely you'll want to deal with us than LeShelle. Muthafuckas tend not to like how her ass asks for a favor. You feel me?"

"Yeah. She's a rude bitch," Pit Bull cosigns.

For the first time, Cleo hesitates. And it's not like I can blame her. Shit. LeShelle's name might make Freddy Krueger pause.

"Okay," I say.

Everyone's head swivels back in my direction.

"I'll go to the hospital and see what I can find out." Of course, I have no intention of telling LeShelle anything remotely resembling the truth. But with LeShelle and Lucifer allowing me to float in and out of the hospital, I can stop sneaking and keep tabs on my girl. LeShelle has another thing coming if she thinks I'm going to help her do a damn thing. If anything, I'm going to do all I can to help bring that bitch down.

22

Lucifer

Mason looks fucked up.

By the time Dr. Cleveland had finished digging and stitching our leader up, there were eight bloody bullets sitting in the bottom of a silver pan. I had hoped by the time I returned today to check on Mason that he would've had a hell of a lot more color than he's showing right now—or at least be awake. My disappointment must show on my face because Bishop takes one look at me and then walks over to try and relieve my fears.

"He's going to be all right," Bishop says, curling up a half smile. "This nigga is like the Teflon Don. You ought to know that shit better than anybody."

I reluctantly pull my gaze away from Mason's still form to look my brother dead in the eye. "Maybe."

"I'm betting every dime I got on it." He throws a light punch against my shoulder. "Now cheer the fuck up before you get all mushy on my ass."

I roll my eyes. "You wish."

"Yeah. Probably. The day your ass sheds a tear, it will likely usher in those 'end of days' that Momma preaches about."

"Ha-ha."

"So what did you find out down at the hospital? Profit awake yet?"

"Nah." I shake my head. "Doctors down there don't sound too fucking optimistic about his ass waking up anytime soon either. Hell, they're still trying to figure out how the muthafucka is still breathing."

Bishop laughs. "It's because him and our nigga here got the same blood rushing through their veins."

"Did the doctor say how long it would be before Mason wakes up?"

"Could be any minute."

"And it could be never," I inject pessimistically. Fuck. I can't help it. It's who the fuck I am. Life has never given me much to be optimistic about.

Bishop twists his face up at me. "I done told you my man is going to pull through this shit, so squash it."

I toss up my hands and back the hell up. I can tell by looking at him that he doesn't even want to consider the possibility of us losing our boy. That shit is odd, given the nature of our business. Niggas fall every day—and there's always another nigga to take their place. It's the cycle of the street life. There's no pension or retirement plans out here. We live by a bullet and the odds are we're gonna die beneath a hail of them. The only questions are, when, and are we going to have the guts to hold our heads up?

Right now, I'm uncomfortable about how still and colorless Fat Ace is. It's too easy to picture his ass lying in a casket like so many other street soldiers before him—my daddy included . . .

Three days after my father was gunned down in our front yard, Momma, Juvon, and I stood huddled together under a lone umbrella while one sobbing person after another stood in front of the closed black and chrome casket and told how my father, the Dough Man, as they called him, either helped pay a light bill or put food on the table when a soldier was either dead or serving a bid. My father was a great man, they said over and over again. The newspapers had it wrong.

"A gangsta? A drug lord? A criminal?" Smokestack thundered in a rising baritone. "These are labels society tries to shackle us with every day. The white man ain't happy unless he keeps us chained down. And trust and believe that it's by any means possible."

A chorus of agreement ensued, despite the few nervous glances we made toward a line of police officers who also stood watch. Momma said they were there for additional police protection, but we trusted the police about as much as we trusted the Gangster Disciples.

"Darcell Washington was the very definition of a man. He was a husband, a father, a brother, and a son. Above all that, he was a good lieutenant with the Peoples Nation. He was a friend when you needed a friend. A brother when you needed a brother."

There was a small ring of "amens" while I sucked in a deep breath and wished that this whole thing would be over soon, but Smokestack was just getting started.

"All I'm saying is that the world outside has forfeited their rights to judge us—how we put food on our table, how we keep the lights on, or how we look out for one another."

"Aww, this nigga gonna start preachin' now," someone said from behind us.

"Well all right now!" Aunt Nicky held up her right hand to Jesus and started waving it around.

Smokestack smiled. "It's important now more than ever that we who have been blessed into the Nation have to stick together and hold the line—even against brothers and sisters who look like us but want to snatch the food out of our mouths—out of your baby's mouth. Those slobs shed Darcell's blood in front of his house—in front of his children." He gestured toward me and Juvon.

I dropped my head lower and prayed that he'd hurry the hell up. I don't want to stand out here all damn day in the rain. I twisted around to see who all came, and it looked like the whole Vice Lord family turned out. I guess I should feel good about that, but so far I still feel nothing. I don't know what it is, but I feel like a huge part of me died when the lights went out of my daddy's eyes.

For the past twenty-four hours, everyone kept telling me that it's okay for me to grieve—like I was waiting around for permission or something. Frankly, all the waterworks was rocking my nerves. All those fucking tears weren't going to suddenly help my daddy rise up from the dead. If they could, then maybe I would've managed to squeeze a few. Meanwhile, it seemed that everyone was putting on a show and I was waiting for the credits to roll.

I started to turn back around when my gaze cut across to Mason Lewis. At first I'm stunned to see him in something other than saggy jeans, a fresh white T, and the latest pair of Jordans he done jacked from the mall. Barely nine years old, the chubby hustler was already a menace to society.

After staring at him for so long, he bucked his head back in his signature, " 'sup, B?" greeting.

For the first time in three days, I actually felt something. There was a tightening in my chest, a flutter in my stomach—but that was the usual when Mason came around. Now, it bothered me that I could still feel that but could feel nothing for the man I've loved my whole life, lying in a cushioned casket.

Maybe there really was something wrong with me. I turned back and faced Smokestack.

"We all know who sanctioned this shit—and you got my word that the Black Gangster Disciples are going to feel the heat of my nine, especially that head nigga, King Isaac." His top lip curled in disgust. "Time to knock that nigga off his make-believe throne. Y'all feel me?"

There was a roar of agreement, and a few niggas even lifted their guns in the air as if somehow asking the good Lord to bless their piece.

But it was Aunt Nicky who hollered out the loudest and waved her hand in the air. "Amen, amen."

She wasn't fooling nobody. While everybody else in the family was dressed in black, she was standing next to Momma in a red dress so tight that no one understood how she could even breathe in the damn

thing. That was Aunt Nicky—always on the hunt for a new man.
Sometimes when she couldn't find an available one, she borrowed
someone else's. Judging by the way she was looking at Smokestack, he
was her next target.

Fuck his white girl, Barbara.

It was funny that for all of Smokestack's militant talk, he always
had this white bitch sniffing shit out of the crack of his ass. At least
that's how my momma put it every time she saw the blue-eyed junkie.

The kids around the block called his wifey Dribbles—mainly be-
cause most of the time she was huddled in the back of someone's house
or gas station with a dirty needle in her arm, her head held back while
a long string of spittle dribbled out the corner of her mouth. When she
was like that, it was just a matter of time before a bunch of niggas came
around and started putting they hands all up her skirt. Once I even
saw her put her mouth on this man's dirty dick outside in broad day-
light, but then she got mad when he took off running instead of letting
her hold five dollars. She raised so much hell out there, screaming and
cursing his ass out that I gave her five dollars out of my allowance to
shut her the hell up.

Mason always got mad and embarrassed when that shit got back
to him, seeing how she was his momma and all. Now, nobody really
believed her lily-white ass was his real momma.

Around here, we may point and whisper, but for the most part we
minded our own damn business. Besides, not too many niggas even
knew or met they damn daddies, so if any nigga wanted to lay claim,
we figured you should consider your ass lucky. Now I didn't have a
damn daddy.

I pulled my gaze away from Dribbles and swung it toward
Cousin Skeet. It was hard for me to stop my lip from curling in dis-
gust. Now more than ever, he had his gaze locked on my momma's ass
throughout this ceremony. He must've felt the weight of my stare or
something because he at long last shifted his gaze in my direction.
When he smiled, I cut my eyes away and returned my attention back
to Smokestack.

Twenty minutes later, he stuck a cork in it and we walked back up to the closed casket to say our final good-byes. As we marched forward, I saw tears gathering in Juvon's eyes again, and I almost wanted to sock him in the face and tell him to cut that shit out. Real niggas don't cry.

Period.

Marching up behind Juvon and Momma, I copied Smokestack's smooth, confident walk, kissed two fingers, and then pressed them in between the blanket of flowers Momma dug out of her garden. I stopped for a moment and waited to feel something. I wanted to. Believe that. But it never happened.

When we all returned home, the sun had come out and there was a huge feast and even more people waiting for us. That was when I knew that this was probably going to be one of the longest days of my life. What made people think that at a time like this, we really wanted their asses all up in our faces? It really didn't make no kind of sense when you got down to it. After like the hundredth person asked me how I was doing, I took my ass outside and plopped down on the back porch. At least today I knew Momma wasn't going to give me no shit about messing up my dress. In fact, this was going to be the last day I was going to wear one of these damn things. What was the point? I only wore them because my daddy liked them.

I had exactly two seconds of peace before the yard was suddenly filled with other kids. No doubt their selfish-ass parents sent them out here so they could get their loud asses out of their hair.

"Bang! Bang! Bang! Nigga, you's dead," Andre shouted, using his hand as a gun.

"Nah-uh. Nigga, you missed me!" Dominic pulled the gold scarf off from around his face. "You know your ass can't shoot anyway."

"I shoot better than you—you stank-breath, cross-eyed, Urkel wannabe," Andre shot back.

Like a flash of lightning, another kid ran up behind Dominic and planted his two-finger gun in the back of his head and shouted, "POW!" And for an extra sneaky move, he swept his foot underneath Andre and then smirked when the stunned kid hit the ground hard and busted his top lip. "Now your ass is dead, muthafucka!"

My interest perked up at the unusual bass pouring out of a kid so small.

With so much blood gushing from Andre's lip, we all waited to see if his ass was going to start hollering like a baby or brush that shit off.

"Fuck!" Andre complained, and then spat out a mouthful of blood and dirt. "Fuck. Nigga, we weren't even playing with you."

The kid kicked him square in his ass and made him eat another mouthful of dirt. "Don't you know what the fuck dead means, stupid muthafucka?"

That shit cracked me the fuck up, mainly because Andre wasn't used to someone putting their foot up his ass. Once I started laughing, I couldn't stop. It felt good to laugh, especially since I'd been surrounded by crying people for three days straight.

Andre's bully looked up and glared over at me. "What the fuck are you laughing at, bitch?"

I blinked at his rudeness, but then decided to match him attitude for attitude. "First of all, your momma is a bitch and I'm laughing at y'all fake-ass niggas playing paper gangstas. Shit. You'd probably piss in your pants if y'all was in any real do-or-die situation."

This miscellaneous nigga scrunched up his face. "Who in the hell are you calling fake?"

Folding my arms, I swirled my neck around like my momma did whenever she got mad. "I'm looking at you, ain't I?" His punk-ass gaze raked me up and down, and I could see that he's debating on whether he'd fight a girl, so I tried to push his buttons some more. "Now what?" I asked. "Whatcha going to do about it?"

"Maybe I'll punch you in your damn mouth," he said, strolling toward me and staring me down.

If he thought I was going to flinch or get up and run into the house all scared and shit, he had the wrong bitch for that shit. "Try it, nigga. There's plenty of time to squeeze in another funeral today." To prove how bad I was, I thrust my chin up and dared his ass to swing. At this point, I'm thinking that it might feel good to hit something— or someone—right now. And this muthafucka was as good as the next.

"Nigga, you better walk away," Mason said, stepping out of the house and shaking his head. "Trust me. You don't want none of my girl Willow. The girl is a devil in a dress." He chuckled.

Had he just called me his girl? That crazy fluttering started again in my stomach as I cut my gaze over to Mason. Gone was his black suit. He was now back in his signature jeans and white T—but more importantly, he looked like that mean muthafucka who even grown niggas didn't want to fuck with.

The fact that he was giving me high praise wasn't escaping these niggas, because that was something he rarely did. If I wasn't so busy staring this nigga down, I might've smiled.

"What's going on out here?" Juvon asked, stepping into the yard with a paper plate loaded down with food. As usual, his ass was a day late and a dollar short.

Mason laughed as he folded his arms. "This brand-new nigga on the block thinks he can take on your sister."

"For real?" Juvon laughed as he shoveled in a mouthful of macaroni and cheese while he peeped out my opponent. "What rock you climbed out from, brah?"

This nigga started to look real nervous.

Mason's and Juvon's faces twisted like a pair of disrespected twins.

"Nigga, you can't talk?" Mason asked, reaching into his pocket and pulling out a gun.

I'm shocked, but I don't act like it. Where in the fuck did he get a gun from?

"Well?" I asked, barking at this deaf-mute muthafucka all of a sudden. In his face, I could see he's calculating on how to back up out of this corner he got his ass into without losing face. I didn't see how that shit was even possible.

Mason cocked his gun and every nigga in the yard froze.

A part of the boy's face twitched. "You really want to fight me, huh?"

I shrugged. "It's something to do."

He stood there for a long time. My ass got tired of waiting, and I *cocked my fist back, mindful to keep my thumb outside of my balled right hand—just like my daddy taught me—and I sent that mutha-fucka flying.*

Crack!

This nigga dropped like a stone.

"Oh, shit," Mason laughed, covering his mouth with his fist.

Juvon nearly dropped his plate, cracking up.

Every nigga in the yard followed suit, laughing and pointing as blood gushed out of this muthafucka's busted mouth. In two seconds, this weak bitch's eyes swelled with tears.

"Niiiigggggaa," Mason howled. "I told your ass!"

My face remained blank, though I was smiling inside. I didn't need no crystal ball to know that I was going to get mad respect over this shit here. The surge of power was heady and potentially addictive.

This nigga scrambled his ass up off the ground and took off run-ning when a tear leaped over his lashes and streaked down his dirty face. What was with these niggas crying all the goddamn time?

Once our little excitement died down, I returned to my spot on the porch. That's the best way I figured for these loud-ass niggas to leave me alone. But Mason ignored my leave-me-the-fuck-alone sign I had flashing on my forehead and sat down next to me.

"Shit, Willow. I was blowing smoke up the nigga's ass. I didn't know those damn bony-ass arms could really knock muthafuckas out like that." He flashed me a smile, and his chubby cheeks dimpled at the corners.

"Fuck. I knew," Juvon said, dropping down next to us and then tearing into a chicken leg like he was afraid the muthafucka was going to try and run off his plate before he could get a taste. "She wails on me all the fucking time. My shit be black and blue, for real."

"Is that right?" Mason smiled at me like he ain't never seen my ass before, and though I'm trying to hold on to my mad face, I get that funny ticklish feeling in the pit of my stomach again.

"What? You can't talk to me?" Mason said, leaning against me and flashing those damn dimples.

"Nigga, get off me." I leaned back, not because I thought he had

cooties but because I was afraid that he was going to hear my heart pounding against my chest. I sniffed the air. "What the fuck you got on?"

Mason's smile spread wider. "You like that shit? I borrowed some of my father's cologne. Since he's a big pimp with the ladies, I figured I'd try to steal a little of his shine."

My nose started twitching faster. "You know you ain't supposed to bathe in that shit."

"Ha-ha. You know you love it." He leaned in again and winked.

I rolled my eyes, unimpressed.

Juvon twisted up his face. "Nigga, stop trying to hit on my lil sister. That shit ain't cool."

Mason eased back. "A'ight, play all you want. But on the real tip, you know I had your back with that lil nigga, right?"

"Uh-huh. Where in the hell did you get a gun at?"

"Yeah. Is that a real gun?" Juvon asked.

Mason puffed out his chest. "What the fuck? You think that I'm going to be working these streets with some fake shit in my pocket? I ain't looking to get white-chalked out here." Then, remembering the day's events, he looked guiltily over at me. "No offense."

"None taken," I said, shrugging my shoulders. My gaze locked on his weapon a second before I reached out to touch it. "Where did you get it?"

"Are you kidding me? My dad has crates of them all over the house. He ain't going to miss this one."

In my head, I replayed those niggas gunning my dad down. I wondered how different things would have played out if he had had his gat at the ready. "You think you can get me one?"

"Say what?" Juvon choked.

Mason twisted up his face. "You? What, you tryna be a gangster now?"

Juvon laughed and shook his head. "Knocked one muthafucka out and now she wants to rule the muthafuckin' world."

"Fuck y'all." I rolled my head away. "I can get my own shit."

"Oh, shit. You serious?" Mason asked after staring a hole into the side of my head.

I turned until our eyes connected. "Don't I look serious?"

He took his time, gazing into my eyes. "Yeah. I think you are serious." His lips hitched up. "A'ight. I'ma hook you up."

"What?" Juvon muffled around his chicken.

I flashed my first smile since the day my daddy died. "Really?"

"Yeah," he said, bobbing his head. "And I'm even going to teach you how to use it. You'll be a stone-cold killer by the time I'm finished with you. Niggas everywhere is going to be calling you Lucifer. Watch and see."

My lips hitch up into a smile as I pull my mind from those good-old days. I reach for Mason's hands, and then my heart drops at how cold and stiff his fingers are to the touch. I shake my head in an effort to ward off the pessimist inside me and embrace the hope my brother is clinging to. In the end, I think it's better for me to concentrate on doing what I do best— killing those muthafuckin' Gangster Disciples.

Knowledge

23

Momma Peaches

Things ain't been right between me and Python for a while now. Mostly because we ain't exactly seeing eye to eye on this whole situation with Christopher. Yes, I know he's his child. Hell. One only has to look at both of them standing side by side to know that shit. But the boy is also the grandson of Memphis's own supercop, who thinks he has a cape flying out the crack of his ass. Shotgun Row is still crawling with police, and the FBI have been through this muthafucka a few times themselves.

Python is gonna have to show his face to these muthafuckas sooner or later, 'cause their asses just ain't going away. Cedric has been riding my ass on what I know about this shit. He can't, or won't, believe that I ain't got nothing to do with this right here. I understand. He doesn't want to get caught up in the mix in fuckin' bullshit. And since I got a record a few miles long, he ain't too quick to believe any of the bullshit that I'm spitting his way.

That's all right. He'll be all right.

Though from time to time, he thinks the best way to get shit out of me is to put me on dick restriction. He doesn't understand why that shit is funny until I told him that dicks come a dime a dozen—if that much. The itch that his ass won't scratch, another nigga will—gladly. He knows that shit is true. He doesn't have to go no farther than my front porch to see Rufus patrolling outside, waiting to see if I'm going to break his ass off a piece before the end of days gets here.

Cedric came around, and now he's hitting my G-spot like it's a part-time job. He knows his ass is addicted to this good shit, showing up in the middle of the night with his eyes as big as his balls and pinching on my titties before he's even in the door good.

This morning, I catch a clip of a teary-eyed Victoria Johnson on a cable news show. She looks like a wrecked, hot mess, clinging to her husband for support in front of the camera. My heart gets all twisted up in my chest because I know exactly what she's going through. When Mason disappeared, my ass looked just like her—crying, begging, and snotting up. The frustrating part is *knowing* that niggas are sitting on information because they are all bound to the code of the streets. Nobody sees or hears shit.

Times like these, you reach out to that one snitch to do the right thing. Normally, you can't stand their asses—but when it's you or your family that has been wronged, there's nothing you won't do for that snitch to crawl out of the gutter and spill his guts. Nothing.

"Sad, ain't it?"

I jerk around to see Cedric, leaning against the wall and staring at the television.

"Yeah. This muthafucka is crawling with sad-ass stories. What's new?"

He stares at me for a long second before his lips start curling up. "You know that you don't have to be so hard all the time. At least not with me."

My brows nearly leap off my forehead at this shit. "Is this the part when you tell me not to worry because you'll never hurt me?"

His lips stretch wider. "If I do, is that where you laugh in my face?"

He's so fucking cute. I can't help but stroll my ass over to him and let him slide his arms around my waist. "See? You've danced to this song before, too."

"Never with someone I wouldn't mind dancing with for the rest of my life."

I sigh. Here we go again. "If you're thinking about making an honest woman out me, you're too late. I'm married, remember?"

"Divorces happen all the time. Haven't you been reading the papers?"

I cock my head. "Well, look at your cocky ass." I try to push my way out of his arms, but he ain't having it.

"Personally, I would've never left something as precious as you chillin' on ice." Cedric shakes his head. "No way. Not ever."

My panties are drenched. Yeah. This is definitely Manny's lil man, talking this fat, smooth shit, trying to get my heart tangled up in some emotional bullshit that I ain't got no business feeling.

"What? Your man got a good dime left?" He pulls me even closer. "There's plenty of time for me to snatch you away from that hustler." He leans forward and kisses the tip of my nose. "Plenty of time." While his hands slide all over my ass and I'm hypnotized by his green eyes, I'm thinking . . . maybe?

Stretching my arms behind his neck, I push his head down and take my time sucking and running my tongue along the bottom of his lip.

Bang! Bang! Bang!

I close my eyes and groan. "What the fuck?"

Cedric laughs. "Must've been feeling good to you." He releases me and then slaps me on the ass as I turn toward the door.

"I ain't never denied that shit."

"All right, then. Get rid of whoever that is and meet me in the bedroom. I'll grab the strawberries and whipped cream."

"All sukie-sukie now. Make sure that you get the bottle of honey, too." I laugh all the way to the door. However, the minute I open it and see Kookie standing on the other side, my eyes damn near roll out of the back of my head. "Why every time I'm about to get my back straight, someone is banging on my door like the muthafuckin' police?"

"Oh. Sorry, Momma Peaches. I didn't mean to disturb you."

"How the hell are you going to knock on someone's door and then claim that you didn't mean to disturb them?" My question clearly throws her off, and for a few seconds, she just stands there and blinks at me. "Child, what do you want?"

She holds up a cup. "I, uh, wanted to borrow some flour."

I look around the porch. "Is there a sign out here that says this is the muthafuckin' grocery store?"

"Uh—"

"Girl. Get on in here." Rolling my eyes, I turn around and shuffle to the kitchen. "This shit is getting ri-damn-diculous. I know if I start shootin' first and asking questions later, then y'all muthafuckas are going to be lookin' at me like I'm wrong."

Kookie twists up her face. "Sorry, Momma P. I didn't mean to set you off or nothin'. I just needed this lil favor."

"Uh-huh." I shake my head. "And since when has your ass started cooking? I know I ain't never smelled no cooking going on over there."

"I can cook," she lies defensively.

I ball my hands onto my hips and stare her down. Why these young bitches try to play me stupid I don't know.

"I just don't *like* cooking," Kookie says. "But I can do it. It ain't like it's that damn hard."

"Uh-huh. You need to borrow my fire extinguisher, too?"

Kookie laughs even though I give her a look that says *I ain't joking*. Fuck. This bitch is liable to burn down the kitchen. I roll my eyes so hard it's a goddamn miracle they don't get stuck at the back of my head. "Whatever. The shit ain't my business. You want some flour, fine." The faster I get her in and out, the better. The minute I take the top off the flour canister, she starts hitting me for what she really came over for.

"Uh"—she clears her throat—"it sure has felt strange on Shotgun Row these past six weeks without Python or LeShelle holding shit down."

I cut my gaze over my shoulder. I know right off the jump that this heifa is working an angle. She got that ambitious look about her.

"Now, I ain't complaining. McGriff and I are down for the cause. We're more than happy to step in and do our part, you know?"

"Uh-huh."

"I mean, McGriff *is* Python's right-hand man—second in command and all."

And there it is. This lil girl is trying to set up a power grab. She's figuring, and probably correctly, that if Python goes down, McGriff steps up onto the throne as the HNIC, and it would make her the head queen.

"I'm sure that Python and LeShelle appreciate you steppin' up." I take her cup and then scoop flour into it. "It's always hard to know who you can trust out here."

"Oh, yeah." She bobs her head. "We don't mind it. Heaven forbid something goes down, but at least there will be a smooth transition—you know what I mean?"

I settle one hand on my hip. "Yeah. I reckon if you keep to simple sentences, I can follow along with what you're saying."

When she reads the suspicion on my face, her hands shoot up. "Hey! I don't mean it like you're thinking. LeShelle's my girl, and she knows that she can depend on me."

"That's nice."

"And you, too," she adds, and starts looking around. "If there's anything you need, don't hesitate to call. I got you."

"As long as I don't need any flour, right?" I thrust her damn cup back at her.

Her smile falters. "I guess I walked right into that one."

"Guess so." I take her by her bony shoulders and turn her around. "Now, if you're finished politicking, child, I got some business to handle."

"Uh, well, I—"

I can't help but shake my head as I push her toward the door. "Save it, honey. You bumping your gums so hard and tripping over your own weak-ass game, I'm two seconds from feeling sorry for you."

At the door, Kookie sputters, "I . . . I think you misunderstood me."

"Nah, baby girl. I got you. So stop trying to outslick a can of oil. I got shit to do." With one last shove, I send her flying out onto the porch and I slam the door. I ain't got time for these children's bullshit. I dust my shoulders off and then refocus my attention on getting my freak on. "Ceddie," I singsong as I head toward the bedroom. "I sure hope your ass got a sweet tooth because I'm about to give you all the peaches you can eat."

Strutting into my bedroom, I pull up real quick when I see Cedric on the edge of my bed, naked but hunched over a photo album. Shit. I would've been less shocked if I walked in here and this nigga shot me. "What the hell are you doing?"

Cedric looks up. "Who is Mason?"

24

Lucifer

July . . .

Rolling my ass up to the federal pen is never a good time, but it's necessary. There's a lot of good soldiers here. All of them putting in their bid with their heads held high while playing a harder game on the inside. They have my respect on that shit.

The moment I stroll into the visiting room, heads turn and then bob back at me, like, *What's up?* They all know that I've been holding shit down, but only the few and trusted got the 411 on where and what is going on with Fat Ace. That's the way I like it and the way that it's going to stay.

The visiting room is loud with women and children. Some are crying; most are wearing their game faces. I cut through the crowd dressed head to toe in Grim Reaper black, my eyes cautious and my lips flat-lined. When I drop into a seat, I take another look around. I strongly believe in being aware of one's surroundings. Everybody in the game knows that it takes only one time to either be too slow or too late and you get white-chalked in the game.

The door opens and another stream of prisoners shuffles

into the visiting room. The man I'm waiting on pulls up the rear.

Still pretty-boy handsome with a mean swagger and a bigger muscular build than he had back in the day, Smokestack enters the place like he owns the muthafucka. I smile before I can stop myself. What can I say? He's still got it, and maybe if I was still wearing Sunday school dresses, I might've stood up and started twirling around for compliments.

"Well, well, well," he says, smiling and shaking his head. "I was wondering what a nigga had to do to get you up in here. What? You ain't got no love for your cousin Smokestack no more?"

"All day, every day. You know that shit. It's that we're in the middle of a fuckin' war and—"

"Hold up before you get started. Squash the excuses," Smokestack says, shaking his head. "You know I've never been one who liked a nigga with a whole lot of excuses. I deserve to know what the hell is going on with my fam. You feel me? I'm hearing so many conflicting bullshit stories up in here I'm about to qualify for a transfer to the mental institution. Nah-whatImean? Now come with it. What's really poppin' out there? Give it to me straight, no chaser."

Straightening my back, I take another look around to make sure that niggas are minding their own business. "It's all good. It ain't great. Both of your boys got banged up pretty bad."

"But they're alive, though, right?" he barks, his eyes bright with hope.

"Yeah. They're alive."

Smokestack closes his eyes and whispers, "Thank God." His shoulders deflate with relief and he pulls in a deep breath. "In my heart, I know one day one of you is going to march in here and give me a different answer . . . but thank God that today ain't that day."

I bob my head because I know exactly where he's coming from. Street niggas ain't got a lot of options out here in this muthafucka. Hustling and grinding is all there is and all there ever will be. I stop myself before I hop onto a mental soapbox. At times I sound like him in his old militant days.

"Thanks, Willow. I appreciate you coming out here to tell me," he says, and then reaches across the table and squeezes my hand.

I don't even correct him on that Willow shit. Some people are afforded the privilege. There's so many emotions racing across his face I feel like I should look away.

"This street shit . . ." He shakes his head. "When word got 'round these steel bars about what happened to Raymond . . . and then no one knew where or what happened to Mason . . . gut check. NahwhatImean?"

I don't respond.

"Of course you don't. You don't have children of your own yet."

Right before my eyes, he ages. That or I'm now noticing all the lines in his face.

"They're not mine. Mason and Profit, I mean." Smokestack flashes me a sad smile. "Doesn't matter. I've always loved and raised them up like they were my own. And as far as they're concerned, I am their real daddy."

Now, that surprising confession confirms one of my lifelong suspicions, but I'm still curious about a few more things.

Smokestack shakes his head. "Mason's momma was a real piece of work. She was an old customer of mine and stayed out in the LeMoyne Gardens area back in the day. Typical crackhead who knew how to suck a nut out of a nigga's sack like a Hoover vacuum."

His eyes cut up toward me. Before he can apologize for the crass remark, I wave that shit off. "Whatever happened to her?"

"Who gives a fuck? She should be happy I didn't bash her muthafuckin' head in for that foul shit she did."

"What did she do?"

"Well, I was one of the few trusted Vice Lord niggas who

was even allowed to roll up in the LMG gang territory. Those young niggas around that way was really feeling theyselves back then. They were body-bagging as many soldiers as the Vice Lords and Gangster Disciples, if you asked me. Since I was slinging the best candy on the street at that time, I was their main connect.

"Barbara was hanging out over there at that time, too. She had a candy problem herself. I always knew that, but I was still feeling her, and from time to time, she would really try to kick the habit. She would get clean for a couple of months, relapse for a while, but then try again to get that monkey off her back.

"Anyway, Barbara hung real tough with her best friend, Alice. Frankly, whenever they got together, I called them Salt and Peppa. They were as thick as thieves because they truly were a couple of thieves. If you turned your back, they would jack you for everything you got. And Alice could pull out a blade like her middle name was Zorro or some shit. I don't know who taught her that shit, but she was good. Any time Salt and Peppa got their hands on some paper, they were blowing up my cell, looking to score.

"After a while, Skeet showed an interest in her, but then that shit was no fuckin' surprise. He's my brother, but he never came across a pussy he didn't want to hit. So he hit it. They had a thing for a hot minute, just as he and Barbara had a thing much later. Anyway, as soon as Alice came up pregnant, he lost interest. Must not have been a big deal to Alice because when he got ghost, she never once even asked about his ass. She kept on keeping on, and that meant partying her ass off. Baby be damned.

"I don't have too many fuckin' rules, but I don't sell product to muthafuckin' pregnant women. I don't roll like that. But what I won't do, another nigga will. You feel me? Alice would get her shit through Barbara or some other lil nigga I was supplying in the neighborhood. I asked Skeet to intervene and shit, but he was adamant that the bitch was fuckin' *way* too many niggas for candy and shit for the baby to be his.

"And he had a fucking point. Plus, there was something off about that girl. I told Barb that I didn't like her hanging around her too much, but Barb was convinced her girl was cool.

"The first time I saw Mason, it was a couple of months after she took him home. I ain't never heard a baby cry so much and so loud in all my fuckin' life. I wondered if she was feeding the kid, you know? For a minute, whenever I popped up around there, it looked like Alice was trying to do right. After a while, all that screaming started getting to her. She started hittin' those rocks in place of her three squares, and her apartment went from halfway decent to smelling like straight-up shit. Barb claimed that she kept going over there to help out. At least her mind was clear enough on occasion to make sure the baby kept eating and diapers got changed. She said her girl had a sister who would come around every so often, but I never saw the bitch.

"Shit. As far as I could tell, her family wasn't worth a fuckin' thing either if they kept leaving the child in her care. A retarded nigga could take one look at Alice and tell that her ass was cracked the fuck out, and she didn't have any business tryna take care of a baby.

"Anyway, one day I rolled over there to the complex to do a little business and then drop in on Barb to see if she was up for some one-on-one time. She was walking out of her apartment door to go party some more with Alice. I put on my best moves, but she claimed she needed to give her girl her package. Thinking that it was just going to take a few minutes, I walk on over there with her.

"We knock, but Alice doesn't answer. Cool by me. I was ready to roll instantly, but Barb tried the door and the shit was open. Now, when I tell you that muthafuckin' place was stank the hell up, that's what the fuck I mean. Barb pulls me inside and I'm twisting my face and tryna block the funk, but that shit was impossible. Hell, I didn't even want to cross the threshold for fear the scent was gonna get into my clothes.

Then I heard the baby crying.

Barb barged right on in and went over to her girl, who was stretched on the sofa on top of a mountain of clothes. Either Barb was used to the smell or her sense of smell was shot to hell.

"Alice, girl. I'm back. I got your shit," Barb kept saying.

I'm still wondering about that baby. It sounded all muffled and shit. Barbara slapped her on the face, tryna wake her up and then shoved the vials of rock into her hand. Alice moaned and slobbered all over herself.

"Meanwhile, I'm concerned about the baby and start moving around the apartment, but the crying seemed to be coming from the kitchen. That shit definitely didn't seem right, so I followed the sound . . . all the way to the kitchen oven. . . .

"You're shitting me," I say, staring across the table at Smokestack. "She fuckin' put Mason in the goddamn oven?"

He bobbed his head at me. "It was just luck I think that she didn't turn the muthafucka on. I mean, you know how fuckin' spaced out your ass got to be to put a kid in the fuckin' oven? Who in the hell does that?"

I can't wrap my brain around that shit either. Knowing Mason, the kid and now the man, all the what-ifs are fucking with me. What would my life have been like without him in it? "So what did you do?"

"Grabbed him, snatched Barbara, and stormed up out of there. It was either that or put a fuckin' cap in that bitch." He shook his head. "Look. The shit hit too close to home. I lost my own damn momma to an overdose. Heroin was her candy. Me and Skeet stayed in that house with a dead body for two weeks before someone came over to check on us. We didn't know what to do, so I sat in that muthafucka, crying and begging her to wake up. After that we were thrown into the system, which was worse than the muthafuckin' streets. In the streets, I found my real family with the Vice Lords. Those niggas are still my heart, even though one is holding it down on high. NahwhatImean?"

I nod, but then something else hits me and I feel sick. "Soooo, Skeet is Mason's real father . . . ?" This is blowing my mind.

"I'm Mason's father! I raised him."

"But—"

"There's no fuckin' *but*. He's *my* kid. Him *and* Raymond. Biological or not. Their daddy stepped out. I stepped up. End of story!"

"I hear you," I say, raising my hands in surrender even though my mind is racing a million miles a second.

Smokestack sits there and huffs for a full minute. "All right. So they're alive," he repeats slowly, calming down. "Looks like I got me two real soldiers, huh?"

"Yeah. A couple of beasts," I cosign, and then get uncomfortable about what I really came here to ask him.

It doesn't take him long to pick up on it. "What's on your mind?"

Sucking in a breath, I come straight out with it. "This fuckin' war, Smokes. It's putting a major crimp on our cheddar, and I need some type of connect that's going to double up our firepower. That Python muthafucka ain't no bitch. He's proving to be as hard to murk as your seeds. You feel me?"

Smokestack bobs his head as he listens. "I've been hearing about that shit. Heard your ass been banging pretty hard, too. Taking those grimy GD niggas out like the muthafuckin' devil." His chest swells. "I'm proud of you, girl. I know your father would be proud, too."

I can't believe this shit, but I'm actually blushing.

"And it's clear that our soldiers respect you as well. I ain't heard one bad word about you stepping in while my boy's down. They following your orders like your balls sag as low as my shit."

I reach down and cup my crotch. "What makes you think that they don't?"

Laughing, Smokestack rocks his head back so far it's amazing that the shit don't roll off his shoulders. "You're all right, Willow. I'm gonna give you that."

"Cool. But I rather you point me in the direction of a new connect." The look he gives me is one of suspicion. "Oh. It's like that? You think I'm miked or some shit?"

"No disrespect but I'm a suspicious muthafucka by nature." He hunches up his shoulders. "But I'm gonna roll with my gut on this one and believe that you're on the up-and-up. Have you checked in with Cousin Skeet?"

Huffing out a long breath, I roll my eyes and slouch back against my chair. "Bad idea. What else you got?"

Smokestack frowns as his light brown eyes scan me up and down again.

"I know he's your boy and all but—"

"But nothing." Smokestack glances around to make sure that no one is listening to our conversation. "Skeet is the best connect we got. Bricks, guns, protection—whatever the fuck you need, he's got you."

I twist up my face, really not wanting to hear this shit.

"Look. I get that there's no love lost between you two, especially when he started hooking up with your momma not too long after your daddy died, but you gotta put your personal feelings aside. We're discussing business, and business always trumps all other bullshit. You got access and a good connect. Use the tools in front of you. If not, another nigga is gonna spot the opportunity and step up to plate."

"And I'll blast that muthafucka off of it, too."

His lips curl upward. "Baby girl, you gonna learn sooner or later that you can't solve everything with a bullet. Nobody likes it, but politics are very necessary in these streets, and as such, sometimes you're going to have to strike deals with your enemies to take down a bigger enemy. You feel me?"

I do, but I don't want to. "Yeah."

Smokestack cocks his head. "Good. Now swallow that lump in your throat and go out there and handle your business with your cousin Skeet. He'll help you out."

"He's not my real cousin."

"I'm not your real cousin either, but we're still fam, right?"

"Right," I say without hesitation.

"Of course, that is until Mason opens his eyes and does the right thing and marries you."

"What?" I choke.

"Aw, man. Save the Oscar performance for someone who bought a ticket. I ain't stupid and I damn sure ain't blind. You've had a thing for my boy since y'all were kids."

"And on that note, I think it's time for me to go." I jump to my feet while he starts laughing his head off.

"Guess I hit a sensitive spot. That must mean the devil has a heart after all."

"Catch you later, Smokes."

"C'mon, sit back down. We still have a couple more minutes."

I hesitate, but I return to my chair, praying like hell that he'll change the subject.

"Don't be sore at your old cuz. I wanted to let you know that I've been rooting for you. But I guess Bishop permanently squashed that shit a long time ago."

"Squash what?"

Smokestack falls back against his chair. "Ain't nobody ever told you?"

"Told me what?"

"Nah-nah." He shakes his head. "I'm not going to be no accidental snitch. You don't know; I don't know."

What the fuck is that supposed to mean? "Great. I guess I'm going to have to dig up the answer myself."

"Guess so." He smiles.

Man, spit it out. "Doesn't matter. Up until six weeks ago, Mason has always had a thing for someone else."

"Well, there will always be other bitches to chase the chill out of a nigga's sheets, but it doesn't mean that his heart can't belong to one woman. That's the way we're wired."

"Yeah, well, up until a coupla months ago, that woman was Melanie."

"Melanie who?"

I cock my head.

"Not—"

"The one and only."

Smokestack's face falls while his color drains. I can tell that his mind is racing now, too.

"He didn't kill—"

"Nah. Wrong place, wrong time." However, my assurance doesn't put color back into his face. In fact, he looks worse. "Smokes, are you all right?"

When he doesn't answer, I look around and call one of the watching prison guards over.

"How long?" he asks.

I'm confused. "How long what?"

"Him and Melanie? They never . . . ?"

I laugh. "Like rabbits, and let her tell it, she was about to have his baby." He continues to grow pale. At least now I know he's thinking and feeling what I was a few minutes ago. "Smokes? Are you sure that you're all right? Do you need a doctor?"

He starts shaking his head. "Did her father . . . ?"

"Clueless—as usual. If the Vice Lords didn't point his ass in the right direction, he wouldn't be able to find his own asshole."

Smokes gives me a hard look, so I shrug my shoulders. "I'm just saying. That supercop bullshit is just that."

"Fuck. I had no idea."

"Looks like I'm the accidental snitch today." I stare at him as I wait for color to return. I want to call the guard again in case Smokes is really having a heart attack. "Look, I'm sorry. I know that you and her dad—"

"Forget it. Just . . . keep me posted on what's going on. You watch your back out there. The streets have taken down harder niggas than you."

I laugh. "Don't be ridiculous. They don't come no harder."

25

Yolanda

Where in the fuck is Python?

I draw in a deep breath and then try to settle my ass down, but this nigga has been MIA for six fucking weeks now. I keep hearing his name in the street, but this nigga ain't returned none of my calls, texts, or muthafuckin' smoke signals for that damn matter. I can't prove it, but I know he's getting my messages. So what's up?

My belly is getting big as fuck, and I've been tapping into my own stash to pay fucking bills that I ain't supposed to be paying. The info I'm getting is off the muthafuckin' streets, and most of that sounds and smells like bullshit. However, some of the other shit got me wondering.

The way Captain Johnson and his badge posse stay on the news looking for his daughter's killer got me believing that Python got the wrong nigga gunning for his ass this time. As usual, ain't nobody seen or heard shit in this case, but Python's real name, Terrell Carver, has been plastered on the news every hour on the hour as a person of interest in the case.

What the fuck does that mean? Do they think he killed the bitch or not? And if he did and they are able to slap him with the charge, surely that shit is like a needle in the arm for killing a cop. Where the fuck will that leave me?

Some niggas say Python is dead and that McGriff is the new head nigga in charge. Judging by the way Kookie has been rolling through, styling and profiling, I figure that she has a lot to do with spreading that fucking rumor. If Python goes down, then so does LeShelle's evil ass as head Queen G.

Again, where the fuck does that leave me?

I close my eyes and curse under my breath for a full fucking minute. I know exactly where that shit leaves me. Up a goddamn creek without a fuckin' paddle. In my mind, I can picture Baby Thug shaking her head and telling me, *Only a retarded muthafucka would keep doing the same thing over and over again and expect different results.*

I can't go back to square fuckin' one. I'd rather cut my own damn throat than have to move back into my momma's house on Shotgun Row and mule shit into the federal pen for some chump change. Maybe I could go back to the Pink Monkey after I have this kid, bounce my ass on the poles again and hope that another high-ranking soldier will get hypnotized by how hard I make my booty clap. Fuck. At this point, I need to be thinking of a plan B, C, D, and even a muthafucking Z.

The way the game keeps flipping so fast out here, it's hard to keep up. One minute I think I can get my kids back, and now I don't even know if that's fucking possible. And if I can't get them now, then when?

A knot grows in the center of my chest while my baby karate chops my bladder for like the millionth time today. I have to do something—something different—to get my ass back in the game.

But what?

What fucking card do I have to play? Python's baby? Shit. Python has an army of ugly lil niggas roaming the streets, and he hasn't wifed none of those bitches that spit them out either. Only LeShelle has been hanging with his ass longer. While she's not wife, she certainly is wifey.

So what's gonna make my baby special? Hell, I was relying on how hard I made the nigga bust his nuts as a guaranteed ride to the top. The shit worked for LeShelle when her ass worked at the Pink Monkey once upon a time. And I refuse to believe that that bitch's pussy snaps harder than mine.

What is it going to take to knock that bitch off her throne?

I have an appointment to go see my kids today, but by the time I climb behind the wheel of my SUV, I've made up my mind to swing by Goodson Construction. Being around the way as long as I have, I know Momma Peaches's man, Isaac, used to use the place back in the day as a business front. Python and McGriff mentioned the place in the VIP of the Pink Monkey a couple of times, and I'm just going to take a chance and see if his ass is over at this muthafucka.

The minute I roll up, I spot Python's ink-black '77 Monte Carlo and nearly piss on myself with excitement. "Got you, muthafucka." The smile on my face is so wide, I probably look like the fuckin' Joker when I hop out of my vehicle and start switching my ass toward one of the metal doors.

As soon as I get halfway to the door, a team of big-muscled muthafuckas start pouring out the door and blocking my path.

McGriff heads the pack as he glances around. "What the hell are you doing here, Lemonhead?"

"Excuse you?" I roll my neck, but I don't stop my stride. "Don't come at me foul, nigga. I ain't in the mood. Where's Python at?"

"He ain't here," he says, grabbing my right arm and damn near snatching me out of my expensive pumps.

"Whoa, nigga. Ease up." I try to snatch my arm back. "What the fuck you doing?"

"Taking you back to your car," he says, jerking my arm so hard that it's a wonder the muthafucka doesn't pop out of its socket.

"Hey! Let go of me!" I twist and jerk my arm, but this

nigga ain't having none of that shit and easily drags my ass back to my ride. "He's in there, ain't he?" That has to be it. Why else are all these muthafuckas out here? "PYTHON! I WANT TO TALK TO YOU!" This time I twist and jerk my whole body tryna get away from this muthafucka. If my man is up in this bitch, he's going to talk to my ass—believe that shit. "PYTHON!"

"Dammit, bitch!" McGriff turns around and slaps his free hand across my mouth.

That's a mistake because I don't think twice to bite down on that thick muthafucka like a starved lion.

"FUCK!" McGriff snatches his shit back, and I have the taste of his blood dripping from my mouth as I holler, "PYTHON!"

McGriff grabs me by the shoulders and shakes the fuck out of me. "Shut the fuck up, you stupid bitch!" He raises his hands, but I keep my jaw up and prepare for the blow that's coming. Shit. It won't be the first time a nigga done knock the shit out of me, and it probably won't be the last. And when he's through, I still ain't going no muthafuckin' where.

When McGriff's fist gets ready to swing like a golf club, Python's voice thunders across the way.

"Yo, nigga! Slow your ass up!"

McGriff releases me, but the look in his eyes says he wishes he could have a couple more seconds alone with me.

"Get the fuck off me." I wrench free and then cut my eyes back over to the warehouse door and see Python's thick, muscled body. The way my body quivers with excitement, it feels as if I've caught the Holy Ghost.

"Python." I smile and race back across the parking lot. I don't give a fuck if I look funny, running in these high heels with this big-ass belly in front of me. I'm happy as fuck to see his ass. "Thank God, baby. I've been so worried." I throw my arms around this nigga and start raining kisses all over his twisted-up face. I pretend not to notice that he doesn't hug me back or even attempt to return a single kiss. I want him to see how happy I am to see him.

"What the fuck are you doing out here? Who sent you?" he asks, looking at me as if I'm some miscellaneous ho on patrol.

I blink and pull back to stare in his face. "What? Nobody sent me. I took a chance and came here to look for you."

His stony expression doesn't change, and I wonder what I did for this nigga to flip on me like this.

"Why haven't you returned any of my pages? I've been worried sick." I touch my belly for emphasis, and his gaze drops and stares at it for a long damn time. I know what this nigga wants to say before he even fixes his mouth. "Now you don't want nothing to do with your child, is that it?"

"Sheeit. That baby can be anybody's."

His hard and emotionless tone hits me like a two-by-four. "What the fuck are you talking about? I ain't been with nobody else but you. You know that shit."

Python shakes his head, humiliating me further in front of his boys. "I don't know shit. And I done had enough of you slick-ass bitches who can't get your damn lies straight. You need to take your ass home and squash whatever bullshit you thought we had going. It ain't happening." He shoves me away from him, and once again, I nearly trip out of my heels.

"What? You can't be serious." I race back over to him, but his big-ass arms come back up and stop me like a brick wall.

"I ain't playing with you, Yo-Yo. Go home, before you get caught up in some bullshit that you can't handle." His gaze sweeps across the parking lot like he's expecting niggas to jump out at any moment.

My heart races because this shit can't be happening to me again. I ain't tryna hear nothing his ass is saying on this shit. "I'm not going anywhere until you fuckin' talk to me. What the fuck you mean, squash this shit?"

He goes on looking around at everything but me.

Without thinking, I reach out and grab the sides of his head and force his big-ass head to turn in my fucking direction. "Look at me, goddamn it! What in the hell are you talking about? How the fuck you gonna put a baby on me and then dip? What kind of fuckin' man is you?"

"Bitch, step!" Python throws one hand up and breaks my hold on his face. I definitely got his attention now, because his face is twisted and his eyes look like straight fire. "I'm *the* muthafuckin' man out here. That's all the fuck you need to know. What we had was cool for a minute. You have some good ass, I'll give you that, but I'm breaking from all the miscellaneous pussy out here and sticking with my true boss-bitch, LeShelle. And until you push that seed out and confirm it's mine, we ain't got shit to talk about. You feel me?"

"WHAT?"

"Bitch, why you keep whating me? I done said what I got to say, now get the fuck on." He glances back at his boys. "Get her ass on away from here. I got some business to handle."

The next thing I know, McGriff grabs me again. "NO! Python, wait!"

He turns his back on me and strolls into the building while McGriff continues to manhandle me.

"Don't do this, Python. Please!" Tears burn the backs of my eyes while all my hopes and dreams blow up in my face. "Let go of me, goddamn it!" I turn and swing. My fist catches McGriff underneath his right eye.

"Oooh." His boys wince and hiss as if they felt the blow themselves.

"Goddamn it!" McGriff loses his grip on me.

I scramble back to the door, trying to catch it before it closes. "PYTHON!" But I don't get there before the door slams in my face. The second I reach for the handle, McGriff is back on his job and once again snatches me up. This time, his arm wraps around beneath my breasts. His hold is tight.

"Let. Me. Go!" I throw both of my hands back over my head and try to beat him in the face that way, but he dodges my blows and continues to drag me.

"Let go! Let go!"

Niggas are cracking the fuck up, but neither one of us is paying them any attention.

"Stop it, you stupid bitch." He drags me closer to my ride.

In a desperate act, I stomp my high heels down and do my best to crush and smash his toes into the ground.

"FUCK!" McGriff roars, but this time his grip remains firm. "You're making a goddamn fool of yourself, Yo-Yo. Stop it!"

"Fuck you!" Next I drop my weight, and at last we both tumble to the ground. From there we wrestle. Fuck the scrapes and bruises. I don't have time to worry about that shit. All I can focus on is getting back to Python so I can convince him that he's making a huge mistake. I can be every ounce of a ride-or-die chick like LeShelle—no, *better* than LeShelle. If he'd just give me a chance.

"Damn, nigga," one soldier pipes up, laughing. "You can't handle one damn bitch?"

"Shut the fuck up," McGriff barks, struggling to get to his feet. When he stands, he has both of my hands in a firm grip so that he can literally drag me and my big-ass belly across the asphalt.

"I bet Kookie wears the damn pants at your muthafuckin' house," another loud-ass muthafucka shouts.

Kicking and screaming, I'm calling McGriff's ass all kinds of muthafuckas my damn self. By the time he grabs me up and shoves me into my car, we're both damn near out of breath.

"Yo-Yo, calm the fuck down," he shouts when I try to get back out of the car. "You're making this shit worse, not better."

He grabs my attention with that.

"You think LeShelle would be out here, making an ass of

herself like this? Have you ever seen that bitch wildin' out of control over a nigga?"

"I ain't LeShelle."

"Exactly!" He gets all up in my face. "A nigga like Python needs a bitch who can hold it down in the time of war. You're out here hollering like some crackhead who has been cut off. Where the fuck is your head at, girl? Pull your shit together and look around. His boys are laughing at you. You think that's gonna convince him to make you wifey?"

The backs of my eyes are burning with tears because I know this nigga ain't speaking nothing but the truth.

"Look. I like you. I ain't forgot how you hooked me and my fallen nigga, Tyga, up in the VIP that one time. But you need to fall back and rethink your position. You ain't gonna get what you want this muthafuckin' way." He steps back and slams my car door. "Go home . . . and think on that shit."

After a few quiet seconds, I stare at him, but then I reach over and start my car. When I pull out of the parking lot and glance down at the blood and bruises purpling my body, my tears flow freely down my face.

LeShelle. LeShelle. LeShelle.

I'm so sick and tired of that fucking bitch that I don't know what to fucking do.

Only a retarded muthafucka would keep doing the same thing over and over again and expect different results. Baby's voice echoes over and over in my head. Then it's clear to me that this fucking city ain't big enough for the two of us.

26

Momma Peaches

"He was here. I swear he was here," Alice repeated, glancing around. "I just . . . got a little taste, you know. Just to calm my nerves," she stressed to the officer who was snapping handcuffs around her wrists. "You don't understand. He wouldn't stop crying and I just needed something to make me relax."

"Who did you buy the drugs from, ma'am?" another cop asked with his notepad out. "Do you remember what he looked like?"

Alice looked at the man like he'd just grown two heads. "Sheeeiit." She shook her head. She was faced with a hard dilemma: snitching or finding her baby. The choice was clear in my eyes, but Alice wasn't seeing it the same way.

"Tell them who was here," I pleaded. "We need to find Mason before . . ."

Alice licked her lips and scratched at her matted hair. "I . . . I just . . . don't . . . remember."

"What the fuck do you mean you don't remember?" I lost it and charged toward my sister. "You stupid bitch! How could you?" Four officers jumped into the mix and struggled to pull me away from her. "You fuckin' sold that baby for a muthafuckin' hit?"

Alice started crying. "I . . . I don't . . . know. I can't . . . I wouldn't." She looked around for a sympathetic face but didn't find one—not even from her son. "Terrell, I didn't. You gotta believe me. I would never . . ."

Terrell, holding his baby brother's stuffed teddy bear in one hand and his pet grass snake in the other, turned his back on his mother.

"Terrell, baby. Please. Listen to your momma."

"All right. Get her out of here." The one cop closed his notepad and shook his head.

"No, wait!" Alice screamed. "Terrell, baby!"

I gathered myself and shook the cops off of me. "Terrell, sweetheart. Come here."

Terrell waltzed over to me with his head down.

"You, bitch," Alice seethed as the police tried to drag her out of the apartment. "You're tryna turn my children against me. You got my baby. I know you do!" She glanced at the police tugging her. "She has my baby. Arrest her! I know she has my baby!"

I shook my head, not believing that she was seriously going to try and pin this bullshit on me. "Not going to work this time, Alice. This shit is all on you! You fucked this up—not me!" I was so angry that I was trembling.

Terrell dropped his teddy bear and grass snake and then wrapped his small arms around my waist. "It's all right, Momma Peaches. The police is gonna find him. You'll see."

Shit. The fuckin' cops in that goddamn city couldn't find their assholes while shitting on a toilet.

"I'M GOING TO GET YOU FOR THIS SHIT, MAYBELLINE! YOU FUCKIN' WATCH!"

More tears burned the backs of my eyes. That bitch was never gonna grow the fuck up. No matter how many times I put myself out to try and help her, she couldn't see past Leroy. It was like his ass was still raping her from the grave or some shit.

Terrell and I had to stay up in that shitty-ass apartment for hours, answering the cop's retarded-ass questions. How many ways can you say that you don't know shit? When we were able to leave the apartment, there were so many news cameras shoved in our faces I could hardly think when reporters started shouting questions.

"Ma'am, can you tell us what happened?" one reporter managed to shout above the others.

"Yes . . . somebody stole my nephew," I said, stopping and looking around. "If anybody knows anything, please, please tell us. We really want him returned to us."

Terrell's arms tightened around my waist.

"Is there any truth to the rumor that the child's mother sold the baby for crack?"

"Who told you that shit?" I belatedly try to cover Terrell's ears. "Do these gossiping muthafuckas got any witnesses?" I don't know what in the hell had me tryna defend my sister, because there was a real possibility that her triflin' ass did just that. "C'mon, baby. Let's get in the car," I told Terrell, directing him to my car.

"B-but . . . what about Mason?" Terrell asked, with his eyes wetting up.

"That's what the police is here for, honey. They are going to find your lil brother." I opened the car door, but reporters still came at us, shouting questions.

"But you said for us to never trust the police," he said, right into this one blond reporter's microphone.

I smiled awkwardly into the camera as I almost shoved him into the car. "Kids say the damnedest things."

"But, Ms. Carver, do you have anything to say to the people who may have taken your nephew?"

Slamming the door behind Terrell, I stop and stare straight into the cameras. "Yes. Please. Bring my nephew back. He's an innocent little boy in all this. I swear we won't press any charges. We just want him back. Thank you." I swiped away a few tears rolling down my face and then thanked the reporter.

"How long has your sister had a drug problem?" another reporter shouted.

I shove past her and rush to the other side of the car so I can climb in.

Terrell watched everyone crowd around us as I started up the car. "Does this mean that we're going to be on television?" he asked.

"I guess so, baby." I swallowed hard as I watched the police car carrying Alice pull away. In the backseat, my sister was still screaming and hollering like a maniac. At the last minute, she turned around and spotted me in my car. That shit made her go into hyperdrive. "This is some fucked-up shit."

Terrell glanced over at me. "Are they going to put her in jail?"

I sighed. "Don't know, baby. Try not to think about that right now." I brushed my hand across the top of his bushy head. "Damn. We need to see about getting you a haircut." I started up the car and then had to creep forward until the reporters got the fuckin' hint and got out of the damn way.

When we returned to Shotgun Row, Terrell shot out of the car like a bullet and raced over to his best friend's house across the street.

I was stunned to see Isaac's Monte Carlo still parked in front of the house. I could've sworn he said he had some business that he needed to handle before I left. I dismissed the shit as my memory fucking with me and headed on into the house. Hell, I didn't even know how I was going to tell him this shit about Alice and Mason. One thing was for sure—he wasn't going to be all that surprised. He had heard all my stories about how much of a fuckup Alice had been over the years. In fact, he didn't miss an opportunity telling me that I needed to cut my ties to her ass and call it a day. I was sure that I was about to hear the same thing.

However, the moment I walked into my house, the hairs on the back of my neck stood at attention. I closed the door and got as quiet as possible. Something told me not to call out for Isaac, and I couldn't say that I felt the need to grab my gat either.

Slowly, I moved through the house, straining my ears for every little sound. When I reached the living room, I heard the first sound and I knew exactly what it was.

Walking faster, I headed straight to my closed bedroom door and threw that muthafucka open. Now, I think it takes one hell of a bold muthafucka to be fuckin' another bitch in my bed, but I couldn't believe my eyes when I saw my best friend, Josie, riding my nigga's dick like she was born on the muthafucka.

"YOU BACKSTABBING, STANK-ASS, PUSSY MUTHA-FUCKA!" I launched toward the bed like a missile, and before Josie could get off my nigga's dick, I got a chunk of her hair in my clenched fist. When I snatched that bitch back, I got a plug torn out of that muthafucka from the fucking root.

"OWWWWW. FUCK!" Josie yelled, falling out of the other side of the bed and then busting her lip on my nightstand table.

I followed her ass right over that muthafucka, landing punches on every part of her body. "You sleeping with my husband, bitch? Is that how the fuck you get down?"

"Peaches," Isaac tried to grab me and pull me back.

The only thing he managed to do was snatch my prosthetic leg off while I whaled on this bitch's ass.

"Peaches, I'm sorry," she yelled, covering her head and scrambling to get off the floor.

"Oh, you ain't sorry yet, bitch. Let me show you how sorry your ass is." I snatched open the nightstand drawer.

Isaac, seeing that I was going for the .38 I kept in the muthafucka, doubled up his efforts to stop me.

POW! POW! POW!

"Aaaaaargh!" Josie screamed, racing toward the bedroom door. "I'm sorry. I'm sorry. I'm sorry."

POW!

The dresser mirror exploded.

POW!

A bullet slammed into the closet door as Josie jetted by it.

POW!

One bullet hit Josie in her ass before she's able to clear the door.

"Aaaaaargh!" she yelled two octaves higher, but she didn't stick around to see if I could hit that other ass cheek.

Isaac is the last to fall over, grabbing me by the waist while—

"You shot her in the ass?" Cedric asks, interrupting my story.

"Damn right I did," I huffed. "That was not the day for that bullshit. With that shit with Alice . . . and Mason." I sniff and then turn to the next page in the photo album to the only picture I have of my nephew. "Here he is. I made a lot of copies—circulated them all over the city. We never found him."

Cedric shakes his head and then leans in for a closer look at five-year-old Terrell holding Mason and cheesing for the camera. "Humph."

"What?"

He shakes his head and then points. "His neck."

I glance to where he's pointing, and another smile drifts across my lips. "Oh, yeah. His birthmark. It's shaped like a horseshoe. Python has one, too, in the same place, but it's hard to see because of his tattoo."

Cedric levels his beautiful gaze on me and then reaches over and brushes my hair back to expose my own horseshoe birthmark.

"You pay attention," I say, smiling.

"Especially when it comes to you." He leans over and brushes a kiss against my lips.

I can't help but smile. Why couldn't Manny have been this attentive back in the day? I stop my roaming thoughts and pull in a deep breath. "Anyway, as far as I know, all the Carvers have that same tattoo. I depended on that small detail to help us find lil Mason, but . . . I was wrong. For a long time, while Alice was in jail, she blamed me for his disappearance, and then once her sentence was reduced to child endangerment, she started blaming everybody else—including some bitch named Drib-bles."

Cedric laughs. "Dribbles?"

"Chile, please." I roll my eyes. "Don't get me started on those crack-high characters she came up with every other week." I think about it some more and then shake my head. "Dribbles. You'd think that she would've come up with something a little more creative than that."

27

Essence

The streets are hot.

There's so many fuckin' bullets flying between Vice Lords and Black Gangster Disciples that the muthafuckin' police stop answering calls and let niggas have it out. At least that's what the fuck it feels like. The few times that the police do come out, it's to interrogate everyone where the hell Python is hiding. Seems they want his ass as bad as the Vice Lords. For the moment that big nigga is ghost. Both him and LeShelle. They pop up every now and again, let niggas know that they are still in charge and running shit, but when you blink they're gone.

Hell, I wish I knew where they are hiding out at—at least then I would get this evil bitch Lucifer off my ass. Because right now she's riding me so hard I'm going to turn dyke any minute now. Since I can't snitch out LeShelle, I gave Lucifer the next best thing: Treasure and Mario. Shit. Those niggas were telling everybody who stood still long enough how they busted the head Queen Gs' sister in on her prom night and watched as LeShelle emptied a whole clip into Fat Ace's baby brother. Fuck. I was happy to do that shit.

Less than an hour after I gave their names to Lucifer, those niggas were found facedown in the back of the Pink Monkey with their own cocks shoved down their throats. That shit let me know that Lucifier's ass is a sadist, and she is certainly not the one to fuck with.

Now when my ass isn't dodging bullets, I'm driving all the way to Memphis Mental Health Institute to visit my girl Ta'Shara. That's where she's been for the past month, sitting in a chair and staring out a window. She hasn't said or done shit since that horrible night. She just sits there.

Like I do every day, I park my car, take several deep breaths, and try to get the energy up to walk into this place. It's depressing. Old people creeping toward you like zombies in a Michael Jackson video. Some talk to themselves, some yell at you, and the others beg and cry for you to take them home. The place gives me the fuckin' creeps.

"Hello, Mrs. Douglas," I greet. She's sliding her purse strap over her shoulder and gathering up her knitting stuff.

She turns and tries to flash me a smile, but it dies before it gets to her eyes. "Hello, Essence."

I swallow and shift my gaze to Ta'Shara, who, of course, is sitting before the window, staring out at everything but seeing nothing. "No change?"

Tracee's large eyes instantly fill with water. "No."

Silence fills the space between us like it does every day. Tracee and Reggie still don't know that Drey and I were the ones who had dumped Ta'Shara on their doorstep, but I sense that she believes that I know more than I'm telling—or maybe that's my guilty conscience trying to trick me into confessing.

"I better get going," Tracee says. "I have a lot of errands to run, but I'll be back in a few hours."

"I'll still be here," I say. She rewards me with another flat smile and then rushes past me and out the door.

"I don't think your stepmom likes me," I tell Ta'Shara.

No response.

Exhaling a long breath, I walk over to Ta'Shara and try to

see whether I notice a change in my friend for myself. I don't. Her eyes are as glassy and vacant as they have been for the past month. "Ta'Shara, please. I know that you're in there some-where. Please, snap out of this shit."

I wait, but there's no response.

"You're wasting your time."

Startled, I jump up and jerk toward the door. There, an old black woman with long silver hair leans against the door frame with a lit cigarette.

"That girl there has checked out," she says. Her voice is low and raspy like she's been sucking on those cancer sticks her entire life. "If I've seen that shit once, I've seen it a million times. She's long gone."

I shake my head. "She'll snap out of it."

The woman stretches her brows up at me. "You want to put some money on that?"

Frowning, I turn up my nose. "You're talking about my friend."

"Oh. I'm sorry. I thought y'all were sisters."

"Fuck. That's how you would talk to me if I was her sister?"

She shrugs. "I thought you should hear the truth. None of these muthafuckas around here is going to tell it to you."

I blink at her and then glance back down at Ta'Shara. "You mean that she can stay this way for . . . forever?"

"It's more likely than not. She's suffering from some kind of shock. What happened to her?" She flicked her cigarette, giving no mind to the ashes that flutter to the floor.

"She, um, was brutally attacked."

"I think the black and blue marks that are still healing on her face told me that," she says sarcastically. "What? Did her man do that to her?"

"What? No." I shake my head and then lower my voice. "Her boyfriend was attacked as well. Took seventeen bullets."

"Fuck." She flicked her cigarette. "Who the hell did *he* piss off?"

Why the hell is she asking me so many damn questions? "What makes you think that they pissed anyone off?"

"Because I'm not stupid, and I know how the streets work." She smirks sarcastically. "Not everybody in the funny farm is crazy, you know."

"You're a patient?"

She rocks her head while she thinks it over. "Let's just say that I'm on an extended vacation. I have a roof over my head, a bed, and three squares a day. All in all, you can't beat it for the money, honey. But I'll be out of here soon."

While she blows out a long stream of smoke, I don't even know what to say to that shit.

"Is the truth too much for you to handle?" she asks, stretching her brows up again.

"That's your truth, not mine. Ta'Shara is a lot tougher than she looks. She'll pull through this."

"You sound like her momma earlier."

"You told Tracee that crazy shit?"

"Figured that she needed to hear the truth. Every time I walk past here, she's crying and beggin' that child to talk to her. I think her father is coming around, though. I ain't seen him in about a week."

I shake my head. "You shouldn't have told them that."

"They're her parents and—"

"They are her *foster* parents," I snap. "What if they throw up they hands and walk away? They can, you know." *Just like they did with LeShelle.*

The old woman is quiet for a long time before she says, "If it's in their hearts to do that, then they're going to do it anyway."

Then Ta'Shara would become a ward of the state. I try to blink back my tears, but one escapes and skips down my face.

"Damn. You really do care about her."

"She's my best friend."

"Then take my advice and find yourself a new one." She gives her cigarette another flick and then strolls off before the ashes hit the floor.

"Now that's one crazy old bitch," I mumble under my breath, but when I turn back to Ta'Shara, I see the same old glassy-eyed stare. *What if she doesn't snap out of this? What then?*

I try to shake the question as I pull up the vacant chair next to Ta'Shara and sit down. "What are you thinking about in there? What's going on inside your head?"

28

LeShelle

I can't believe my life has come to this. Python has pulled me off my throne on Shotgun Row, and he's hidden me in this piece-of-shit warehouse in West Memphis, Arkansas. And to add insult to injury, I'm in this bitch taking care of his and Melanie's wet stain, Christopher.

Maybe I could put up with this shit better if I had at least gotten my fuckin' ring by now. But for two months all I've gotten from Python are sweet words and a wet ass. Sure. We're in the middle of a gang war and shit. Blasting crabby-ass Vice Lords is part of the fucking job. It certainly ain't no reason to be reneging on promises.

"Word is bond, my ass," I mumble under my breath while I roll a fat joint. Shit, I need something to relax me before I snap, crackle, and pop up in this bitch. After I put some fire to the end of this herb and fill up my lungs, my body chills the fuck out, but my mind is still tripping on this bullshit. How can it not? There's so much of it piled all around me.

All this shit is my fault. This is what the fuck I get for believing his lying, snake-wannabe ass. Time and time again, I put my shit on the line, proving how down I am, and this is what the fuck I get? It's time to stick a fork in this shit because I'm done. So done. I ain't going to stay out here in Bum-Fuck Egypt forever. What the fuck is a queen without her throne? And my fucking seat is in the heart of Shotgun Row. I ain't scared of those crabby-ass hooks or Captain Johnson and his tarnished badge. I wish they would bring their asses back down Shotgun Row. I got something for them—especially that young nigga Profit. Whatever deal his ass made with the devil is only fucking temporary. Believe that.

This inconvenient war is getting to Python, too. His ass ain't sleeping right—well, at least when he's in my bed. Now that I think about it, he ain't been doing much of shit in that muthafucka. So if I'm not fucking a big pussy monster like his ass, then that means Yolanda's retarded ass is still in the mix. Fuck. Who am I kidding? It could be any number of bold bitches in the set, smiling in my face while tossing pussy at my man like candy.

That's how these bitches roll.

Not so long ago, I was one of them, waiting for his ex-wifey, Shariffa, to fuck up and lose her spot. I didn't have long to wait either—six months tops. Python caught her ass creeping, too. He murked her nigga with so many bullets that he *and* his car looked like Swiss cheese on the side of the road.

Shariffa ended up in the hospital, fucked up, but at least her ass is still breathing. Most Queen Gs, my ass included, believe that she should consider herself lucky. Bones heal and oxygen is more valuable than gold any damn day of the week. Last I heard, Shariffa slithered her ass on over to the Crips. She's at the bottom of the pile, making pennies on the dollar, muling shit in and out of the pen. Course, the Crips ain't the pickiest of muthafuckas. *Muthafuckas don't come to the Crips. The Crips come to you,* they like to brag. Sheeeiiit. Don't believe the hype. They recruit more crackheads than soldiers, and that's keeping it real.

Before the escalation in this current gang war, I thought of

Shariffa as some silly bitch who got caught slipping. I mean, who the fuck would risk losing all the fucking power and respect that came with being Python's main bitch for some dusty nigga who ain't about shit?

But now? My ass is starting to see shit from a whole new perspective. The longer I'm with Python, the lonelier I get. If he ain't out hustlin' up some paper, he's out blastin', and if he ain't doing either one of those two things, he's out choking and fucking a new bitch. *Muthafucka.*

Another thing me and Shariffa have in common is also starting to fuck with me: no fuckin' babies. No babies make it easier for his ass to bounce. I'm convinced of that shit.

But with Melanie? Frankly, I can't tell if he's more upset that he didn't earth Fat Ace when he had a chance or if he's missing that double-crossing pig he's been fucking since high school. Oh, this nigga thinks I don't know, but I see his ass walking around, staring at Christopher's ugly future mug shot while about to trip over his damn bottom lip. That muthafucka was stuck on that pig.

Real stuck.

That shit has me fucked the hell up.

The last time I caught his ass in a daze, I took him to the bedroom and gave the nigga my best Super Bowl head game. That nigga couldn't stay hard for more than three minutes. THREE FUCKING MINUTES. That shit ain't never happened. EVER.

My main question now is, Where is this nigga getting his dick wet? Which bitch needs to be put down so I can get what's coming to me—my *fucking* ring.

Jacki-O's "Sleeping with the Enemy" blasts from my cell phone, jarring me from my mental argument. When I look at the caller ID, I feel another nerve snap, but I answer it, sounding cool as fuck. "Yo, bitch. Whassup?"

Kookie ignores my rude ass with a snicker. "Gurl, you do not sound like a happy camper."

"You don't fucking say," I respond flatly. Though I'd love to sit here and spill out all my problems, I know the minute I end the call this mouthy bitch will be on three-way putting my business on blast all up and down Shotgun Row.

Two months ago, Kookie was my main bitch. Now I'm starting to hear shit that's fucking bothering me. While Python and I are hustling outside our zone, he's put more and more responsibility on his right-hand man McGriff. With his ass looking like he's in charge of shit on ground zero, Kookie has been bossing and flossing like her ass is the new head of the Queen Gs.

Oh, sure, she calls every day and tells me how much Shotgun Row hasn't been the same since we've rolled out—*temporarily*. Other bitches talk, dropping dime on my girl. She and McGriff are laughing it up and partying with a bunch of governors, overseers, and enforcers. All that shit is highly suspect. Yet, when I bring this shit to Python's attention, he tells me that McGriff is doing this with his sanction. He wants the set to still feel that everything is everything, especially after Treasure and Mario were found fucked the hell up out behind the Pink Monkey. Niggas are jumpy as hell.

Right now, Python and McGriff ain't having the same ease at picking off Fat Ace's top soldiers. Those muthafuckas got ghost real quick. At most, we've been able to take out a few corner boys—nothing major. Suddenly these muthafuckas are strategic with their shit. Hitting us with laser precision instead of coming at us whole hog. That shit ain't like Fat Ace. Makes me think that Lucifer bitch has taken over their soldiers and playing this shit like a master chess game.

Personally, I know it had to be a couple of bitches who got to Treasure and Mario—probably some onion-ass Flowers sent in to lure their always-horny asses out back with the promise of some pussy. Everybody knows that niggas can't think straight when their dicks are hard. Shit. Nobody but a bitch would cut off a nigga's dick, and that's keeping it one hundred.

Regardless of all of that, I can't believe that Python is allowing his boy to play head nigga in charge. Once muthafuckas get a taste of power, they can't scrub that shit out of their mouths. Next thing you know, niggas be plotting and scheming to move your ass out of the way—if not, their bitches certainly are.

"LeShelle!"

"Huh?"

"Girl, is you even paying attention to me?"

"Fuck. Not if I can help it." I suck in another dose of this good weed while Kookie laughs, thinking my ass is just being funny instead of being for real.

"I was asking if your ass is going to Pit Bull's birthday party? I've contacted the high-ranking Queen Gs, and so far everybody is coming."

"*You* contacted them?"

"Girl, I knew your ass was stressed the fuck out dealing with that pig's bastard, so I figured I'd step in and help a bitch out." She laughs, but that shit sounds phony as fuck.

I blow out a huge smoke cloud while envisioning pistol-whipping this heifer all the way back into her momma's pussy. Instead of raging, I kick this shit to her real calm. "Kookie, I'm going to tell you this one time." I pull in another toke. "You listening?"

"Now, LeShelle, don't get upset."

"Stop bumping yo gums and listen," I tell her, stopping her before she buries me in bullshit. "You need to stay the fuck in your lane. I know what you're doing. Back the fuck up."

Silence hangs over the line while my shit either sinks in or she gets busy thinking up some countermaneuver to convince me that my ass is being paranoid.

"All right, LeShelle, but I think you're tripping. I was trying to help you out," she insists.

My eyes damn near get stuck at the back of my head. *Silly bitch.* "So where the fuck is this party gonna be?" I sit on the edge of my unmade bed.

"Passions, gurl. We gonna toss it up big. I got these new Gucci boots I copped out at Saddle Creek."

"Damn, Kookie. Since I've been gone, you keep your ass up in the mall."

"Shit. I've needed some new clothes for a minute."

"Yeah, but since when did your ass become a label ho?"

Kookie huffs.

"What? You got something to say? Say it." I'm ready to jump in her ass.

"Nah-uh. 'Cause you ain't in the mood to hear it."

"I can handle anything that you toss my way." I cobra-neck while clutching the phone.

"Fine. I want to know if Python is breaking yo ass off any fucking dick, 'cause you're seriously tripping, and I'm getting tired of having to watch every muthafuckin' word I say, because you always at the ready to dig in someone's ass. It's getting ridiculous. It ain't my fault that you're in this mess. You're the one who wanted to play Dirty Harry and dump a clip of ammo into the Vice Lord's chief's *brother.* What the hell did you think was going to happen? Or were you so high off the testosterone that your imaginary balls were giving you that you didn't think the whole thing through?"

"Look. I ain't scared of those Vice Lord slobs," I snap. "In fact, bet your ass I'm going to be at that fucking party with my Glock cocked and my imaginary balls sagging real low."

"What about Python?"

"He can suck on these nuts 'cause I'ma be out. Watch."

29

Lucifer

"**W**e found that muthafucka," Bishop hisses through my phone. I lower the gat I have pressed up against the head of this Gangsta Disciple nigga, Killa Kyle, and step back so I can focus better on what my brother is saying. "Come again."

"You heard me. We got his ass."

My heart nearly leaps out of the center of my chest, and I turn and smile at this barely breathing nigga that Droopy and Monk are holding up. "We got him."

My people smile back at me while Killa Kyle's knees fold. He knows what time it is. He ain't ever gonna leave these woods alive now. "Where you at?" I ask, giving this nigga my back.

"Out here at the old Goodson Construction building. Looks like your snitch came through on our finding and following that yellow pregnant bitch Yolanda around. Her ass finally led us straight to him. Though it looks like there is no love lost between the two. Nigga had his boys drag her kicking and screaming across the muthafuckin' parking lot like she was last year's trash." He laughs.

"TMI I don't need to know all that shit." I check to make sure that I have a few clips in my pocket.

"Yo, ease up. It's been a fuckin' while since I've been able to watch my stories, so this nigga's ghetto bullshit drama is going to have to tide me over."

I roll my eyes. "Yeah, whatever, pussy-punk muthafucka."

"A'ight. You gonna get tired of talking out the side of your neck at me. One of these days your ass is gonna—Yo, what the hell is this?"

There is a brief pause over the line, and my brows dip with concern. "Talk to me. What is it?"

"Damn, Willow. I think this nigga's connect is rolling through. There's like an army of SUVs pulling up to this muthafucka right now. Hold up. Yeah—gotta be. I don't think that there's this many Latinos running across the border right now."

"They moving weight?" Jacking this muthafucka's trafficked shit could make this a really damn good day.

"They're hauling something, baby girl. What you want us to do?"

I make the mental calculation on how fast we can get out our own troops to that spot, but then my excitement starts dwindling. "Shit."

"What?" Bishop barks.

"Sit on that nigga. We don't know what's going down, and ain't no way we can get the muscle and firepower we need to get at him and his crew on such short notice. I got niggas spread out."

Bishop swears into the phone. "C'mon, Willow. We may not get an opportunity like this again. I say we go at this nigga with everything we got *NOW!*"

If this was any other nigga, he would've been cussed the fuck out, but instead I draw in a deep breath and let my silence do the talking for me.

"Fine. Whatever," Bishop says. "We'll sit out here until we hear word back from you, *boss.*"

He really can try my nerves sometimes. "Don't lose him. I'm gonna wrap this shit I got going here and I'll holler back at you."

"Yeah. Whatever." He disconnects the call.

I pull the phone away from my face and stare at it. Sure enough, he hung up on my ass. "I swear to God . . . any other nigga." I pocket the phone and turn back to this piece of trash who I've spent the last half hour carving up. I would say he's been pissing on himself, but after I'd relieved him of his impressively big cock, I'd say that he was bleeding more than he was pissing.

Smiling, I trudge back over to him and my boys.

"We rolling out?" Tombstone asks.

"In a sec." I cock my head at this Killa Kyle. "I got to tell you. I don't think that you're going to make it."

Tombstone and Monk shrug and bob their heads in agreement.

Killa Kyle starts panting real hard, and given the wild look in his eyes, I'm guessing that his ass in about to go into shock. But this nigga glares over at me. "I'm not fuckin' scared of you, bitch." Blood spews from his busted lips.

I level my unimpressed gaze on him. "If I had a nickel for every time one of you dying muthafuckas told me that, I'd be a rich bitch right now."

Killa Kyle gulps down a mouthful of blood while desperately trying to hold on to his courage. "I'm not . . . I'm not . . ."

I cock my head again and then take aim at his left kneecap. "Are you the nigga who dumped that clip into my boy Profit?"

"F-fuck you."

POW! The nigga's kneecap explodes.

"Uuuuuugh!"

"I asked you a question," I say, taking aim at his other knee. "Are you the one who shot up our man? Yes or no?"

Killa Kyla pants, sounding like a freight train, but he clearly is determined to go out of this world a soldier.

I'm interested to see if he makes it. *POW!*

"Fuuuuuuccckk!"

My boys let him drop to the ground.

"No dick, no knees—this interrogation is not going well for you," I state the obvious.

Tears pour out of this muthafucka's eyes, but still there's no whining and begging.

Impressive. I take aim at his left arm.

POW!

Right arm.

POW!

"Aaaaarrrgh!"

While Killa Kyle rolls onto his back and stares up at the sky, I step over him so that my legs are planted on both sides of his hips, and I block any view of heaven that he may be thinking of.

"Now, the way I see things, Kyle, I can either let you lie here and let nature take its course—which could take hours—*or* I can help you out and plant this next bullet right here in the center of your skull. And like that"—I snap my fingers—"it will all be over with." I lock gazes with him. "Would you like that? Would you like for me to take all your pain away?"

More tears leak from the corners of his eyes, but he stares at the barrel of my gun like it's a long-lost lover. "Please," he finally begs.

"Please what?"

He tries to swallow but chokes on his own blood for a few seconds. "Please," he gasps. "Shoot . . . shoot me."

"Ah. So you do want the easy way out." I lift one foot and press it into his bullet-wounded arm. His pain-filled roar is like music to my ears. After he empties the air out of his lungs, he tries to squirm away. "I'm still waiting for an answer. Tell me what I want to know and I'll help you out."

"Okay . . . okay," he pants. "I'll tell you."

I remove my foot but aim my gat at the center of his head. "Were you the trigger man?"

He shakes his head.

"But you were there," I say.

"I was doing what I was told. That's all." He keeps chugging in air while staring at my gun.

"Were you told to rape that little girl, too?"

He swallows hard while guilt covers his face.

I adjust my aim and plant a bullet in each of his shoulders. *POW! POW!*

"Arrrrgh. Fuuuuuck."

"We can be at this all afternoon if you want. Me and my niggas ain't got nothing but time."

Killa Kyle's face twists with pain while he continues to choke and gag on his own blood.

"If you want"—I reach over to my left hip and ease my bloody Browning hunting knife out of its leather sheath.—"I can go back to lopping off some more body parts. Your choice."

"Le-LeShelle," he spits. "LeShelle shot your boy."

My eyes narrow. "LeShelle . . . as in LeShelle Murphy—Ta'Shara's own sister?"

Killa Kyle bobs his head. "She ordered the sex-in." He huffs harder as more blood streams out of the corner of his mouth. "And to make sure that her sister never hooked up with her lil boyfriend again, she . . . she dumped that clip in that nigga."

I cock my head.

"Swear to God," he adds before his gaze starts shifting between the gat and the knife.

Why would this nigga lie?

"P-please," he begs.

"Where are they?"

"I . . . I don't know. I s-swear to God I don't know where they hiding out. P-please."

Making my decision, I swoop down and slice open his neck. "Sorry. I lied." I watch in great satisfaction as his eyes bulge with surprise. The gurgling and choking is an added bonus. This shit goes on for a solid minute before death claims the light in his eyes. That part never ceases to fascinate me.

"You think that nigga was telling the truth?" Droopy asks. "Her own sister?"

I mull the question over in my mind, and I have to admit that as crazy as that shit sounds, it sort of fits with all I've heard about Python's lil wifey. "I guess the only way to find out is to ask her ass."

30

Essence

Profit is never going to wake up.

The more time that passes, the more I'm convinced that he will never be more than what he is right now: a living, breathing vegetable. After all, it's been a little over two months and he hasn't so much as twitched a finger when I hold it. I've been telling myself that I want him to wake up so that I'll at last have some good news to take over to Ta'Shara. Maybe his recovery will somehow spur hers—or vice versa. Shit. I don't know. I'm not a damn doctor.

While I'm sitting here in the room, rubbing cocoa butter into Profit's arms and hands, I'd be lying to myself if I didn't admit that I didn't feel . . . something for the cute brother. Hell, maybe I've always felt something, even as far back as the day that he and Ta'Shara met at the mall. I was the first one to peep him out, but he was staring at my girl so hard, I brought it to her attention.

I was a little jealous at how he threw money around, buying us anything our hands touched. But when he let it be known who his damn brother was, I was honest when I told my girl to squash any and all thoughts about hooking up with his ass. I'd been in the game too long not to believe that nothing but trouble was going to come of it.

While I'm being honest, I completely understand why Ta'Shara didn't listen to reason. Profit ain't like any of other niggas I've ever come across. He has this smooth, old-time gentleman flavor to him, but his ass also knows how to flip the script the next minute and be like the hardest gangsta walking. If his ass was a GD, then I'd say that he was the total package and I might've given my girl a run for her money.

Realizing that the thoughts racing through my head are seriously fucked up, I lower Profit's hand and step back from the bed. Even then I can't pull my gaze away from his still face. Like Ta'Shara, I can't help but wonder what is happening inside his head. Wouldn't it be something if they were somehow together in their weird comatose state? Maybe they're dreaming that their limo hadn't got jacked on prom night and that they made it to the Peabody Hotel.

I can only imagine how well Profit can work a woman's body. Shit, I've already stolen my fair share of looks at what type of equipment he's working with underneath his hospital gown.

My jealousy is complete.

That was what my girl has been riding all that time? No wonder her ass couldn't think straight. I creep back to the side of the bed and lift up the sheet.

"Well, I'll be damned," a voice thunders.

I drop the sheet as my gaze jerks up to Qiana. Pulling up the rear are a couple of her roughneck Flowers. My hand inches back into my jacket and then wraps around my gat.

"I heard that some fucking Queen G bitch was coming up here every day, but I thought that was some street bullshit." Qiana cocks her head as she struts into the room. My eyes are drawn to the ugly, crude gashes that Ta'Shara's razor blade made on both sides of her face a few months back. "I mean, you got to be a real stupid muthafucka to roll your ass up here."

I take another step backward. "Look. I ain't looking for no trouble."

"That's too muthafuckin' bad now, ain't it?"

She makes it to the foot of the bed while I inch my way back near the top. These bitches are ready to jump and whup my ass, and frankly there's not a damn thing that's going to stop them. I bump into Profit's IV stand and then trip when I try to move around it. Falling, my hand squeezes the trigger on my gun.

POW!

I hear a gasp, but by the time I hit the floor, these bitches are on me like white on rice. We scrap, and we scrap hard. I catch a couple of hard blows against my head, but I land a few of my own. Hell. I got brothers. I ain't no punk. But let's face it. I'm still outnumbered, and these stank hoes are punching body blows like heavyweight champions.

"Grab that bitch and let's head out," Qiana barks.

That shit ain't going down. If they manage to get me out of this room, it's lights-out and my ass will be standing before Jesus within the hour. I go for my gun again but discover that the muthafucka has fallen out of my jacket. I try to feel around as these bitches are lifting my ass off the floor. Kicking and punching with everything I have, I catch two of these bitches dead in their mouths, and it's enough to stun them and make them drop me.

When I hit the floor again, hip first, pain like I've never known ricochets throughout my body, and I scream out like the punk bitch I was trying *not* to be. The tears that rush my eyes blind me for a second, but still have the presence of mind to feel around the floor for my gat.

"Fuck it. Just fuck that bitch up!" Qiana barks.

In the next second, these bitches are back on me, knocking down poles and machines that almost crack my skull open.

I'm vaguely aware of a loud, beeping noise filling the room, but that shit is so not important compared to my ass struggling not to black out. When my fingers brush against my

Glock lying underneath the bed, the door bursts open and a voice thunders, "What the fuck is going on in here?"

I keep throwing aimless punches and clock Qiana upside her head before grabbing one of her big door-knocker earrings and yanking that muthafucka clean off.

"Fuuuuuuck!" Qiana rears back and then punches me so hard that my mouth fills with blood.

After that, this big nigga I've seen off and on guarding the door lifts this screaming bitch off of me. I scramble to get up but end up slipping and sliding in a pool of blood. Whether it's mine or someone else's, I don't know. I want to get the hell out of here.

A foot away from me, Qiana is rolling around and gripping her arm.

"That bitch shot me!"

"That's not all I'm going to do." I grab the gun again and swing the muthafucka her way so I can put this bitch down once and for all. When I squeeze the trigger, this big, gorilla-looking muthafucka kicks the gun out of my hand, and the shot goes more toward the bed where Profit still lies.

Horrified, I slap a hand over my bleeding mouth and try to stand again.

Everyone holds their breath and leans over to see if my stupid ass shot a comatose body. When it's clear that the bullet completely missed him, we all go back to breathing again. However, I'm still the most unpopular girl in the room.

Get the fuck out of here. I push the pain in my hip to the back of my mind and scramble again to get to my feet. By that time, doctors and nurses start pouring in.

"What in the hell is going on in here?" one of the dudes in a white coat asks as another Vice Lord grabs me by my waist and lifts me effortlessly into the air.

"Get off me, muthafucka!"

I throw more punches, not giving a damn about where

they land. I may be small, but I'm not going to let these muthafuckas kick my ass, and if I'm gonna cop a charge, then I'm going to make sure that it's for something that I can pump my chest out with pride while I'm in the clink.

"Pipe the fuck down, small fry. Your ass is in enough trouble as it is," this nigga barks, and gives me a good shake. "Ain't nothing going on," the nigga lies with a straight face. "We were having a little family disagreement."

The small staff scatters. The two nurses rush to pick up the beeping machines and poles off the floor.

"We heard shots," the doctor says, looking around. When his eyes land on the puddle of blood on the floor, he starts to inch back toward the door.

"It's nothing. The little girl here fell and busted her lip. She's going to be all right." He gives me another shake. "Ain't that right, shawty?"

He's looking to me to back up that stupid lie? When I open my mouth, this angry nigga gives me another hard shake that rattles around the few marbles I have left in my head. I bob my head along to cosign whatever lie this nigga wants to tell.

Across the room, Qiana's jaw is clenched tight and her narrowed glare says this shit ain't over by a long shot. From now on, I'll have to be looking over my shoulder for this bitch.

The doctor pushes up his glasses. "Look, this is a hospital, not a—"

"Oh my God!"

Everyone's head swivels toward the gasping nurse, and our eyes follow her line of vision to the bed.

31

Lucifer

As much as I want to give the green light to Bishop to make a move on Python and his pussy-ass paper gangsters, I know that it's no longer my call to make. After putting down Killa Kyle, my boys and I roll over to Ruby Cove to check in with Mason, who, by all appearances, has survived another dance with the devil—barely.

"Did that nigga talk?"

The question is thrown at me the second I stroll out of the sliding glass door and into the backyard. I look over to see him concentrating on moving his silver walker an inch at a time across the back patio.

Sweat is pouring down his face like a waterfall. "What are you doing?"

"What in the fuck does it look like I'm doing?"

Oh yeah—his attitude sucks, too. I turn around and give Monk and Droopy the *give us a few minutes* look and then slide the glass door closed again so that we can talk privately.

"You're going to overexert yourself," I warn him.

"I didn't ask for your opinion, *Doctor*," he barks as he inches the walker along. "I think I know what my body can and *cannot* handle." He barely gets the sentence out before his legs buckle and he and his trusted walker go their separate ways.

I jump into action and rush to help.

"I got it," he says, but when I don't back away fast enough, Mason damn near takes my head off. "Goddamn it, Willow, I said I got it!"

I lift my hands up in the air and move back.

Turning away from me, he struggles to right his walker and pull himself up. After a while, his upper body trembles and quakes so bad that he looks like a human earthquake. Cutting him a break, I reach over and loop one of his arms around my shoulder and lift him off the ground and over to a nearby chair.

"You're welcome," I tell him after it's clear that he's not going to say anything.

He grunts.

"What was that?" I challenge.

He cuts a hard look over at me but then spits out, "Thanks."

"Don't mention it." His mismatched gaze meets mine, and his apology is clear in his softening expression.

"Really. I mean it," I add before grabbing his sunglasses up off the patio and handing them over.

"Thanks," he says again.

I nod while an awkward silence hangs between us. If I'm not careful, I'll fuck up and tell this nigga, my best friend, how I feel about his ass—about how tired I am of being scared that the next bullet he takes might be his last. I mean, damn, I'm no mathematical genius, but common sense would tell a nigga that he can't keep outsmarting the devil every time you roll through his crib.

Sooner or later, he's gonna trap his ass down there, and where would that leave my ass—blasting through the city seeking revenge? And what happens after that? It hasn't been easy holding shit down this last time. Sure, I have my people's respect and loyalty, but I was as much a wreck on the inside as Bishop, thinking that we—I—was going to lose him.

"So whassup? You get that nigga to talk or what?" Mason asks again.

I push up a smile. "They always talk."

"When you're doing the wet work—no doubt." He leans forward and rubs his hands together. "So who was the fucking trigger man?"

"Trigger *woman*. The rumors on the streets might be true."

Mason twists up his face. "No shit?"

I shrug. "Apparently."

"How come your snitch didn't toss her ass up then?"

"Maybe she didn't know."

"Bullshit." Mason shakes his head. "That's all right, though. I got a muthafuckin' bullet with that bitch's name on it." He removes his Mark-23 from beneath a towel lying on the patio table. "Believe that. I'm going to handle her ass right after I earth her nigga Python. This muthafuckin' city ain't big enough for the two of our asses no more. I'm tired of playing with him and his fucked-up crew on the south side. I say that we blast up the whole heart of their organization—right now. Smoke that nigga out. We fire enough bullets, we'll hit someone his ass gives a fuck about."

"Is this about Profit . . . or Melanie?" I ask.

His gaze cuts back over at me with enough fire to blaze my ass up.

"Dead is dead. You feel me?"

I choke on a sudden surge of jealousy. The bitch has been dead and in the ground for damn near two months. "Whatever."

"What?" His voice is as hard as his glare.

"Nothing." I stand. "Bishop called in. He found Python over at Goodman Construction. I told him to sit on his ass while I check in with you."

Mason bolts up onto his feet. "And you're just now saying something? Fuck!" He grabs his gat. "We're rolling the fuck out." He takes one step and is falling again. "Shit! Fuck! God-damn it!"

I bite my tongue and go to help him again, but this damn time he pushes my ass away. "Goddamn it, Willow! Leave me the fuck alone. Shit!"

"Fine. Stay your ass down there, then! See if I give a fuck!" I march toward the sliding glass door. "You can just stay a crip-pled muthafucka since you don't need no damn body." I jerk the door open and stroll back into the house with my eyes stinging with what feels like acid tears. I pop Monk on the shoulder and tell him, "Let's roll out."

He and Droopy jump but then cast a hesitant gaze back to-ward the backyard.

"I SAID, ROLL OUT!"

They get their asses moving this time.

"Lucifer," Mason yells.

I keep marching toward the door. "Don't you fuckin' stop," I warn Monk and Tombstone, though I can tell by their slouching shoulders that they're torn.

"Goddamn it, Lucifer!" Mason barks again. "Don't leave me out here like this!"

I stop as Monk opens the front door. He and Tombstone cast me this weird look, and I'm so irritated that I'm actually thinking about busting a cap in both of their asses for dragging their feet. Instead, I take several deep breaths to calm down. "Shit," I mumble, and then jerk back around to see if Mason can now talk like he's got a little damn sense.

"What?" I say, entering the backyard again and folding my arms while I hover above him.

"Don't *what* me. Help me up."

"Why the fuck should I do that? You don't *need* me. You can handle all this shit all by yourself, *right*?"

"Willow—"

"Don't fuckin' *Willow* me either. It's Lucifer. Use the fuckin' name you gave me."

Mason sighs, but it's way too late for me to feel sorry for his rude ass. "Let's get something straight, right here, right now. Despite what your goddamn ego tells you at night, you didn't get on top by your damn self. If it wasn't for me, your ass would've been dead and buried waaaay before you got the crown. You feel me?"

"I know."

"If I hadn't rolled up when Python tried to blast you and Juvon at that little corner at the mall back in the day, that nigga would've fucked up more than just your fuckin' eye. . . .

"I don't care what you say, Willow. You ain't coming," Juvon yelled as he stormed around his dirty bedroom. "You ain't locking down no corner, blasting no niggas and getting your thirteen-year-old ass in no bullshit out here in the street."

I rolled up on him and mushed him in his fucking head. "Don't be talking to me out the side of your neck, Bishop—or whatever the hell you're calling yourself this week. The last time I checked, you weren't my damn daddy!"

Leaning against a wall on the other side of the room, Mason chuckled and flipped down his shades. "She got a point there, Bishop."

"You stay out of this," Bishop barked at his boy.

Mason tossed up his hands, signaling that he was going to mind his own business.

"Traitor." I jutted my chin and folded my arms. Every damn time Bishop and I got into it, Mason acted like his ass was Switzerland and wanted no part of it. It would be nice if someone had my back every once in a while, especially since he spent as much time at our crib as he did with Smokestack. Sometimes I wondered if he regretted not moving to Atlanta with Dribbles and his younger brother, Raymond. I knew that he missed them.

"You're not going," Bishop shouted again. "And that shit is final."

"Blah, blah, blah. Talk that bullshit while you're walking. You

can't stop me. I'm gonna do whatever the fuck I want to do. If there's paper to be made, then I'm gonna get mine just like y'all."

Juvon clenched his fists, but if he even looked like he was ready to start throwing those muthafuckas around, I had something for his ass—and he knew it, which was why his hands stayed at his sides.

"You ain't got to worry about making no paper. I'm the fuckin' man of the house. I'm handlin' the bills around here."

"What bills? Nigga, please."

"I'm serious, Willow," Bishop warned. "Stay your ass here."

"Stop calling me Willow. I done told you about that shit."

"I'm not going call you no fuckin' Lucifer. You need to stop smoking whatever the fuck you've been smoking and get your head right."

Out in the driveway, Tombstone laid into his car horn.

Bishop glanced at Mason. "Nigga, you ready to roll out?"

Mason pushed up his sunglasses and twisted his ball cap to the back. "Yo, I've been waiting on you, nigga." They exchanged fist bumps and headed toward the door.

I thrust up my chin, puffed out my small titties, and followed right behind their asses.

"Willow, I ain't playing with you," Bishop warned without turning and looking back. "So don't fuckin' try me."

I didn't answer his ass. I kept marching right behind them.

Once we reached the front door, Juvon roared, "GODDAMN IT!" He whipped around with his fist raised; just when he launched that muthafucka toward my face, Mason's hand came up and caught it in midair.

"Nah, my nigga. I can't let your ass do that shit."

I didn't even flinch, but had he landed that punch, it would've been the last muthafuckin' thing he ever did in life.

"What's going on in here?" My mother thundered into the room, and we all broke apart like she'd caught us stealing money out of her purse—again. Since we looked suspicious, her eyes narrowed and scanned each one of us.

"Nothing," Bishop lied, forcing up a smile. "Me and Mason are heading out. I done told Willow she can't go, but she won't listen."

"Tattletale," I hissed, because I knew what was coming next.

"Willow, leave your brother alone. You're getting too old to be following him around everywhere," Mom yelled, settling her hand on her hips.

"Exactly." Bishop gave me a smug look. "Catch you later, Willow." He jerked open the door and then blew me a kiss.

I cocked my fist, but my mother barked, "Willow!"

My punch hung in the air, but I gave Bishop a look that told his ass that this shit wasn't over by a long shot. "Willow Elizabeth Washington!"

I dropped my fist and turned back toward my mother. It couldn't have been a worse time, since Cousin Skeet chose that moment to stroll his ass up into the living room, wearing my father's old robe and pair of slippers. Smiling, he wrapped his arm around my mother's slim waist and kissed her upturned cheek.

"Morning, baby."

Whatever annoyance my mother felt toward me melted away, and a big-ass smile covered her face. "Morning, honey. You hungry?"

"After what you put me through last night? Hell yeah." He slapped her on the ass. "Morning, Willow. Don't you look . . . nice this morning."

I glanced over my shoulder to see whether Bishop and Mason were getting a load of this shit, but those two niggas had already crept out the fucking door. In the driveway, I heard a car pulling off.

"Dammit."

"I don't know why she insists on wearing black all the time," my momma complained. "She always looks like she's on her way to a funeral." She turned and headed into the kitchen.

Cousin Skeet remained rooted in the living room, his eyes raking over me like an X-ray machine. "Damn, Willow. If you keep it up, you're going to be a real looker like your mother. You're not going to be able to keep the boys off of you—or the men."

"Eww."

Cousin Skeet laughed.

It took everything I had not to hurl right there on the spot. That muthafucka must've thought I was dumb, but I knew exactly what he was getting at with all those long stares on my titties or touching my knee whenever my mother or brother wasn't around. Pervert.

"Willow, did you clean your room?" my mother yelled from the kitchen.

"I gotta get out of here." I turned and rushed out the front door.

"Yo, Lucifer," Dominic hollered from way down the street.

Since I wasn't raised in a barn, I wasn't about to be hollering back down the street. But I did jog down off the porch and headed toward Hoskins Road, where Juvon and Mason usually held down their corner.

"Lucifer, wait up," Dominic yelled again.

Since I don't wait up for miscellaneous niggas, I kept walking until he caught up with me, all out of breath and shit.

"Damn, girl. Didn't you hear me calling you?"

"What the hell do you want, Dominic? I don't want niggas thinking we hang or nothing."

"Damn. You're cold, girl." He shook his head. *"Where your nigga, Fat Ace, at?"*

"Why?"

" 'Cause he better not take his ass back down to the Mall of Memphis. Word is that the Gangster Disciples are rolling through to take their territory back."

"Get the fuck out of here. That mall ain't been there in like three years. Where you hear that shit?"

"Up at the package store. I was getting my moms her Friday bottle of Crown Royal, and I overheard these nigga talking about how that new nigga they got running things is trying to make his mark."

"What new nigga?"

"Sheeiiit." Dominic frowned as he gripped his cock. *"Where the fuck you been? That ugly muthafucka who always got a fucking snake wrapped around his neck or some dumb shit."* He leaned closer while I leaned back from his stank breath. *"I even heard that he had his tongue surgically altered to look like a snake's tongue."*

I frowned. "You're lying."

Dominic crossed his heart. "If I'm lying, I'm dying."

"When are they supposed to be doing this?"

"Today!"

"Shit." I glanced around. "We got to get over there!"

Dominic tossed up his hand. "I ain't got to do shit but stay black and die. I came over here to warn Big Man. If he's already gone up there, two tears in a bucket. You feel me?"

I reached out and grabbed this scary nigga by his ear. "I said we got to get over there and that's what the fuck I mean."

"Ow. Ow. Ow."

I looked around, tryna figure out what the fuck to do. Then it hit me. "C'mon." Still holding on to his ear, I raced back to my house. "Stay here," I told him. When his gaze darted around, I added, "You move and I'll hunt you down and carve you up into little pieces."

His eyes grew wide as fuck because he knew I meant business.

I crept back into the house and for once was glad that Mom and Cousin Skeet had returned to her bedroom for another afternoon quickie. Momma is screaming "Oh God" while her headboard slammed against the wall. Despite that, I tiptoed to her purse that was sitting on the coffee table and pulled out her car keys. I was headed back to the door when another thought occurred to me. Turning around, I went over to the coat closet by the front door and retrieved the metal box in the back of the top shelf.

The minute I had my daddy's old gun in my hand, I felt this wonderful surge of power. This was my gun now. I knew at that moment that it had been waiting for me.

When I rushed back outside, Dominic was about to take one step off the porch.

"Where the fuck are you going?" I challenged.

"I . . . uh . . ." His eyes dropped to the gun in my hand. "Look. I'm sorry. I didn't think you were going to come back out."

"Whatever, nigga. Get in the car." I raced off the porch and headed to my momma's car.

"What?"

"You're working my nerves, Dominic. Get in." I hopped in on the driver's side and jammed my momma's keys into the ignition.

"Do you even know how to drive?" he asked, getting in on the passenger side.

I started up the car. "How hard can it be?" I shifted into reverse and slammed my foot down on the accelerator, and the car jetted back so fast that I jerked the steering wheel and took out the mailbox.

"FUUUUUCK!" Dominic roared.

"Oh, calm down. I got this."

"Willow!" my momma screamed, clutching her robe and running out the front door. "What in the hell do you think you're doing?"

"Sorry, Mom. I'll be back." I shifted into drive.

"Girl, you get back here!" She nearly reached the car before I slammed my foot back down on the accelerator and peeled off.

"Whoa, ho, ho," Dominic said with his eyes growing bigger by the second. "Your ass is grass when you get back home."

"What the hell ever. We have to get over to the mall and warn Fat Ace and Bishop." I cut another corner and hug that muthafucka so tight I know niggas on the block got to be impressed.

"Girl, you wild. I'll give you that shit," Dominic said, getting supped up. "Damn. You're my getaway driver if I ever decide to rob a bank."

I blocked his silly ass out while I concentrated on floating out to the mall. I tried to calm myself down by rationalizing how much bull-shit got shoveled around on the street. It was probably nothing but gossip. I could get over there and—

POW! POW! POW!

"Aw, shit!" Dominic grabbed the dashboard as I whipped into the parking lot.

Niggas scattered every which way as they returned fire toward a line of old-ass cars. I scanned the crowd, trying to find my brother and Mason.

"There they go!" Dominic pointed toward the corner of the Dil-

lard's store, and once again, I jammed the accelerator all the way to the floorboard.

"Shit. You're driving straight into the line of fire!"

I ignored him and grabbed my daddy's Glock.

"Lucifer! Are you crazy?" His voice climbed into a bitch octave. "Lucifer!"

"Roll your fucking window down," I yelled.

"What?" he screeched.

"Fuck it!" I aimed my gun at the passenger side window and then pumped two bullets into it.

"Fuck, fuck, fuck," Dominic freaked out.

A black car sped toward Mason and Juvon. I spotted at least three guns taking aim at them. "ALL IS ONE!" they yelled.

For a split second, I'm that little girl in the yellow dress again.

Mason saw them, too, and instantly tackled Juvon to the ground.

Bullets flew as I shake those old memories off and jetted up onto the sidewalk and directly into the black car's line of fire where I blast at the muthafuckas myself. I caught one nigga straight across his dome and watched him propel backward into the car. The nigga in the rear of the car ducked back into the car, but not before I caught sight of his ugly face.

"Goddamn."

After our cars passed one another, I hung a hard right and spun the car around as that muthafucka popped back out of his window and started blasting again. I leaned out the driver's side window and started dumping again. Those grimy Gangster Disciples got the picture and took off.

This time I spun the car around and doubled back toward my people. I kicked up my own smoke when I slammed on the brakes. I kept my Glock clutched in my hand as I jumped out of the car. I'm scared as fuck at the amount of blood painting the sidewalk.

"JUVON! MASON!" I reached their huddled bodies and peeled Mason off of my brother.

Juvon was fine, but Mason's right eye was fucked up.

"What the hell happened?" Juvon asked, pulling himself off the concrete and looking dazed and confused.

"What you think? I saved y'all's asses. Now help me get Mason in the car."

To Mason credit, he ain't out here hollering like a bitch while he bled out, but at the same time, he looked as stunned as my brother.

Juvon jumped into action and helped me get Mason into the car. However, there was another surprise waiting for us. Slumped back against the passenger seat was Dominic, the light gone from his eyes.

"Yeah," Mason says, bobbing his head while he still sat there on the ground. "You came through for us that day."

I lifted my brows.

"Correction: You *always* come through. You always got my back. And you don't deserve me tryna bite your head off every time you turn around." He sucks in a deep breath. "It's just . . . I feel so fucking guilty, you know? My ignorant ass was out in these damn streets, chasing after that fucking . . ." He stopped himself and drew in another deep breath. "I was supposed to be looking after Profit. He was my responsibility."

"Look. It's hard out here—"

"Don't give me that shit. My name should've been enough to protect him, but instead that nigga Python came after me while his girl tried to take my lil brother out on the same night. This shit can't stand. The showdown between me and that nigga has been a long time coming."

I can't let another I-told-you-so moment slip by. "I warned you. Like father, like daughter."

"Yeah. You did." He bobs his head and looks up at me. "You were right. You're always right."

"Careful. You gonna give me a big head."

He cocks his head. "Too late for that shit."

We laugh as my cell goes off.

"Yeah?" I'm not sure I heard the caller right. "Say that shit again."

Mason frowns up at me. "What?"

"All right. We're on our way." I disconnect the call and then stare at the phone for another second.

"What? Don't leave me hanging."

I look over at him. "It's Profit. He's awake."

32

Momma Peaches

"Right there, baby. Right there. Momma's coming. Momma . . . ahhhh." I clutch the back of Cedric's head and smash his face into my pool of pussy juice.

Even then, his tongue doesn't stop flicking and rotating. When I think I can't take any more, this nasty muthafucka thrusts two fingers into my ass, and I shoot off back-to-back orgasms and make sure that everybody on Shotgun Row hears. The aftershocks of that shit have me panting and trembling so hard that the entire bed shakes.

"You like that, baby?" Cedric mumbles around my pulsing clit.

A lazy smile eases across my lips while my eyes grow heavier than a muthafucka. "What have I told you about talking with your mouth full?"

"My bad." He laughs as he climbs up my body, peppering kisses along the way.

For a brief moment, I think my ass is about to get a small break. Silly me. My ass should know by now that when it comes to pussy, Cedric is a fiend. Fuck. I'm starting to wonder if the muthafucka got batteries shoved up his ass. Some time later, I pass the fuck out. Hell, I don't even know if he was finished or not. I'm just gone, dreaming about getting used to this shit for the rest of my life.

Then in the dead of night, my eyes fly open. *What was that?*

Glancing to my right, I verify that Cedric is passed out next to me, snoring.

Creak.

I bolt up in bed and instantly go for my .38 that I keep in the nightstand drawer next to the bed. "Cedric," I hiss.

When this nigga doesn't move, I rock his shoulder. "Cedric, wake up. I think there's someone in the house."

Creak.

"Huh? Hmm?"

"I said— Fuck it." I peel the sheets off of my sweaty and sex-funked body and grab my prosthetic leg. The floorboards in the front of the house are creaking like a muthafucka by the time I slip into my robe and creep my way out of the bedroom. "These niggas gonna get tired of fucking around with me," I threaten under my breath as I work my way toward the living room. Whoever these kids are in my house, I'm going to shoot first and ask questions later. Muthafuckas out here know that I don't play this jacking bullshit. I've worked too hard for my shit.

Something clangs in the kitchen, and then a second later my refrigerator door pops open. I take aim at the big nigga who's headlong into my fridge and then hit the light switch. "What the fuck?"

Python stands up, shoving the last of my pecan pie into his mouth.

"Nigga . . ." I roll my eyes and lower the gun. "Do you know how close you came to having a cap in your ass?"

He cocks a grin. "I missed you, too," he mumbles, and resumes chomping on that piece of pie.

I frown and shove my gun into my robe pocket. "Don't talk with your mouth full."

"Yes, ma'am," he says, dropping crumbs all over my floor.

"Boy, sit your ass down." I pull out a chair, and while he pops a squat, I grab plates and silverware and then pour two glasses of milk. "I don't know why you insist on acting like I didn't raise you with *some* home training." I snatch a few sheets of paper towels while I'm at it.

"I take it that you're still mad?"

"Just because I'm still thinking about shooting your ass doesn't mean that I'm still mad."

Python reaches for his glass of milk. "Good to know."

I sweep my gaze over his face, and I feel a great deal of comfort at seeing him alive and well. "Where's the boy?"

"With LeShelle."

"Oh God." I roll my eyes.

"Don't be like that. She's doing all right with him."

I fold my arms and shake my head because I ain't buying that bullshit. "You keep fucking up, Python."

"Momma—"

"Don't," I warn him. "I'm too old a cat for the fuckin' games." Our eyes lock, and I swear to God I want to take him by his shoulders and shake some sense into his ass. "What are you doing here? You know the whole city is looking for you for . . ."

"Killing Melanie," he finishes.

"For killing a cop. For killing Captain Johnson's daughter. If they catch you, that's the fuckin' needle, baby."

Python huffs out a breath and plays with his second pie serving. "I didn't go over there to kill her."

"Dead is dead, Terrell. You need to roll up out of here. Go to Mexico or some shit."

"Nah. And give up the throne? It ain't happening."

"What throne, Terrell? You boss around a group of niggas and you think that makes you king? Shit." I go back to shaking my head. "Look. I know better than most that there's no love out here in the streets. We all do what we have to do to eat and provide. I could take all this shit better if you were in trouble for those things—but not no baby momma drama bullshit. You want all these girls to be loyal to you while you're out here fucking anything that moves? I *warned* you that you were gonna get caught up. You got too much dirt out here not to. Now you done dragged that innocent child into the shit that you let pile up. How the fuck is that fair? Fuck. For all we know, we lost your baby brother because of some bullshit like this. Lord knows your momma kicked up about as much unnecessary dirt as you do."

"I hear what you saying."

"Do you?"

"Yeah. I mean . . . I'm handling my business."

"Nah. You're moving pieces around the board and hoping that no one checkmates your ass. You need to be watching your back—and start looking at those around you."

"Momma Peaches, ease off that LeShelle nonsense. If anyone is really down for the cause, it's her. I'm thinking that I'm really going to do this thing and marry her."

My eyes start rolling again. "Baby, it's too late at night for you to be trying to give me heartburn."

"I'm serious, Momma Peaches."

Our gazes meet again, and I know he's telling the truth. "Great. Bonnie and Clyde ride again."

He chuckles.

"Uh-huh. Remember how that story ended, Terrell. You know, just because something creeps inside your head doesn't mean that it's a good idea," I tell him.

"Why don't you like LeShelle?"

I turn up my nose but choose my words carefully. "I never said that I didn't like the girl."

"You don't have to. It's written all over your face. I've been with her for almost five years, and you ain't warmed up to her yet."

"Terrell, it ain't up to me to like her. She ain't sleeping in my bed."

"But?"

"But . . . watch yourself. I got a bad feeling about the trouble you're in this time."

"I'm gonna be a'ight, Momma. Ain't I always?"

"You keep playing with the devil and eventually you're going to lose. That's a fact." I reach over the table and take his hand. "About Christopher, baby, take him back. For me." Terrell eased back in the chair and even attempted to pull his hand from mine, but I hold on to it. "Please?"

"I can't do that. He's my son and he belongs with me. I'm gonna raise him up. I'm gonna take care of him."

"What makes him any different from the fifty-eleven children you got running around the city? Or even the one you got coming with Yo-Yo?"

Terrell groans and rolls his eyes to the back of his head. "Man, Momma Peaches. That whole situation is squashed."

"What the hell is that supposed to mean?"

He sucks in a sharp breath and shakes his head. "Squash as in done. Over with. Hell, I don't even know if that baby is even mine."

"Ah. I see. So since Melanie supposedly did you wrong, everybody else is suspect?"

"Pretty much," he spits. "Shariffa had a nigga on the side. Melanie was sleeping with my number-one enemy—for all I know, the bitch was a Flower from the jump. Why should Yolanda be any damn different?"

"What about you, Mr. Clean? I've told you I don't know how many times that fuckin' around with these little girls was going to come back and take a chunk out of your hardheaded ass. *Now* you don't know whether you're the damn daddy? Nah. You ain't squashing shit. You're gonna man the fuck up and you're going to take care of Yo-Yo and her child as long as you're drawing air into your lungs—or you're going to have to start worrying about me busting a cap in your ass."

"But, Momma—"

"Don't 'Momma Peaches' me. You knew what you were getting into when you hooked up with that girl—just like you knew what you were getting into when you hooked up with the captain of police's daughter. Boy, you ain't the only mutha-fucka in these streets running game. You will *not* run all over Yo-Yo. You hear me? I know she's not the sharpest tool in the toolbox, but I like that girl, and you're going to do right by her and take care of that baby before it ends up with Children's Services. You don't want a relationship, fine. But you're taking care of that baby. As for all those other bitches, if you want a faithful woman, then you need to be faithful. Not only are you fuckin' all these bitches, but you're also putting babies on them and then you just expect them to keep takin' your bullshit. It doesn't work like that."

"Since when? You ain't never left your man and his ass jug-gled you and my momma like a fuckin' pimp."

I whip my hand across Terrell's face so fast and hard that it sounds like a gunshot. "Get the fuck out of my house!"

"Momma Peaches, I—"

"GET. THE. FUCK. OUT!"

He holds my gaze for half a second to see that I mean busi-ness. "All right," he says softly, and then stands up.

"And next time you roll your ass over here, knock before you come into my house! I'm gonna start shooting first and asking questions later around here."

"Yes, ma'am."

I watch him as he strolls out of the kitchen. It's not until I hear the click of the front door that I allow a tear to roll down my face.

33

Yolanda

I've never owned a gun before, but I've seen enough niggas use these muthafuckas to do what I gotta do. The way I figure it, murking LeShelle's ass is gonna be a twofer. Justice for Baby Thug and getting my ass back in the game. All I need now is a way to smoke the bitch out, and then this beautiful semi-automatic I got for a couple of Benjamins is going to do the rest.

I know that Pit Bull is having a birthday party at Passions. I could roll over there and see if LeShelle puts in face time. If she does, I can be right there waiting to blast her ass back to the devil.

My smile grows as I take a couple of practice aims at the sixty-inch television screen in my living room. I keep imagining that the news anchor is LeShelle's big monkey head. "RAT-A-TAT-TAT-TAT! You're dead bitch."

Fuck. What I would give to see her head exploding in front of my eyes. If I could, I'd run up and spit on her ass, too. Shit. I should've done this shit a long time ago. Maybe if I'd wised up after LeShelle had pistol-whipped my ass at FabDivas, Baby would still be here with me now.

I suck in a deep breath while regret crashes around inside

of me. It shouldn't have been up to Baby to defend me. This gun right here could've easily rock-a-byed LeShelle's ass with quickness. Once LeShelle is out of the picture, I know Python will come back over here, looking for a shoulder and some ass to bury his troubles away in.

Shaking my head, I realize more than ever my mistake in rolling over to the construction company and making a big fool of myself. I wasn't expecting Python to come at me sideways. I'm going to fix everything.

I kiss the tip of my gun.

"You're going to fix all my troubles, aren't you, baby?" I smile. "Baby. That's what I'll call you. My new Baby Thug."

There is a rattle at the front door, but the chain on it stops my uninvited guest from just strolling into the apartment.

Who in the fuck? I jump straight up from the sofa and clumsily drop my new gat. Thank God the muthafucka isn't loaded or I would probably have shot my damn foot off.

"Yolanda," Python barks. "Why the fuck is this chain on the door?"

"Oh, shit." I glance around the apartment and then try to bend over and pick up my gun, but I'm still sore and stiff from being dragged across concrete, and this big-ass belly isn't helping matters either. I end up kicking the muthafucka under the sofa. "Here I come!"

"What the fuck are you doing?" he hollers back. "You tryna hide a nigga up in here?"

"What? Don't be ridiculous!" I rush toward the door, doing this running wobble kind of thing. It's the best I can do since my whole left side is still sore like a muthafucka. When I get a few feet away, Python throws his shoulder into it and breaks the chain right off.

I stop and stare at his big ass as he strolls into this muthafucka like he owns the fucking place.

"You took too damn long," he says, walking past me and looking around.

"Sorry," I say, but then slide on a smile. I rethink my whole program. Maybe I did do right by going out to see him. It got his ass over here. I want to launch into his arms, but clearly that has to wait until he checks out the entire apartment to make sure that I really don't have some nigga stashed up here somewhere. "Satisfied?" I ask when he makes his way back to the living room.

Python grunts.

I ignore his sour mood and throw my arms around his thick neck and rain kisses all over his face. "I've missed you, baby, so much. Muah. Muah. Muah."

He rolls his eyes, but I can tell that he loves this shit. All niggas love attention—forget what you've heard. "All right. All right."

"You scared me, baby. I would never do no stupid shit like cheat on you. You got to know that. You got my word on that shit." Before I know it, tears stream down my face. I can't help it. The stress of the last couple of months hits me all at once.

Python looks at me and my tears and doesn't say anything.

Fear pricks my heart again. Am I reading too much in his ass showing up here? I ease my arms down from around his neck and step back, but I keep my smile in place. "Can I get you something to eat?"

"Naw. I'm good."

That fear spreads. Niggas don't turn down food. "How about a beer?"

"Yeah. A'ight. Cool." His black gaze settles on me, and I try to tell what he's thinking, but the muthafucka is blessed with the perfect poker face.

"Okay. Make yourself at home," I tell him, and then rush off to grab him a beer. While I'm in the kitchen, I pull myself together by taking several deep breaths. The shit doesn't work. Regardless, I return to the living room with his cold beer and a smile on my face. "Here you go, baby."

Python made himself comfortable, stretched out in the center of the sofa with his arms spread across the back. His eyes lock onto my bulging belly.

I've seen that look before. It's the same one my other baby daddies got when they were trying to convince themselves that the baby you're carrying ain't theirs. Typical bullshit.

"You know we're getting a blood test, right?" Python says.

"Whatever you want, baby." I ease down next to him, but it turns into something more like a plop.

"Uh-huh." He stares at me. "Since you supposedly ain't fucking nobody else, what have you been doing this last couple of months while I was gone?"

I shrug. "Nothing. I've been waiting on you." I slide against him, as close as I can, and then walk my fingers up his chest. "I've been waiting for you to come back home—where you belong."

His black gaze roams over to my big titties. "Damn. Those muthafuckas have gotten big as shit."

I cup them up and give them a big squeeze. "You like them?"

"What's not to like?"

He reaches over and pinches my shit hard. The pain that ripples across my face gives him an instant hard-on. "I've missed playing with you," he says, and then pulls the top of my gown off. My big titties bounce free, and the next thing I know, he's biting and gnawing on my shit like a starved animal.

Sex with Python has always been a painful event, but tonight it's even more so because every ounce of my body is either sensitive from the pregnancy or sore from McGriff dragging my ass around. My painful whimpers and sharp breaths just play like music in Python's ear.

I watch as his dick creeps down the inseam of his jeans. That's all right. I'm going to handle whatever this muthafucka tosses my way like a damn soldier. I can't afford not to.

When he rips the rest of the gown off my body, his head pops off my glazed and chewed titties, and he stares at the large scrape marks across the left side of my body, which are black and blue now. Python reaches over and presses a hand against it.

I suck in a sharp breath.

His gaze shifts to my face, and then he presses down again.

I hold my breath, but I can't do anything about the pain rippling across my face.

Then he surprises me by saying, "Sorry about that. I'll talk to McGriff about this shit." He pulls away and stretches back with his beer.

Is that it? He's not going to touch me now?

To confirm that shit, he sets his beer down and stands up.

I scramble to grab his hands. "Wait. Don't go!"

He looks down at me.

"I . . . I was hoping that I'd get the chance to show you just how much I've missed you." I tug him back down onto the sofa and waste no time trying to get his dick free of his pants.

"Nah. Nah. I didn't even come over here for this. I want to let you know that until the blood test—"

"Python, I ain't been fuckin' no other niggas since we hooked up. I wouldn't do that shit. So squash whatever the fuck LeShelle has been spitting in your ear. She just wants your ass to herself—that greedy bitch!" Realizing that I might have crossed a line, I look up at him with pleading eyes. "She don't know that a powerful nigga like you needs a lot to be satisfied.

I'll cook for you, clean for you, and give you all the babies you want." I'm hitting all the right notes, because my nigga is smiling as he caresses the side of my face.

"You really care for a nigga, huh?"

I grab his hand and kiss it. "More than you'll ever know."

"Then show me." He thrusts his hips forward.

Shit. He doesn't have to ask my ass twice. I spring that fat monster out of his jeans and start slobbering and choking on his meat the way he fucking likes it.

"Sssssssss." Python runs his hands through my hair until he grips the back of my head and holds me in place.

After that, my mouth is another pussy to him. He starts pounding against my tonsils like a boxer on a speed bag. When I think I'm getting used to the rhythm and can steal some air, he changes up and holds his shit against my windpipe and grinds his hips.

I can't breathe, my chest hurts, and I'm starting to black out.

"That's it, baby. Show your nigga how much you love this shit."

I resist the temptation to push his hips back.

"That's it, baby. Sssssssss. You love me?"

Since I can't speak, I nod my head.

"You'd do anything for me?"

I nod again.

"You'd blast niggas for me?"

Nod.

"Lie for me?"

Nod.

"Die for me?"

Nod.

He laughs and grinds his hips some more. "If I asked you to die choking on this dick, you'd do that shit, baby?"

What?

He laughs again. "I asked you a question, Yo-Yo. You think your ass is better than what I got at home, so answer the muthafuckin' question. If I fuckin' choke you out with this dick right now, that's okay with you?"

Is he fucking for real? My mind scrambles for something, but I'm starting to get a pain in my head and I feel weak. I muster up the courage to nod. As clear as a bell, Baby's voice comes to me: *stupid ho.*

Above me, Python's entire body shakes while he laughs, but at least he releases my head and whips his cock out of my mouth. I collapse onto the floor. The first gust of air is as painful as my scraped-up ass. After a while, my head clears, but I'm panting like a dog with tears rolling down my face.

Python gets down on the floor behind me and delivers a slap on my ass so hard that I cry out. "Get on your knees."

I almost ask for him to give me a couple more seconds, but I'm supposed to be proving myself worthy to be wifey, so I squash that shit. Trembling and shaking, I get into the doggy-style position.

"Ahhh. Look at this ass," he praises, and then delivers a second slap. "I've fucking missed this muthafucka."

Slap!

He spreads my ass cheeks. "This fat bitch, here. Sssssss." Python leans forward and swishes that forked tongue around the rim of my asshole, and I fucking melt like butter.

"Mmmmm," he moans. He reaches down and jacks his dick while his tongue makes a deep Dumpster dive.

That choking shit floats right out of my mind as Python washes all four walls of my ass, but minutes later when he crams his thick, mushroom-headed cock through that same hole with one stroke, the pain roars back to life.

"Oh, fuck yeah," he groans, stroking and slapping my ass like I fuckin' owe his ass money.

"You like that, baby?" I ask, my voice raspy as fuck.

"Work it, Yo-Yo." He holds his hands up in the air while I make my booty clap around his dick. "Yeah, get that shit, girl. Sssss."

It's like old times up in this muthafucka. A few times I get his ass to call out my name, and other times I'm in so much pain that it actually feels good. One thing for sure—we stay at it for hours until there's cum dripping out my ass, off my back, and out of my hair.

I'm definitely back in the game.

Hours later, I lift my head and see we've made it to the bed. We've jacked it up, and the room smells like musk and pussy, but that's okay. I put his ass to sleep, too. Smiling, I wiggle my fat ass against his growing hard-on until he starts to wake up.

Python moans and stretches behind me. Without even opening his eyes, he reaches between our bodies and slides his dick back into my ass, lifts my leg high into the air, and strokes for another nut. After he blasts off, he looks around to see where the fuck he is. "What time is it?"

"I don't know. Late."

"FUCK!" Python springs out of bed. "I gotta go."

"Oh," I moan disappointedly. "Do you have to?"

"Hell, yeah. I don't want to hear LeShelle's mouth that I left her with Christopher again."

"Humph. Since she can't have babies, the least she can do is babysit from time to time."

Python's gaze cuts back over to me.

I fold my arms and keep my funky attitude in place. "What? It's the truth. I don't know why you put up with half a woman anyway."

"That's the last one. I done told you about staying in your lane. Keep my girl's name out your mouth."

"I'm your girl, too."

"Yeah. But I'm giving *her* my last name."

"What?" This nigga didn't say what I think he said.

He shrugs his big shoulders as if he just told me the weather. "I'm making it official. Before the summer is out, LeShelle is going to be Mrs. Carver. Deal with it."

34

LeShelle

"**P**lease, please, I'll be good," Christopher whines, backing himself into a corner.

I roll my eyes. "Oh, God. Here you go. Stop whining. Ain't nobody hurting you. Get over here in this bed, boy."

"I don't like it when you tie me down in the bed."

"Did I ask you what the hell you liked?" I yell through gritted teeth. This boy seriously doesn't know how close I am to bouncing his ass off every wall in this bitch. He's nothing but a spoiled brat who doesn't know how good his ass has it up in here. "Get over here, Chris. You won't like it one bit if I have to chase your ass around this muthafucka."

Christopher inches toward me.

"And if you piss on yourself again, I'm whupping your ass. You hear me?"

"Yes, ma'am." His lips tremble as he swipes away his tears and climbs into the bed.

I start tying him down with nylon rope. Still he has the nerve to be up in here sniffing and crying. "Cut it out," I snap. "I wouldn't have to do this shit if your damn daddy knew how to bring his ass home some damn time. But nooooo. He thinks chasing pussy is more important than taking care of his own damn kid. Well, fuck that shit. I ain't the bitch to be sitting on a damn shelf, flicking my clit until he feels like rolling his ass over here. If he's going to be out in the streets, then, dammit, so am I."

"Ow!" Christopher yelps. "That's too tight."

"Boy, if you don't man the fuck up . . . It's tight because I don't want your ass to move."

Fat crocodile tears roll down the boy's face.

"Your damn momma should be rolling around in her grave. She ain't done nothing but raise a big fucking crybaby." The smell of piss hits my nose. "What the fuck?" I look down and see this big fucking pee stain spreading across my good white sheets. I reflexively pop this nigga on the side of his big-ass watermelon head. "What the fuck did I tell you?"

Christopher breaks down whimpering and crying.

"You know what? You want to be a big baby and piss on yourself, then fine. You're going to lie in that piss." This muthafucka starts crying harder and working my nerves.

"Please, Ms. LeShelle. Don't tie me down. I won't go nowhere. Please."

"I swear to God. You don't know how good your ass has it. You got a roof over your head. We feed you. Ain't nobody beating your ass or sneaking in here in the middle of the night and doing all kinds of perverted shit to you. I wish all I had to do was lie in bed and go to sleep. Now shut the fuck up and take your ass to sleep before I really give you something to cry about."

Christopher presses his lips together, but he still sniffs and whines like a little bitch. I shake my head. This little cum stain is the spitting image of his father, right down to the horseshoe-shaped birthmark on his neck.

I turn and storm out of the room before I do something to his lil ass I'll regret. In my bedroom, I grab this sexy black lace see-through dress and shimmy it over my silver rhinestone pasties on my nipples and matching thong. Afterward, I take one look in the mirror. I feel and look like the fuckin' queen that I am. After sliding my feet into some cute Louboutin heels, I grab my clutch bag and then stroll my fine ass out the door, tossing deuces to an empty bedroom.

The minute I roll up into Passions, I see the club bumping with all the usual suspects. "Goddamn it feels good to be home," I shout above the music, and watch as niggas' heads whip around.

"Damn, bitch," Kookie and Pit Bull say in unison as they plow through the crowd to get at me.

Kookie takes the shit one step further. "Does Python know your ass is out here naked and shit?"

I roll my eyes. "I ain't studdin' that nigga. I'm out here doin' me." Turning my smile toward Pit Bull, I reach into my clutch and hand her ass a small box. "Happy birthday, bitch. Don't say I ain't never got you nothing."

"Thanks, girl. C'mon over to our booth. We're tossing up bottles of Cristal and puffing on some of that blueberry AK-47 that you like."

"Puff, puff, pass, bitches!"

"Holler!" Pit Bull holds up her glass and takes me by the hand.

As we make our way through the club, I grin and cheese my ass off as niggas damn near give themselves whiplash as I walk by. Some of them are even licking their lips and twisting up their faces as if I was putting a hurting on their damn hard-ons. Now the game is to see which of these muthafuckas are going to be man enough to step to me and not fear the blow-back from Python. Shit. There's no crime in dancing with a muthafucka.

"Here you go, girl," Pit Bulls says, handing me a drink. "Happy birthday to me and hallelujah that you came out of your cave to come hang with your girls tonight."

The family of Queen Gs sitting at the table all hold up their glasses and shout, "Cheers, bitches!"

After I toss back a few sips of my drink and hit one of Pit

Bull's fat blunts that's been in serious rotation a couple of times, I'm relaxed as fuck and scanning the crowd again looking for the right nigga to man up.

"Shit. I don't blame you for bouncing tonight," Kookie says, reaching for the blunt in my hand. "With Lemonhead back on the scene, I'm sure you need to blow off some steam."

I twist my neck around. "What the fuck are you talking about?"

Kookie pretends to look shocked. "What? You don't know, girl? McGriff told me that jump-off had the nerve to roll her retarded ass up over at the construction warehouse, demanding to see Python. Showed her ass off real good."

This bitch just blew my muthafuckin' high. "Girl, I ain't studdin' that yellow bitch," I lie.

"I know you ain't, girl. And I don't blame you. Python probably rolled over there tonight to set her ass straight."

"He did what?"

She continues with her innocent act. "Didn't you know? McGriff texted me before I left tonight that he and his niggas are parked outside on security." She glances at her diamond Rolex. "Shit. That was a while ago." She presses the blunt against her lips and takes a deep toke and then slowly blows that shit into my face.

No this bitch didn't.

Knowing exactly what this bitch is doing, I pop up out of my chair and pimp-slap her ass straight out of the muthafuckin' booth.

"DAMN!" the entire table roars as they bounce up out of their seats to try and get a better view.

"What the fuck?" Kookie yells, clutching the side of her face.

"I'm getting sick of your ass tryna rise up, bitch!" I rear back and kick her upside the fuckin' head. "Have you forgotten who the fuck I am?"

Dazed, Kookie tries to scramble away, but I grab hold of the back of her head and snatch out two of her tracks.

"LeShelle, please—*stop!*"

"You want me to stop, then apologize, bitch." I deliver a second kick to the side of her gut that she has strapped down with a couple gridles.

"I'm sorry. I'm sorry," she says after I've chased her ass all the way to the fuckin' dance floor.

I force myself to stop kicking, but I stand over her while blood drips from her mouth and nose. "If you *ever* come at me sideways again, I'll put a fuckin' bullet in the back of your goddamn head and then piss on your muthafuckin' grave. You hear me, bitch?"

Kookie nods while she tries to breathe with a cracked rib.

Not until I turn to storm back to the booth do I even realize that the music has stopped and the entire club has formed a huge circle around us. "What the fuck? I thought we were having a fuckin' party up in here?"

On cue, the DJ pumps the music again, and niggas part to let my ass through. When I make it back to the booth, I pluck the blunt out of rotation and grab my clutch. "I'll catch up with you bitches later."

"You're leaving?" Pit Bull asks, unconcerned about her partner in crime still bleeding over by the dance floor.

"Yeah, girl. This fuckin' club is whack. You do you." I stop. "Consider my ass not stomping you into the floor with your lil buddy over there as another birthday gift."

"But—"

"Bye, bitch." Puffing on their shit, I strut out of the club. The minute I walk out of the fuckin' door, my mind zooms back to Python and his creeping ass. Once again, every miscellaneous bitch on the street knows what time it is before my ass does, and I'm getting fuckin' tired of this shit.

Calling Python all kinds of muthafuckas as I march back to

the car, my ass actually slips up and I don't even hear muthafuckas coming up behind me until it's almost too late. My
hand dives into my clutch, and when I turn around, I have my
cute .38 ready to blast.

"Yo, white flag," this young bitch yells at me.

I frown at her scarred-up cheeks and then glance at the
two chicks standing behind her. "Start talking because I don't
know you bitches."

"That's all right because I ain't looking for no new friends,
especially with a bitch whose sister fucked up my face."

She got my attention with that. I take another look at the
ugly gashes on the chick's face, and I feel a certain level of
pride in Ta'Shara's handiwork. Who in the fuck knew that she
even had that shit in her? "So what the fuck do you want, and
why the hell are you rollin' up on me in the middle of the
night if you're not looking to get blasted?"

"Look, if I wanted to blast, I would have got your ass the
minute you strolled out of that muthafuckin' club. Shit. I'd
even be a hero, considering the price on your head for dumping a whole clip into our chief's lil brother—especially now
that his ass is awake."

"What?"

"Oh? You didn't know about that, did you? Yep. Ta'Shara's
boyfriend is up and talking. Shit. If you think we've been
painting the streets with your soldiers' blood, you ain't seen
nothing now that Fat Ace is rehabbing, too."

"Well, ain't you the muthafuckin' snitch?"

"You mean sort of like that lil bitch Essence you got patrolling the hospital?"

I smile. "I don't know what you're talking about."

"Of course not. Just like you don't know that she's been
snitching on you to Lucifer."

My eyes narrow on this bitch.

She cheeses at me. "She's the one who gave up those niggas who raped Ta'Shara. It's just a matter of time before Lucifer

comes after you. C'mon, after what the fuck you did, you think we'd let a Queen G visit Profit without a reason?"

Damn. I can't even find a good-ass snitch in these streets.

"So what do you want?" I ask, tired of waiting for her to get to the point.

"I want you to dust the bitch off."

I laugh. "You come to me to do your wet work?"

"Orders on high say that the girl can't be touched, but if you knocked her off . . ."

"The last thing on my bucket list is to do a muthafuckin' Flower a favor," I sneer, opening the car door. There's a piece of paper taped onto the steering wheel. I pick it up and read, *TICKTOCK*.

Suddenly there's a squeal of tires, and I look up in time to see a silver Terrain blazing down the street. "FUCK! GET DOWN!"

We all dive for cover.

RAT-A-TAT-TAT-TAT!

RAT-A-TAT-TAT-TAT!

Bullet after bullet slams into my Crown Victoria, shattering the windows and causing glass to cascade over us.

"TICKTOCK, BITCH!"

A second later, we all lift our heads with our gats cocked and ready to blast back, but the silver SUV is gone.

"Who in the fuck was that?"

I look down at the piece of paper in my hand and laugh. "You know what, ladies? I think that we can do business together."

Justice

35

Essence

August . . .

"She's in a mental hospital?" Profit asks with his face twisting in pain. From the moment he was pulled off the respirator, he's been asking about Ta'Shara nonstop. When Lucifer and Fat Ace can't distract him or get his mind focused solely on getting better, they turn to me to give him the bad news.

"I'm sorry," I tell him. "But she sort of checked out. The doctors say that she may snap out of it at any time or she . . ."

"Can remain that way for the rest of her life," he finishes my sentence, and then turns his gaze back up to the hospital ceiling.

I get uncomfortable at the sight of tears rolling out of the corners of his eyes, but for the first time, I think I actually *get* it. After months of telling Ta'Shara that she was crazy for risking her life to be hooking up with this boy, I think I understand what she couldn't explain.

And I'm jealous.

"I want to see her," Profit says after a long silence. "I called her parents, but Mr. Douglas screamed at me for not telling them that I was in a gang, and then he said something about polishing me off if I ever even think about seeing Ta'Shara again. Funny, huh? I'm lying in this hospital because of her sister and yet somehow *I* get blamed."

He sucks in a deep breath and then swipes at his tears. "I couldn't do anything. There were just too many of them and . . . they made me watch. How? How could she do something like that to her own *sister?*"

"First you'd have to understand that LeShelle isn't exactly human. She'll do anything to stay on top, and you two together threatened that for her. I tried to warn Ta'Shara, but she clearly kept remembering a different sister than the one she has now."

Profit shakes his head as more tears roll. "At one point, Ta'Shara stopped fighting. The look on her face . . . I'll never forget it as long as I live."

Without thinking, I reach over and squeeze his hand. I want to say something, but what? I saw Ta'Shara that night—I saw what those muthafuckas did to her body. I can't begin to imagine having to go through anything like that, let alone live with the knowledge that my own flesh and blood ordered the deed done.

"Right now I wish that I could explain to her foster parents what really happened that night."

"Please don't blame them. They're really hurt right now. I'm sure if they knew that I was a Queen G, they would ban me, too."

Profit tilts his head. "Hey, maybe you can get me in to see her?"

"Me?" I blink stupidly at him. "I don't know about that."

"What? Why not? You're on the guest list—you can get me in."

I throw my hands up and shake my head. "No, no. I'm already in over my head in this shit. I don't like the fact that two of the meanest bitches on the street even know my fuckin' name, and now you want me to risk getting put on the Douglas's shit list, too?"

Profit levels his puppy-dogs eyes on me and then flashes me his cute dimples. "Please? I have to see her."

I shake my head, but I'm already caving—and he knows it.

Two hours later, I get Profit situated in a hospital wheelchair. Since there is no way I'm going to get him past the two large Vice Lords posted outside the door, we included them in our scheme to take him over to the mental hospital to see Ta'Shara. Frankly, I didn't think either of them would go for it, but clearly the VL soldiers have developed a weak spot for Profit and actually help me get him past the nurses' station and drive us to the hospital.

The entire time, I'm calling myself every name in the book. I know that continuing to be involved in all this is dangerous, but here my dumb ass is, hanging with the Vice Lords more now than with my own set. That shit is not good.

"Stop beating yourself up," Profit says, snickering. "No woman can say no to this face."

"I see all those bullets didn't do shit to your fucking ego," I say.

He laughs and I have to admit that I like its rich sound. During the short drive, I can't stop sneaking looks over at him. His six-foot-three frame is leaner than usual, and he looks white instead of his usual honey color, but none of that takes away from him being fine as hell. While I'm staring, he glances over at me and smiles.

"What?" he asks.

"Huh? Oh. Nothing." Feeling the heat in my face, I jerk my gaze back around so I can pay attention to the road.

There's a weird silence between us for a couple of miles before Profit says, "If I haven't said it already, I really want to thank you for being here these last few months. I know this shit has put you in an awkward position between the sets."

"You have no idea."

"Are you kidding me? I've met LeShelle. I have more than a *damn* good idea, but I'll tell you what—her ass needs to be checking for me, 'cause I'm coming after that ass. I done told my brother and Lucifer to step back off that bitch. I personally want to handle this shit."

I draw in a deep breath and shake my head.

"What?"

"This is how this shit keeps going. A nigga shoots one nigga and then his family come hard at the shooter to take him out. But then that family gets pissed and wants revenge, so they come in hard after that family, and on and on and on it goes. The shit never stops. We stay at war.

"And you want to talk about scary? How about that bitch Lucifer? What the hell is up with her? I toss her a few names and she goes after muthafuckas by cutting off their dicks and shoving them down their throats? That's sick."

Profit shrugs. "She likes doing wet work. Other than that, she's a sweetheart."

"Right. These bitches out here are as crazy as the niggas, if not more so. It's like they got something to prove. Like you don't need balls to have balls."

He laughs, but this time it annoys me.

"What's so fucking funny?"

"You. If you feel that way about it, why the hell are you a Queen G?"

"Because I was born into this shit," I snap. "That's why and I'm sick of it. And after seeing what happened to my girl Ta'Shara . . ." I shake my head. "I got to get the hell up out of here." I glance back over Profit. "That used to be Ta'Shara's goal until she met you."

Profit's large caramel-colored eyes look wet. "So you think this shit is all my fault, too?"

"I didn't say that."

"Actually you did. If Ta'Shara never hooked up with me, then she wouldn't be sitting in a crazy hospital right now."

What the hell am I supposed to say to that shit? No, I didn't intend to say it, but the truth is the truth, right?

We squash the conversation and ride the rest of the way to the hospital in silence. Once we park, Profit's guardians climb out of their SUV and help me get Profit back into the wheelchair so I can roll him into the hospital.

The receptionist pulls her nose out of a book as we stroll in. Her eyes widen at the sight of the two big niggas strolling in behind me. "Uh, hello, Ms. Blackmon. You're here late."

"Yeah. Busy day," I say, signing my name on the guest list.

"Are all them with you?" the woman asks.

"No. Just my brother here," I say, and then flash the bodyguards a sweet smile. "You two don't mind waiting out here, do you?"

They glance at each other.

"It's cool," Profit says, and gives them a look that tells them to chill.

They still look like they want to argue, but the biggest muthafucka bucks his head at me and says, "Thirty minutes." He pulls back his jacket so I can see his gat in his waistband. "After that, we come in to get you."

I roll my eyes and then resume pushing Profit toward Ta'Shara's room. Halfway down the hallway, I can tell that Profit is getting anxious by the way he keeps shifting around in his chair.

When we reach Ta'Shara's room, I peek inside first and see that she's still sitting in the dark in a chair next to the window and staring out at the city. It's like time is standing still for her.

"Is she in there?" Profit asks.

"Yeah. C'mon." I hip bump the door and then roll Profit in backward. I go to hit the light switch.

"No," Profit barks, and then softens his voice by saying,

"Leave it off." He cocks his head and then proceeds to roll himself over to the window.

I glance at Ta'Shara to see if Profit's voice pulled her out of whatever shocked state that she's in, but she doesn't even move. Standing silently by the wall, I watch as Profit rolls to a stop beside her chair.

"Shara?" he whispers softly. "Can you hear me, baby?" He takes one of her hands and presses a kiss against the back of it. "Oh, baby. Please snap out of it. I don't know what I'll do if you don't come back to me."

Tears roll down my face at a clip that is fucking embarrassing. At the same time, I can't get myself to look away.

"I'm so sorry, baby." Profit's voice is choked with emotion. "This shit is all my fault. I should've protected you better. I should've . . . fought harder . . . I should've . . ." He presses her hand back against his lips, kisses it, and then drenches her hand with his tears. "Come to me, baby. I promise I'm going to set all this shit right. I'm going to prove that I can protect and love you the way you deserve to be loved. Come back to me."

Profit brushes Ta'Shara's hair back over her shoulder so that he can stare at her in the moonlight. "I love you," he whispers over and over again. "Please come back to me."

36

Momma Peaches

It's time.

I've been putting this shit off for far too long. I can't believe my ass is nervous, too. However, this morning, I wake up knowing in my heart that today is the day I need to see Isaac. For weeks now, I've let that last argument with Terrell fuck with me. Yeah, I'm sorry that I blew up at him, but shit. He hurt my fuckin' feelings, and that shit doesn't happen often. I'm wrong for jumping on him when all he did was spit the truth.

Cedric senses my change in mood, and even after a good dicking down, I'm not even in the mood for flapjacks. "Are you ever going to tell me what's up?" he asks, sipping on his coffee and staring at me from across the table.

"Nothing's up. I got a lot of shit I got to do today."

"What kind of shit?"

I stab him with a sharp look.

"Look. I ain't trying to get in your business or nothing. It's just that you've been walking around with your bottom lip mopping the floor. C'mon, talk to me."

Staring into those beautiful green eyes, I want to crack my chest open and confess everything, but now ain't the time.

"Later," I tell him, getting up. "Right now I got to get over to the Big House."

Cedric's thick brows jump up, but he doesn't say shit when I finally turn to get my purse and car keys.

An hour later, my ass is sitting in a metal chair, waiting for my husband to be led into the visiting room. For the hundredth time, I'm thinking my ass should've smoked something to relax my nerves before I rolled up in here.

At last the doors open, and a stream of niggas are directed into the room. My eyes zoom to the nigga who still holds the biggest part of my heart: Isaac. Six-five with shoulders the size of mountains and there isn't an ounce of fat to be seen nowhere. His muscled thighs and arms have me itching to stand up and rip my muthafuckin' clothes off right here and now—fuck the consequences.

Ain't that the damn reason I've put up with his bullshit for so damn long? Yeah, he did a lot of good shit, too, but his ass was careless when it came to handling my heart. I ain't mad because his ass used to slang or gangbang with the best the streets had to offer. Neither one of us wrote the rules on how to survive out here. But I do fault his ass for whispering those sweet lies into my ears night after night. I'm equally mad at myself for believing them.

"Well, well, well. If it ain't my baby girl. You've come out to see me, huh?" Isaac's eyes twinkle like black diamonds as he settles down into his chair behind the Plexiglas. "You're looking good, Peaches. Then again, you always did take good care of yourself."

"Thanks. You look good, too," I say, raking my gaze over his shaved head and remembering what it used to feel like when I gripped the back of that muthafucka when he was fuckin' the shit out of me. I look around and complain, "Goddamn. It's hot in this bitch."

Isaac chuckles. "Yeah. I miss you, too. Believe I'm counting the days until I get some of that homemade peach pie."

I roll my eyes, but my damn smile remains in place. He has that effect on me.

"I've been hearing some disturbing things from the street. How's Terrell holding up?"

"Like a soldier," I tell him, not wanting to get too into that shit in case muthafuckas are listening.

Isaac bobs his head, while a half smile slopes one side of his mouth. "Good. Glad to hear that shit. The war behind these damn bars is as heated as it is out there on the streets. These fuckin' hooks in here are strutting with they chests all out because I hear some bitch has been taking out a lot of Terrell's crew."

I shake my head. "Look, I didn't come up here to rehash all that gang bullshit. I've come to talk to you about some other shit—our bullshit, as a matter of fact." If my getting heated bothers him, it doesn't show on his face.

"A'ight. Say what's on your mind."

I shut down. My throat closes the fuck up.

Isaac cocks his head. "What? Am I supposed to be a fuckin' mind reader now?"

"Fuck you, Isaac."

"Hell. I wish you could. Maybe it would work out some of that stress in your face."

"The stress I feel right now, baby boy, is all on you."

"What the hell have I done from behind bars that's supposedly causing you stress now?"

"Don't be an ass. It's what you did *before* you got in here. It's what you did the entire time we were together."

"Aw, shit. Not this again."

"Yes, this shit again. It's about all those fuckin' bitches you fucked in all those other area codes that I let slide."

"Look, Peaches. I've apologized for all that shit. What else do you want me to say? Shit. I'm a man, and a man has fuckin' urges and needs that you and all those man-hating bitches out there will never understand. So if you ain't got shit else to do but be sitting up in the house and getting mad about shit that happened *years* ago, then you do you, boo. Personally, I don't want to fuckin' hear about it no goddamn more." He jumps up out of his seat and starts to head to the door.

"Get your ass back over here, nigga. I ain't finished talking to you."

Isaac, as well as every nigga up in here, whips his head around.

"Y'all mind y'all's fuckin' business," Isaac barks.

Everybody turns away, but we both know they're watching to see what the fuck he's gonna do.

"A'ight," he says, though I know if he could reach through this damn fake-ass glass right now, he would slap the taste out of my mouth for disrespecting him like this in front of so many people. "Speak your piece, Ma. Clearly you got a lot on your chest." Isaac plops down into his chair.

I take another moment to try and calm down, but at this point, it's impossible. "I need a simple yes or no."

A muscle twitches along Isaac's jaw as he folds his arms. "A'ight."

Heart hammering, I lock gazes with my love, my husband, and pray like hell that I'm wrong in my suspicion. "Are you Mason's father?"

37

Essence

"**Y**ou're in over your head," Cleo says.

I plop two peanut butter and jelly sandwiches down on the cluttered dining room table and holler, "Jamie, Kay, come and eat!"

Cleo switches her hips and folds her arms as she glares at me. "E, don't fuckin' ignore me. I'm serious about this shit. You've been rolling up there to that damn hospital long enough. That nigga ain't your problem, and I'm sorry to say, but your girl Ta'Shara is as fucked up in that damn mental hospital."

I cut my eyes over at her as the kids run to the table.

Cleo throws her hands up. "Sorry, but I'm keeping it one hundred. Stop running your ass up there, tryna play inch high private eye for LeShelle. The girl is our leader and shit, but everybody knows her lightbulb ain't screwed in too tight. When you deal with crazy, you get crazy."

"I know that," I say, shaking my head. "But it ain't like I got a choice."

Kobe strolls his ass into the mix. "Fuck. Niggas always got choices. You got to learn how to make the right ones."

Cleo gestures toward our brother like, *See?*

I roll my eyes and try to storm away from the table, but my sister blocks my path.

"We ain't done talking," she says, rocking her neck.

"I don't know why. I done said all I have to say."

"And what's that? I'm a stupid muthafucka? Is that what you're saying? Because that's what I'm hearing." Cleo turns toward Kobe. "What about you, brah?"

"Not only that but you have 'Re-Re' stamped across your forehead."

Insulted, I reach over and pop him on the arm. "I'm not *retarded*!"

"Then how about you stop acting like it?"

Like a couple of parakeets, Jamie and Kay start pounding their hands on the table and chanting with their mouths stuffed with peanut butter. "RE-RE! RE-RE! RE-RE!"

I mush Jamie in the back of the head. "Y'all shut the hell up and eat your lunch."

The kids giggle while I roll my eyes and try to get past my sister, but she and Kobe still ain't budging.

"C'mon, y'all. I got to get going if I'm gonna go."

"That's the whole fuckin' point," Cleo says, now mushing me in the center of my forehead. "You ain't going no more. Game is game, but family is family and I'm putting my foot down on this."

I grind my teeth.

Cleo looks ready to whup my ass. "You can catch an attitude all you want, lil girl, but I'm doing this to save your hardheaded ass. I ain't gonna be the one to tell Grandma that your ass is in the morgue because of some other bitch's bullshit."

Kobe shakes his head. "I can't figure out why those crooked hooks let you stroll up in the hospital to see that nigga any damn way. How the fuck you gettin' a Vice Lord pass?"

His boys in the living room playing on the PlayStation pause their shit and eyeball me in my damn mouth.

"Like I said, they know that I'm best friends with Ta'Shara.

Everybody knows how Profit loves her ass, so they're letting me slide."

Kobe's eyes snap back so fast it's a wonder they ain't rolling around on the floor. "That sounds like some weak-ass bullshit to me."

"Exactly," Cleo says, shaking his head. "Either those niggas are playing you or you're tryna play LeShelle. Either mutha-fuckin' way, you're going to come up shorter than you already are."

"Yeah," Kobe cosigns. "That's going to bring heat over to this crib, and it's time-out for all of that bullshit. I ain't having it. Fuck. Did you forget how they found Treasure, Mario, Killa Kyle?" He grips his shit as he shakes his head. "That shit was fuckin' foul."

Heat burns up the side of my face. I'm the one who served those bastards up to Lucifer, and I ain't sorry about that shit. Not one damn bit.

Cleo's eyes narrow on me, and for a split second I'm scared the bitch can hear my thoughts. "What's the fuckin' problem? You've peeped in on him for months. Surely that's enough to satisfy LeShelle. Tell her that the Vice Lords canceled your free pass and get the fuck on."

"Shit," Kobe says. "If they hit Treasure and Mario, them niggas already know LeShelle was behind the attempted hit on their man. Get your ass up out of this shit."

"I'm not doing this shit for LeShelle," I snap, tired of the sermon.

Cleo's brows jump, but her eyes light up like I confirmed something. "Then who in the hell are you doing it for?"

I hesitate and then blurt out a half-truth. "Ta'Shara."

My sister's face twists. She ain't buying that shit.

Doesn't matter, I'm sticking to that lie for all it's worth. "When I go and talk to Ta'Shara, I feel that hearing about Profit hanging in there is giving her encouragement to do the same thing. I want her to snap out of this shit."

I may as well be talking to a brick wall.

"So excuse me," I say, shoving past them and storming back toward my bedroom. "I don't abandon my friends like you fair-weather muthafuckas." As I pass the living room, I flash all those nosy muthafuckas the bird. "Damn. Why don't y'all take your asses home?"

Two minutes later, I'm cramming my feet into my Nikes when Cleo strolls into our bedroom, clapping her hands. "You need to get out of here and take your ass to Hollywood."

"Will you squash this shit already? I'm tired of talking about it."

"We will when you admit that the real reason you keep creeping your ass over to that hospital is because you're falling for your girl's man."

I stop wiggling my feet into my sneakers and look up at her.

Cleo's smug smile grows bigger. "Yeah. I got your mutha-fuckin' number. If you want to keep your fuckin' secrets, you need to stop talking in your sleep."

I blink at her.

"Close your mouth before flies come flying out of that muthafucka."

Hell, I didn't even know that the muthafucka was open. "What in the hell do you expect me to do when you say some dumb shit like that?" I rebound.

"Uh-huh. Girl, stop playing yourself. Didn't you warn your girl about this same bullshit? What the fuck is it with this nigga that got you two stuck on stupid?"

Silence.

"HUH?!"

"Look, Cleo, I gotta go." I hurry up and get my ass out of there. Pulling out of my grandmomma's driveway, I can't help but note how quiet the street is. No lookout boys, no corner hustlers, and no hoes on patrol.

It's dead out here. A hood ghost town, waiting for night to

fall so some shit can pop off—and our bloody war with the Vice Lords can resume with its regularly scheduled program.

I fly out toward the hospital but then notice my gas tank is sitting on empty. I roll up into a corner station, hoping I got some money in my pocket. I pull behind a rusted-out '72 Buick Electra. I'd know this muthafucking car anywhere. I take a second to look at the nigga pumping gas and can't believe my eyes.

"Drey?"

He turns his head and I still don't recognize his ass. I climb out from behind the wheel and remove my shades. This nigga's face looks like it's been put through a meat grinder.

"What in the hell happened to you?" I rush up to him to get a better look.

Drey sneers or at least I think he's sneering. It's hard to tell since he is missing a left ear, his right eye looks permanently swollen, and his lips look as if they are busted or completely allergic to one another.

"Fuck," he groans, and steps back. "You need to stay the fuck away from me."

I blink. To top it all off, this nigga is missing about four or five teeth. "What the fuck? It ain't like I'm the one who rearranged your face."

"The fuck you didn't." He looks around. "It's because my stupid ass listened to you and helped you with that psycho bitch that those grimy hooks showed up at my muthafuckin' front door. "THEY FUCKIN' TORTURED ME!" he roars.

Muthafuckas turn and look at us. "Damn. Calm down," I say.

"Calm down? Bitch, look at my face! Since they peeped our asses dumping that girl at her front door, they assumed that *I* had something to do with that nigga Profit lying up in the hospital. None of my screaming and bleeding convinced them otherwise."

I suck in a sharp breath, but then as fast remember Lucifer

knowing all about prom night when she snatched me up in the hospital hallway that day. "Fuck."

"Yeah. Fuck." He bounces his head as his one good eye narrows on me. "How the fuck is it that you are walking around looking like the perfect picture of good health? Those niggas didn't come after you?"

"I . . . uh . . ." I can't think of anything to say. I'm certainly not about to spit out the truth. Unfortunately, my lack of defense or a plausible lie only makes him angrier. "You a fuckin' snitching bitch. You sicced those niggas on me, didn't you?"

"What? Don't be stupid. Why would I do that?"

"Something is up. So spit it."

"Yo, nigga. Calm down. I don't know what to tell you. They didn't come at me like that."

"That's the second damn time you done told me to calm down." Drey starts walking toward me, and I start backing up. "I don't believe this shit! I should've put two and two together a long time ago, but I've been too busy trying to learn how to breathe with a collapsed lung. I told your ass that I didn't want to get involved with that bullshit. Now look at me!" He grabs me by the arms and shakes me. "LOOK AT ME!"

His fucked-up eye twitches and shit, and some weird puss oozes out of the scar on his right cheek.

Cringing, I pull away, but Drey's grip tightens to the point he's about to break my arm. "Let me go, goddamn it! Let me go!" I snatch my arm away and then turn to run back to my car, but I pull up short at the figure standing behind me.

"LeShelle."

She smiles. "You've been a bad girl."

Fear chokes off my air supply. "What?"

LeShelle cocks her head. "That's all you got?"

I try to inch my way around her. "Well . . . I don't know what you're talking about."

"Fuck. No wonder you and Ta'Shara are best friends. You

bitches got the same muthafuckin' problem: thinking my ass is stupid."

"Look. I don't know what—"

"Spare me. I had a little talk with your friend Qiana. I know your ass has been double snitching. You gave up my boys Treasure and Mario."

"What?" I desperately glance over at Drey, but he folds his arms and shakes his head. "Wait now. LeShelle—"

"Save it. You done made your fuckin' bed—now lie in that bitch." She snatches the gas pump out of Drey's tank and then hoses my ass down with gasoline.

The strong fumes singe my nostrils and burn my eyes but not so much that I don't realize that I need to get my ass away from this crazy bitch. I break away and run back toward my car.

"Where the fuck you going, E?" LeShelle rushes behind me.

I hop behind the wheel and turn the key, but my car stalls.

"Run, rat, run!" LeShelle laughs.

I turn the key again and then hit the button for the power window.

"I got something for your snitching ass." LeShelle flicks on a lighter and tosses the muthafucka.

I watch in horror as it stays lit and sails through my window.

"NO! NO! NO!"

WHOOOSH!!

38

Momma Peaches

"What the fuck are you talking about?" Isaac thunders, throwing his weight back against his chair and mean mugging me like I've lost my mind.

"It's a simple question," I say, and go back to holding my breath.

"I ain't answering that bullshit," he barks. "That's what you brought your ass down here for? You wanna sweat me about some bullshit that floats around in your mind?"

I can't help but laugh. "Is this seriously how you want to play this?"

He twists in his seat and looks everywhere but in my face.

A sharp pain stabs me in the center of my chest. "You know what? You ain't even got to say shit. How you actin' is all the confirmation I need."

Isaac shakes his big, bald head as if by doing that shit he can avoid taking responsibility for the dirt he wallowed in while he was roaming the streets.

"Look. I'm far from stupid, Isaac. And it ain't like I don't know that your ass was addicted to pussy the entire time we were together. Me walking in on you and Josie was confirmation enough that you didn't have any kind of respect for me."

"And what about you? You gonna tell me that you weren't

dishing your dirt? You got that pussy on lockdown while I'm up in this bitch, serving my bid?"

"Hell fucking naw. I'm getting plenty of dick, fuck you very much. And don't change the muthafuckin' subject. While you were out here like every other ho on patrol, did you knock up my sister? Yes or no?"

"I don't fuckin' know!" he shouts.

We stare at each other while his words linger between us for a full minute.

"You don't fuckin' know?" I repeat. "But you *do* know whether or not you put your dick into my sister, right?"

Isaac sucks in an impatient breath, but then finally leans forward and plants his elbows on the counter. "Peaches . . . it was a long time ago. The shit didn't mean nothing to me."

"FUCK. YOU." I jump up from my chair and slam my fist against the Plexiglas. "Be glad this muthafucka is here because I would seriously fuck you up!"

The guards jump to attention. Two come charging up behind me and grab me before my fists fly again. "You worthless piece of shit. I fuckin' hate your ass."

Isaac is on his feet, staring at me like I've really lost it.

Meanwhile, I keep hollering. I have to do something to avoid the guilt that is threatening to crush my chest in. Of all people, Isaac *knew* how fragile my sister was. I had poured my heart out to him about how guilty I've always felt for the part I played in her being raped when she was a teenager. I told him through my tears about my struggle of dealing with her drug problems and juggling that with taking care of my ailing grandmother. I shouldered the burden of caring for Terrell while she was doing God knows what with God knows who. And he what, ran his ass over there and possibly put another baby on her?

"Where's Mason, Isaac?" I shout while being dragged backward. "What the fuck did you do with Mason?"

"I didn't have shit to do with that bullshit," he shouts back with his own guards trying to extract him from the room.

"Bullshit!" How the fuck can I believe anything this nigga says now? All these fucking years, he never once said or acknowledged that maybe it was *his* son who had gone missing. Never once did he even try to look for him. He watched me day after day go crazy, wondering where that poor child could be. Who Alice sold him to or what sick bastard stole him out of his home.

All these years, I let my fucking heart ignore and dismiss a whole lot of things because . . . what? What the hell was I thinking? I can't even remember anymore. By the time I'm back at my car, I'm literally sick to my stomach. For all my fucking street smarts, how come I always pick the worst men? Why have I always picked liars, addicts, and rapists?

I sit there a long fucking time, feeling sorry for myself before my mind drifts back to the man I got waiting for me at home. Cedric. Sure he's the son of my first love and technically my parole officer, but at least he's got his shit together. He ain't out here in these streets chasing fifteen cents and slinging bullets around like life is one big-ass video game. No. He's a grown-up.

"And he loves me." I lift my head and meet my eyes in the rearview mirror. "*And* he wants to marry me," I remind myself. Though I seriously doubt my ass really wants to get married again, I do feel better knowing that I got somebody at home who cares for me.

"Fuck you, Isaac." I start the car, flip the prison building the bird, and then blaze up out of there.

By the time I get to Shotgun Row, I'm feeling a little more like my old self. I push Isaac and all his lies to the back of my mind as I park and climb out of the car. In case Betty or Josie is hanging around, I push on a smile so that those haters don't get the ghetto grapevine going.

However, as I stroll up the porch steps, I get this weird feeling churning in my belly, and the hairs on the backs of my arms and neck stand up. When I push open the door, those feelings only intensify.

"Cedric?" I call out, shutting the front door behind me. "Baby, I'm back." I move through the house. *Maybe he's taking a nap?*

I hold still for a second and then strain my ears to catch any strange sounds. The whole thing gives me a sense of déjà vu as I creep toward the bedroom. Yet, when I step into the bedroom, I see Cedric stretched out on the floor with blood pooling around his head. "Shit!"

Rushing over to him, I drop down to check and see if he's even breathing. But the minute I touch him, I know he's gone.

"Oh, fuck, fuck, fuck." *I need to go get help.* I jump to my feet and turn, but then gasp aloud when I see this bitch standing behind me.

"Hello, Maybelline."

Despite the long silver hair, recognition settles in. "Alice?"

She gives me a thin smile. "Glad to know that you remember me."

Before I can say another fucking word, this bitch swings and hits me with something so hard that it knocks me the fuck out.

39

LeShelle

The small spikes on my chain collar dig into my skin and intensifies the pleasure coursing throughout my body while Python focuses on tearing up my G-spot from the back. It's been a hot minute since his ass has handled this pussy the way I like it, but he's on his muthafuckin' job now.

"Your ass is always talking shit," Python growls, and reaches around to tug and twist one of the heavy nipple clamps locked onto my titties. "Now look at you. You're loving this dick, ain't you?"

"Awwww, shit," I moan. I can't do much either, since my hands are handcuffed behind my back.

Python switches it up and jerks the chain on my collar. My neck is pulled back while those spikes dig in deeper. "Uh-huh. Your ass needs to be trained again. Lately you've been rolling around this muthafucka thinking your ass got the bigger dick."

I try to answer, but I feel a powerful nut rising all the way up from my big toe. "Aw, shit," I repeat, ready to pass out from both the pleasure and the pain.

"Ain't that right, baby? You think your ass has a dick bigger than mine?"

Fuck, yeah.

Python pulls the chain harder. No doubt my ass has blood oozing beneath my collar. Still, I don't want to answer his question. I want to hold out for as long as I can because I'm addicted to pain. I don't know how it happened or when it happened, but it did. I'm no longer that little girl who used to cry herself to sleep at night with her panties full of blood. Where I once was weak, I now am strong.

Two more hard strokes and I'm screaming up toward the ceiling while honey gushes down my legs and around his cock.

"Did I tell your ass to come?" Python asks, sliding out of my wet trenches and slapping the back of my ass with it. "Hmm? You think you can do whatever the fuck you want to do, huh?"

I turn my head and grin devilishly at him.

He shakes his head. "Yeah. You need to be trained again. There's only room for one muthafucka to be sagging up in this bed." He dips his thick finger into my asshole and twirls that bitch all around. Before I know it, he shoves in another and then another. More honey flows down my leg in anticipation of him cramming in his monster cock and splitting my shit wide open, but Python wants to play some more.

"C'mon. Get your ass up." He stands up from the bed and then drags me by my chain over to the metal hook we got hanging from the ceiling. Next, he hooks my collar onto it and then walks over to the corner of the room and pulls the hook up like a pulley until I'm standing on my tiptoes.

A new level of pain shoots throughout my body, and my clit thumps in double time. "Ahhhhh."

"Yeah. Yeah. This is much better," he says, locking the chain in place and then stroking his dick as he approaches me again. "Now this is how I should keep your ass, strung up all day every day."

I choke and gag while he picks up a leather riding crop. My heart races while I struggle to stay on my tiptoes.

"Get ready, baby. Because I'm about to light that ass up," he promises. "I want to hear your ass tell me who the fuck wears the pants in this muthafucka." Without even waiting for my ass to respond, he sends that crop flying across my ass.

Smack!

I jump at the burning sting and then lose my balance. My collar digs so deep into my neck that I almost black out.

Python laughs while I scramble to get back on my toes. However, my relief lasts less than a second before the next series of blows takes my breath away.

Smack! Smack! Smack!

My entire ass and thighs feel like they're on fire.

And still I'm coming like a muthafucka. To change it up, Python strolls around in front of me and starts hitting me across the nipples, which are already straining from the weight of the nipple clamps.

Smack! Smack! Smack!

"Sheeiiiit," I yell.

Smack!

"Who's the fuckin' man, Shelle?"

Smack!

"Sheeiiitt." I turn and try to get away from the blows, but it doesn't help. Python is happy to chase me in a complete circle.

Smack! Smack! Smack!

"I'm waiting." He laughs.

Smack! Smack! Smack!

I can't take the shit no more. "You are!"

"Who?" Python presses. "I didn't hear you."

Smack!

"YOU, BABY! You're the man!"

"Damn muthafuckin' straight." He gives me one last, hard smack that literally makes stars dance in front of my eyes.

Still this nigga ain't through. He moves up behind me.

"Spread your legs," he says, using the riding crop to slap in between my thighs until I obey. "Yeah. There you go." He rubs his cock between my legs until it's coated with my pussy's thick honey.

It gets harder by the second to remain on my toes, and every time I slip a little bit, I'm gagging and choking like a bitch seconds from meeting her maker. I can't say that I completely trust this muthafucka not to murk my ass up here, but it's that not knowing that adds to the danger and gets me off.

Python's thick finger pries open my ass cheeks, and then with one thrust, my ass is on fire again.

"Sssssss. Oh." He locks his hands on my hips while I dangle like a slab of beef.

More stars start dancing behind my eyes. My entire body is radiating with pain. "Awwwwww. Awwwww." I'm at my limit. I can't take any more, but I no longer have the ability to beg for mercy. Hell. I barely have the ability to get air into my lungs. Python isn't in any hurry to reach his nut, so the pain just intensifies to a whole new level.

"Sssssss. I fuckin' love your ass, girl," Python hisses, catching my attention. "I don't know why the hell you still fuck with me, but I'm glad you do."

I blink. *What the hell did he say?*

In the next second, he whips his cock out and blasts all over my ass and then smears his warm nut into the skin of my burning ass.

"Sssssssss."

Ten minutes later, I'm unhooked and a funky mess lying across our bed.

"You're a real fuckin' soldier," Python says, leaning over to kiss my shoulder. "You really have proved yourself over and over again."

"Glad you recognize."

"I've recognized it for a long time, but . . . bullshit clouded my judgment."

Bullshit named Melanie Johnson. I roll my eyes.

"Anyway, I made a promise to your ass, and I'm a man of my word." He reaches for the chain attached to the collar around my neck and removes something from the end. "This is for you. You earned it, baby."

Stunned, I stare at a beautiful diamond ring.

A smile hitches the side of his face. "Let's do this shit."

"Fuck, yeah." I jut out my left hand so that he can slide this fat rock onto it. While I'm doing this, my heart is racing like a muthafucka.

"You happy now?"

Fuck, yeah. But I tell him, "Not until I get yo ass in front of a minister and say 'I do.' "

"Just like a woman—never satisfied."

"What the fuck ever," I sass back, and then lean in to suck on his bottom lip to get round two started. "Chronic" starts bumping from his cell phone. I groan because this shit keeps happening. "Let it go to voice mail," I tell him.

"Sorry, Ma. Business before pleasure." He rolls to the other side of the bed and picks up his cell.

"Talk to me."

I sit up and hold my hand out to admire my ring again. *This shit is finally going to happen.*

"WHAT?"

I jump at Python's roar and then start scrambling out of bed in case it's time for me to grab my gat and haul ass.

"I'm on my fuckin' way," he says, and springs up out of the bed, too. When he hangs up, he announces, "Something's gone down at Momma Peaches's. Stay here."

"No. I'll come with you."

"Nah. I need you to stay with Lil Man. I'll be back once I know something." He snatches up his clothes.

"But—"

"STAY HERE!"

Before I can say shit else, his ass blazes out of here like there's a fire lit under it. Once I hear the front door slam, I roll my eyes and shake my head. Then my attention is drawn back to the ring on my finger. I know just the person I want to see this muthafucka.

40

Yolanda

My babies Malcolm, Amin, and Vivian act like they don't re-member me. That shit has thrown me for a loop as I watch them run around the park. They each treat me like I'm a stranger trying to offer them bad candy or some shit.

"Don't worry," Ms. Terry says. "Give them more time."

I cut my gaze back at her as she sits next to me on the park bench. "Don't play me. Y'all got to be turning them against me. Malcolm and Amin are six and seven. Why wouldn't they remember me?"

"They remember. They were five and six when the state took them. They're not going to make it easy for you." Ms. Terry sighs. "Vivian is another story. She's probably following her brothers' lead on this."

I shake my head and cross my arms. "This is some bullshit."

Ms. Terry draws in a deep breath. "Look, Ms. Turner. I know this is hard on you, but you got to know that it's even harder on them. So far your children have been bounced around from one foster home to another. Your boys are show-ing signs of ADHD in school and lean toward violence when they don't get their way in certain situations."

"Yeah, yeah. I'm a bad mother. I got it." I roll my eyes up to the sky, but it's not enough to stop the tears from streaking down my face. I'm a complete fuckup, with my kids, with Python, and even with taking out LeShelle's evil ass. *Shit. I can't do nothing right. Let everybody else tell it.*

"Ms. Turner, are you all right?"

"Yeah." I backhand the tears off my face and return my attention to my children. Despite ignoring me, they look like they're having a great time running around chasing each other. Little Vivian is holding her own. Now more than ever, I'm happy that I named her after Baby Thug. Even though there's no blood relation, it's still a little reminder that Baby was once here.

Vivian's big brown eyes settle on me before she races across the grass to come and talk with me.

"Careful," I say. "You don't want to fall down."

"Malcolm says that we're going home with you," Vivian says, sounding way more grown than her three and half years.

"Well . . . not yet," I tell her. "I'm working on it."

"If you're our momma, why can't we go home with you?"

I glance over at Ms. Terry, looking for some help, but she just quietly folds her arms and lets me handle the question.

"It's a long story," I tell Vivian.

My little girl blinks up at me like she has nothing but time to wait for my answer. "Well, Momma just had a little problem being able to . . . afford taking care of y'all right now."

"I got some money in my piggy bank," she says. "I can give you some."

"That's sweet of you, honey. But you go ahead and keep your money. Okay?"

Vivian twists up her face. "What? You don't want us, then?"

"Of course I do. I didn't say that."

"Uh-huh."

More tears spring to my eyes while shame spreads throughout my body. My ass has been out in these streets, worried about the wrong things—locking down soldiers and trying to become the head Queen G.

"Malcolm says that you're about to have another baby," Vivian continues, interrogating me and staring at my belly.

"Yeah. I am. In the next few weeks."

"Is it going to be a boy or a girl?"

"The doctors say it's going to be another boy."

Vivian pokes out her bottom lip. "I hate boys. Can you send it back and get a girl? I want a sister."

Ms. Terry and I laugh. "Sorry. That's not how it works."

"Is he going to come live with us at foster care, too?"

Stunned, I suck in a breath. "I . . . uh . . ." Now how do I tell her no when I just told her that I couldn't afford children?

"Vivian, why don't you go back and play with your brothers some more?"

"Okay." She shrugs and then takes off back toward the jungle gym.

"Sorry about that," Ms. Terry says, reaching over and touching my hand. "Are you okay?"

"Yeah. I'm fine."

"You have to know that you're going to be getting a lot of questions like this from them in the future."

I nod, even though Vivian's question cracked open my chest and yanked out my heart.

"Ms. Turner?"

"Yeah." I sniff. "I'm fine. It's okay."

"Look. You're doing the right things now. You're going to classes, putting in face time with the children. Everything is going to be fine. You'll see."

"Thanks. But . . . I don't need for you to blow smoke up my ass. The chances that a judge will give me my kids back are damn near zero. Muthafuckas don't believe in giving people like me second chances. And look at them." I gesture toward the kids playing. "They look a lot happier now than they ever did with me. They're eating; they have on decent clothes—"

"C'mon. Don't put yourself down," she urges, scooting closer to me and wrapping her arm around my shoulder. "I ain't going to lie and say that this is going to be a walk in the park for you, but it can be done. And damn near zero ain't zero. You can do this. I've seen others do it. Keep doing your best. The rest will take care of itself."

I can't believe it, but I actually take comfort in her words. For a few brief seconds, I actually believe that I can pull this shit off.

Before I know it, my two hours are up and Ms. Terry calls the kids to her minivan.

"All right, now. I'm still going to see you in my office on Monday, right?"

"Right." I swipe my eyes dry and then turn my attention to my children. "Now, y'all give your momma a hug. I stretch out my arms, and Vivian is the first to try to stretch her arms around my big belly. They don't even get halfway around, but I do manage to lean over and press a kiss against her chubby cheeks. I have to step to Amin and brush a kiss against his forehead while he looks everywhere but at my face. Malcolm stands back with his arms folded and his eyes daring me to step to him.

"What? You're not going to say good-bye to me?"

"Bye," Malcolm says with a big attitude.

"C'mon. Give me a hug and a kiss like your brother and sister."

"No. I don't want to."

I lower my arms while my eyes burn again. "All right. If you don't want to, then . . . I guess I understand."

Without sparing me another look, he marches right past me and climbs into the minivan.

Ms. Terry closes the door and tosses me another sad look. "It'll get better. Give him some more time."

"Sure." I stand there while she walks around to the driver's side and then climbs in behind the wheel. When she pulls away from the curb, I'm still standing there, waving. Amin and Vivian wave back while Malcolm ignores me.

Once the van is out of view, I lower my hand and place it against my belly. "Please, please, say that you'll never hate me." I draw a deep breath and then turn toward my silver Terrain. Opening the car door, I plop into the driver's seat, and my heart stops at reading the Post-it note on the steering wheel.

Ticktock.

41

Lucifer

All is well.

Ever since Profit opened his eyes, Mason is back to being the leader our people love and respect. As a result, the Vice Lords have ramped up the war on the streets and are moving niggas off GD blocks that they had long held down on the south side. Thanks to Bishop tracking Python's ass for the past three weeks, we know where this nigga does his business, who all his lieutenants are and where they live, and even some of Python's resting places around town. Nigga got so many damn baby mommas, it makes my head spin.

Tonight we're going to take it to these niggas hard. Go at them with everything we got and rip the heart out of the GD's stronghold by taking out Python and all his lieutenants on the same night. Mason wants to play with his food for as long as he can by choking off their life blood: the money and their connect. Once that's done, he wants to watch these niggas eat their own.

We still got a couple of hours before the sun goes down and Cousin Skeet rolls through with some new firepower.

Right now, I'm chilling my ass in the tub trying to relax and get my mind right. Now that everything is everything, and we're going to settle all this beef tonight, I keep asking myself, what's next?

How long am I going to be Mason's ride-or-die chick? Is being his right-hand bitch enough for me, or is it time for me to seriously get back down to earth and find something else to do while I'm still able to draw breath and ain't serving no bid nowhere?

Yet, at the same time, I don't want to leave his ass. I can't leave his ass.

Shaking my head, I lean all the way back in the tub and watch as the few remaining bubbles in the water circle around my full titties. *Should I stay or should I go?* My thoughts circle around that question until there's a loud bang on my bathroom door.

"Damn, girl. How long are you going to be in there?" Mason barks.

What the fuck is his ass doing over here? "What the hell do you want?"

"I told you that I wanted to go over this shit one more time before our people roll out tonight. I don't want shit to go wrong."

I roll my eyes. "I'll be out in the minute," I say, and don't even bother to get up.

This muthafucka must have had his ear up to the door because he barges his ass right on in.

"What the fuck?"

Mason looks down at me in the tub, and his eyes instantly land on my bubble-capped titties. "Fuck. Nice rack."

I'm not a shy bitch at all, but my neck and face grow warm beneath his intense stare. "Why don't you take a muthafuckin' picture? It'll last longer."

Grinning, Mason scoops out his cell phone and does exactly that.

"Nigga, is you crazy?" I push myself up and stand. Water

and bubbles cascade down my curves. "Hand me my towel," I tell him.

Mason doesn't move.

My annoyance chills a bit at noticing his reaction to my naked body. After a few seconds, I settle my hand on my hips and strike a pose. "Are you through?"

A smile curves up the side of Mason's face. "Damn, girl. Just . . . damn."

I step out of the tub and walk over to him. When I'm inches away, I reach and brush my left wet titty against his arm and grab my towel. "Thanks for nothing."

"No. Thank *you*." His mismatched eyes roam over me while his face softens.

The thing is, I'm willing to let whatever is flowing between us happen, because despite having the towel in hand, I don't attempt to dry off or cover up. After another couple of seconds pass, Mason reaches up and removes my elastic twisty and lets my hair fall down around my shoulders.

Still neither of us says anything while he combs his thick, meaty fingers through my hair. One thing's for sure—the air in my chest gets thinner and the butterflies in my stomach flutter around like they're on crack.

When his gaze finishes mapping out every inch of my body, our eyes lock.

"You're fuckin' beautiful. Do you know that?"

I reach up and touch the side of his face, brushing my fingers against the small scar beneath his milky eye, and say with all honesty, "So are you."

Together, we lean forward until our mouths connect. Instantly this warm feeling seeps into my soul, and it heats up into a fire and then sweeps through my body. My towel falls to the floor while I wrap my hands around his thick neck. I press my wet body against his hard frame, and before I know it, there's more than water making me wet. He gets no protests from me when two of his fingers slide down both sides of my throbbing clit. In fact, all I can do is quiver. No shit. I've been starving for his touch for so long that the second his slippery fingers brush over the top of my clit, I come unglued.

"Ooooh, Mason," I moan, dragging my lips from his and then tilting my head all the way back.

With my neck exposed, Mason peppers kisses all up and down the column. I've never pegged myself as the romantic type, but I swear my head is blown while his hands and mouth cast a spell on me.

"God," Mason whispers as his mouth drifts toward my left earlobe. "Why didn't we do this shit a long time ago?"

"You tell me," I answer, tugging on his baggy jeans and working them off his hips.

He sucks in a ragged breath while his mouth dives down and captures one of my rock-hard nipples in his mouth. Mason doesn't just suck on them; he does this nice, gentle biting and chewing that drives my ass wild. By the time my hand wraps around his thick cock, I'm convinced that I know what it's like to be a crack addict. I need this man inside of me now in the worst way, and I don't think I'm above selling my soul to make it happen.

Mason turns me so that I'm backed up against my bathroom sink. In the next second, he spreads my legs open and kneels down before me. Before I can take advantage of the fresh oxygen, Mason's thick tongue slaps against my clit.

"Fuck." My hands grip the sink while I reflexively prop my legs up around Mason's head. Now, I've had my share of head jobs, but the tornado action this nigga touches down on my shit has me feeling like Dorothy spinning her ass all the way to the land of Oz.

"Shit. Shit." I need him to slow down so I can catch my breath, but I can't get myself to pull my hands away from the sink for fear that my ass will fall down and embarrass myself.

Yet, at the same time, if I don't do something about his unmerciful tongue slapping my clit around, I'm really going to embarrass myself by screaming like a banshee.

"Awwwwwwwww." I take a chance and rip my hands away from the sink to lock them around his head so I can try to push him back, but that sexy head of his refuses to budge, and I'm hit with one orgasm after another. "Awwww."

By the time Mason ends his assault on my pussy, I'm as limp as a wet noodle and his mouth is glossy like he's finished a whole bucket of fried chicken on his own.

"How you like yo boy now, baby?" Mason stands up, cock in hand while I try to catch my breath. "Hmmmm? You ain't had no shit like that before, have you?"

"You a'ight," I pant with a crooked smile. I ain't about to let this nigga's head get any bigger than it is right now. He can forget that shit.

"A'ight?" He laughs and then locks an arm around my waist. He lifts me up and then slowly slides me down on his cock like we've been doing this shit for years. His shit is so fat that it literally takes my breath away. After watching my mouth drop open and my eyes damn near roll out the back of my head, Mason is back to feeling cocky. "How you like me now, Willow? Hmm? Still think that I'm just a'ight?"

For the first time, I love the way he says my name. I don't feel like the bad chick who needs to be in control or dominated. I feel like . . . a fucking girl. But I do have something up my sleeve for his ass. After a few wonderful strokes, I take full command of my vaginal muscles and lock my shit up.

Mason gasps. His mouth drops into a perfect circle while he squeezes his eyes tight. "FUUUUUCK."

"How you like *me* now?" I use his shoulders for an anchor and then bounce my ass up and down and even throw in a few circles as well. This muthafucka's knees buckle, and he nearly drops my ass. "What's wrong, nigga? Pussy got your tongue?"

"Damn, Willow. Damn."

We tumble to the floor, but that shit doesn't stop our flow.

With my knees planted on both sides of his hips, I lean forward and smother his face with my titties while simultaneously churning his precum into a thick, creamy concoction. My ride on top doesn't last long.

Soon I'm facedown against the linoleum, and Mason is stuffing me from behind. He hammers his hips with the same velocity as he can twirl his tongue. I had no idea that his dick game was this fucking tight. If I had, I might've raped his ass a long time ago. By the time my nut explodes and tries to drown his one eyed–monster, I know for sure that my ass is good and sprung.

I say something about taking this shit to the bed, and the next thing I know, my legs are wrapped around this nigga's waist while he crawls on all fours into the adjoining bedroom.

In bed, our shit gets slow and tender. It's as if we just needed to get those first couple of nuts out of the way. The softer touches and kisses take our minds to a deeper level. We explore each other's bodies like we have all the time in the world. I learn that he doesn't like his nipples sucked, and he learns that there's not a damn thing I don't like. But I do love kissing him on his neck, right against his adorable horseshoe-shaped birthmark. I can tell he loves it, too, by the way his moans deepen. We eventually pass out—but not for long.

Bang! Bang! Bang!

My bedroom door vibrates.

"Lucifer," Bishop shouts through the door. "Have you seen Mason?"

Mason and I pop up and then glance at each other.

Bang! Bang! Bang!

"Boy, if you don't stop pounding on my door!"

"Well, have you seen him?"

I stare at Mason for a hint as to what he'd like me to say,

but his face is as blank as mine. When I open my mouth, Mason cuts me off. "I'm in here, man."

That apparently gives Bishop permission to waltz into my room, but he gets more than an eyeful when he sees me and Mason, naked and tangled up in my funky sheet.

"What you need, my nigga?" Mason asks, pulling me an extra inch closer.

Bishop stands there open-mouthed for a few seconds. A smile curls up at the corners of his mouth. "It's about fuckin' time." He rolls his eyes and starts backing out of the room. "Y'all two hurry the fuck up. Cousin Skeet is on his way over."

Mason and I relax against each other as we bob our heads.

"A'ight. We'll be out in a few," Mason says.

"Mason and Willow kissing in a tree," Bishop sings. "K-I-S-S—"

"Nigga, get out of here!" I throw a pillow and smack him dead in the mouth.

Bishop laughs and then slams the door.

Mason and I look at each other again and grin.

"I guess he approves," Mason says. "This evening is full of surprises."

I laugh but make no move to climb out of the bed.

He doesn't either. "We finally fuckin' did it."

"Yeah, we did."

Mason bobs his head some more and then clears his throat. "And how does it feel?"

"You still fishing for a compliment?"

"No . . . well, yeah, but that shit can come later. What I want to know is how you feel about this shit?"

"Oh. We're about to have 'the talk'?" I laugh to try to hide my nervousness.

"Yeah," he confirms. "I want to know how you feel about this shit. Am I just something to do, or are we going to try and make something happen here?"

"I don't know . . . I mean—"

"What? You ain't got feelings for a nigga?"

"Of course I do. But . . ."

"But?"

"But you did just get out of a . . . situation. And I ain't interested in being a rebound bitch. You feel me?"

"I feel you," he says, leaning forward. "*But* this shit didn't just crop up overnight. I've had feelings for you for a long damn time."

My eyes narrow suspiciously. "You have?"

"Yeah," he answers without hesitation.

"Uh-huh. Whatever happened to 'one bitch is just as good as the next'?"

Mason shakes his head. "C'mon. I was just blowing off steam that night."

I'm going to let him have that. "So why didn't we—"

Bang! Bang! Bang!

"He's here," Bishop shouts.

We sigh in annoyance.

"We'll continue this conversation a little later," Mason promises.

"A'ight."

He leans forward again and kisses me deeply. No shit, I wish that we could lie in this bed forever. We have business to tend to, so we pop out of the bed and rush for a quick shower.

Strolling outside so we can head over to his place a few doors down, we don't quite know what to do with our hands or even know how to behave.

"This shit is going to take some getting used to," Mason says.

"You ain't never lied," I joke.

"There you two are!" a voice booms as we approach Mason's driveway.

My stomach clenches, but this time in disgust. I hate it when we have to do business with this muthafucka.

Mason allows Captain Melvin Johnson to throw his arms around him while I stand back. When the pig shifts his gaze to me, his smile twists slyly.

"Hello, Willow." He throws open his arms. "Where is the love for your old cousin Skeet?"

42

Yolanda

*T*icktock.

I'm paranoid like a muthafucka and peeping around every nook and corner like a crazy bitch now. I thought I was ready for this fight to knock Python's wifey off her throne, but it turns out that I've highly underestimated LeShelle. She has made it clear that she isn't afraid to toe-tag any bitch who gets in her way, and my stupid ass couldn't leave well enough alone. Now what am I supposed to do, walk around with a gat strapped around my big belly everywhere I go? Would she really come at me though I'm still under her man's protection?

Why not? I went at her.

My cell phone buzzes, and when I look down at the screen, I see: Ticktock.

Oh, this bitch is fucking with me now.

Should I call Python and tell him what's going down, or will that have me looking like a whiny bitch who can't handle my own problems?

Better a whiny bitch than a dead one.

You'd think LeShelle would have better things to do now that her sister is in a mental hospital, drooling and staring at a fucking wall. If the shit that's buzzing on the street is to be believed, that bitch is foul for orchestrating her own lil sister's sex-in into the Queen Gs. Then again, I shouldn't be surprised. It's clear that the bitch will do anything to stay on top. What the hell was I thinking putting myself in her crosshairs?

Ticktock.

I feel like a beach ball as I walk up and down the grocery store aisles, looking for something to satisfy all my sweet and sour cravings. And what I end up lugging out of the store is enough junk food to send my ass into a diabetic shock. As I step out into the dark parking lot, the hairs on the back of my neck stand up. *Someone is watching me.*

My nervous gaze darts around, but I don't see anyone lurking in the shadows. I remain paranoid as I head over to my car. I need to stop making these late-night trips. This city isn't safe when the sun goes down. I climb into my SUV and lock the door. I feel a little safer knowing that I have my new gat tucked under the driver's seat. There's a loud *bing* from my purse. Before pulling out of the parking lot, I scoop out my cell phone and check the text message.

Ticktock.

"This fuckin' bitch is getting on my nerves." I toss my cell phone aside and shift the car into gear. But I'm not on the road for more than two minutes before that feeling comes back over me. Now there's a strange anxiousness, and my blood seems to be speeding through my veins, leaving me light-headed. My gaze shoots to my rearview mirror and then to the side mirrors. There are a few cars on the road, but I'm suddenly suspicious of all of them.

"Calm down. This bitch got you tripping." I readjust my sweating hands on the steering wheel and concentrate on hurrying up and getting home. However, no sooner do I shove my paranoia to the back of my head than the black SUV behind me speeds up and rear-ends me.

I jolt forward; my belly rams against the steering wheel. "What the hell?" I look into the rearview when the muthafucka hits me again. "Fuck!" Instead of pulling over, I jam on the accelerator. I almost shit myself when someone springs up from my backseat and presses a gun to my head.

"Ticktock, bitch."

Shocked and scared shitless, I shoot my gaze to the rearview mirror. A pair of dark, sinister eyes glares back at me from beneath a black wool ski mask.

"Pull this muthafucka over," the woman hisses.

Blinking, I don't react. I was expecting it to be LeShelle, but it isn't. "Who are you?"

"I'll splatter your brains all over the fuckin' dashboard if you don't pull this muthafucka over right now!"

I don't doubt her ass for a minute. I ease my foot off the gas and pull the vehicle over. Two things I *don't* do is beg and cry. Once I'm on the side of the road, the other SUV pulls up behind me.

"Look, I don't know what you want, but if you let me go, you can take my purse, my car . . . whatever."

"Shut the fuck up, bitch!"

My door flies open, and the next thing I know I'm being shoved over into the passenger seat. "Ow. My baby. I'm pregnant!"

"No shit," the woman in the backseat says a second before wrapping duct tape around my mouth. After that, she shoves some kind of cloth over my head and presses a gun against the back of my head again. The bitch next to me binds my hands with plastic cuffs that bite into my skin, as someone climbs behind the wheel. By the time we peel off from the side of the road, I can no longer hold back my tears.

They just want to scare me. No way would LeShelle enlist these girls to actually hurt me, especially while I'm still carrying Python's child. That would be too crazy even for her. I rethink that shit after we drive for a long time. These two bitches haven't said another word. A few more minutes pass, and we turn off the main road and onto a rocky path.

A few more minutes tick by and my full bladder bursts. I sit in a puddle of piss while tears stream down my face. The car stops. My two kidnappers jump out and then open my door. I tumble and fall onto sharp rocks. Pain explodes through my body, but I'm unable to scream or push myself up. Are they planning to leave me out here like this—in the middle of nowhere?

I hear tires crunch over the gravel. It must be the other SUV. I'm full-on crying as two women pull and tug me onto my knees.

"What the fuck?" A car door slams and a third woman's voice shouts, "Have y'all done her yet?"

Oh, shit! My mind races as I struggle to get to my feet, but I'm shoved back down. I scream, "Please don't do this," behind my taped mouth to no avail.

"I ain't knocking off a pregnant woman," one says. "That shit is foul. The baby ain't done shit to nobody."

"Count me out, too," another voice says. "Shit. I didn't know this bitch was this far along. I don't understand why we're doing the Queen Gs' dirty work anyway."

Relief sweeps through me but then is snatched away when the third woman says, "I owe that bitch LeShelle a favor for getting rid of Essence, and I pay all my debts. So we're going to do this, but we're going to take some insurance."

"What type of insurance?"

"We'll cut the baby out and take it with us."

My eyes bulge beneath the bag, and I double up on my efforts to get away, but I'm completely and utterly defenseless.

"Hold this bitch down!"

No! No! No!

Cold steel is stabbed into my flesh. My scream breaks through the duct tape, but I drown in a sea of pain as this bitch's blade carves around my belly. Before I slip into nothingness, I hear my baby's cry.

43

LeShelle

You can't keep a good bitch locked up and babysitting miscellaneous bastards. So after strapping Christopher to his bed, I roll over to Memphis Mental Health Institute. I've put off this visit to see Ta'Shara for months, and now that Essence's double-snitching ass is put out of commission, I can refocus my attention on my other problems, two of them being my sister and Profit.

Profit. That lucky muthafucka. I still can't believe his ass is not only alive, but also awake and talking. That's okay. A bitch like me ain't never scared. I'll be waiting for that ass.

Strolling into the hospital, I sign my name on the guest list at the front desk. I'm halfway expecting the bitch behind the counter to take one look at my name and sound off an alarm. Instead, the chick doesn't even pull her eyes out of the magazine she's reading.

"Which room is Ta'Shara Murphy in?" I ask, pressing my luck.

"You'll have to ask one of the nurses at the station," she says, flipping through pages.

Rolling my eyes, I stroll past this lazy bitch and go in search of my sister. It doesn't take long, but when I approach her door, my gaze lands on Tracee. I slow up and roll my eyes. I can't stand this fucking bitch. The last thing I want to do is deal with her ass right now, and if I walk through this door, it's going to be a situation and some fucking furniture moving.

Instead of turning around and walking my ass back out of here, I stand there and watch this bougie bitch bump her gums about nonsense while she knits some crazy-looking thing in her lap. Every once in a while, she looks up at Ta'Shara and strokes her hair as if she were some life-sized doll. Watching the two of them churns my stomach, but still I can't look away.

After a while, tears streak down Tracee's face and she puts her knitting down and rushes toward the door.

I jet toward another room until Tracee blazes past me to get to God knows where. A poke my head out first, glance around to make sure she's gone, and then dip back into the hallway and head into my sister's room.

"Hello, Ta'Shara," I say, closing the door behind me.

She doesn't respond.

Cocking my head, I take a closer look at her. I try to see if I can catch this bitch faking this shit. I ease closer. "Surprised to see me here?"

No response.

Cautious, I move all the way over to the chair Tracee had been sitting in and move her knitting to the bed. Now that I'm up close and personal, I lean into Ta'Shara's face so that I can block her view out of the window.

Nothing. Ta'Shara looks straight through me. It spooks me, and I lean back out of her face. Unexpectedly, guilt rushes through me like a freight train, but then I try to derail that muthafucka by shaking the shit off. "I'm not going to feel guilty about this shit," I tell her. "This is *your* fault. You pushed and pushed." I roll my eyes and suck in another long breath.

Silence.

"I mean, what the fuck did you think was gonna happen,

huh? You thought that I was gonna ignore that you were sleeping with the enemy? I mean, I fuckin' ask soooo little of you, and you . . . you just had to show me your ass."

Silence.

"Whatever. It is what it is," I tell her. "This shit ain't on me. I ain't gonna feel guilty about none of this. And as for your lil nigga, if his ass wants to continue where we left off, that shit is fine with me, too. It'll be a cold day in hell before I'm scared of a fuckin' hook. If he wants to get at me, then he can find my ass right where I belong—at the muthafuckin top." I flash my ring in front of Ta'Shara's face. "Choke on that, bitch. I got my family now. I don't need you anymore."

Silence.

"You hear me? I. Don't. Need. You." I lower my hands and then ball them at my sides. I fight the urge to knock her out of that damn chair.

I want her to acknowledge what I've accomplished on my own. I want her to see that no matter what, my ass is going to land on top. After the silence stretches too long, I move in on her again. "You know what? Maybe you sitting in here like a vegetable is the best thing for me all the way around. At least this way you're out of my hair. I don't have to look after your ungrateful ass anymore." Clenching my jaw, I suck in an angry breath. The guilt I felt earlier is now a low, simmering anger.

"You got just a lil taste of what I've been through in the past. Just a *little* taste—and what do you do? Check out? Shrink into your lil shell." I tap her on the side of her head. "Hello? Anybody in there?"

Silence.

"Look at you. Weak. How in the hell are we even related?" My eyes narrow. "If the roles had been reversed, you wouldn't have lasted one day out here on the streets. Not one *fucking* day."

Silence.

"Oh. And don't be looking for your lil girlfriend Essence

to come around here anymore. I took care of her disloyal ass—just like I'm going to take care of your man, Profit, once and for all." I flip Ta'Shara's hair into her face and then turn toward the door.

I don't get more than two feet before I hear this deep, guttural voice behind me.

"You fuckin' bitch!"

Stunned, I turn around and barely comprehend Ta'Shara charging toward me or those two large knitting needles swooping down and plunging into my chest.

"Aaaaargh!"

We fall to the floor as Ta'Shara jerks the needles out and then jams them back in, over and over while her scream rings in my head.

"DIE, YOU BITCH! DIE!"

44

Lucifer

Melvin Johnson stands proud while our people open crate after crate of new weapons for tonight's bloodbath. As usual, I hang back while Mason and Cousin Skeet discuss business. During the entire time they're talking, I can't help but steal sideway glances at them and wonder.

Could they be?

The idea doesn't sit too well with me because that would mean that this whole time Mason was fuckin' his . . . no. I don't even want to think no shit like that. But it's not impossible. I knew Skeet got around, my mother and Aunt Nikki were testimony to that shit. But damn.

I'd long thought Skeet was just slumming in Ruby Cove. Skeet and Smokestack had the perfect setup—one brother neck-deep in the game while the other ran the police department and made record busts on our main enemies the Gangster Disciples. To complete his double life, Skeet raised and kept his perfect, bougie family on the other side of town. That was another reason why I couldn't stand his ass. His family was too good for us, including this Gangster Disciple–fuckin' daughter.

Irony.

You'd think with my ass giving him Python's name for plugging his daughter that he could've at least dragged his ass in for questioning, but as usual, if the Vice Lords don't hand shit to him on a silver platter, he's worthless.

So tonight we're going to handle this shit ourselves.

Street justice.

I think that's what Skeet wanted this whole time. He wants Python dead, not behind bars.

Tonight, we're hitting two hot spots to let the street know that we're taking this shit to another level. Dressed in my usual Grim Reaper black, I turn to join up with my peoples on Ruby Cove. We have seven black Escalades lined up with plates off. Mason dubs them the Murder Train.

It's fitting.

When Mason and Cousin Skeet slap palms together, shoulder bump and separate, it's time for us to roll out.

"Looking good, Willow," Skeet says, shooting his handgun at me and hopping into his vehicle.

I glare at him while he rolls out and then disappears down the Ruby Cove.

Mason strolls back out from his crib, in his own black gear and with his flag draped around his neck. My heart starts hammering at how good he looks and how well he's walking. "Let's do this!"

Niggas break and head to their vehicles.

"Yo, Lucifer," Mason calls out. "You ride with me."

I stroll to the front of the line and climb in with Mason. "I'm honored."

Mason starts up his shit. "You know you're my right hand . . . and my fucking lucky charm."

" 'Bout time you recognize."

"Oh, I've recognized that shit. Didn't want your head to get any bigger than it already is." He reaches over and surprises me by taking my hand and squeezing it.

Smiling, I slip on my shades. "If that's your backhanded way of telling me that you can't live without me, then I guess it'll have to do."

"Hard-ass." He slips on his own shades and then pulls away from the curb. It doesn't take us long to reach our first spot: the Pink Monkey.

One by one, we all pull into the parking lot and block entrances and exits. Next we jump out, armed to the teeth and ready for the slaughter. Half of us march toward the door. The bouncers inside take one look at our asses and go for their weapons. That's the last muthafuckin' thing they do on this earth. My new .22 LR semiautomatic blows the biggest muthafucka back nearly ten feet.

Bitches scream and run, but their naked asses get blasted, too. What the fuck, I'm an equal-opportunity killer. The only time we get some exchange of gunplay is when some niggas come running out of VIP, but other than that, this shit is an easy hit. We're in and out in less than four minutes.

Heading back outside, there are a few more bodies facedown on the concrete. They must've tried to escape out of the back door but were picked off by our soldiers who remained outside.

"Cutty, man. Do you," Mason yells.

"You got it, boss." Cutty gives a mock salute and then runs into the building while we all load up again and roll out.

Three minutes down the road, we hear Cutty's bomb explode.

"That eyesore is officially out of business," Mason chuckles as we hug a right turn. Our next stop: Goodson Construction. If Bishop is right, tonight Python will be doing his weekly pickup with his connect. There should be two armed cars from his connect and two cars loaded with Gangster Disciples—we would still overwhelm them by three.

"You ready for this?" Mason asks.

I'm not used to his ass asking me such a question. "I was

born ready." His gaze lingers on me, and after a while I become self-conscious. "You want to pay attention to the road?"

"About what we were talking about earlier—"

"When?"

Mason swings a left. "When I told you that I couldn't live without you."

"Oh."

"Yeah. Oh." He draws in a deep breath. "Look. It ain't like me to beat around the bush, but me and you . . . well, shit is complicated. NahwhatImean?"

I debate on whether to let him off the hook. "No. Not really."

He laughs. "You're not going to make this shit easy on me, are you?"

"Not if I can help it."

Still laughing, he shakes his head. "A'ight. Cool. Well, here goes. I have feelings for you, Willow. Putting all cards on the table, I always have, but Bishop made it clear a long time ago that you were off-limits."

"What?" I shift around in my seat, but then I remember something that Smokestack had said. "I don't believe this. First off, why in the hell would you discuss something like that with my brother?"

"Are you kidding me? That nigga stepped to me from the jump. He did that shit with damn near everybody back in the day. Hell, he even fucked up a few niggas who said anything out of pocket around him. He even checked Cousin Skeet one time."

"You're shitting me."

"Fuck naw. He ain't never liked that nigga. Me neither, you want to know the truth, but the nigga is a handy muthafucka to know. I understand why you didn't want to deal with him while I was . . . out of commission. But business is business. NahwhatImean?"

"Yeah. Whatever."

"You'd rather put a bullet in the center of his head?"

"I wouldn't pass it up if the opportunity presents itself."

"See. This is what I'm talking about. You always say exactly how you feel. There's nothing fake or phony about you, Willow. Unlike a lot of females I've dealt with in the past." He shakes his head.

"Like Melanie?"

He shrugs.

"Yo, look. I'm flattered, I guess. But don't be looking at me like I'm some fucking consolation prize. Old girl played you—oh, well. Shake that shit off and move on."

"Oh, it's like that?"

"What? I'm supposed to faint at your feet because once upon a time you might have stepped to me, but because my big, bad brother stepped up, you changed your mind? Get the fuck out of here with that bullshit before I shoot you my damn self."

"A'ight. That shit didn't come out right."

"You don't say." Our conversation is cut short when we arrive at our spot. We're barely up in the lot before these muthafuckas unleash heavy artillery at our asses. Instantly, I hit the automatic window and then I'm up out of my seat and on the passenger side door, returning fire. Bullets whiz by my head. A new surge of adrenaline gives me a high that you just can't buy on the streets.

RAT-A-TAT-TAT-TAT!
RAT-A-TAT-TAT-TAT!

Once these niggas see how much firepower is being returned, they all scatter like cockroaches when a light comes on. "Damn muthafuckas. Where ya going?" I laugh while enjoying the feel of the kickback from the semiautomatic. I don't waste a fuckin' shot as I pick off one nigga after another. So far I don't see that nigga Python nowhere.

When Mason hits the brakes, I ease off the trigger and brace myself so that I don't tip over and fly out the window.

Once we stop, I'm out of the SUV *Dukes of Hazard* style and slapping in another clip. I've never feared getting shot or killed in these fuckin' battles, and as a result, I've yet to take a hit. Not even once.

I'm not Superwoman, but I sure in the hell feel like the Terminator while I unload on these assholes.

Mason's out of the vehicle, rock-a-byeing muthafuckas right next to me with his TEC-9. To no surprise, the battle is short, with most of these muthafuckas dropping to the ground and folding their hands behind their heads as a signal of surrender. Unfortunately for their asses, only the Vice Lords are leaving this muthafucka breathing.

"Where that muthafucka at?" Mason roars, grabbing one nigga by the back of his head and jerking it up. "Where that nigga Python?" he barks in his face.

"He's . . . he's not here," the nigga croaks.

"Bullshit!" Mason plants his gun at the top of the nigga's head and blasts his brains all over the concrete.

The nigga lying next to his murked friend starts cursing, "Fuck, fuck, fuck."

Mason systematically goes to the nigga and grabs him by the back of the head. "Same question, nigga. Where he at?"

"He told you the truth. Python didn't sanction this deal. McGriff set this shit up, wanting to cut Python out."

"Bullshit!" Mason plants his gun at the back of that nigga's head.

"NO. I SWEAR!" the nigga screams, and then squeezes his eyes shut to prepare for his brains to be blasted, too.

Mason looks up at me. "Are you buying this shit?"

I take another look at the shaking nigga and nod my head. We all scan the ground until we see McGriff lying facedown by one of the car's shipments. Both Mason and I stroll over to his ass. This nigga's back is coated in blood, and he wheezes for air.

"Damn, nigga. I don't think you're going to make it," I say, squatting down next to him and cocking my head. "You really look fucked up."

McGriff raises his head. "Fuck you, bitch."

Placing my hand over my heart, I gasp. "Such language. I'm hurt. Truly."

He sputters out blood while his body starts to tremble violently.

I see that familiar light dimming in his eyes. "Any second now," I tell him. "But while we're waiting, why don't you tell me why you're out here, dealing behind Python's back? Ain't you supposed to be his right-hand man?"

Blood oozes and drips out of this fallen soldier's mouth.

"You're a fuckin' snake, aren't you?" I ask, shaking my head. "You're trying to knock your man off his throne, aren't you?"

"Great," Mason mumbles, rolling his eyes skyward. "We just did that ugly muthafucka a goddamn favor, blasting these fools."

Still shaking, McGriff gives us a bloody smile. "It's time for new leadership. J-j-just a matter of time before he goes down for killing that cop. Johnson is not going to s-s-stop until he brings him in."

"So you figure that you'd position yourself to be the next leader in your piece-of-shit gang," I finish for him. "Pathetic. I had more respect for that nigga Killa Kyle while I was carving him up."

McGriff fixes his mouth to say something else, but I'm tired of hearing his voice and simply remove my handy Browning knife and carve a permanent smile across his neck.

Mason's face is still twisted up for our having killed the very niggas who were planning to dethrone their own leader. "Shit. We could've made this a movie night and let these muthafuckas do our work for us."

"I ain't gonna cry if there's a few less GD bastards in the world. Believe that," I tell him.

Bishop and his team of niggas stroll out of the warehouse building. "Yo, man. You should see this huge muthafuckin' snake up in this bitch."

"I ain't interested in that nigga's pets! I wanted that muthafucka dead—tonight!"

Bishop tosses up his hands. "I ain't had no way of knowing his ass wasn't going to be here."

"You *should* have fuckin' known." Mason moves toward Bishop and chest bumps him.

Surprised, Bishop steps back. "What the fuck?"

"You get one fuckin' job and your ass can't do that?" He bumps Bishop again, while anger twists his face.

Hopping up, I get in between them. "Y'all squash it. This ain't the time or the place."

Heat radiates off Mason in waves while my brother's confusion remains highlighted on his face.

"Let's take care of this shit out here and then we roll over to his crib."

"Shit," Mason swears. "The nigga stays at different places all the time. He got so many baby mommas. Do you want to guess where he's resting his head tonight? Hell. That's if Bishop actually has been following him to the right addresses," Mason growls, storming away.

"Damn." Bishop turns to me. "What the hell is up with him?"

"Forget it. Let's blast these fools and get out of here."

The minute I say that shit, niggas jump up and try to make a run for it, but it's like shooting fish in a barrel, and we mow these muthafuckas down in twenty seconds flat.

When it's done, we all slap palms and shout, "Five for life!"

Glancing over at Mason, I see that he's still pissed as shit. "Fuck it," I say. "Let's keep the Murder Train rolling. We got the crew, the firepower, and the element of surprise on our side. Let's hit these muthafuckas at their heart."

"Shotgun Row?" Mason says with an excited light in his eyes.

My smile stretches wider.

"My people, load up," Mason yells. "We're rolling this train through Shotgun Row."

"No shit?" Bishop asks, smiling.

"No shit," I confirm, and hop back into Mason's bullet-riddled ride. Seconds later, we're headed south. The moment we cross enemy lines, a silent alarm must've gone off because niggas come at our murder train hard.

RAT-A-TAT-TAT-TAT!

RAT-A-TAT-TAT-TAT!

Hoopties from four decades back jump out of nowhere while bullets hammer our vehicles. I handle my business, taking out the drivers of two cars and then watching as the runaway car carries the shooters in the passenger's seat careening into one light pole and one parked car.

Behind us, there's more tires screeching and cars crunching together—some of them our own crew. "Shit!"

"So much for the element of surprise," Mason says, hanging a sharp left to take us deeper into the Gangster Disciple territory and closer to Shotgun Row.

"All is well," I say, trying to comfort him . . . and me. But he's right; these niggas now know we're coming, and getting to ground zero will be like trying to bust into a military compound.

Mason hangs tough. He's as good a driver as I am, so I have no doubts that he can get us where we need to go. If either of us is having second thoughts, now is the fucking time to voice them. However, one look at the determined set of Mason's jaw, and I hold back my concerns and continue firing away at anything and everything that's moving. A lot of couples brag that they would go through hell together. Mason and I are doing that shit literally.

Shotgun Row looms straight ahead, and Mason presses the accelerator all the way to the floor.

"THERE THAT MUTHAFUCKA GO!" Mason points to Python's infamous black Monte Carlo.

Seeing this big muthafucka in his car, my heart starts hammering with excitement. *We're actually going to get this muthafucka.* "Go! Go! Go!"

Python opens fire back at us, his bullets wasted on our bullet-proof windshield. Now there's police sirens added to the mix. I know we're going to have to wrap this shit up real quick.

"Tires," Mason shouts. "Take out the tires."

I'm already on that shit, but Python is ahead of the game and rocking the same honeycomb, bulletproof tires that we have on our shit. "Shit! Shit! Shit!"

"Take the nigga out, then!"

"I'm fuckin' trying!"

Python hangs a tight left and then jets down I-240, going the wrong muthafuckin' way.

Car horns blare while Mason stays right on his tail.

Still blasting while we bob and weave through oncoming traffic, I have serious concerns about how this shit is about to play the fuck out. As soon as I think that shit, a huge eighteen-wheeler lays on his horn. Python tries to swerve out of the way, but he gets clipped and ends up spinning off the shoulder and then flipping down into a ditch.

I don't even get a chance to celebrate the sudden turn of events because Mason also has to swerve hard to the right, and before I know it, we're barreling toward Python's flipped car. I drop my weapon and try to sink back into the car, but before I'm halfway in, our SUV is airborne, too.

Next thing I know, I hit the ceiling, then the floor, and then I think the steering wheel. Then everything goes still.

There's nothing but pain, the taste of blood, and the stench of gasoline. I try to look around, but it's almost impossible because of the way my neck is bent.

"You muthafucka," a voice roars shortly before there's the unmistakable crack of bone hitting bone.

I may not be able to move, but I manage to open my eyes and see around the blood streaming from my head. Python is whaling on Mason's bloody head. "You thought you were going to take me out, muthafucka?"

Crack!

"I should've taken care of your ass the night I put a bullet through that pig's head!"

Crack!

"M-Mason," I groan, but it sounds more like a gurgle of blood.

Crack! Crack! Crack!

He's going to kill him. "M-Mason."

Python pulls out his gat and plants it in the center of Mason's head.

My tears now blend with the blood flowing down my face. "N-no." I hold my breath, waiting for the sound of Python's gat firing, but then the nigga lowers his gun. "What the fuck is that on your neck?"

Python takes a second look. "Is that a fuckin' birthmark?"

There's a long pause while Python's hardened face begins to soften. In the distance is the wail of police sirens.

"I asked you a fucking question. Is that horseshoe a fuckin' birthmark?"

What the fuck is he talking about?

"ANSWER ME, GODDAMN IT!"

Mason spews a mouthful of blood into Python's face. "Fuck you!"

Python wipes the shit off and keeps on interrogating him. "What's your fuckin' name? What's your real fuckin' name?!"

When Mason doesn't answer this time, Python shakes him. "WHAT'S YOUR GODDAMN NAME?"

My heart stops at the way Mason flops around. I desperately search his bloody face, wanting to see his eyes, needing to see that light. But I can't find it.

"NOOOOOOOOOOOOOOOOOOOO!"

Discussion Questions

1. Did you understand LeShelle's motivation for ordering her sister's rape? Can she ever redeem herself?

2. Essence finds herself exactly where she doesn't want to be, in the middle of her best friend's gang drama. Is there ever really a good reason or time to become a snitch, or was she dealt a raw hand from the jump? Was there a better way for her to seek justice for her friend?

3. How much of Momma Peaches's lifestyle contributed to Python's life choices? Is she a good or bad influence on him?

4. How much did seeing her father's murder shape Lucifer's life? Why do you think she never approached Mason with how she truly felt?

5. Who do you think Mason's father really is?

6. How much did Ta'Shara contribute to her circumstances? Do you believe that she's completely innocent? What about Profit?

7. Do you think that anything would change if Fat Ace and Python knew that they were brothers—or is the gang affiliation too deep?

8. Where do you think Alice has been all this time?

9. Do you think that Smokestack was right to take Mason from Alice's apartment?

A sneak peek . . .
GANGSTA DIVAS

Ta'Shara

"All is well." That's all that Profit ever says nowadays. Somehow we both have made it through hell only to become ghosts in our own lives. If you can call what we do now living.

I don't.

Love sustains our hearts while revenge consumes our souls. It's been more than six months since the Vice Lords lowered their leader, Fat Ace, into the ground. And since then, Profit hasn't missed a Saturday where he comes out to his brother's grave to shed a few tears and give the proper respect.

Him and Lucifer.

They are a solemn pair—Profit with his broadening shoulders and mounting muscles and Lucifer with her growing belly. More than once, people have mistaken them for a couple, and more than once I've wondered if I'm out of place for remaining by his side. I can't bring a smile to his face or hope to his heart anymore—hell, I can't even do that shit for myself.

There is chaos in the streets. The Gangster Disciples and Vice Lords have the entire city on lockdown. The minute the sun goes down, scared citizens run into their houses and lock up their shit. The rest of us spill into the streets, hunting each other down like animals.

And I'm no different.

Once I dreamed of escaping this life, these streets, and now they feel like a second home. While Profit busts his ass making moves, I'm right by his side, proving how much I deserve to be his ride-or-die chick. If I don't do it, another bitch will.

That's not to say I don't have to watch my own back. I've racked up plenty of enemies in a short time. Some even before I escaped the hospital. I know my leaving the way I did has hit the Douglases hard, but I did the right thing, and in time they'll see and understand it.

I close my eyes while the rain continues to pelt my body. Add the cold February wind and you have three potential Popsicles on the verge of catching their deaths. At long last, Lucifer is the first to turn away from the gray tombstone to slosh her way back to the waiting vehicle. I glance over at Profit and have to reach out for his hand to try to bring him back to earth with me.

"Baby, let's go." I might as well have been talking to myself because I'm sure that my words don't penetrate. Stepping back, I gently tug his hand. After a few tries, he turns toward the car.

"It's time," he says, barely above the sound of the increasing rain. "I'm ready."

His words are like an ice pick to my heart. It's not that I didn't know this moment was coming. I did. It's that the stakes are so high, and to be honest, the odds are stacked against us. After all, Python is a legend out here, and his killing Fat Ace has elevated him to icon status. It doesn't help that the rumors running through the streets are that the Crips have taken sides in our civil war and are plugging in the holes that Lucifer and Fat Ace managed to blast into the Gangster Disciples' strong-hold before the big fall.

"Are you sure, baby?" I ask.

Profit pulls his hand from mine so that he can walk to the other side of the SUV and climb in behind the wheel.

Sighing, I climb into the vehicle as well without looking into the backseat, where Lucifer stares out the window toward Fat Ace's grave. I don't know why I thought that Profit and I would resume our conversation, but after he turns over the engine and pulls off, I see that I'm sadly mistaken.

During the drive back to Ruby Cove, there is just the soft, steady whir of the car's heater struggling to fill the thickening silence. Again, I find myself stealing glances over at Profit and seeing the same rock-hard expression, the same intense stare, and the same raw anger.

I understand that anger. I've lived with it for months now . . . and I'm exhausted. I twitch in my seat, wanting to say what's on my mind, but not in front of Lucifer. Then again, the times that she's not with us are few and far between. She has taken it upon herself to train Profit, to get him ready for some big showdown that they both claim is inevitable.

For months now I've watched Profit put himself through hellish rehab. Nearly all the bullet holes LeShelle had scarred him with are now covered with tattoos—five stars, bunny rabbits, pyramids, but most importantly the name MASON stretched across his heart. Once Profit was able to walk again, he spent hours weight training, target shooting, and studying the art of war.

Niggas started eyeballing him and whispering about how he should take Fat Ace's place as the people's leader. Others thought the title belongs to Lucifer, but until they both come out of their self-imposed mourning, Bishop stepped up.

We turn down on Ruby Cove and pull up outside Lucifer's crib. When she doesn't jump out, Profit turns to look back at her. "We're here."

He says it gently enough to jar her out of her little world. And without saying a word, she climbs out of the vehicle.

I watch Lucifer as she slowly walks toward her house. *That's going to be you if anything ever happens to Profit.* I've lost count of how many times that thought has crossed my mind, and each time that ice pick chips another huge chunk away from my heart.

"Baby, we need to talk," I say, turning back around in my seat.

Profit sucks in a small breath as he cruises down to one of Fat Ace's old businesses—Da Club, ten minutes out.

Since he doesn't stop me, I take it that his silence is a cue for me to spit out whatever it is I got on my mind. The problem is, I have so much to say that I don't know where to start. "Let's just leave," I say. I reach across the seat and take his hand into mine. "I know and understand that you want—"

"No." He looks over at me. "I don't *want* to do anything. I *need* to murk that ugly nigga Python. He killed my brother," he stresses with venom seeping into his voice. "I know blood don't mean shit with you and your family, but it's a little different with mine."

That jab hurt.

"Smokestack will be out soon. Let him handle it."

Profit pulls his hand from mine. "What the fuck? Do you think your nigga's a punk or some shit? You want me to run out of this city with my dick tucked in between my ass and let other niggas fight my battles?"

"No. That's not what I meant."

"That *is* what you meant. Be woman enough to admit it."

"WHAT?"

"Don't think that I don't know that you've been plotting and planning to dump this emotional bullshit on me. Your heart has never truly been down for this shit. You're walking the walk and talking the talk, but it's all bullshit. Your heart ain't VL. You ain't no true Flower."

"How the fuck can you say that shit to me? After what I've been through to be with you? What *we've* been through. Now your entire world is about running with the Vice Lords? Shit.

Whatever happened to us not wanting to be sucked into this street bullshit?"

"My fucking brother died—that's what happened! All that other shit is squashed. If you're down, you're down. If you're not . . ."

My shock grows. "If I'm not what?"

Profit jerks his gaze away.

"No. Finish your muthafuckin' sentence. If I'm not what, Profit? You want me to go? Leave? Then maybe you and Lucifer can hook up since clearly she's the fuckin' kind of bitch you like?"

"Ta'Shara—"

"No. Fuck you, Profit!" I jerk the car door open and race through the pouring rain and into Da Club. However, the minute I run in there, an army of guns jerks up and points toward me. Two seconds later, Profit runs in behind me.

"Ta'Shara, I didn't mean—" For a moment, he freezes at seeing that we're surrounded, and then he goes for the gun on his hip.

"Ah. Ah. Ah. Ah," a low baritone warns. "I wouldn't do that if I were you."

Profit stops, waits, and then heeds the warning and lets his hands fall back to his sides. "What the fuck y'all niggas want?"

A man steps forward. My eyes are instantly drawn to his big, bulky frame donned in black ink. But it's the man's face and that damn forked tongue that slithers across his thick lips that gets my blood boiling and my hands balling into tight fists.

Python smiles as he locks gazes with Profit. "Hey, Superman. I heard that you've been looking for me. . . ."

CPSIA information can be obtained
at www.ICGtesting.com
Printed in the USA
LVHW08s2053290618
582299LV00001B/172/P

9 780758 247575